UNQUIET SOULS

When those you love betray you, who can you trust?

D.I. Gus McGuire Book 1

By

Liz Mistry

D1269806

This edition published in 2019

By
Murder Book Publications

PUBLICATIONS

First Published in 2016 by BHB

PRINT ISBN: 978-1-9161835-6-8

DI Gus McGuire Series:

Uncoiled Lies
Untainted Blood
Uncommon Cruelty
Unspoken Truths
Unseen Evil

DS Nikki Parekh series:

Last Request
Broken Silence

Praise for Liz Mistry

'I have great admiration for Mistry's skill, this is one of the best crime thrillers I've read in ages.'

'Absolutely fantastic read.'

'Simply unputdownable.'

'Devoured in two days.'

PUBLICATIONS

DEDICATION

To Nilesh, my light through the darkest times and to Ravi, Kasi and Jimi, who each shine with their own unique sparkle, brightening my life every day.

Xxx

PROLOGUE
1998

When he flexed his fingers, they cracked and a spiral of rusty flecks floated onto the cream duvet. For a second he stared at them, each piece testament to his actions the previous night. His blood was unwired now, his heart anguished and guilt-filled. The crushing, numb awareness of the way he'd snapped was all too clear. He knew what he'd done and he felt sick.

His hands were still covered in her blood – a hard patina over a sticky smear. His wife lay amid the carnage, a motionless, amorphous bundle. Her hair, sweat-matted and bloody, hid the worst of the damage. She moaned. Crossing himself, he sent up a quick prayer of thanks. Cautiously, he left the bed to run a bath, then returned to lift her broken body through to the rose-scented bathroom. Impervious to the tears flooding his cheeks, he lowered her listless body into the warm suds. He flinched when the sting of the water against her raw body made her whimper.

Despite everything, she lifted a trembling hand, reached out and squeezed his arm lightly. Their eyes met and his heart shattered when her swollen, cracked lips broke into the sweetest smile. Leaning forward, he kissed her forehead and, blubbering like a post-tantrum toddler, swore that *this* was the last time. Never again would his uncontrollable demons force him to hurt her, *punish* her, for not being what his unquiet soul craved. No, he'd find his release elsewhere. He'd never hurt her again, no matter if the devils called or how dark his soul became.

He fussed over her with chicken soup and Lemsip as if she had flu, then much later, left her sleeping and took his first decisive steps forward. The phone calls he made would change his life forever. They heralded the hell that was to descend on so many... Strange that each lasted only minutes.

The first call, to the builder, was easy and, at the time, he didn't realise just how profitable it would be in the long run.

'I want it done as soon as possible.'

He could hear the sound of paper being flipped over then, 'Mmm, yes, ok I can juggle a bit. I'll come this afternoon.'

As quickly as that, the fate of both men was decided. Of course, it didn't happen immediately. As the progress on his Decompression Room continued, they became aware of a common interest. Initially, they skirted tentatively around the subject, each conversation leading ever closer to the revelation that would ultimately unite them.

The second phone call proved even more profitable. Individual anger management sessions created a familiarity with the counsellor that highlighted their similar interests. They were like-minded people – fellow travellers indeed. Their patient–client relationship soared to a whole new level.

Within the year he'd pulled together a small group and created his own private sanctuary. His wife was safe, and, for now, his unquiet soul was sated.

CHAPTER 1
Present Day,
Somerset House, Shipley
Friday

Detective Inspector Angus McGuire looked around the waiting room. He hated it, from its cloying vanilla-scented candles to the china clutter on the mantelpiece to the seaside paintings on the chimney breast. The only thing remotely bearable was the oversized aquarium that stood dead centre, providing a 360-degree view of tank life. He didn't particularly like fish, but, in *this* tank, he'd found one he could relate to. He'd named him Nemo out of sheer bloody-mindedness because *his* Nemo was neither a clown fish, nor orange and white. His Nemo was, by aquarium standards, a monster, lurking in solitude near the bottom of the tank. Its lazy eye blinked rarely. Cold and dead, it reminded him of Becky's eye. The one without the knife protruding from it. The one that blinked reproachfully at him in his nightmares.

He tapped the glass and Nemo moved, the frondy things springing from the back of its head floating in the water. They reminded him of his own short dreads which he kept at the regulatory 'above-the-collar' length to avoid hassle from DCI Hussain. Gus' finger trailed across the tank. He'd happily spend the whole hour painting abstract patterns for Nemo to follow. However, such carefree indulgence with a friend – a bottom feeder, but no less of a friend for that – was not to be.

The door opened and Dr Sabrina Mahmood beckoned him into her lair. Gus walked past her, quads clenching painfully, forcing himself not to limp. Ever conscious of her role in his future and resentful of it, he'd trained himself to exhibit no weakness. For Gus, these bi-weekly sessions were the equivalent of a siege. She was the negotiator trying to worm her way under his defences and he would not comply. Not when so much depended on her assessment of his mental stability.

Despite his pain, he strode towards his usual chair, opposite her desk. In here, vanilla was replaced by occasional wafts of Chanel No 5. No amount of careful lighting and magnolia paint could disguise the age of the building but, Gus had to admit, she'd tried really hard. Little touches, like the fluffy turquoise rug thrown over a threadbare blue carpet, and the coffee table with fresh flowers in the corner were an obvious attempt to humanise the process. Dr Mahmood took her place behind the desk and waited for him to sit. Gus stretched his legs, feeling the pull of scar tissue in his upper thigh. Immediately, he found the damp spot on the wall above her right shoulder. With a practised half-smile, he focussed on the spot and waited for the usual ducking and diving to begin. These sessions were like a strategic ballroom dance and Gus wasn't a great dancer. All he wanted was to immerse himself in his sole salvation – work. Dr Mahmood, he felt, was hell-bent on making him dance to her tune. A dance Gus was determined not to share.

Elbows on the desk, fingers steepled against her lips, Dr Mahmood studied him. Efforts to disguise his limp probably hadn't deceived her but, it *was* less pronounced and his physiotherapist had given him the all-clear to return to work. Shoulder, still cushioned in a sling, was healing as expected. His thigh was improving daily but his physical improvements weren't her remit. *Her* concern was his mental health. Gus felt sure that, despite the well-meaning concern in her brown eyes, she'd have him carted off to Linfield Mount psychiatric hospital if she realised *just* how fragile he sometimes felt.

She tapped her pen on the desk, her varnished nails flashing in Gus' peripheral vision. She looked tired today, less effervescent. Thank God, no woman in her sixties, no matter how well preserved, should display quite so much vitality. It drained him.

'How have you been this week, Angus?'

Gus shrugged. 'Fine. And you?'

He heard the smile in her voice. 'This is your session Angus, not mine.'

'Thought you looked a bit tired today, that's all.'

'Thanks for your concern, but let's crack on with the session.'

'That's why I'm here.'

'Have you had any night sweats since our last session?'

Eyes on the damp spot, Gus shook his head. *Well, none he was telling her about!*

'Panic attacks or palpitations?'

'No.' *Only at night, when he had the nightmares.*

'Insomnia?'

'No.' *But his heavy eyes belied this.*

Her skirt rustled as she got up and moved to the front of the desk. With a small grunt she hefted her ample bottom onto it. This was different. He risked a glance at her. She'd hoiked her skirt up slightly and her chubby legs dangled a few inches from the floor. Her smile was motherly but Gus thought her tone sounded distinctly sarcastic. 'Since we've made *such* good progress over the months, I thought we'd try something different today.'

Gus' eye twitched. He hated this shit but he'd no choice.

'This is about you getting fit for work, Angus. I'm on your side.'

When he didn't reply she continued, 'Right, this is how it works. Close your eyes.'

Stifling a groan, he did as she asked.

'I want you to respond to what I say, ok?'

Automatically recreating the wall with the damp spot in his mind's eye, he strained to hear her quiet words.

'Tell me about when Greg plunged the knife into his wife's eye.'

His eyes sprung open making the wall with its damp spot disintegrate. Not believing he'd heard her correctly, he glared at her but she nodded. Closing his eyes again, fingers clenched over the arms of the chair, he deliberately slowed his breathing.

'How do *you* think I felt, doctor?'

'These sessions are about you Angus. You've *got* to give me something to work with. Please answer the question.'

He wanted to shout 'fuck off!' but instead, he complied, his tone robotic. 'I felt angry and frustrated, but I'm sure you probably guessed that already.'

'Good start. Now, tell me how it happened?'

Feeling the colour drain from his face, he hesitated. He could feel the tell-tale sweat under his armpits and, concentrating even more firmly on his breathing, remained silent. The last thing he wanted was to have a panic attack in front of her. That would really screw up his chances of returning to work.

Eventually, voice low, he opened his eyes and stared right at her. 'I don't remember.'

Licking her lips, she held his gaze. 'Sometimes, talking about our traumatic experiences helps us to heal.'

He responded through tightened lips. 'Yes, so you've said, doctor. But, the operative word is 'sometimes' isn't it? Not everyone responds to baring their soul. Not everyone needs it.'

'How do you know *you* don't if you've never tried?'

CHAPTER 2
2003,
Cambridge,
Sunday

T he Matchmaker inhaled deeply each time he pulled himself up: chin to the bar, toes pointed, naked sweaty torso rigidly straight, the smell of his own perspiration giving him an almost sexual pleasure, spurring him on to complete each agonising repetition. Finally, he was done. Dropping gracefully to the floor, he towelled his soaking body and, frowning at the silent phones on his desk, walked through to the en suite. A cursory two-minute shower, change of clothes and he was back at his desk.

Leaning back in the soft leather chair he waited, his impatience betrayed only by the jig of his right knee and his fingertip's measured tap on the polished mahogany desk. It had taken years, combined with the creation of his Decompression Room, to achieve this level of self-control.

He pumped the number into a safe phone and waited. The idiot *still* wasn't answering. Deliberately, he replaced the phone on the desk. His fingers and knee continued their languid dance, but his breathing was strained. Leaning over, he pressed a button. Immediately, relaxing music filled the room. Eyes closed, hands resting on his abdomen he allowed the calm to embrace him until his anger receded.

At last, pulling his chair closer to the desk, he looked at his computer. The order form was on the screen. Granted the client *had* made a particularly difficult request but, he'd also paid handsomely for their delivery agreement. Now, three days before the due date the acquisition form remained invalidated. The client was becoming nervous. So was he *and*, to make matters worse, The Provider was uncontactable. Not acceptable… not acceptable at all. It was beginning to look like the delivery would fail or, at the very least, be delayed. The resultant financial loss would be catastrophic, to say nothing of the damage to their reputation.

The phone dedicated to his extra- curricular business rang three times before he answered. 'Speak.'

It wasn't the voice he'd expected but, nonetheless, the call was important.

'Client 21 has returned damaged goods again.'

The Matchmaker frowned and pulled the relevant file up on his computer. 'That's becoming an issue.' He listened. 'You're right. Client 21 is becoming careless and arrogant, putting us all at risk. We'll make him pay.'

The Facilitator laughed. 'Yeah, hit him where it hurts most... in his pocket.'

The Matchmaker considered the client's file before responding. 'I think a £100,000 damage fee should teach him. No more supplies till he's settled, ok?' Hanging up, he typed a note on the file and glared at the silent phone.

'Fuck!' He spat the word into the empty room, grabbed the phone and hit redial. This time it was engaged.

He stood, filled his lungs with air and held it for ten seconds before slowly releasing it. Before he'd finished exhaling, the phone rang. Allowing the remaining air to spew out, he paused before lifting the receiver. 'Where have you been? We've been awaiting confirmation.'

The Provider laughed. 'You are *so* easy to wind up, my friend. Relax, chill out. Everything's under control.'

'You have the delivery?'

'Well, not exactly ...'

'You knew how difficult this would be. The rest of us deferred to *your* decision. *You* assured us *you* could meet the demand. *You* told us to accept the order and now you tell me you don't have the delivery.'

Another laugh. 'Let me finish will you? It's all in hand. It'll be en route to our client as scheduled.'

'Then why the silence? Why haven't you filled in the acquisition form?'

'God, give me a chance. Everything's ok'

'Fine, so long as it *is* ok. There's a lot of money at stake, not to mention our reputation.'

'Yeah, yeah, yeah... So you keep–'

The Matchmaker hung up. He breathed deeply until he was calm. Then, he smiled.

Gorce, Poland
Monday

This was the third time he'd observed the boy and his big sister traipsing down to the village, but today was different. Today was D-day. His abdomen tightened and a surge of adrenalin flooded his huge body. He trained his binoculars on the girl and felt a responding tingle in his scrotum.

'Mmm, Mr Happy, you are one lucky boy.' His oil-stained hand drifted to his crotch and briefly rubbed his erection through his jeans.

With her dark hair and soft tanned skin, she was perfect. How lucky was he to have found her? It had taken him a fair amount of time. The client was a fussy bastard. Bloody pervert wanted a boy, younger than eight, with blue eyes and brown skin. The Provider couldn't understand some of the clients they supplied to. *'Dirty poofter bastards! It wasn't normal, not right.'* Never mind, as long as *he* got paid for his efforts and had a few little bonuses in the process, he was happy.

He started the engine. *'Not long now, Mr Happy, not long now.'* By the time they reached the car park near the village he'd be in position and they'd be his. No questions asked. *'After all, who cares about two mucky Roma kids?'* That was the beauty of this job: one for the client and one for him. It was the proverbial win–win situation.

Gorce, Poland,
Thursday

Sergeant Jankowski, overcoat pulled tightly round his skinny middle, watched the crime scene team process the rocky hillside. The girl's body had been taken away, but horrific images of ten-year-old Magdalena Lauk would give Jankowski nightmares for months.

Abruptly, he walked away, signalling his constable to follow. When they were out of earshot, he turned frosty eyes on the man. 'So, Magdalena Lauk was reported missing *three* days ago, and what…' He flung his arms in the air, 'You did *nothing*?'

The young constable, hat in hand, looked distraught. He mumbled something indistinguishable.

'Speak up! I can't hear you.'

Risking a sideways glance at Jankowski he said, 'She was Roma, sir.'

Jankowski swore. 'And?' He stepped closer, his jaw tight. 'You're saying that because she was Roma, you didn't investigate fully?'

The constable paled. 'I thought she'd turn up, sir. That sort usually do.'

Jankowski stepped back, fists clenched. He was tempted to punch the constable's face. Instead, he spat on the pebbles at the man's feet. 'Well, you were right, constable. She *did* turn up, didn't she?'

He strode off, but the constable called his name.

'Well?'

'What about her brother, sir? Where do you think he is?'

'Fuck!' Jankowski turned slowly. 'Her *brother*?'

'Yes, sir. They were both reported missing.'

Without stopping to reprimand him, Jankowski, spun on his heel and headed up the track, bellowing orders to extend the search for a boy.

CHAPTER 3
Present Day,
Shay Lane, Bradford,
Saturday

With sheets tangled round his sweat-drenched legs, Gus lurched upright, painfully jerking his shoulder. Breathing unevenly, his heart pounding, he swung his legs over the side of the bed and, elbows resting on knees, supported his head in his hands.

Movement in the hallway told him he'd wakened his parents. He cursed. The dream was somehow more vivid tonight. He blamed Dr Mahmood. Why the hell did she have to keep banging on and on about it? He wanted to forget the whole fucking thing not hash over every bloody stab wound Greg had inflicted. It was bad enough that he revisited the incident most nights without having to put up with her solicitous enquiries over his mental health. He didn't need anyone to confide in and, if he did, it wouldn't be a fucking shrink.

He took a slug of water from the glass on the bed side table and downed two naproxen before getting up and walking naked to the en suite. Allowing the warm water to trickle through his dreads and soothe his aching shoulder, he stood arms splayed against the tiled wall. Head bowed, he thought about Greg pacing up and down the living room, a kitchen knife in his hand. Off his meds and out of control he didn't know what he was doing. Greg loved his wife Becky and adored little Billy. If he'd been in control he'd never have done it. Slapping his palm against the wet wall. Gus railed against the sobs that clogged his chest. He could still hear Greg raving on about Satan and devil's spawn. As vividly as if he was still in the room, he saw him thrust the knife into Becky. The hilt quivering from her eye. The other

11

blinked twice and then she was gone... Just like that. Gone. Little Billy, head against her breast, her arms still round him, screamed as she died. And then Greg began thrusting the knife into Billy's small body.

This was Gus's last memory of Billy and he saw it every bloody night. In his mind he could see the blood, smell it even now. He'd never forget it, or what he did next. Knowing only too well that when he jumped over that coffee table he had to stop Greg, he did the only thing he could. He dived on top of Billy, hoping that the weight of his body would staunch the blood. He barely felt the rain of knife blows to his own body. Twisting onto his back he saw the insanity in his friend's eyes and did the only thing he could. Stretching up, he yanked the knife from Becky's eye and plunged it into his best friend's neck.

CHAPTER 4

Heaton
Sunday

Detective Sergeant Alice Cooper's boot connected with the car tyre, sending a puff of snow into the blizzard. 'Fuck, fuck, fuckity, fuck, fuck, fuck!'

She stomped, covering her trousers in slush and yanked open the door of her Mini Cooper. Scrunching her coat round her waist she flung herself into the driver's seat and gripping one woolly fingertip between her teeth, she teased her glove off, before jabbing the number into her phone. The last thing she wanted was to ask newbie Detective Constable John Sampson for help, but she had no choice. Her Mini couldn't stutter up a feeble cough, never mind propel her to the crime scene.

In more temperate weather, Alice hand-washed and valeted her beloved car each week, but in the freezing Bradford winter she'd been neglectful and now her treasure was retaliating. She couldn't really blame her. She had been lashed by rock salt and now scum covered her beautiful green body. The hand-painted black flowers billowing over her doors, along her roof and across her bonnet were filthy. Cursing the northern weather, she waited for Sampson to answer. It wasn't that she disliked Bradford. On the contrary, she loved it. As cosmopolitan as London, but with much more heart and warmth, well... not at *this* precise moment, she acknowledged, shivering in her frozen tomb. Sampson answered at last.

'Pick me up at my house, ASAP.' She hung up before he could reply. She didn't dislike Sampson. He was keen and competent; what was there to dislike? She just felt out of her depth. 'She had been effectively running the Violent Crimes Unit ever since her boss Detective Inspector Angus McGuire

13

had gone on sick leave six months ago. She feeling less out of her depth lately, especially after what happened in Brent last year. Truth was she was still reeling from that and but she did not need the added pressure of mollycoddling a newbie.' for the Violent Crimes Unit since her boss, Detective Inspector Angus McGuire went on sick leave. She was in charge and she didn't need the added pressure of mollycoddling a newbie. When Sampson arrived, she tramped over like a miniature Michelin man, her scarf hiding her disgruntled expression as she got in. 'Let's go.'

Obediently, Sampson edged onto the icy road. Slipping into second gear he said, 'Good morning, DS Cooper.'

Alice, fiddling with the heater, muttered a reluctant greeting and sank deeper into her seat. Sampson edged up the hill, wipers frantically battling the sloppy drops of snow that landed relentlessly on the screen. Nearing their destination, the snow slowed and the juddering screech of wipers across the drying windscreen made her fingers itch to flick the wipers off, but she contained herself. Instead, she studied the row of shops that made Heaton a village in the heart of inner city Bradford. A café, chippy, chemist, post office, pub, Chinese takeout and One Stop grocery store – what more did a community need?

'The gates at the bottom of the graveyard are open, so park in there,' she advised Sampson. 'You don't want to get stuck on those cobbled side streets.'

Edging between the ornate gates, Sampson parked beside a Mercedes. Alice knew it belonged to Gus' dad, Dr Fergus McGuire, the pathologist. They got out and signed the crime scene log. The graveyard stood on a slope, with Emm Lane running along the bottom. Sandstone terraced houses dominated the right and a row of newer houses stood on the left. A low drystone dyke stretched along the top with a gap leading to the children's playground. The white forensics tent rose like an incongruous igloo amid the tombstones with an ice-covered climbing frame looming behind.

'Damn creepy, having a graveyard next to a kids' playground.'

Sampson laughed. 'Bet the kids love it. Playing hide and seek round all those spooky graves.'

'*Morbid little bastards*,' thought Alice with a shudder, as she braced herself to face the crime scene. She trudged towards the tent, Sampson trailing behind. A raised walkway allowed them access without contaminating evidence. Outside the tent, a police constable with a runny nose thrust body suits and bootees at them. Alice struggled to pull the suit over her bulky coat. 'What do we have?'

'Woman,' said the constable, launching into a coughing fit. When it finally subsided, he added, 'She's in her night clothes. Wound to the head. Bloke who found her, a Mr Bates, lives over there. Says she's local.' He gestured to the houses behind them. 'He's in a police car on Quarry Street. He was out looking for his escaped pet rabbit when he found the body. Doesn't want to go home till he's found the rabbit. Trying to avoid a ticking off from his wife, I reckon.'

Wishing a missing rabbit was her only worry, Alice poked her head through the tent flap. 'Alright to come in?'

A lumbering yeti, encapsulated in a crime scene suit, turned round, arms spread wide. 'Och Alice, grand to see you!'

Alice grinned at the bulbous turnip face peering at her from inside the white hood.

'Hi Doc, what've we got?'

Dr McGuire moved to offer her a clearer view of the body. Alice had trained herself to deal with the horror of murder by starting at the victim's feet, which were rarely the most horrific part of a murder scene. By focussing on them first, the rest became more manageable. Still awful, but less in your face.

A soggy pink slipper hung from one of the woman's feet, the other slipper protruded from the snow nearby. Her toes were skinny and looked as if they'd been mangled by years of being crammed into too-small shoes; chipped varnish clung to raggy nails. Emaciated legs with the blue thread-lines associated with drug use, escaped from her sodden nightie. A sad polyester dressing gown lay open under her body like a picnic blanket. Pock marks and macabre drizzles of mascara, tainted pink with blood, lined her face. Her hair, like rats' tails, surrounded her head. She looked forty, but experience told Alice, she was probably in her twenties. Doc McGuire would find out during the post-mortem.

'Poor sod.' She turned to Sampson. 'What's your feeling?'

'A bit unusual to be out in just your nightie.'

Alice nodded. 'Yeah, for you and me maybe, but she shows signs of being a junkie. Societal conventions aren't top priority when you need a hit and, according to our witness, she's local.'

She turned to Dr McGuire who was packing his things away in his battered old case. 'What can you tell us, Doc?'

'Well, as you can see, we've got two blunt force trauma injuries to the head. The first, just above the eye, knocked her over and the second, to the back of the skull was caused by hitting her head on the gravestone as she fell.'

Alice opened her mouth, but before she could ask her question, he spoke. 'Och, Alice, you know I can't tell time of death with any accuracy yet.' He patted her arm, 'Come to my post mortem party later and find out more but, for now, I'll leave you in the capable hands of Hissing Sid.' He lowered his voice, 'And believe me he's in excellent *hissing* form today.' He leaned forward, kissed Alice's cheek and executed a skilful shuffle past her on the narrow boards. Alice saw Sampson raise an eyebrow and smiled. 'I lived with the Doc and his wife when I first moved up from

16

London. DI McGuire gets really pissed off by his affection, but I think it's funny.'

They followed Dr McGuire outside and Alice caught up with him. 'How's Gus, Doc?'

For a second the pathologist's smile faded. 'He's *physically* fit to return to work, but that bloody shrink is farting about. She doesn't understand that the best therapy for Angus is to get back to work.' He shrugged. 'Bloody experts!'

Stripping the nitrile gloves from her hand, Alice shoved them in her pocket. She knew that his physical injuries were the least of Gus' worries. It was what was going on in his mind that mattered and that cow Gabriella hadn't helped by ditching him. She kicked one of the plastic boards and felt marginally better. Then, catching Sampson's eye, she turned her attention to the Chief Crime Scene Officer, Sidney Denby, nicknamed Hissing Sid because of his ability to foully contaminate every crime scene with his noxious farts.

Barely five foot two, Sid strutted over to Alice and pulled his mask down, revealing a neatly trimmed goatee. He handed Alice a plastic bag containing a bloodied sandstone chunk.

'We've found the weapon. It's the right shape and of course the blood smear's a dead giveaway.'

Alice took the bag, then abruptly covered her nose. 'For fuck's sake Sid! You've bloody dropped one haven't you?'

He grinned. Alice handed the bag back as he moved away, laughing.

She surveyed the surrounding area before speaking to Sampson. 'Look like an opportunistic crime to you?' She blew on her hands. 'Reckon she brought a punter back here for a shag and it all went wrong?'

Sampson hesitated. 'You don't think she was dumped here then? She's not wearing the usual prostitute gear is she?'

Alice shrugged. 'We'll have to consider every possibility.'

She stripped off her 'abominables', her name for the cumbersome white suits, and pulled on her woolly gloves. 'Not a very private dump spot is it? He'd have to have parked in Garden Street, and then lugged her up those narrow steps.' she pointed to the entrance, 'then get her into the park, in full view of those houses, before hauling her into the graveyard.' She brushed her hair back from her face. 'Or, if they parked in Quarry Street, they'd have to lug her past people's front doors to get to the park entrance over there.' She shook her head. 'I'm not buying that. I think it's a local crime and, going by the blood on that stone, probably an opportunistic one. Come on, let's go and see what Mr Bates has to tell us.'

Alice and Sampson climbed the few steps into the park and made their way through the gap onto the playing field. Unusually for a snow covered park, it was unblemished. The first responders had done a good job securing the scene and the hordes of eager sledgers that would normally have made their way through the park down towards prime sledging ground in Heaton Woods had been thwarted. As they trudged over the raised pathway to the park entrance, Alice was aware of anonymous faces in the upstairs windows of the houses overlooking the crime scene. They took a right into a cobbled ginnel that led them alongside snow covered gardens, before turning left onto Quarry Street itself where the police car waited, its windows steamed up and the engine on for heat.

Alice tapped gloved fingers on the driver's window and it immediately cracked open. She nodded at the PC behind the wheel. 'Off you go and join the house-to-house, while I chat with Mr Bates here.'

She stood back to allow the PC to scramble out of the car and then took his place behind the wheel, while Sampson slipped into the back seat beside Simon Bates. Mr Bates was in his forties, slightly balding, unshaven and wearing a pair of baggy joggers with a slice of striped pyjama escaping from the elasticised cuffs. He'd slipped his anorak off and now sat slumped against it in the back seat, an empty takeaway coffee cup in one hand. He looked expectantly from Sampson to Cooper as they introduced themselves.

Alice turned sideways in the driver's seat so she could see him and smiled. 'Just tell us in your own words what happened this morning, Mr Bates.'

He rubbed his hand over his stubble. 'Well, I fed the rabbit, Floppy, yesterday and mustn't have latched the hutch properly. She's always trying to escape, is Floppy. Anyway, when Jane went to feed her this morning she was gone. Jane wasn't right happy, so she dragged me out of bed to go and find her.'

Alice nodded sympathetically and he continued. 'She told me not to come back till I'd found her or she'd make me sleep in the office. She's done that before and it's not that warm. So I got up and started trekking through the graveyard. That's usually where the stupid thing goes when she escapes. Anyway, I'd done all of the area nearest to our house.' He grinned and for a minute his worried frown disappeared. In a proud voice he said, 'I used that grid method like they do in CSI, you know?'

Sampson smothered a giggle which earned him a frown from Alice who continued to smile encouragingly. 'Good idea, but no luck, eh?'

The worried frown returned. 'No, damn snow hid any rabbit tracks, so I wandered further up towards the park and that's when I saw her.'

He shuddered and pinched the bridge of his nose. 'I could see she was dead. You know with the snow covering her and the blood on her head? So, I phoned 999 and then Jane came over to see what I was doing.'

Alice frowned. 'You mean your wife came over to see the body?'

'Eh? Oh no. No, she came over to see why I'd stopped looking for Floppy. She saw me on my phone from the back bedroom window and she was in one of her *moods*.' He used his index fingers to emphasise the word.

Alice and Sampson exchanged amused glances. 'Did either of you recognise the woman?'

He nodded. 'Oh yes. She's always hanging around the pubs, trying to get money from folk and that, she's a bloody nuisance. Jane says she's a...' he raised his eyebrows, 'you know... a prostitute?'

Alice raised one eyebrow as if surprised, 'Oh?'

Mr Bates folded his arms over his chest and nodded. 'She's got kids at the school. He gestured behind in the direction of the primary school at the back. Not right, her being allowed a kid when she's like that, is it?'

Alice shook her head in acknowledgement. 'Don't suppose you know her name do you?'

'Oh yeah, Jane did a bit of phoning around and found out she's called Sharon Asif.' He pursed his lips. 'I sometimes see her when I'm working late. She's always drunk or stoned or something. Jane says the kids were always in a right state.' He lowered his voice, with a look that reminded Alice of her long dead Nan who'd always thought the worst of everybody and enjoyed a damn good gossip. 'Nits and smelly clothes and stuff.'

'Do you know where she lived?'

He delved into his pocket and brought out his mobile. 'Yes, Jane's just texted me her house number. She asked the neighbours, you know?'

Alice bit back the sharp retort that came to mind and tried not to imagine the crowds that would turn up in the next hour, not only at the crime scene, but also at the dead woman's house now that the news was out.

'Yes here it is, 9 Inkerman Street. That's just opposite the bottom end of the graveyard, near the Catholic boy's school.'

Alice thanked him for his time and was just about to open the door when someone knocked on the window. She pushed the door open and saw a massive PC holding something in his hands.

'What's that, Ken?' she said, recognising him immediately. 'Something for us?'

The huge PC grinned and held out his arms. 'Not exactly, boss, more of a surprise for Mr Bates. We've found his rabbit!'

CHAPTER 5
2003
Cambridge

Sergeant Hedges scratched his belly and yawned. Only an hour till his shift ended, then a couple of pints and a pie down the White Horse before home and bed. For now, the waiting room was empty. From the holding cells, he could hear the distant yells of Jacko, a harmless drunk, who was being processed for urinating against an ornamental tree by the entrance to Marks and Spencer.

Just as he thought he was going to have a quiet changeover, the station door opened and a skinny woman with a sleeping baby balanced against her shoulder walked in. The first thing Hedges noticed was her eyes. They bulged from puffy, red cheeks: two dull discs floating in misery. She looked barely old enough to have a child. Hedges, with twenty years' experience under his rather extensive belt, instinctively knew she'd come to report an abusive husband. He smiled encouragingly, hoping that she'd have the courage to go through with her complaint; so many of them lost heart, gave up and went back to their abusive spouses.

'Can I help you, dear?' Just watching her discomfort made his eyes crinkle. At first, her voice cracked, so Hedges quickly poured her a plastic cup of water and pushed it across the partition towards her. She took a sip and tried again. 'It's my…' her eyes flitted around the room, double checking they were alone. 'It's my husband.' Her face hardened and she raised her hand protectively to her baby's back, before spitting her next words out as if they were toxic.

'He's a paedophile.'

Before Hedges could respond, she continued hurriedly, 'I have proof.'

Expertly balancing the baby in one arm, she fumbled in her jacket pocket and pulled out a CD. Immediately, she thrust it towards Hedges as if it was a live flame. 'It's all on there. I downloaded it from his PC.'

Hedges took the item from her trembling fingers and studied her face for a moment. Satisfied that she was genuine and knowing that this was well above his pay grade, he rang the bell for another officer to staff the front desk and buzzed her through the side door. Gently, he guided her and her baby into the lift.

Cambridge CID was housed in a huge room on the top floor with glaring fluorescent lights and startlingly bright walls. It was divided into cubicles, by a series of shoulder-high dividers, set at strategic angles that, supposedly, created an illusion of privacy. Hedges hated it, but there was nowhere else for Cathy Clegg and her daughter to wait. Embarrassed by the noise and activity in the room, Hedges watched as, using her bundled up coat and a cushion, she barricaded her sleeping child safely against the back of a soft chair. Mrs Clegg looked barely the same age as his niece, Shannon, who was doing her GCSEs this year. Like Shannon, Cathy favoured baggy hoodies and skinny jeans that made her frame look emaciated and fragile. As she sat down on the uncomfortable plastic chair near the desk, tugging her cuffs over her fingers, he deposited a mug of sweet tea in her shaking hands.

Whilst the experts analysed the CD, Hedges listened to her story.

'I was only using his damn computer to get a recipe 'cos my laptop crashed. I got impatient and kept clicking to try and hurry it up. Suddenly this completely new window opened with a whole load of weird labels. It asked for a password.' She took a sip of her tea.

'He never lets me near his techie stuff when he's at home… but he's away on business at the minute.' She grimaced and her face paled. 'Oh my God! What if he's not on business? What if he's hurting some poor boy? Oh my God.' And she picked up her phone and frantically flicked through it.

Sergeant Hedges grabbed her hands 'What are you doing, Cathy?'

She glared at him wide-eyed. 'What do you think I'm doing? I'm phoning James so he'll stop. I've *got* to stop him hurting any more kids.'

Hedges gently prised the phone from her unresisting fingers and she collapsed against him sobbing.

Hedges mumbled meaningless words of comfort and patted her back until his soothing words calmed her. Red-eyed and spent, she hiccupped to a shuddering stop and took another sip of her tea before continuing the story.

'I saw him typing his password one day. I didn't intend to ever use it, you know? It was just sort of good, knowing that I had it and he didn't know about it. He could be a bit of a control freak.' She clenched her fist tightly and spoke through gritted teeth. 'I wish to hell I hadn't gone near his fucking computer. I wish to hell I'd never met the bastard'

Sergeant Hedges reached over and gently squeezed her arm. 'Look Cathy, when CID have finished with the data one of them will come and speak to you. You'll be here for a while so, if there's anything you need, just let me know.'

***

Development like this necessitated speed and Detective Inspector David Wentworth was nothing if not fast. He stalked across the room, a vision of colour co-ordinated perfection, from the tips of his expensive leather shoes right up to the diagonally pin-striped tie, which echoed the exact hue of his cashmere socks. To Detective Sergeant Nancy Chalmers, this sort of affectation was unnecessarily showy and she seriously questioned the sanity of any man who dedicated that amount of time to his wardrobe. She had noticed with amusement, how he surreptitiously appraised other officers for their dress sense, often following up with a barely concealed smirk and a preening puffed out chest that made him look like a fat canary.

To Nancy, Wentworth's almost colourless eyes made him appear cold and distant, which, in fact, he was. At present they were intently focussed on Cathy Clegg. Behind him, Nancy made no attempt to match his speed as she glided across the room with a smile and a friendly wave to fellow officers. Nancy was well aware that her blouse was slightly crumpled around the shoulders and the hem of her Marks and Spencer skirt was beginning to unravel. Despite her inability to iron, she'd never been one of those masculine, trouser and jacket-type women officers who hid their femininity behind a patina of angular cuts and dark colours. Instead, she'd held her ground in the male dominated environment and been herself; slightly scatty, very feminine and as honest and straightforward as she could be. It worked because she was well liked *and,* more importantly, well respected

By the time Chalmers reached the cubicle, Wentworth was already mid-flow. His staccato voice reminded her of a persistent woodpecker, chipping unsympathetically at Cathy. Nancy could almost see the younger woman shrink into herself. Inwardly she cursed Wentworth. She'd been working with him on the child abuse unit for six months now and couldn't get used to his inability to empathise with fellow humans. She sat down and listened with a sinking heart. 'Tonight, our surveillance equipment will be installed throughout the suspect's house and you will be moved back before your husband returns from his business trip.' Wentworth rocked back on the heels of his Italian suede shoes and rubbed his hands together, like a gleeful banker foreclosing on a loan. 'Then, we settle in for the floorshow. You just carry on as usual. We'll do all the hard work and sooner or later the bastards will slip up and we'll catch the lot of them.'

Turning to Cathy, Nancy noticed globules of sweat dotted her forehead, despite the shivers that wracked her small frame. Suddenly, Cathy lunged forward, grabbed a bin and vomited into it. The acrid stench enveloped the quartet and a few stray flecks of vomit landed on Wentworth's shoes. His face contorted and he jumped back with an annoyed squeak.

Nancy rubbed Cathy's back, murmuring soothingly until she finally leaned back, clutching a handful of tissues to her face.

Nancy glared at Wentworth and said, 'Perhaps I should take over here for the time being DI Wentworth? Mrs Clegg is obviously distressed and needs time to understand what we'd like her to do'

Wentworth, preoccupied by the sick marks on his shoes, was suddenly all too eager to pass the responsibility of Cathy Clegg over to his sergeant. He nodded and without another word to Cathy turned on his heel and strutted away, no doubt heading to the toilets to attempt a rescue operation on his shoes.

Nancy sat down opposite Cathy, her legs wide open, her floral skirt scrunched inelegantly between them. 'He's a bloody arse isn't he?'

Cathy's head jolted up and her eyes met the sergeant's uncertainly. Then, raising her eyebrows, she conceded. 'Yeah, that's one way to describe him.'

Nancy smiled. 'Right, now we've got that out of the way, I'll explain what's going on.' She leaned forward and held Cathy's gaze. 'Basically, the information we are currently collating from the data you copied indicates that James is a key member of a child trafficking ring we've been trying to track down for months. Now, this is where it gets tricky. We've enough evidence to ensure your husband goes away for a long time...' she paused '...but we *don't* have enough evidence to identify the other key members and the clients they've supplied... not yet anyway.'

Cathy's eyes narrowed and Chalmers nodded. 'This brings me on to what DI Mr Tactful blurted out earlier. Basically we've got three options: One, you refuse to co-operate with us and we're forced to arrest James now. Which would give the other traffickers the heads-up. They would disband and regroup later on, resulting in hundreds of children and their families suffering.' She paused to allow the implications of her words sink in.

Cathy bit her lip and Chalmers continued. 'Option two, you leave Cambridge with your daughter without seeing or contacting your husband and we continue to investigate, hoping he doesn't suspect you know anything and then, when we've got our evidence on the rest of the group, you can return and testify at trial. The risks of that are that any sudden, unexpected changes in your behaviour will make them jittery. Maybe they'll panic and disband before we have a chance to nab them. But, and this is the crux of it Cathy, they won't stay disbanded. They'll re-form and start doing it all again.'

Nancy sighed. 'This brings us round to option three, which is the one we'd really, really like you to take.' She hesitated and then took Cathy's hands in hers 'I'm not going to deceive you Cathy, this option will *not* be easy, but I promise you we will put things in place to protect you *and* your daughter.'

Cathy held Nancy's gaze then nodded for her to continue.

'What we want is for you to return home and try to live normally until we get our evidence. As DI Wentworth already explained we're already setting up all sorts of surveillance and monitoring equipment in your home. We just need you to keep things 'normal' for as long as it takes us to compile more info on the other traffickers. Then, after the trial, you can leave this all behind you and start again.' Chalmers raised her hand as Cathy opened her mouth to interrupt

'I know, I know. You're wondering how you could possibly go back home as if you don't know about your husband's seedy perverse hobby. I'll be honest with you Cathy – that's the hard part and I'd completely understand if you said no.' She sighed and lifted her hands palm up. 'But, and I'm being honest with you – these bastards kidnap children from Eastern Europe and sell them to the highest bidder. They steal kids to order for paedophiles throughout Europe. They have been responsible for hundreds of abductions and many of these kids end up dead and thrown into a canal after suffering unspeakable indignities. You've seen for yourself what they do!'

Cathy bit her lip, leaned away from Chalmers and folded her arms defensively over her chest. Tears rolled unchecked down her cheeks.

Chalmers pushed home her advantage. 'We don't just want the ring. We want access to their clients so we can close the whole thing down once and for all. *And* put every single one of these perverted bastards away.'

Cathy shook her head 'I can't do it. I can't. I never want to see him again. There's no way I can go back there and live like normal and I won't put Ali at risk. My baby's going nowhere near that pervert ever again.'

CHAPTER 6
Present Day,
Heaton,
Sunday

Despite the layers of snow and ice, it was clear that Inkerman Street was well cared for. The two facing rows of large terraces, many with loft extensions, were in good repair. Most paths were shovelled clear of snow and gritted. Alice allowed herself a smile at the jaunty snowman that stood guard in one of the gardens. Even before they reached number 9, she knew which house they needed. It was the only house in the street that looked dirty and unkempt. The windows were mucky with closed curtains hanging half off their rails. The windows in the loft extension were boarded over with plywood and nobody had bothered to clear a pathway to the door.

Even with the snow covering, it was clear that the little patch of grass was overgrown. The paint on the rotten front door was flaking off. The gate was ajar and judging by the yellowing snow near the gate post, something had left its mark. Alice and Sampson trudged through the ankle-deep snow and climbed the steps. Alice pressed the doorbell, but not trusting it to work, also rattled the knocker a few times and added a couple of bangs with her fist for good measure. She didn't know whether to expect an answer or not. She knew that the victim, Sharon Asif, had two young girls at primary school, an older boy who was at high school and a toddler. Alice, concerned the children were home alone, was desperate for access to the house.

A voice came from behind them. 'Why don't you try the back door? That's the one the kids use to go in and out, poor little buggers. It won't be locked.'

Alice turned round and held out her warrant card, 'And you are?'

The woman tugged gently on the dog lead she was holding, 'Wait a minute, Shaggy.' Then turning back to Alice she frowned, 'Oh! She's not got summat to do wi' you lot being in the graveyard has she? I'm Lola Jones by the way.'

Alice ignored the question. 'Do you live nearby?'

Lola Jones nodded. 'Yeah, next door to her, for my sins. She's a foul-mouthed bitch and she shouldn't be allowed those kids. Poor Jamal does his best but he's only a kid himself, you know?'

'Jamal?'

'Yeah, her eldest. He's fourteen but he tries his best to look after the kids when she's drunk or stoned or high. Bloody disgrace, it is.'

'When was the last time you saw Mrs Asif then, Mrs–'

'*Ms* Jones. Last time I saw her? Now, let me think? Yeah, it was last night.' She nodded and folded her arms under her substantial boobs. 'I was just taking Shaggy,' she gestured to the highland terrier that shivered morosely by the kerb, 'for his last walk and it had just started to snow again. The stupid bitch came flying out the front door wearing nowt but her bloody nightie and a dressing gown.' She snorted and pointed a stubby finger in Sampson's direction, 'and she wouldn't be running to get some food for them kids, you know?'

Ms Jones turned to smile at an elderly woman in a heavy coat with a black and white PLO scarf covering most of her grey hair. She was pulling a sledge along the snowy pavement, much to the glee of the toddler, who was so well wrapped up the only part of his body visible were huge mischievous eyes and the tip of a red nose. 'Hello there, Mrs Khalifa. Damn cold today isn't it?'

Mrs Khalifa smiled.

'Looks like all the bother over on the hill is to do with her.' And she jerked her head towards Sharon Asif's house and snorted.

The older lady stopped pulling the sledge and spoke in Urdu to the toddler on the sledge. The child responded with an exaggerated sigh and then directed his attention to Ms Jones's dog, who was now licking his nose enthusiastically. His nan smiled at the two police officers and, in good but accented English said, 'Are the children alright? My worry is always for them. I often hear them crying as if their little hearts will break.' She shook her head 'Poor things. She shouldn't have them but social services do nothing. Nothing! I have called them and my daughter-in-law Nusrat has called them. Sometimes they send people out, but she refuses to let them in and they just go away again. It's not right.'

Alice smiled sympathetically and leaned over to pat the elderly lady's arm.

'Don't worry now, I'm sure you've done all you can and we'll make sure the children are taken care of now. A police constable will be over later to take a statement, if that's ok?'

Gesturing for Sampson to follow her, Alice headed to the ginnel at the end of the row of houses, while the two neighbours watched.

Alice counted the back gates as she passed until they arrived at number nine.

When Sampson pushed the gate there was an ominous screech. The gate listed to the side and hung, half off its rotten hinges. A furrow of snow had gathered behind it holding it at a lop-sided angle and frozen it tight. Alice poked her head through the gap and groaned when she saw what lay in the yard. 'What a fucking state.'

Inches of snow covered discarded bin bags that clogged up the cramped space. Ripped open by the four legged scavengers that prowled Heaton at night, their guts spewed out rotten food, filthy nappies and empty vodka bottles.

Alice noted that no human prints were visible in the snow as they picked their way around the detritus. She hammered on the door.

Sampson leaned over cupping his hands on the glass to peer through the grimy window. 'Can't see a bloody thing through this muck.'

'Never mind, we'll have to go in regardless. Can't risk leaving her kids in there alone.'

She tried the wobbly handle and was pleased when the door opened easily. 'Fuck!' She stumbled back from the stale whiff wafting through the door. 'Bloody stinks!'

With Sampson following, she entered the kitchen. Their feet stuck to the lino and it didn't take long to identify the source of the stink. A pile of soiled nappies flung haphazardly in the corner of the room. Alice raised an eyebrow as Sampson coughed and cupped his nose with his hand.

'Yuck, how the other half lives.'

She shook her head. 'Welcome to the real world, Sampson.' Then, frowning she cocked her head to one side. 'You hear that?'

The muffled sound of a TV drifted through from behind the door leading into the hallway. Alice sneaked over and pulled the door open revealing a dark hallway with a staircase going up to the right and a door leading into the living room just beyond it. She put one finger over her lips and edged forwards.

'Peppa Pig.' Sampson had joined her by the door and his breath tickled her ear as he spoke.

'Eh?'

'Kids TV programme. My sister's kids love it. It's about a pink pig called–'

'Peppa. Yeah, yeah I get it. If her kids are in there, get straight on to social services and get someone over here. ASAP!'

With Sampson on her heels, Alice moved along the threadbare carpet to the living room door. She pushed the handle down and the door opened to reveal a huge flat screen TV in one corner of the room and a grubby sofa opposite with three young children huddled on top. The oldest of the three, a girl of around eight, glanced at Alice for a second before turning back to Peppa Pig. 'She's not in.'

Alice smiled and glanced surreptitiously at Sampson, who with a brief nod, got out his phone and edged into the hallway to make the call. The oldest girl sat in between two younger children; a girl of around five and a boy who, judging by the eye-watering shitty smell that had Alice gipping, was clearly still in nappies *and* in desperate need of a change. All three, wearing too-small well-worn pyjamas, huddled tightly under a thin blanket.

The older girl held an open tin of best buy baked beans in one hand and, in the other, a spoon which she loaded with cold beans before offering it to each sibling in turn. Alice's heart hitched momentarily. As an only child with no cousins and parents whose only friends were of the four-legged variety that ran around cages in a sterile science lab, she felt hopelessly out of her comfort zone. She could hear Sampson murmuring behind the door and knew she was on her own. Teeth gritted, she willed herself to ignore the smell and stuck a smile on her face. 'Think someone needs their nappy changing.'

The older girl, eyes glued to the screen said, 'None left. *She* was meant to get some last night but she didn't come back.'

'Okaaay.' Alice mentally cursed Sampson for taking so long. 'What are your names?'

Still focussed on the antics of the pink pig, the girl sniffed and shoved an overflowing spoon of lurid orange sauce into her brother's mouth. 'I'm Rehana.' She pointed, first at her sister, then at the toddler. 'That's Maryham and he's Imam.'

Alice released a long slow breath, desperate now for Sampson to get his arse back into the room. Children were an alien species to her and she'd no idea how to proceed. Give her a dead body any day over this. As he came back into the room Alice sighed and raised both hands upwards in a *what should we do with the kids?* sort of gesture. Sampson's grin, in her mind, was a bit too gloating but as he quickly moved past her, crouched down next to the couch and began speaking to the kids she decided she'd let him off.

'You know, if Imam doesn't get his bum changed it'll get really sore.'

No response.

Alice raised her eyebrows. Sampson shrugged, 'I know it's not strictly procedure but we're going to have to sort this out.'

Alice blinked rapidly. 'We?'

Sampson turned to Rehana. 'Well, me.' He winked at the girl, '… and Rehana.'

Rehana continued to shovel beans into mouths that opened as automatically as chicks in a nest receiving regurgitated worms from their mum's beak.

'So, can you help me clean him up?' said Sampson

Rehana glared at him, then, just when Alice thought she was going to refuse, she shrugged pitifully bony shoulders and said 'Okay.'

Alice watched Sampson lift the small wriggling boy who immediately began to sob, arms stretched towards his sister. Sampson held him at arm's length, manfully managing not to grimace. Alice shuddered when she saw the brown sludge trailing down the leg of the toddler's Thomas The Tank Engine PJs.

She followed them through to the kitchen, cleared mouldy dishes from the sink and stood back to watch as Rehana, with the air of an expert, put on the tap and let it run for a minute, flicking her hand under the flow of water

34

periodically. She turned to Sampson, who was making faces to distract Imam. 'It's as warm as it'll get'

Holding her breath against the foul smell, Alice watched Sampson remove the nappy flinching at Imam's screams when the dried up shit pulled the tender skin. Ferocious blisters caked in faeces covered his butt. Alice, bit her lip as Sampson lowered the boy into the barely warm water. Imam whimpered and struggled in Sampson's arms until, finally, he lifted him from the water. Alice handed him the cleanest towel she could find and watched as he gently dried the open sores before wrapping a tea towel loosely round him.

They returned Imam to the settee, where Rehana hugged him close, murmuring soothing words as she rocked him. Alice, copying Sampson's earlier actions, squatted beside the children and spoke quietly. 'Someone will come soon to take you somewhere safe.' Then, remembering that there was an older, fourteen-year-old brother, she asked, 'Is there anyone else in the house?'

Rehana bit her lip and shook her head, but Maryham, who'd remained silently till now spoke for the first time. 'Rehana…?'

Rehana, glared at her sister and in a sharp tone said 'Choop curr.'

Maryham stuck her thumb in her mouth and pulled the blanket up to her chin.

Alice pursed her lips and exchanged a glance with Sampson.

CHAPTER 7
2003
Cambridge

The Matchmaker was at work. Wary of the flow of people around him, he channelled his anger into his tapping fingers as he re-read the damning report. *'Fucking idiot, fucking damn idiot.'* The refrain pulsed in his head until, unable to bear it any longer, he thrust the report into the shredder imagining it was the idiot's head. He hoped it wouldn't come to that, but if it did… so be it.

Desperate for fresh air, he slung on his coat and left the office. He walked briskly through the drizzle towards the canal and turning into a park three streets from his office, found a secluded seat before pulling out his safe phone.

The Facilitator answered almost immediately. 'You just caught me. I'd just finished with a client. What's up?'

'Two things,' said The Matchmaker, his voice low as he glanced around making sure no one was in earshot. The first is annoying and concerns The Provider. Fortunately, for his sake, it should be relatively easy to deal with, so I won't bother you with that. The second is much more serious and needs urgent attention.'

'Hmm, sounds ominous.'

'You could say. My sources tell me that The Treasurer has been compromised. He has been careless. His wife discovered incriminating data and reported it to the police, who now have access to his computer activity. Fortunately, thanks to your genius, we are safe. However, many of our clients will be compromised and scrutiny of his activities will be intense.'

'Damn!'

'Exactly.' The Matchmaker's leg did its involuntary jig as he once more glanced around.

'What shall we do?' asked the other man.

The Matchmaker laughed. 'That's easy. We cut him loose and let him take the fall for all of us, but, I'm telling you now, I *will* exact revenge on the idiot's wife. We will lie low for a while till I discover the extent of the damage. Dispose of this phone, transfer the accounts, leaving only shadow ones so as not to alert him and then sever all links with The Treasurer immediately.'

'Right, I'm on it.'

The Matchmaker hung up and took a deep breath, before dialling a different number. It rang for ages but just as he was going to hang up, it was answered. He spoke quickly not allowing The Treasurer to speak first. 'We've got a couple of issues to resolve.'

The Treasurer sighed. 'Hold on, let me get my laptop and some privacy.'

The Matchmaker heard a child's voice in the background and then the sound of his colleague repositioning the phone before he spoke. 'Sounds serious, what's up?'

A moment's silence as The Matchmaker chose his words. He wanted The Treasurer to deal with The Provider's mess before he cut him off completely.

'The Provider has left a smell in Poland.'

'Fuck! Traceable back to us?'

The Matchmaker frowned. 'Well, the murder of a young Roma girl and her missing brother have been referred to Interpol and then circulated to Europe. It's potentially trouble for us, but if he can be contained it might blow over.'

'Stupid little fucker. Why does he always take extra for himself?'

'Hmph! Because he lacks finesse, that's why. His appetite needs curbing.'

The Treasurer grunted. 'What do you suggest?'

'His behaviour warrants a freeze on his cash flow till he toes the line.'

'Ok, I'll sort it now.'

'See you do.' He paused. 'Dump your phone too, time we used some new ones.' He hung up, took the battery out of his phone and walked back along the river towards his office. Stopping on the bank, he dropped the battery into the water and then repeated the process with the phone a few hundred yards later. Shoulders back, he headed away from the river, feeling satisfied that, once more, things were under control.

CHAPTER 8
Present Day,
Heaton,
Sunday

Alice and Sampson crept upstairs and were faced by three closed bedroom doors, a bathroom door and one that led up to an attic space. The door was padlocked. Alice could hear the two social workers' voices, drifting upstairs, as they escorted Sharon Asif's three children out of the house. She turned her attention back to the doors, her heart thudding as she eyed the heavy padlock. Biting her lip, she made her decision and turned to the first of the unlocked doors. Catching Sampson's eye she nodded towards it and in unison they moved to either side of the door. Alice raised her voice. 'Police! If anyone is there, please make yourself known to us now!'

Silence.

'We're coming in, please make yourself known to us.'

No response. Alice quickly turned the handle and pushed. In the darkness she fumbled for the light and quickly flicked the switch. The single bare lightbulb emitted a jaundiced glow, revealing a double bed with no sheet and a dishevelled duvet. The broken side board held a scattering of cruddy make up and cheap jewellery. Empty spirit bottles and dirty clothes were strewn over the threadbare carpet. Alice scrunched her nose and moved in to look under the bed.

Nothing.

With a shrug she gestured to the second door and was about to repeat the process when a bang from above made her pause. She looked at Sampson. 'Upstairs? Attic room?'

He nodded and Alice studied the padlocked door. 'Where's the fucking key?'

She moved towards the bedroom, but turned back at Sampson's sudden, 'Got it!' She watched as he stretched his hand up to a ledge above the door and grinned when he turned and presented her with a small key.

Taking the key, she slotted it into the lock. Soundlessly, she threw the padlock aside, yanked the door open and peered up the dark narrow staircase. There was just enough light for her to see another padlocked door at the top. With Sampson following her, she crept up listening for any further sounds, but the silence hung heavy.

Nearing the top of the stairs, a familiar smell hit her. She'd smelled that smell once before when she worked in London. She'd been one of the first responders to a crime scene involving a homeless man who'd set up home in a huge disused pipe. Trying not to breathe in too deeply, she took two pairs of nitrile gloves from her pocket and silently handed one pair to Sampson.

On tiptoes she reached up and felt along the door frame for the second key. With trembling fingers, she undid the padlock and thrust both the lock and key into an evidence bag.

With a final glace at Sampson, she thrust the door inward till it hit the wall, fully releasing the contained stench. Behind her, Sampson slapped his hand over his nose and coughed. Alice schooled herself to take shallow breaths through her mouth and, when her breathing settled, she stretched her hand into the darkness and flicked the light switch. Her eyes darted round the room and, before she could fully absorb the scene, an anguished cry escaped her lips. She stepped back, knocking Sampson off balance and sending him stumbling backwards down the stairs to land in a wide-eyed heap at the bottom. She looked down at him. 'Get an ambulance and DCI Chalmers down here now!'

CHAPTER 9
Shay Lane

Fergus McGuire opened the door of his refurbished, fully modernised farmhouse and was greeted by the aromas of singed meat and over-boiled vegetables and by the sight of his diminutive wife coming out of the kitchen, afro hair wild and even more tightly curled than usual due to the humidity.

He'd signed the body off at the morgue and dropped in to check on Gus' house on Marriner's Drive. Gus hadn't been back there since the incident and Dr McGuire took it upon himself to check it out at least once a week. As always, when he saw his wife Corrine, his heart lifted and a smile tugged at the corners of his lips. She stood on tiptoe, kissed his chin and with a hand on either side of his stubbly cheeks, she pulled his head down till she could repeat the kiss on his lips.

'You're just in time. Lunch is ready when you are.'

Enveloping her in a bearhug which allowed him to bury his face in her coconut scented hair, he hid his grimace. Much as he adored his wife and marvelled every day at his good fortune in being her husband, he had a hard time coping with her culinary endeavours. Intelligent as she was, she was unable to master the art of cooking edible food and equally unable to realise that, what she considered culinary masterpieces were actually indigestion-inducing atrocities that her doting family felt unable to reject. As he continued to inhale her special scent, Fergus McGuire knew he would rather eat her worst concoctions than ever be without this remarkable woman.

Laughing she patted him lightly on the arms till he reluctantly released her.

'That bad, was it?' she asked.

He shook his head and followed her towards the kitchen. 'Actually, no. Well, no more traumatic than the usual waste of life from a drug-propelled existence.'

'Prostitute?'

He nodded. 'Probably. Definitely a drug addict though. Where's Angus?'

Corrine McGuire's face fell as she flicked the kettle on. 'He left an hour ago for one of his walks.' Her blue eyes, unusual for a black woman and so like their son's, studied him intently. 'Did you hear him again last night?'

Fergus grimaced, he'd been wakened at around 3am by his son thrashing about in bed, and had been unable to get back to sleep even when Gus' nightmare had abated. He nodded. 'It was bad last night.'

Corrine wrung her hands and her blue eyes filled with tears 'What can we do Fergus? He can't go on like this for much longer. Whatever happened with that psychiatrist on Friday has just made him worse.'

'I know, my darling.' He moved over to hug her but was interrupted by his phone ringing. With a 'tut' he grappled in his pocket for the offending item. 'McGuire!' Head cocked to one side, he listened intently. 'Ok, Alice, I'll be right there.'

He turned to his wife. 'Seems they discovered a lot more than they expected when they visited the dead woman's house.'

Corrine frowned, 'Another dead body?'

Fergus nodded. 'Two it seems.' He shrugged back into his jacket, 'and they're both children. Alice seems upset. Very upset indeed.'

Corrine leaned over and patted his arm 'Off you go, then. I'll save your roast dinner for later.'

Fergus grinned 'Don't wait for me. You and Angus eat yours. Don't know how long I'll be.' He headed back out to his car, knowing he could grab a burger or something on his way home.

Just as he was about to climb into his car he saw his son approach the house from the woods. Fergus hesitated for a moment, studying him, noting that although he still had a slight limp it was less obvious than it had been a month ago. But what worried him was Angus' rounded shoulders and sullen expression. Even his usually ebullient dreads seemed flatter and less awry somehow.

Fergus lowered himself into his car and decided he would exert pressure to get his son signed fit for work as soon as possible. He knew his son and he knew he needed something to occupy his mind, never mind the namby-pamby stuff the shrink spouted about 'sharing' the experience. Why the hell should Angus have to share the gory details of the day he failed to prevent his poorly childhood friend from executing his wife? Why should he relive the moment he stabbed his sick friend to death to save his own life, whilst trying to stop his godson bleeding out?

No, an active case was what Angus needed to help him move on and he'd bloody well pull in favours until they let his son back to work.

CHAPTER 10
2003
Cambridge

DS Nancy Chalmers sat with a tall man who wore a Colombo raincoat despite the sun that had penetrated the last few days' drizzle. She wore her trademark floral dress slightly too tight over her breasts, a pair of wedge heel sandals and no tights. Her blazer, flung haphazardly over the back of the chair, had on the lapel a blob of strawberry jam that had fallen from her doughnut earlier. She glanced up as the door to the CID room opened and Sergeant Hedges walked in, accompanied by Cathy Clegg. With a half-smile on her face, Nancy stood up and moved to greet the other woman. Cathy, she noted, looked dreadful. Already skinny the woman had become positively emaciated over the past few weeks. Her face was haggard and pallid with wrinkles around her mouth and across her brow.

Nancy directed her to a chair next to the other man, asked Hedges to bring coffee and then sat down. 'This is Sergeant Jankowski, Cathy. He's from Poland and he has come here for a very specific reason that we'll discuss in a bit.'

Jankowksi smiled at Cathy, his hand extended in greeting. Nancy waited till the greetings were complete before she continued. 'How have things been?'

Cathy snorted. 'If you're asking what it's like to share your bed with a paedophile and act like you don't know how sick he is, then it's fucking shit.'

Nancy nodded, but kept her face neutral despite her pounding heart. She felt for the woman, she really did, but she knew that Cathy was their only hope of reeling the bastards in. 'You're doing really well Cathy, really well.'

Cathy put her head to one side and crossed her legs. When she spoke her tone was accusatory. 'So, does that mean you've made progress? Have you nailed down the rest of the gang? Are you going to arrest him so my daughter and I can get back to normal?' She rapped her finger on the table to emphasise her point. 'It's been three fucking weeks and I'm not sure how much longer I can do this.'

Nancy waited till Hedges had deposited mugs of coffee and a plate of digestive biscuits on the table before gesturing for him to join them. He and Cathy had built up a rapport and she wanted him there to support her when she disclosed the new information they had.

'Well Cathy, it's not as easy as that.' She lifted a folder and tapped it lightly on her desk. 'We've been working closely with Interpol and about a month ago two young children from the Roma community were abducted in Poland. There have been similar abductions throughout Poland and Eastern Europe over the past year and we think your husband's paedophile ring is responsible for this. What makes this momentous for our investigation is that normally the children disappear completely. When they've been found it's been in another country and usually dead.' She paused. 'This time a girl, ten-year-old Magdalena Lauk, was sexually assaulted, killed and dumped near her home. Her brother Paul was taken. The only good thing to come out of this is that Magdalena's post mortem revealed DNA evidence that we can use to convict her killer and her brother's abductor.'

Cathy, face taut, jumped to her feet. 'Good news? Not for her parents is it? Not for that poor girl's parents.'

Sergeant Jankowksi cleared his throat, then in good but accented English said, 'Cathy, nothing can bring Magdalena back. Nothing. Her parents are desolate by her death. The fact that we now have some physical evidence is a good thing. Combined with the information we are gaining daily from your husband's computer activity we are much closer to shutting these animals down.' Cathy looked at Jankowski, nodded briefly and sat back down, shoulders hunched, fingers clenching and unclenching in rapid succession.

Nancy bit her lip and leaned forward, elbows on the desk. 'Cathy, we found Magdalena's brother Paul.'

Cathy's head jerked up, the expression in her eyes hopeful.

Nancy quickly shook her head. 'Oh Cathy, I'm sorry but Paul was found dead in the Thames estuary. His body had been what we call 'sanitised'. In other words, whoever dumped him removed any physical evidence we could use to identify his killers. We feel sure he was brought over here by your husband's colleagues, sold to a 'client' and then dumped.'

Cathy groaned. 'Why are you telling me all this?'

Nancy glanced at Jankowksi before she replied. 'We need you to stay on track, Cathy. We need you now, more than ever. Through James' activity we've identified some of the people who're ordering these children. We just need a bit longer, that's all.'

CHAPTER 11
Present Day,
Heaton,
Sunday

S leet drove at a 45-degree angle onto the muddy alley. It hammered relentlessly on the sides of the ambulance and police cars that were squashed into the alley and it rattled against the buildings. DCI Nancy Chalmers moved rapidly through the trampled snow, her coat flapping behind her like a super hero's cape, her sturdy winter boots sploshing through puddles. Her gaze was intent on Alice huddling against the fence, a polystyrene coffee cup in her hand, her black hair matted and damp. Spheres of hail mottled Alice's coat and clung to her woollen scarf. Her eyes looked huge in her ashen face and Nancy noted the slight tremor in her hand as she lifted the cup to her mouth.

Nancy followed Alice's gaze and saw that her eyes were trained on the ambulance that was parked, one wheel embedded in a slush-filled pothole, as if it had been abandoned. The back doors were ajar and a huddle of children with vacant eyes, wrapped in blankets, sat unmoving on the row of padded seats in the back. A small female paramedic leaned over to fasten their seat belts and the smallest child flinched. The paramedic smiled reassuringly, muttering nonsensical soothing words as she completed the task and moved on to fasten the other kids' belts. Nancy saw Alice's fists clench at her side and guessed she wanted to slam her fist into the wall. The paramedic slammed the doors shut, blocking out the final huddle of children waiting to be transported to Bradford Royal Infirmary.

An angry thrum pulsated in the air. Paramedics, social workers and translators worked professionally but without their customary ribaldry. Each one was profoundly horrified by the discovery of the children and each was directing their anger into doing their best for the victims. Chalmers knew the aftermath of today would have long and lasting repercussions for each and every professional here. The attic crime scene had been compromised in deference to treating the children DS Cooper and DC Sampson had rescued. Most of the children were in a fugue state, all were irreparably damaged physically and mentally. Two were dead.

Chalmers stepped in front of Alice. Deliberately removing all emotion from her voice she said, 'DS Cooper, fill me in.'

As Chalmers had intended, Alice responded to her authoritative tone. She pushed herself away from the wall and straightened. Hesitating only to take a sip of coffee, Alice, her tone dull, summarised. 'Eighteen living, ten boys and eight girls. Two dead. All abused, malnourished and severely traumatised. From what we can gather so far, none are British; most appear to be Eastern European.'

Chalmers bit the inside of her cheek and stamped her boot into the icy ground. 'Fucking Hell!'

'I don't think I'll ever forget this,' said Alice, her voice trembling.

Chalmers drew her coat around her and with fumbling fingers began to fasten the buttons. Giving up after three, she put her arm round Alice and hugged her firmly. 'No, you won't ever forget this, Alice. And nor should you. But what you can, and *will* do is your best to find the sick fuckers who did that to those kids.' She turned and saw Sampson approaching. He looked equally shaken but she noticed with approval his firm determined stride. 'Not the best initiation into CID is it, Sampson?'

He shook his head and she placed her hand on his arm. 'Both of you have done good. Bloody good!'

Alice nodded abruptly. 'Yeah, but I wish Gus was here.'

'Well, he's not here so you're just going to have to hold it together till he gets back. Hopefully that'll be soon. Anyway, what's the state of play?'

'Social services pulled in huge favours and have managed to secure a weekday only ward at BRI for most of the children. The Yorkshire Clinic have provided two rooms for the most traumatised. We've kept them as near as we can in national groups and where possible have employed female translators. The hospitals have pulled in as many Eastern European nurses as possible and we've asked for secrecy, but as you can see the lions are already prowling.'

Chalmers turned to see that already the Yorkshire-based representatives of the national papers were already congregating behind the barrier alongside their local news counterparts.

Alice continued, 'Forensics are working the attic. Doc McGuire, the pathologist on call, has already been and he's fast-tracking the PMs on the two dead children. Says he'll start first thing tomorrow.'

Hissing Sid approached, still wearing his white suit but with the hood pulled down. He nodded at DCI Chalmers but directed his words to Alice and Sampson. 'You can come up if you like. We've got what we can from the stairs and, for what good it'll do, we've paved off a viewing area.' He turned to Chalmers. 'It's not pleasant, you know.'

Chalmers bristled. 'Don't you patronise me, Sid. I've seen more fucking crime scenes in my thirty years on the force than you have. Cheeky bloody brat!'

Sid smirked. 'I stand corrected, DCI Chalmers. Didn't mean to offend.'

Hissing Sid and DCI Chalmers moved towards the dilapidated gate leading into the yard. They'd almost reached it when Nancy realised Alice wasn't with them.

She turned and saw her, hands in her pockets, scarf bundled haphazardly round her neck. Her head was tilted towards the upper window of the row of terraced houses that sandwiched the alley they stood in. Chalmers followed her gaze and saw that most of the windows were filled with the silhouettes of ghoulish bystanders gazing down on them. She took a step towards Alice and saw her small body tense as a flash from one of the windows evidenced the extent of their morbid curiosity. Before she could intervene Alice's hand was out of her pocket and her small fist waved angrily at the offending photographer. 'What the hell are you sick fucks doing?' she yelled. 'You didn't fucking notice what was going on in your own back yards, but now you want to document it!'

Nancy strode over, grabbed Alice by the arm and pulled her towards the gate. She nodded to one of the constables. 'Go to that house and threaten the bastards that if we find evidence that they've spoken to the media, allowed them access or posted anything pertaining to this on social media, we will lock them up for perverting the course of justice. In fact, get that message over to all these bloody people.'

The constable hesitated, then turned abruptly on his heel and scurried away. Alice, breathing heavily leaned on the gate. 'I'm sorry.'

Chalmers shook her head, 'You're not the ghoul taking photos Alice. You don't need to apologise.'

CHAPTER 12
Manchester

The Green Man pub nestled under the arches beneath Victoria train station in Manchester. With its reclaimed wooden pews it could have been an old church; a chapel for worshipping real ale, with a congregation praising the good fortune that led them into its holy precincts. It was dotted with incongruous Starbuckesque, sinky-soft leather couches. Before each stood hefty coffee tables, sprinkled with scriptures offering advice on motorbikes, 'sins of the flesh' and Mary Berry recipes. The fervour of students intent on debating testament, chapter and verse buzzed throughout.

After that drug-whore was found in Bradford, The Facilitator had panicked like the girl he was and, as usual, The Matchmaker had been obliged to meet him. Preferring a bit of distance from Bradford, he'd suggested Manchester because here he could remain anonymous. Looking round the pub, he nodded in approval and, with his overcoat slung carelessly over one arm and his expensive leather man-bag hanging over his shoulder, he was satisfied that he blended perfectly with the other patrons. Carrying a pint of Theakston's, he made his way toward his friend who sat uncomfortably on the low couch, skinny knees bent awkwardly and a pint of soda water and lime on the table. The Matchmaker's grin widened as he approached, savouring the fact that his friend felt the need to keep his wits about him for this meeting.

He slid gracefully into the empty space beside him, took a long sip of his real ale, sighed appreciatively and licked the froth from his lips with relish. He turned to the man beside him, amused by his nervousness. For all his keen organisation and dedication to their business, he knew that

The Facilitator still hadn't found a way to master his stress and he relished his obvious discomfort. It kept him on his toes and gave him the edge.

He waited, a benign smile curving his mouth and his head cocked enquiringly until the other man coughed and glanced furtively around the pub. He leaned in so closely that The Matchmaker caught a waft of mint on his breath. He covered his grin by taking another long draft of ale, amused that they looked as guilty as a couple of old faggots sharing illicit drinks whilst their wives explored the Sunday shopping malls.

Finally, The Facilitator spoke. 'You heard the news? She's dead! Murdered! Don't know what the fuck we're going to do now.'

The Matchmaker frowned watching as the other man shredded a napkin with his long fingers. Flakes of it fell on to his trousers like desiccated skin. He waited without speaking until the other man continued.

'We won't be able to fulfil our orders and who knows *what* they'll find in her house.'

The Matchmaker took another sip before replacing his glass on the scarred coffee table. With one finger he idly traced the 'I love sex' logo that had been etched into the varnish, encapsulated in a love heart. Then, he turned and, casually feeding the gay scenario he'd already built in his mind, he flung his arm round his friend's shoulder before speaking. 'On the contrary, we know *exactly* what they'll find in her house.' He laughed and, much to the other man's disgust, leaned close, kissed his cheek and winked lewdly at him. Rising to his feet, he swung his bag back onto his shoulder in an exaggeratedly camp manner, casting a regretful glance at his still half-full glass and continued, 'After all, *we* deposited the packages there, did we not? You and I both know that there's no trail back to us and, as for fulfilling orders,' he shrugged, 'The commodities are ten a penny. Anyway it's time to move on to operation revenge.' Seeing The Facilitator's grimace, he rubbed his hands together and grinned. 'I can't wait.'

CHAPTER 13
Haworth

'Charles… is that you?'

'No, No. Charles is, em, well he's unavailable at the moment I'm afraid.'

'It's Fergus McGuire here. Is that you Hazel?' He didn't wait for the woman's response before ploughing on. 'What do you mean he's not there? Where the bloody hell is he then? I've been trying to catch him at The Fort but he's not there either and DCI Chalmers says he's not at the crime scene, so where is he?'

Hazel's voice trembled as she spoke and Fergus felt contrite. He could imagine the woman biting her lip and wringing her hands which, in his experience, seemed to be her default mode. Fergus had always thought Detective Chief Superintendent Charles Bowles and his timid wife, Hazel, an unlikely pairing. Bowles himself was self-assured, some would say arrogant, yet, despite his frequent peccadilloes, he seemed to genuinely care for his rather nondescript wife.

'I'm not sure. He left after lunch, just after Nancy phoned to tell him about the house in Bradford. I thought that's where he'd gone. I'm sorry.'

'No, no, Hazel, hen, there's no need to be sorry' Fergus said, 'I didn't mean to snap but it is important I speak to Charlie, ASAP.'

He listened for a minute as Hazel executed a stammering apology ending with the promise to pass on his message as soon as her husband made contact. He was just about to hang up when Hazel's voice, raised in agitation, stopped him. 'Oh hold on a minute, Fergus.'

He heard her wittering tones, followed by a deeper tone and then Charles' voice boomed down the phone. 'Is that you Fergus? What can I do for you? I'm just about to head into The Fort so you better be quick. We've got a lot on at the moment, you know.'

Fergus pursed his lips. He didn't like the other man, but now wasn't the time for a pissing contest, so he responded in a mild tone. 'Yes I appreciate you're busy, I've got three bodies lined up myself, but I just wanted a few words.'

DCS Charles Bowles sighed, 'Look, Fergus, I know why you phoned.'

Fergus frowned. 'You do?'

'Well of course I do! It's the same bloody reason you always phone. You want me to exert pressure on Gus's psychiatrist to get him signed fit for work. And you think that the current discovery of abducted foreign children, as well as the murder of the prostitute, who rented the property where they were found, is reason enough for me to do so.'

Fergus chuckled. Through the phone he could hear the other man's relentless tapping. It was such an irritating habit, but he'd more important things to think about. 'Couldn't have put the argument better myself.'

Fergus heard the other man's slow exhale before he responded 'I know your boy's an excellent detective. He shows initiative, thinks outside the box and has exceptional closure rates. The question is whether he's mentally fit to return to work'.

'Poppycock, Charles. You'll not get a better detective to lead on this than Angus. He needs to get back to work and no amount of pussy-footing around with a bloody shrink is going to help him. He needs to be on the job. Using his brain, getting things done.'

'Dr Mahmood is a well-respected psychiatrist. If she has reservations, it's with good reason.'

Fergus's voice got louder, his already flushed face becoming hot. 'That's just it. The physio has signed him physically fit for work but that damn shrink's playing silly buggers. Fannying about wasting his time. How the hell does she know what will help him? He *needs* to be back at work and this case will help him. You *know* he'll deliver on this. He always does.'

Charles sighed. 'What do you expect me to do, Fergus? You know he can't come back to active duty till he's been signed both physically *and* mentally fit. Dr Mahmood is excellent at this sort of PTSD stuff and if she thinks he's not ready then, he's not ready.'

'Och, come on Charles, you know as well as I do that all that touchy feely stuff doesn't work with everyone. She doesn't know him like I do. He's *my* son and I know that what he needs is to get back in the saddle. And more to the point, *you* need him now.'

The continued drumming of fingers drifted down the line, then Charles spoke. 'Look this is a Catch 22 situation. I desperately need Gus back at work but I can't go against the psychiatric evaluation. The last one I read said that Gus was uncooperative and so, in Dr Mahmood's opinion, was still not ready for active work. Besides this is going to be a highly emotional case *and,* it involves children. Is Gus really ready to be thrown into such a horrific case after what he's been through? Christ man, he's probably still grieving the death of his godson; what was his name now… Bobby?'

'Billy. The wee laddie's name was Billy not Bobby.'

'Billy, then. That's what I meant. Look Fergus, my hands are tied, there's nothing I can do, sorry.'

Fergus bit his lip then, phone clenched tightly, he lowered his tone to a whisper. 'Oh, by the way, how's Nancy, Charles? Haven't seen her for a while, have you? After all I know you two work *very* closely together, some might think *too* closely perhaps.'

Charles paused, then, 'Are you blackmailing me, Fergus?

Fergus laughed. 'Who me? No, no, not at all. I'm just looking out for my boy, Charles. Just looking out for Angus. You'd do the same if you had kids, I'm sure.'

CHAPTER 14
The Fort

Surveying his kingdom was rather fanciful but, it was how DCS Charles Bowles regarded his office in The Fort, in the heart of Manningham. He had an enviable 180-degree view. To his left stood the large and newly renovated Lister Mills, with its sandstone tower and Scandinavian-style one- and two-person flats securely snuggled inside a gated complex. Why the hell anyone would want to pay a fortune to live in bloody Mannigham, he just couldn't understand. Straight ahead, past the medical centre on the corner and down Oak Lane was a clear view beyond Manningham Lane to Bolton Royd woods. He loved watching the ant-people toddle round their daily business. Tonight, however, the streets were quiet because of the snow. Charles enjoyed watching the white flakes dance against the dark sky and amber street lights. It was a welcome distraction from the earlier phone call from Fergus McGuire. God but that man was insistent.

Sighing, he settled himself into the chair behind his desk and swung it round so he could continue to look out the window. A familiar sense of anticipation surged through his body and, knowing this was neither the time nor the place to become agitated, he concentrated on his breathing and the soothing effect of the softly falling snow. The scent of L'eau D'Issey reached his nostrils before he'd even registered her footsteps entering the office. He quickly stood as she slammed the door behind her, flung herself into his arms and held tightly. Charles flicked a glance to make sure the office blinds were closed before returning her embrace. He felt himself harden as he did so.

DCI Nancy Chalmers was everything his wife was not. She was confident self-assured, sensuous and completely natural. His wife on the other hand was reserved, nervously solicitous and, he hated to admit it, bland. He loved Hazel. Of course he did. She was his wife and he'd do anything for her, but for years now there'd been something lacking in their physical relationship. He knew why and accepted that it was his fault. Her reticence plagued him, her dutiful acquiescence unsettled him and her obvious disassociation filled him with guilt... So, he had Nancy. He frowned. Actually, he wasn't entirely sure he *did* have Nancy. Not fully anyway. Their relationship was tantalisingly uncomplicated and impulsive. No strings, and yet Charles was hopelessly addicted to her. After all, a man in his position was used to being in complete control.

Reluctantly he extricated himself from her grip and reached over to flip the lock on the door before guiding her over to the sofa in the corner of the room. He sat down and pulled her down onto his knee, enjoying her delicious curves. She pushed herself slightly back from his chest and ground her buttocks against his erection. Then she twisted her body round so that she straddled his thighs. Ever so gently she nipped his lip with her teeth. His groan deepened. She raised her hips and he gently tugged her skirt up.

As his fingers found her naked beneath her skirt, she whispered, 'You like my surprise?'

Before he had a chance to reply, she unzipped his trousers and impaled herself on him. He held her frenzied gaze as she worked him like a rutting pig until she was spent. Then, he climaxed. Still breathing hard, he felt her lean away from him.

'We need Gus back. Now, Charles. Now!' Her words had the same effect as a bucket of icy water.

Trying hard to refocus, he watched her stand and smooth her skirt down. Fuck, but the woman was unpredictable. She'd barely finished fucking him and already she'd moved on, leaving him feeling like a horny school boy. He swallowed the angry words that sprung to his lips and began to put his trousers to rights. He felt thoroughly used. With a lingering frisson of desire still twitching at his penis, he watched her pour the coffee he'd prepared earlier. If it wasn't for her mussed hair and the delicious flush spreading over her cheeks he could almost believe he'd imagined their perfunctory mating. She added milk and sugar to his drink, handed it to him and then sat down in one of the two leather chairs on the other side of the coffee table.

Gazing seriously into his eyes she continued. 'I mean it, Charles. We need him back. Rogers is still out of action and Aziz and Panesar are tied up with the drug ring in Thornbury. We need Gus back ASAP. That stupid bloody Mahmood woman is dragging her heels. I've spoken to her and Fergus has spoken to her but she won't budge.' She lifted her coffee and took a long sip. 'This one's bad. Twenty kids imprisoned on our doorstep, two of them dead and the rest… well,' she placed her cup back on the coffee table with trembling hands. 'Well, the rest of the poor sods have been used every which way you can imagine and many ways nobody but those sick bastards could imagine.'

With a long sigh, Charles lifted his cup, crossed his legs and leaned back on the sofa before drinking. He met Nancy's eye and in a slow drawl said, 'Most of my DCIs just put in a written request for things like this, you know? Not saying I didn't enjoy the extra attention to detail but, if I didn't know you so well Nancy, I *could* feel decidedly manipulated.'

Nancy frowned and then laughed. 'Oh the sex wasn't for *you,* Charles. No, *that* was for me.'

He raised his cup in a 'touché' gesture.

She smiled and continued, 'Anyway, I know you well enough by now to know that you don't kowtow for sexual favours.'

He inclined his head. 'Good to know you think I'm incorruptible.'

They drank their coffee in silence and then she stood up. 'So, will you put a bit of pressure on Mahmood then?'

Charles studied the tense way she held herself as she paced in front of the coffee table. 'Why is it all so imperative now, Nance?'

She flopped down next to him and threw her hands in the air. 'Apart for Gus being the best there is?' She hesitated, biting her lip. 'Today... just took me back to Cambridge, that's all. Seeing those kids made me think about The Matchmaker again.'

Reaching over he placed his hand on her knee and squeezed. 'That was in 2003. You need to let it go. You can't keep letting it affect you. You didn't let Cathy Clegg down. Her husband did that.'

With a tremulous smile Nancy placed her hand over his. 'You're right, of course.' She shrugged. 'I've got a bad feeling about this case and I'd feel better if Gus was back.'

Placing his empty cup on the coffee table, he picked up a folder. From it he took out a print out of an email conversation and handed it over.

She glanced at it and then smiled. 'You've already made the request and she's agreed.'

Returning her smile, he nodded, noticing the tension leave her shoulders. Leaning over, she kissed him before heading for the door leaving behind the lingering smell of their sex mixed with undertones of expensive perfume. As the door clicked closed, his smile faded and his eyes darkened. Charles Bowles did not like to feel controlled and now, twice in the one evening, he felt out-manoeuvred.

CHAPTER 15
The Fort,
Monday

lice massaged her throbbing temples. She'd just got off the phone to the last of her Interpol connections and had established initial contact outlining the highlights of their findings in the attic room in Heaton. She'd called in their technical whizz kid, DC Compton – Compo to his mates – who was working to match the attic children's photos with missing children from Poland, Romania and Croatia. DCI Chalmers had provided another detective constable, Sadia Hussain, who to date, had looked down her supercilious nose and isolated herself in the corner inputting witness statements. Alice felt like she was swimming upstream through mud, with rabid crocodiles nipping her feet.

DC Sampson, on the other hand, was proving to be her saviour. He supported her decisions, made relevant and useful suggestions and above all worked like a Trojan. Still, she wished Gus was back. He'd know exactly what to do. Despite Sampson's support and encouragement, the uneasy feeling that she'd missed crucial actions hung heavily on her mind. She stood up and walked over to the coffee machine in the corner of the room. Caffeine was the last thing she needed with her headache, but she had to keep going. With treacle-thick coffee in her Mini Cooper mug she went back to her desk, pushed her chair back and sat, feet on the table, eating an out-of-date Mars bar she'd salvaged from the bottom of her handbag.

Images of those staring, expressionless eyes kept popping into her mind, distracting her. Maybe if she let them in and 'owned it' she'd be able to move on. She closed her eyes and took herself back to that attic room. The first thing was the smell. She'd identified it correctly before they'd even opened the door. She was expecting a corpse. What she hadn't expected was eighteen pairs of eyes blinking at her through the semi-darkness. As her eyes moved round the room she'd seen that the most animated bodies in there were the dead ones; putrid and writhing with maggots. The living bodies were empty, soulless, drained of vitality and so beaten they were accepting of anything. Two buckets in the middle of the room overflowed with human waste and around the walls of the room huddled on filthy mattresses were twenty children. All were clearly victims of horrific abuse. Their clothes, sodden by pus leaking sores, fell in rags from their emaciated frames. She'd spoken to them but they didn't respond; not a flinch or a blink or the turn of a head. Stepping forward, Sampson close behind, one child, a boy of maybe eight or nine, raised his head. She stopped and knelt beside him. 'You're safe now. We are the police.'

He uttered one word in a hoarse voice. 'Polski.'

Glancing at Sampson she saw the same shock reflected in his eyes. How had Sharon Asif managed to keep twenty children captive in a terraced attic in Heaton with nobody noticing? How long had they been there? And where did they come from?

CHAPTER 16
Somerset House

Gus had been looking for Nemo in the aquarium when Dr Mahmood came out from her office and wordlessly gestured for him to come in. She'd perched on the edge of the desk like she'd done on Friday, tucked her hands under her thighs and stared at him. 'Right Angus, no messing about, how have you been since our session on Friday?'

Frowning at the damp spot on the wall, he tilted his head to meet her gaze, puffed out a breath of air and shrugged his good shoulder. 'Same as usual.'

Despite her usual professionalism, Gus noted the slight tightening of her lips. He guessed she was frustrated with him, but didn't care. He couldn't spill out his woes like the rest of the bleeding hearts she treated. It just wasn't his way. Looking away from her he sighed. 'Truth is Dr Mahmood, we both know these sessions are going nowhere, yet still I've turned up religiously for every single one. Surely it's time to let me go back to work.'

Cocking an eyebrow, she tapped a finger on her lip. 'Would you say you've participated fully in the sessions, Angus?'

'Yes, of course. To the best of my ability.'

Smiling, she shook her head slightly before reaching behind her to grab a cardboard manila folder. Tapping it once on her thigh she hesitated then, with a resigned expression handed it to him.

Slightly puzzled, Gus took it. 'What's this?'

Splaying her hands before her like a conjurer, she said, 'Ta Da! Your wish fulfilled.'

Intrigued, he flipped the folder open and there, at the top, was a single sheet of paper with the words 'Detective

Inspector Angus McGuire is hereby certified fit to return to active duty.' Underneath was Dr Mahmood's sprawling signature.

'You signed me fit for work?' His voice held a note of scepticism.

She nodded. 'With a few provisos.'

Still unconvinced, Gus read the paper once more. 'You'd already signed me fit for work before this session?'

Jumping down from her perch, Dr Mahmood sighed. 'Seems somebody was impatient for your return and, in all honesty, after Friday's session I was at a bit of a loss how to deal with you. Maybe you're the exception to the rule. Maybe immersing yourself in work *will* be your salvation.' Looking unconvinced she shrugged. 'Well, we'll see now, won't we?'

Slowly, he got to his feet and, aware that he was grinning like an idiot, only just managed to quell the urge to lift her off her feet, twirl her round the room and kiss her cheek. 'Thanks, Doc.'

Smiling sardonically, she waited till he opened the door, then said, 'Oh Angus, same time Friday?'

Eyes narrowed, Gus stopped abruptly. 'But, I thought you said—'

She waved her hand at him. 'I said there were provisos, Angus, and that's one of them. You still need to see me twice a week for as long as I think you need to, ok?'

It was far from ok. But, with as much good grace as he could muster, he nodded and opened the door. Before stepping out, he turned back. 'Well, since we're into provisos Doc, do you think you could lose the vanilla smell? It's truly nauseating.'

Dr Mahmood blinked twice. Feeling that he'd got the upper hand for once he continued. 'How about a rose-scented candle or jasmine even? I don't mind jasmine.'

Her face transformed into a huge smile that made Gus feel good. He winked at her and left the room. 'See ya Friday.'

Now, after his adrenalin-fuelled meeting with the psychiatrist, he felt like a fizzled-out firework. His leg ached, and, as was typical of Bradford in the snow, no buses were running so he was destined to walk. With a longing glance at The Branch pub, Gus hefted his bag onto his shoulder and began to limp towards Manningham. His joy at being allowed to return to work sped him on, in spite of the sleet pebble-dashing his face as he walked.

His relief when he reached the welcoming statue of Sir Samuel Lister at the gates of Lister Park pushed him on and, as he entered the bottom end of the park he smiled, ignoring the pain in his hip and groin. This was his territory now. His old house, which he'd avoided since the attack that nearly cost him his life, nestled at the end of Marriner's Drive, opposite the park. His habit had been to jog through Lister Park and up Oak Lane to work whenever possible. He grimaced as his foot caught some ice and he slipped sending a shooting pain through his leg and into his shoulder. He wouldn't be jogging for a while but maybe it was time he moved out of his parent's house and back home. Gabriella, according to his dad had taken everything she wanted from the house so there was no reason not to reclaim it.

As he skirted the boating lake, he watched two young lads dressed in woolly jumpers and hats tentatively make their way onto the frozen water. They appeared to be coaxing and daring each other in an Eastern European language to move further onto the ice where it was thinner. Gus was about to holler at them when from behind a stream of angry-sounding words flew past his ears. The boys, faces stricken, glanced up and then scrambled quickly to the side, before running off laughing.

The old man nodded at Gus and spoke in accented English. 'Bloody fools. They forget that in Poland the winters are harsher and the ice thicker.'

Gus smiled, as the old man shook his head and lit up a cigarette. This was the Bradford he loved – a melting pot of culture, variety and life.

Slowly, he walked up the slight incline that ran between the statuesque Moghul Gardens and Cartwright Hall Art Gallery. He felt envious when a trio of women, chatting in Mirpuri Punjabi, power-walked past him. The contrast between their black burkhas and the flash of neon pink and orange Nike trainers made him smile. They were followed, at a more leisurely pace, by the group of elderly men Gus often spotted playing crown bowls on the green in summertime.

For months, Gus had adopted a strict regime of exercise to strengthen the muscles shredded by Greg's attack, and the truth was he had improved greatly. His mobility was certainly better and the fact that he'd just walked about five miles battling through snow and ice should have made him happy. A month ago he'd barely been able to walk to Somerset House in Shipley because the pain had been excruciating. Now he'd even managed to reduce his pain meds. However, he was well aware that the journey ahead would be a long one. Reaching the top of the incline, he chided himself for being defeatist and determinedly trudged along the path that was lined with flowerbeds neatly tucked under a snowy duvet. When he reached the main gate leading to Oak Lane he knew he'd finally be able to rest for a bit.

CHAPTER 17
Bradford Royal Infirmary

Two tiny bundles lay abandoned on steel trolleys, flanked by another one containing a larger bundle. Fergus McGuire stood in between the two smaller bundles, suited up, masked and ready to go. His assistant, Hardeep, completed the final preparations and then they were ready. Alice, pale beneath her mask, stood to the side, her eyes filled with a steely determination not to succumb to the anguish she felt.

Fergus walked round to the gurney containing Sharon Asif. 'Might as well do them in order.'

With Alice watching he began. Two hours later, three Post Mortems complete, Alice felt like she'd been subjected to a head on assault by a four-by-four. Her shoulders radiated tension and she felt sure her face shared the hue of the corpses.

'Come on, Alice. A recuperative drink is in order, I think. Get rid of your scrubs and we'll go to my office.'

After a toilet stop, during which she sluiced her face in ice cold water, a dazed Alice found herself in the only comfy chair in Dr McGuire's office, with a fine Glenlivet in her hand.

Fergus held his crystal glass up to the light and studied the amber liquid with as much concentration as he'd studied the bodies earlier. Then, when she felt his gaze shift to her, Alice took a single restorative sip of the whisky. Immediately, she felt the warming sensation drift down to her stomach, chasing the chill she'd felt since the previous day. She looked at Dr McGuire with a smile. 'Go on then Doc, I'm ready now.'

Swirling the whisky round his glass, Dr McGuire sighed and settled his bulky frame comfortably in the chair. He took a sip and rolled it round his tongue before speaking.

'Basically, Sharon Asif died from blunt force trauma to the back of the head from when she landed on the gravestone. The strike to her forehead is consistent with a blow from a heavy rock or stone, as evidenced by the granules of, what appear to be, sandstone in the wound. It sent her flying backwards with such force that, when her head hit the gravestone, it caved in. She would've died almost instantaneously. Hardly unexpected, were the usual indicators of a drug addict; mashed liver, malnourishment, kidney and heart damage.' He waved a hand in the air. 'My report will have all the technical details when the lab results come back.'

Alice placed her glass on the table and leaned forward and waited.

Dr McGuire took another sip and continued. 'The first child, Child A, a girl of around eight or nine, pre-pubescent certainly, was severely malnourished. External signs despite the condition of the body, show extensive bruising and cuts to her torso and limbs. She had been sexually assaulted both vaginally and anally and her insides were ruptured. We'll know more when the entomologist has processed the maggots we took from the body.' He slopped more whisky into his glass and offered Alice some more which she declined. Doc McGuire may be finished for the day but she still had an investigation to lead.

Inclining his head, he said, 'I already phoned Corrine to collect me in a bit. I've had enough for one day.' He gazed into space for a second then continued. 'The wee lassie has been dead for at least a week. She probably died of a combination of infection caused by the abuse and starvation. Again the lab tests will tell us more and hopefully some of the fibres and fluids we managed to find will help when you catch the bastards!'

Alice said nothing. What could she say? She'd seen what had been done to those children and now she needed to use whatever Dr McGuire could tell her about the dead children in order to get justice for the living.

Dr McGuire looked at her, 'You know Alice, maybe I'm getting too old for this. Or, maybe I've just seen too much of it.' He shrugged. 'Whichever it is, I find it increasingly difficult to deal with, to paraphrase Rabbie Burns, 'man's inhumanities to man' than when I was younger.' He reached over and patted her leg. 'Ignore me, I'm just being maudlin.'

Alice was unsure how to respond. She knew it had been a difficult few months for Dr McGuire, with Gus's injuries and the situation with Gabriella as well as his own grief for Greg, Becky and Billy. She'd thought he handled it all with his usual bluff optimism, but apparently not. She placed her hand over the older man's hand and said, 'We've just got to take strength from the fact that we make a difference. Sometimes not a very big one, but all those little differences add up, Doc.'

He took a handkerchief from his pocket and blew his nose before continuing. 'The second child, a boy, Child B, exhibited similar signs of abuse and malnourishment. He was slightly older than the girl, twelve or thirteen maybe and hadn't been dead for quite as long. Maybe a week tops. Again, trace evidence will help nail the perpetrators.'

Alice sighed. 'I don't really understand this. From what I can gather Sharon Asif was a nobody, a petty drug addict, sometime prostitute, certainly no criminal mastermind. So, how the hell did she come to be housing twenty trafficked children?' She shook her head angrily. 'It doesn't make sense.'

Fergus shrugged. 'Maybe she was just a pawn in the trafficker's game. Do you reckon she was killed by the traffickers?'

Alice shook her head slowly 'I don't think so. Why would they kill her and leave the children in that attic for us to find? No, I reckon her murder was coincidental; it seems more personal to me. If she'd not been murdered, those poor kids would still be there.' She closed her eyes and shuddered. 'It just doesn't bear thinking about.'

Dr McGuire leaned over and rested a huge hand on her arm. 'Don't dwell on this Alice. Focus on the important thing, catching these animals.'

CHAPTER 18
The Fort

*P*alpable, Alice thought as she glanced round the room; the tension was palpable and her stomach was knotted.

Compo, as usual sat behind his array of IT equipment with a smile on his face and a bacon butty in his hand. The new DC, Sadia Hussain sat with her body angled away from Compo as if he was infested with a contagious disease. Sampson leant against the wall near the boards ready to add to them as the briefing continued. He nodded encouragingly and winked. Alice narrowed her eyes and frowned. What the hell was he playing at, winking at her like he was her friend?' She barely knew him after all *and* she was senior to him.

She took a deep breath and ignoring Hussain's sullen stare, she began to outline the key points. 'We've identified ten of the children, thanks to Compo's liaison with Interpol, and their database of missing children. Three come from Estonia and the other seven from Poland. Their parents are en route as we speak. A senior detective from Poland, Inspector Detective Jankowski, who DCI Chalmers has worked with in the past, has been seconded to help liaise between the countries. He'll arrive with the parents later today.'

She paused and took a moment to order her thoughts. 'This is a two-pronged case. We've got the investigation into who murdered Sharon Asif; and the investigation into how and why those children were in her attic and who was responsible for it.

'The priority is to find her older child, Jamal. Her ex-husband is in Pakistan apparently. We've arranged for a trained officer to interview the younger children and we're still compiling information from house-to-house enquiries. We've got a DCI Wentworth coming up from the serious child crimes unit in London to input on organised child trafficking links.

'Oh, and on a positive note,' she smiled, 'DI Angus McGuire is returning to work later and will head up the rest of the investigation.'

Studying the crime board with all those haunted faces staring at her left Alice feeling sick to her stomach so, when she sensed DC Sadia Hussain sidling up to her, she was relieved to have a distraction. Her smile, however, was met with a sullen look and a curt monotone. 'Got an address for Jamal Asif's half-brother,' said Sadia, handing Alice a sheet of paper with a scribbled address on it. 'He lives up Great Horton. Road. You should send somebody up there in case Jamal's with him.' And swivelling on one foot, she walked away.

Alice, already stressed, was irked by the other woman's attitude and the mild directive in her wording and she responded more aggressively than she would normally have done. 'I'm the senior investigating officer on this one, DC Hussain, and I'll issue the directives, if you don't mind.'

Sadia paused for a second and then turned to face Alice, a slight flush blooming over her cheeks. 'Well, excuse me for making a suggestion. I thought you'd appreciate the advice, what with you being new to the job and so inexperienced.'

Aware that both Sampson and Compo were ear-wigging and annoyed that her cheeks were similarly flushed, Alice stood up and stepped towards Sadia. Her smile was sugar-sweet and her tone deceptively conversational. 'I didn't know you suffered from IBS, Sadia. How unfortunate for you.'

Sadia frowned, her eyes darting between Alice and the other officers. She shrugged. 'IBS?'

Alice's smile widened and she winked. 'Irritable Bitch syndrome.' Then, before Sadia could respond she added. 'You might think you're too good for us because of who your Dad is but, believe me, when DI McGuire comes back, he won't stand for your rude sullenness. In this team we work together co-operatively, regardless of how we come to be here.'

Sadia's face darkened. 'How do you know who my dad is? It was supposed to be kept quiet.'

Alice tapped the side of her nose 'DI McGuire trains us well and I like to know who I'm working with.'

Sadia glared at her, then with barely contained anger said, 'My dad's got nothing to do with me being here. I'm here on merit, ok?'

Alice moved away. 'If you say so, but if you want to be accepted here then start showing a bit of team spirit. Now *you* go and interview Jamal's brother and if Jamal is there, bring him back for interview. You'll need to organise an appropriate adult to accompany him if his brother can't make it. Take a PC with you. Singh's good with kids. Oh and while you're at it, double check that Jamal's dad really is in Pakistan will you? Be good to get at least one suspect ticked off our list.'

Sadia bit her lip, then turned on her heel and marched out. Alice waited till she'd left the room before looking over at her colleagues. 'No, don't ask me who her Dad is. It's up to her to tell you, even if she is a bitch.'

Compo mumbled something that sounded like 'spoilsport' from behind a Kit Kat, making her laugh. She winked at him. 'Of course it wouldn't require a degree in rocket science to work it out, Compo, especially if you're a clever detective.'

Sampson grinned. 'IBS? Sure that wasn't just a bit too much Alice?'

She grimaced. 'Yeah, it was really. She got my back up.' Alice settled in her chair behind her desk and looked at Sampson. 'So, what are your thoughts on all this?'

Sampson perched on the edge of Alice's desk so they could both study the board. 'I reckon you're right about it being two distinct cases with an overlap.'

Alice nodded. 'The way I see it is that Sharon Asif was killed by someone with a personal motive – maybe a relative, maybe a punter or dealer. Shame really, that both of her ex-husbands are out of the question, considering the first is in Pakistan and the second died of a drug overdose a couple of years ago.

'Sharon Asif's not had much luck has she?'

'Nope, but maybe her kids'll get lucky now she's dead.'

'I hope so. How do you reckon the children came to be in her attic?'

'Damned if I know. Hopefully young Jamal will be able to shed a bit of light on this. All I know is that it reeks of child trafficking on a grand scale and Sharon Asif didn't have the brains to be a key player in it. Maybe we'll be able to repatriate some of the kids and if we're damn lucky, find the bastards behind this.'

CHAPTER 19
Oak Lane

The bright red sign proclaiming '*MO's sa MO'sas the best in Bradford*' beckoned from across the road. Gus waited for a break in traffic then crossed and peered through the steamed up window. Inside, he could see his friend, Mo. Greg, Gus and Mo had become inseparable during their high school years at Belle Vue Boys' School and even though they chose different career paths after school, they'd remained staunch friends. Well, that was until Gus killed Greg. He didn't know how Mo felt about that, having avoided him since the funerals, and truth be told, he'd been too drugged up on painkillers to have a meaningful conversation then anyway.

When Gus had gone on to university to study forensic psychology, Mo had set up his first café here in Oak Lane, got married to his high school sweetheart and had four beautiful daughters. Greg began a law degree, dropped out, held down a variety of different jobs, met Becky, got married and had Billy. Somewhere in amongst all that, Greg's mental health declined.

Mo, short and burly with full tattoo sleeves visible below his T-shirt, crashed the till drawer shut and began wiping the counter. Two young Pakistani lads, jeans halfway down their buttocks, Calvin Kleins thankfully covering their arses, swaggered over to the plastic tables by the window carting yellow polystyrene trays filled with samosa and, what looked to be, mushy peas in one hand and cans of Rubicon mango in the other.

Gus pushed the door open. A bell tinkled, alerting Mo to his arrival. He glanced up, did a comical double-take cloth paused mid-sweep on the counter and said nothing. Gus immediately felt like spinning on his heel and leaving.

Stifling the impulse, he raised his good arm in a half wave. 'Hi'

A huge grin broke over Mo's face and in one fluid movement he braced an arm on the counter and effortlessly jumped over. 'Fucking hell, Gus! Good to see you, mate.' He enveloped Gus in a hug that, despite the pain it caused in his shoulder, filled him with love. When Mo finally pulled away both men wiped away a tear causing the boys by the tables to dissolve into juvenile giggles. Mo mumbled 'Shut the fuck up' as he and Gus moved over to the high stools at the end of the counter. Mo left Gus taking off his coat and approached the kitchen door where he swept aside the beaded curtain that dangled in the doorway. He poked his head through and yelled in for some chai and samosas, before joining Gus at the counter.

Neither said anything until after the tea was delivered by a young Asian woman wearing salwar kameez and an apron. Mo studied Gus's face, his expression full of concern.

'You alright, Gus?'

Gus shrugged and sipped the near-scalding spicy chai. 'Ah missed this Mo, nowt better than spicy chai.'

Mo tipped some of his chai into his saucer, and blew on it before drinking straight from the saucer. 'Ok, so you've missed the chai, but what about you? How's your leg and arm? Have you seen Gabriella yet? When will you get back to work? Heard there's been a murder up Heaton Hill and some kids or something found in a house. Sounds like they need you back.'

Gus grinned, happy to hear his old friend's infectious chatter. 'Yeah, Dad got called out twice yesterday. Won't say what's gone off but … he had a few more whiskies than usual for a Sunday.'

Mo gestured to Gus's tea and Gus obediently took another drink before he said, 'So, you heard about Gabriella leaving, did you?'

Mo snorted. 'Bitch! Picked her fucking time well didn't she? Naila and me were furious. Wouldn't have killed her to wait till you were better!'

Gus leaned over and squeezed Mo's arm, ignoring the jeers from the boys by the window. 'You're a good mate, Mo' and for the first time in what seemed a lifetime, he flung back his head and laughed. Mo studied his friend with an indulgent grin on his face.

When Gus finally stopped laughing he said, 'Your wife leaves you at death's door and you find it funny?'

Gus shook his head. 'To tell the truth, it didn't matter much when she left. We'd drifted apart and even before all this I thought she'd found someone else.'

Mo looked away.

'You know something I don't, big man?' said Gus, blowing on his tea.

Mo shrugged and began to clean the counter. 'Not my place to say, Gus. Ask her yourself, eh?'

Gus inclined his head and bit into the meaty samosa that had been deposited on the table. He sighed in pleasure. 'Anyway, I've just been to see the psycho– oops I mean psychiatrist and… drum roll please….'

Mo obediently tapped a rhythm on the counter.

'At long last she's signed me fit for work. After this I'm heading up to The Fort.'

Mo grinned and clicked his fingers together 'Yeah, man. Now you can get back to normal and move on.'

Unexpected tears filled Gus's eyes and the thick samosa pastry clogged up his throat. Mo averted his gaze. 'That's something I'll never forget Mo. Never! Killing Greg was bad enough.' He shrugged 'but not saving wee Billy and Beth… Well that kills me, bloody kills me!'

Mo nodded and squeezed his arm again. 'I know, Gus, I know.'

Fiddling with the samosa crumbs, Gus said, 'I miss him. I really miss him.'

Wiping a tear from his own eye, Mo squeezed his friend's arm. 'I do too, but it happened and I for one am bloody glad it panned out the way it did. If he'd killed you, he'd have been locked up for good and medicated. He'd know what he'd done. It would have been hell for him and, being purely selfish, I'd have lost *two* best mates not just the one.'

Considering the veracity of his statement, Gus sipped his drink savouring the warm spiciness as it spread down to his stomach.

Mo, got out photos of his girls and for a while the two of them chatted. Then, with a furtive glance towards the beaded curtain, Mo leaned over and lowered his voice so much that Gus had to hunch over to hear his words. 'I've got a bit of a problem.'

Cocking an eyebrow, Gus waited whilst Mo again looked towards the beaded curtain. 'Business has gone through the roof recently and I've not been able to keep up with the samosa-making. Understandably, Naila doesn't want to help out after working all day so we decided to get some women in for a few hours a day to mass produce the samosas.'

Mo's wife, Naila, was a social worker and worked long hours with the fostering service. When Gus nodded, Mo lowered his voice even more and leaned towards his friend. 'Well, their samosa making's fine and they work hard, but …'

Gus swirled his hand in front of him in a get a move on gesture.

'They sit round the table in there.' He gestured towards the curtained kitchen. 'They've got a sort of production line going. One rolls the dough, the second shapes them into triangles, the third fills and the fourth seals them.'

'Yeah, yeah Mo, I get it; they make bloody samosas. What's the problem?'

'That's just it.' Mo caught up in his tale, forgot to lower his voice. 'I've got no problem with their samosa making. It's their...' he swallowed and lowered his head, 'It's their *conversation.*'

Gus frowned, not getting it. 'You can't expect them to work in silence, Mo.'

Mo wafted his hands in front of him. 'No, no, I don't. Course they can talk.' He flung his hands up into the air. 'It's not them talking that's the issue. It's *what* they're talking about that's the problem.'

From the corner of his eye, Gus saw the beaded curtain twitch and was about to warn his friend, when Mo said, 'They're *always* going on about their *underwear* and what their husbands like them to wear and Ann Summers and stuff.' Mo raked his fingers through his thick hair. 'It's not like I can talk about it to Naila, is it? And if I say owt to them they'll think I've been ear-wigging into their conversations. They might think I'm a pervert and tell their husbands. It's driving me bloody mad.'

Gus, aware that the women from the kitchen were gathered in the doorway listening with huge grins on their faces, tried to shut Mo up, but he was in full flow now. 'I'm no prude. I couldn't care less about their red thongs and black bras and what not. But, it's just a bit … TMI, you get it?' He shifted on his stool. 'Especially when I see their husbands at the mosque.' He wrung his hands. 'I shouldn't know that sort of stuff about my friends' wives. I wouldn't want you to know stuff about Naila's... you know... knickers.'

Gus, really struggling not to laugh, saw one of the women put a finger over her mouth and wink. She crept quietly up behind Mo, carefully positioning the curtain behind her so the strands wouldn't click together.

Oblivious to Gus's amusement, Mo continued in a pleading voice. 'What shall I do, Gus?' and then nearly fell off his stool when the woman behind him spoke right in his ear.

'Oh, get a grip, Mo. We've been winding you up! Do you really think we'd discuss our knickers with you around?'

The other three women high-fived each other as she prodded Mo's arm. 'You're bloody daft Mo. Your Naila put us up to it, you know?'

Mo gawped at them, speechless then wiped the back of his hand over his forehead. 'So, Naila's behind this is she? I'll get my own back on her later. Thank God it's all a joke. I was seriously thinking of changing mosques because of you lot. Now instead I'll just dock your wages for cheeking me.'

The women laughed and traipsed back through to the kitchen.

Grabbing a napkin to wipe his streaming eyes Gus said, 'You know, Mo? I've not felt so good for ages. Thanks for this.'

Mo, hands on hips looked indignant 'Thanks a lot for your support, mate. I think it's about time you got back to work now. Get some normality back in your life. Go on, piss off.' And he made shooing motions with his hands as, still laughing, Gus shrugged his coat back on, hugged Mo, and left.

CHAPTER 20
Bradford

The Facilitator studied the spreadsheet on his computer. 'This is a disaster. Losing those assets has made a huge dent in the profits. Knew we shouldn't have trusted that whore, but The Distributor vouched for her.'

'Hmm.' The Matchmaker lounged on the double bed, not caring that his shoes, still wet from the snow outside, left muddy, damp marks on the white duvet. With his fingertips he rapped a rhythm on the bedside unit. 'It's not as if we need to justify our losses with the taxman, is it?'

'Suppose not; but it's a fucking mess. We're going to need to acquire more assets to meet the current orders.'

'Don't worry about that: The Provider has it in hand. What's more important now is moving forward. It's time to deal with that other bitch. Her comeuppance is long overdue. Twelve years overdue, in fact. We need to get that little job started.'

The Facilitator's voice rose, 'Look, you know I'm not convinced about this. Can't you just let that lie? Our business is flourishing again now. Why rock the boat?'

'I spent ages locating her and now that things are in place I'm not walking away. I *will* have my revenge. Have you forgotten how close we were to being caught? How much revenue we lost, not to mention the damage to our reputation? All because of her interference.'

Head bowed, The Facilitator's next words were spoken in a quiet voice. 'I still think we should focus our energies on the current problems, namely reassuring our clients and acquiring new assets.'

The Matchmaker's mouth opened in a silent snarl. With effort, he relaxed his facial muscles before speaking.

'There's nothing to say we can't combine the two, is there?' He stood and took the single step necessary to reach the Facilitator and gripped the other man's arm just a little too tightly. 'Are you with me on this?'

The Facilitator's nervous swallow satisfied him that his lead would be followed. He released his grip and sat down on the edge of the bed avoiding the damp patch left by his shoes. Crossing his legs, he waited for the other man to speak.

'Are we ready? Is everything in place?' said The Facilitator, fiddling with the strap of his laptop bag.

The Matchmaker grinned. All trace of his previous displeasure eradicated from his face. 'Oh yes everything's in place. It'll happen tomorrow!' He rubbed his hands together and jumped to his feet. Retrieving his coat from the flimsy wardrobe, he slipped it back on. It was still faintly warm. Sensing his colleague's anxiety, he said, 'Don't worry. Everything's under control. Trust me.'

The Facilitator nodded once. Satisfied, The Matchmaker turned and left the hotel room. It had been risky meeting in a rooms-by-the-hour hotel, but he knew they weren't too fussy. And, of course, he'd taken the usual precautions to protect himself, and he assumed The Facilitator would have done the same. Striding back toward Bradford City centre, beanie hat pulled over his forehead and scarf wound round his mouth, he knew he was unidentifiable. As he walked, he planned his next conversation. When he was ready, everything clear in his mind, he stepped inside an empty bus shelter, speed-dialled The Distributor's number from his safe phone and waited.

'Yep!'

The Matchmaker scowled at the abrupt greeting, imagining the other man's graceless bulk lounging in an unsavoury stained couch, beer cans and discarded food scattered around, the air soured by the pervading odour of days-old sweat. He began without preamble, his tone clipped and disapproving.

'Yet again you've fucked up and, yet again, I'm not impressed. Damn shoddy work if I'm honest, damn shoddy.'

Hearing the other man's laboured breathing down the phone, the Matchmaker, added the presence of a drugged-up whore and the lingering stink of stale sex to his previous image. His mouth curled in distaste as he paced back and forth in the confined space of the shelter. The Distributor really was an abominable creature.

When he'd caught his breath enough reply, The Distributor sounded defensive. 'Well, it's not as if we've lost much is it? Most of the little buggers were well used. Past their sell by dates. I think we got our money's worth from them.'

The Matchmaker snorted. 'That's really *not* the point, is it?' he said, his voice curt.

The Distributor remained silent.

'This is bad management and now the problem isn't that the police have our assets. It's that they've also got a credible witness. One that isn't too traumatised to speak!' He paced his office and waited for The Distributor to realise who he meant.

It took a minute, then in a stunned whisper, The Distributor said, 'Shit, you mean her son?'

'Exactly! Now we need to nullify the risk of him revealing crucial information.' He hesitated then delivered his final thrust. 'Like a detailed description of the idiot who delivered the kids to his mother's door. Do you understand?'

The other man swallowed, and a satisfied smile spread over The Matchmaker's face.

'What shall we do?'

The Matchmaker laughed. '*We* won't do anything. *You,* however, need to nullify him.'

'Me?'

'Yes, you! You messed up, you sort it out. Today!'

A moment's hesitation, then reluctantly, 'Yes, yes, ok, I'll deal with the boy.'

'Good, that's sorted then.' The Matchmaker smiled and, pacing suspended, delivered his sucker punch in a conversational tone. 'Oh and we'll be moving on to phase two tomorrow, by the way.'

'What?' Disbelief resonated through the phone. 'Tomorrow? You can't be serious!'

'Oh but I am. Perfectly serious. School's on holiday and they're vulnerable right now. It's the perfect opportunity. Don't let me down.'

CHAPTER 21
Oak Lane

Mo's samosa and spicy tea sat nicely in Gus's stomach as he began the hike up Oak Lane to Lilycroft Police Station, home to Bradford CID. As he passed the bright blue painted medical centre he saw a group of women with pushchairs approach it and realised it must be baby clinic day. A faint cry from one of the buggies made him smile.

A crossroads marked the end of Oak Lane and the start of Lilycroft Road. Waiting for the lights to change, Gus studied the towering building opposite that he and his colleagues nicknamed The Fort. He sympathised with the local communities who'd protested that the huge sloping walls surrounding the station gave it a threatening air. So much for community policing, huh? Even the few children's drawings, blown up and stuck to the walls failed to soften the 'Big Brother' feel of the building. Opposite The Fort, in complete contrast was the sand-blasted, newly refurbished Lister Mills Apartment Complex. Maintaining the outward appearance of the old wool mill, the complex consisted of up-market apartments. The force's local greasy spoon, The Chaat Café, was situated just along from it.

Gus's older sister Katie had bought one of the apartments, yet, despite its close proximity to his work, Gus rarely visited her. Something about the minimalist, too clean, too sparse décor made him yearn to muss up her Laura Ashley cushions and leave sweat marks on her glass coffee table by propping his feet on it, preferably after a long jog. Maybe he reverted back to childhood roles with Katie because they'd always been so different. He loved to annoy her and she loved to be annoyed with him… Natural sibling rivalry according to his mum.

85

Since 'the incident' he'd avoided everyone, including Katie, whose insistent hovering had gradually reduced to the odd phone call and occasional family Sunday lunch, in light of his steadfast refusal to interact. He felt guilty that despite her best efforts, he'd shut her out, just like everyone else.

The green man beeped and Gus crossed the road, the twinge in his hip telling him he'd overdone the walking today. A sudden impulse to see his sister, combined with the need for pain relief before facing his team, made him cross the road to her apartment complex rather than continuing up the incline to The Fort. Maybe he'd be lucky and she'd be home. If she was in, he'd share his good news, pop some painkillers and then head over to the station.

Gus pressed the buzzer at the gated entrance and before long he saw a figure wearing a security guard uniform approach. The navy jumper stretched over the man's generous belly and his peaked hat was tipped at a jaunty angle. If he hadn't already known about ex-copper Frank Hobson's leg injury, he wouldn't have noticed the slight drag of his right leg.

'Well, well, well, if it isn't DI Dread McGuire. Hold on and I'll buzz you through.'

Gus grinned, as the gate opened. He stepped through and was immediately pulled into a gentle hug. 'Good to see you, Frank, didn't know you'd started here. How're tricks?' he said, extricating himself.

'Started last week. Wife got fed up with me at home.' Frank grinned. 'What about you? Heard you'd been through the mill a bit yourself.'

Gus nodded and pointed to his shoulder. 'On the mend now, Frank. I've only popped in to see my sister, then I'm headed over there. Signed fit for work again at last.'

'Didn't know your sister lived here,' said Frank. He lowered his voice. 'Bloody tragic, that case your team caught yesterday. Bet they'll be glad to have you back. Young Alice looked drained when I saw her in Chaat's this morning.'

Gus frowned. 'I'm not up to speed yet. I know my dad looked pretty frazzled yesterday and Mo says it's something to do with kids?'

'Yeah, that's what I heard too. It's always a fucker when there's kids involved.' He pointed over Gus's shoulder. 'Must be serious because the vultures are out.'

Gus glanced back towards The Fort where Frank was pointing. A huddle of hacks stood on the pavement, smoking and laughing, whilst a young Muslim woman with a pushchair struggled to edge past them without stepping onto the road. A yell came from the top of the station's steps. Gus recognised the duty sergeant shouting at the reporters to stop causing an obstruction or risk spending a few hours in the cells. Gus smiled when he heard one of them shouting back that 'It'd be a damn sight warmer in the cells', whilst the others apologised profusely to the woman and moved to the side, leaving the pavement clear.

With Frank, Gus walked across the square open-topped atrium that nestled under the surrounding flats. When they reached the shiny new lifts that snuggled discreetly near the entrance to the underground car park, Gus pressed the button.

Frank jerked his head upward. 'Can't be doing with them flats, Gus, too damn clinical for my liking.'

'God, I know, I prefer my own shabby, cluttered gaff to this, but each to their own, eh?' said Gus, wondering what clutter he'd find when he returned to his own house.

The lift door opened silently and with a nod to Frank, Gus stepped in and was whisked to the second floor. He exited and walked over to Katie's front door – expensively fashioned from Nordic wood with overly-shiny chrome fittings – and pressed the bell. Moments later the intercom buzzed and a distorted female voice spoke.

Gus, presuming the disjointed voice required identification, replied. 'It's your younger and *much* more attractive sibling, Katie, open up and let me in before I collapse in a heap at your door. My leg's killing me.'

There was a moment's silence before Gus heard someone fumbling with the lock. Then the door was pulled open. The smile on his face faded. 'What the fuck are you doing here?'

The woman gripped the door tightly and said, 'You look well, Gus.'

Absent-mindedly rubbing his throbbing thigh, he studied her, trying to make sense of his estranged wife's presence in his sister's flat. Last time he'd seen her had been when she had told him she was leaving him, just before he was released from hospital. Now, three months later here she was. He released a guttural laugh and clicked his fingers together. 'Do I? Of course you wouldn't *know* how I am, Gabriella, because you haven't seen me for three months, have you? Not since you dropped your little bombshell and then fucked off.'

Gabriella's eyes flashed at his words, but she remained silent, which annoyed Gus even more. What the fuck was she doing here, in Katie's flat? He knew she'd cleared all her belongings from their marital home because his dad had told him, but no one seemed to know where she'd gone. Except Katie? Why the hell wouldn't Katie tell him if she knew where she was? It didn't make sense and now here she was looking up at him with those enormous chocolate button eyes shimmering with unshed tears. A flash of irritation made him glower at her. No way was her 'poor little me' act going to work on him. No fucking way. He'd been there and done that during their tempestuous marriage and, despite feeling let down when she'd walked out, his overwhelming feeling had been one of relief. He wouldn't fall for her tears now. She'd behaved despicably and he wanted to know why her exit from his life had been so abrupt. 'Aren't you going to invite your *husband* into his sister's flat, huh, *darling*?'

He saw a spark of anger in her eyes, but she opened the door wider and stepped back. 'Come in then. Katie's at work, though.'

Stepping through the door onto the virgin wood floor he momentarily considered removing his shoes to protect the polished surface, but, all of a sudden, he felt drained and it seemed like just too much effort. Besides he felt angry with Katie for providing a safe haven for his estranged wife without telling him. A bit of melting snow on her beloved floor felt like just retribution.

In tracksuit and slipper socks, brown hair tied in an untidy knot on the top of her head, Gabriella led the way through to the open-plan sitting area. Without waiting to be asked, Gus plonked himself down on the cream leather sofa and began to massage his thigh. She walked over to the adjoining kitchen area, leaned against the breakfast bar and folded her arms across her chest. Her fingers clenched and unclenched repeatedly against her upper arms. With a wary expression, she gestured to Gus's leg. 'You ok?'

His dreads bounced as his head jerked up and he lasered her with a look. 'What the fuck do you think, Gaby?'

Her face paled and before she could reply Gus pushed himself from the soft cushions and walked over, stopping just in front of her. 'Don't try to excuse your behaviour, Gabriella.' He said, each word staccato. 'Three months you've had to make contact, three fucking months!' His voice rose, 'but no, not as much as a letter or a phone call. Nothing! Not a fucking thing!'

Gabriella flinched as miniscule drops of spittle hit her face.

He snorted and took a backward step. 'What? You think I'm going to hit you?'

She shook her head. He watched as a single tear ran down her cheek and he felt drained. When he finally spoke his voice was low. 'Have I *ever* touched you? Hit you? Beat you?'

More tears ran down her face and she shook her head furiously. 'No, no of course not Gus. It's just…' she wiped her sleeve over her cheek and tried to control her breathing. Gus studied her face and then, stepping back, returned to the sofa and flopped down. 'Just what, Gaby?'

Her chest heaved, she whispered. 'I'm sorry, Gus, truly sorry.'

Running fingers through his dreads, he sighed. 'You and me both Gaby. But fuck, you shouldn't have done it the way you did.' He shook his head and smiled sadly. 'I'm not stupid. I know things weren't going well with us. I knew it was only a matter of time, but fuck's sake, what made you do it like that?'

Hands shaking, she walked round the breakfast bar and switched the kettle on. 'Coffee?'

Knowing how much Gabriella detested the smell of coffee, Gus usually opted for tea. This time though, no longer the dutiful husband, he nodded, adding, 'and a glass of water.'

She gave him his water and he popped a couple of painkillers from his packet swallowing them with a slug. As she busied herself with the kettle, he studied her. Her head was bowed and tension radiated from her shoulder muscles as she spooned coffee into a cafetière.

Finally, she spoke. 'Things were complicated Gus, really complicated and…' she sighed. 'I panicked when you got hurt and was scared that if I didn't leave straight away, then I'd never leave.'

'Thought you'd be too guilt-ridden to leave a cripple, is that it, Gaby?'

She glanced at him over her shoulder. 'Yes, maybe. It's not as if things were rosy between us, is it?' She poured boiling water into the cafetière and took a mug from the wall unit. 'I'm sorry. I should've been in touch, should've explained things before now.'

'Damn right you should. Five years of marriage, I think deserved an explanation at the very least. Not a kick in my already rather painful groin!'

She carefully placed his drink on the coffee table and moved back to her previous position by the breakfast bar, as if in need of its support to hold her upright.

'I don't get why you're here though, in Katie's flat.'

Exhaling slowly, she bit her lip and looking directly at him, said, 'Don't you? Can you *really* not guess?'

Gus frowned and glanced round the room, knowing he was missing something. Dotted about along the window sill and on the book shelves were a few familiar objects. Ornaments that had once been in his home. Next to a vase of lilies, was a photo frame with two radiant people smiling from the top of The Cow and Calf rocks. He moved his eyes back to her face. She held his gaze as the pieces began to slide together. Then she nodded.

Gus swallowed hard to release the lump that had materialised in his throat. 'No, Gaby, please, not that.'

Wringing her fingers, Gabriella looked straight at him as she spoke. 'I'm sorry, Gus. We both are. We didn't mean it to happen.' Her gaze fell to the floor. 'I'm sorry.'

Ignoring the protests from his stiffened muscles, Gus stood up. Swinging his man bag onto his shoulder, he knocked his coffee cup over the cream rug that lay beneath the coffee table. His lips curled in a sneer as he walked towards the door. 'Fuck you, Gaby, and fuck Katie too!'

He slammed out of the flat and down the stairs, not responding to Frank's cheerful 'Goodbye.' Fighting for breath, he stopped when he reached Lilycroft Road and looked up at Katie's flat. Gabriella watched him from the window. He turned away and dodged through a gap in the traffic and, with a sudden surge of relief, climbed the few steps to The Fort and, ignoring the insistent jabber of the journos, he went back to work.

CHAPTER 22
Rosalind Street

Jamal Asif stood on the top step in front of a house halfway along the row of terraces. His clothes were mucky and he knew he stank. His head had been pounding since the previous morning and he knew it was because of his hangover. He hoped Ishaq wouldn't smell the alcohol on him.

Driving sleet had emptied the street of all but a few locals determined to buy their cigs or booze from the One Stop at the end of the road, but still, he glanced up and down before pounding on the door with his clenched fist. His entire body shook and veins of dried tears slashed his face and as soon as his half-brother Ishaq opened the door he threw himself into his arms, reassured by his familiar soapy scent.

'What's wrong, Jamal?'

Jamal felt himself being hefted through the door and into the warm house. The familiar smell of pakoras frying made Jamal's stomach gurgle. He was starving. He'd slept in the village hall doorway the night before because Frankie's mum wouldn't let him sleep over on a school night and he hadn't dared go home. Anyway, it hadn't been much colder than it was at home and he'd managed to get a newspaper and a smelly blanket in exchange for a blowjob from the old perv that lived near the chippy. He wouldn't tell Ishaq that though – he wouldn't understand. He'd just think he was a poof and make him go to the mosque and pray. The Imam would go on and on about upholding the faith and shit. They'd no idea… no idea at all.

As Ishaq released him, Jamal fell to the carpeted floor, curled into the foetal position and all bravado gone, sobbed like the fourteen-year-old boy he was. He heard Ishaq calling in a panicky voice for his wife. Asma ran from the kitchen and then she was on her knees by his side, her cool hand pushing his hair back from his eyes. She looked concerned and the small frown crinkling her forehead made him feel guilty for bringing his troubles to them when they had a new baby to look after. He allowed her to rock him back and forth until his sobs faded to sporadic hiccups and then, when he was spent they helped him through to the small cellar head kitchen at the back of the house. He slid into a chair at the table next to the high chair, dropped his head into his palms and groaned.

'What's wrong, beta? Has that bitch done something to you?' Ishaq raked fingers through his thick black hair and, unable to pace effectively in the small space, he fell into the chair opposite Jamal. 'I'll kill her! I bloody will. I'll kill the bitch!'

Fresh tears rolled down Jamal's cheeks and he saw Asma direct a stern look at her husband. Ishaq pushed himself away from the table as she spoke to Jamal. 'Sssh, beta, ssh! Your brother will sort it all out. Just tell us what's happened. What has she done this time?'

Jamal looked from his brother to his sister-in-law. His head felt heavy and his eyes sore. Exhaustion descended on him like a dark cloud and his shoulders slumped. Then, a cry from upstairs made him sit up. His nephew was awake. What was he thinking of troubling Asma and Ishaq like this? He grabbed a handful of tissues and scrubbed his face as Asma, with a final quick hug left to tend to her baby.

Jamal, hands clasped on the table waited till she'd gone before speaking. 'She's dead, Ishaq! My mum's dead. They found her yesterday and they've taken the kids into care!' Tears rolled down his cheeks and dropped onto the table as Ishaq stared at him before saying, his tone resigned, 'Well, it was only a matter of time before she ODed. It's no loss to us, Jamal. Now you're free of her and the children will have the chance of a half-decent life.'

Jamal wiped an already grubby sleeve over his snotty nose and glared at his brother. 'Fuck off Ishaq, just fuck off. I know you hate her but she's me mam. She was me mam.' Fresh tears rolled down his cheeks, his fists clenched on top of the table as he stared his brother down for a second before lowering his gaze.

Ishaq moved round and put his arm round Jamal. 'I'm sorry, Jamal.'

Nodding abruptly Jamal said, 'It weren't drugs, Ishaq – she were murdered.'

'Murdered?' said Ishaq exhaling a long slow breath.

Jamal nodded. 'She were drunk on Saturday, so I stayed over at Frankie's in Frizinghall. When I went back this morning the house was all covered in crime scene tape and Mrs Khalifa told me what had happened.'

For a minute or two the only sounds in the small house were the muffled tones of Asma comforting her baby upstairs. Then, Ishaq pushed his chair back from the table and stood up.

'You need to get cleaned up. You stink of alcohol and Allah knows what else.'

Jamal, head bowed said 'I'm sorry, Ishaq. It were Frankie that made me.'

Ishaq tutted. 'I've told you before. You can't hang out with the white boys, Jamal. There's too much temptation to stray. Now that woman's dead you'll start coming to the mosque with me and learn how to be a proper Muslim.'

Jamal's heart sank. He loved his brother dearly, but he wasn't sure he wanted to live the devout life Ishaq did. There was nothing he could do about that now, so he dutifully nodded and headed upstairs to shower.

CHAPTER 23
The Fort

There's an odour that pervades most police stations and Lilycroft police station, home of Bradford's CID, was no exception. It was a mixture of sweat, disinfectant, urine and hard work. Gus breathed it in eagerly as he walked through the doors. He'd missed this smell. It signified purpose and justice to him. The place where, above all others, he felt at home, felt that *he,* personally, made a difference. He was damn glad to be back. Regardless of Dr Mahmood's reservations, Gus knew this was the one place capable of healing him.

With the same single-mindedness that had always been a bone of contention between him and Gabriella, he put their earlier encounter to the back of his mind. Walking unnoticed into the incident room he took a moment to devour the scene before him. Without warning his eyes welled up and with an angry shrug he blinked the tears away. Compo, surrounded by a complicated system of IT equipment, drink cans, mugs, a variety of food containers ranging from Chaat's cafe sandwich bags to Tupperware containers, rocked to whatever beat thrummed from his earphones. Casually dressed, as per usual, in jeans and a retro band t-shirt – today's was Bowie's Aladdin Sane. The beanie hat, which, combined with his unusual computer talent, had earned him his nickname, sat firmly on his head.

DS Alice Cooper, unfortunately named by parents who lived a sheltered existence in the labs of academia at Oxford University and had no idea that another more famous Alice Cooper existed, had her head immersed in reports and interviews. She was his right-hand woman and he had utmost faith in her abilities; a faith she occasionally lacked. Clad in gothic black from her black skin tight polo neck jumper down past her black dress trousers to her black kick 'em in the head bovver boots, sat in front of the crime board. His gaze was drawn to the twenty pairs of bruised eyes that looked back at him. Momentarily, he was reminded of the confused look in little Billy's eyes, before they'd fluttered closed forever, but he quickly shut the thought down. This was work, no time for sentiment.

The new addition, DC John Sampson, recently recruited to CID and requested by Gus for the team months ago, was typing rapidly on his computer in the corner. Suddenly, a scuffle of chairs, a high pitched screech and a hug that squashed his sore arm, told him he'd been spotted. Gently, he pulled away from Compo's limpet embrace, smiling as Alice and Sampson jumped up to greet him in a clatter of enthusiastic chatter.

Practically stammering in excitement, Alice jumped up and down. 'You're back. Great. We weren't expecting you till tomorrow.'

Grabbing Alice in a one-armed hug, he said, 'It's good to be back, Al. Hope you've got everything under control.'

Her face clouded and she tapped the floor impatiently with her foot. 'Don't know about that, Gus. This one's bloody bad.'

Shaking hands with Sampson, Gus, itching to crack on, flicked a glance at the children on the board and nodded. 'I can see that, Al. Come on, get me a coffee and fill me in.'

Alice pouted. 'Get your own bloody coffee, Gus. I've got a murder and a paedophile ring to investigate *and* I'm expecting some VIPs, at DCI Chalmers' request.' She paused and grinned at him. 'Of course, you're perfectly welcome to sit in. It'll bring you up to speed and then you can take over, ok?'

'Who are the VIPs?'

'Well, the first one is a Detective Jankowski from Poland who was investigating the disappearance of three of the children we've discovered.' She pointed to three faces on the wall. 'He's bringing the parents with him. One set of parents will be identifying their dead child.'

She bit her lip and then turned back to Gus. 'The second guest is an ex-colleague of Nancy's from Cambridge, a DCI Wentworth who specialises in this sort of thing. Nancy's got it into her head that there are similarities to a case she worked in 2003. They should be here any minute.'

Gus walked over to the coffeemaker, poured himself a coffee and depositing his bag on the floor next to his chair, slouched out of his jacket and flung it across the back of the chair as he listened carefully to Alice's update, the PM findings and the actions she'd initiated. When she finished he said, 'Good job, Al. I think you've covered everything for now.'

He walked over to the children's photos and, reciting each name silently to himself he committed their ages, details and images to memory. His responsibility was to them now.

CHAPTER 24
Rosalind Street

A t *least there's usually two pigs in the car when they're staking out a house,* thought The Distributor, fidgeting in his seat. He was desperate to piss and wasn't sure there was enough room left in the coke bottle he'd brought with him for that purpose. He'd been here for over an hour now and despite his bulky coat, gloves and hat, he was freezing. He didn't dare risk putting the engine on. Didn't want to attract attention, even if the car was stolen. No doubt some nosy git would question what he was doing and the last thing he needed was to be noticed.

Trying to distract himself he peered through the slightly iced windscreen and scowled at the loved-up couple, snuggled together, oblivious to the wet sleet that froze as soon as it landed. Jiggling his leg, he hoiked up a glob of phlegm, cracked the window a slit and gobbed it out onto the slushy road. The lad suddenly stooped, scooped up a handful of snow and shoved it down his girlfriend's neck, dancing away laughing as she screeched and jumped on the spot trying to dislodge the snow. Then she too started to giggle, scooped up a handful of snow and ran after the lad.

'Idiots!' said The Distributor and tilted his head to glare once more at the terraced house with its cheery red door. Nothing, not a bloody thing. He dipped his hand into the gap in the door, grabbed the coke bottle and cracked the window again. Within seconds he'd upended the bottle and a flood of piss cascaded onto the road forming a trickle that froze into a puddle like a discarded lemon ice lolly. Shuffling his hand down his trousers to release his penis, he sighed with relief as he peed into the receptacle. Glancing at his mark, he cursed, jerked upright dislodging his penis and depositing droplets of urine over his hand and trousers.

'Fuck!' he quickly screwed the lid back on the bottle and watched as two police officers approached the house he was watching. '*How the fuck can you have a bloody wog with a turban over his uniform and a bloody Paki bitch in a man suit enforcing law and order? No wonder the country is in a fucking recession if they are depending on the likes of them to keep crime at bay.*'

He rested his hand on the steering wheel, hesitated and then reluctantly took his phone out of his pocket and pressed redial on a familiar number. 'We've got trouble,' he said when his call was answered. 'Two oink-oinks just went into the kid's brother's house. What'll I do now?'

The silence from the phone filled him with foreboding. The Matchmaker was completely ruthless and he dreaded being told to '*Off the pigs and, the kid.*' He was still holding his breath when The Matchmaker responded. 'Wait and watch. You might get an opportunity to intervene when the police leave.' He paused for a second and then continued. 'I've reconsidered by the way. Don't kill the boy. Bring him to the depot. We may be able to recoup some of our losses.' He laughed. 'Some of our clients like a, shall we say, slightly more mature challenge. I'm not averse to that myself.' He laughed again and hung up.

The Distributor shuddered and took a deep breath. Thank God. Abduction was more his thing than killing. When the police left he'd knock on the door, push his way in, threaten them with the gun and take the boy. He reached over and pulled a black balaclava onto his lap. Yes, that was a much better solution all round.

CHAPTER 25
The Fort

The visitor strutted into the incident room like a prize ram suffering from testosterone overload. Gus winked at Alice indicating that she should take the lead. She turned, hand outstretched to greet him. 'DCI Wentworth? So pleased to meet you. We really could do with your help on this one. I'm DS Cooper and this is …'

Wentworth placed his hand momentarily in hers and then, without bothering to disguise his actions, wiped it down his trouser leg, walking away before Alice could introduce Gus. She raised an eyebrow, but said nothing. Instead, she gestured to the pictures pinned on the crime board. 'These are the children we found in Sharon Asif's attic. We've already made headway into identifying some of them and repatriation is in process.'

Wentworth nodded dismissively, hoisted his bottom onto the edge of Compo's desk and, rubbing his chin with one hand, studied the photos. Alice stood by his side until from the corner of her eye she saw Sampson discreetly waving his hand at her. She stepped out of Wentworth's line of vision and mouthed, 'What?'

He pointed at DCI Wentworth's bottom wedged on Compo's desk. Alice frowned and looked. Then, understanding dawned. Protruding from beneath Wentworth's expensively suited bottom was the greasy remnants of Compo's latest bacon butty. Her face tensed and she glared at Compo who didn't seem overly concerned that his bacon wrapper was now stuck on the arse of a visiting DCI. Her eyes fluttered up in disgust and then she shrugged, plastered an insincere smile on her face and spoke to their guest, 'Coffee?'

Wentworth grunted and Alice, assuming it meant 'yes', gestured to Sampson to get it for him. She glanced at Gus who, with a small shake of his head, indicated he wanted her to continue. Alice cleared her throat. 'Is there anything else I can get you, DCI Wentworth?'

He swivelled his bottom on the table and Alice inwardly cringed at the damage he was surely inflicting on his very expensive looking trousers. Folding his arms across his chest revealing sparkling cufflinks he said, 'DCI Chalmers not about?'

Alice shook her head. 'No, she had another appointment. She said she'd drop in when she got back.'

His lips tightened and he tugged gently at his jacket sleeves. 'Not important enough for her to cancel her appointment, huh?' The smile he flashed nearly blinded Alice as he continued. 'Left me with her minions, *despite* me heading up from Cambridge at a moment's notice.'

Alice's eyes narrowed. She was tempted to take the coffee Sampson had made, fling it over his supercilious head and watch it cascade down his designer Italian suit. Instead she kept her face expressionless. 'I'm sure DCI Chalmers appreciates your prompt arrival and I'm sure she'll be here just as soon as she can.' Thankfully the door opened interrupting her before she clicked her heels together and sieg heiled Wentworth. A haggard, dishevelled, bald man in his fifties entered, escorted in by one of the duty constables.

'Detective Jankowksi, from Poland, DS Cooper.' The constable spotted Gus behind his desk and his face broke into a grin. 'Nice to have you back, DI McGuire.'

Wentworth immediately turned to Gus, a look of annoyance on his face. 'Why didn't you introduce yourself if you're the senior officer? Why are you allowing a sergeant,' he spoke the last word with distaste, 'to brief me?'

Gus remained seated, his ice-blue eyes scouring Wentworth's face for a few seconds before he spoke. 'DS

Cooper, is more able than I to brief you. In fact, she's just done an excellent job of briefing me as I've only just returned to work an hour ago.' He allowed his gaze to drift up and down Wentworth before adding. 'Oh, and by the way, in Yorkshire we don't tolerate arses lightly, no matter their rank. Show a bit of respect for my team whilst you're here, please.'

Wentworth's face flushed and he opened his mouth to respond, but Gus already turning to greet the new arrival, said, 'DS Cooper will brief you both.'

Complete silence reigned until Wentworth stood and pointedly turned away from Gus, issuing a 'We'll see what DCI Chalmers has to say about your behaviour,' over his shoulder. He then nudged Alice out of the way in order to greet the Polish Detective.

As he turned away from her Alice noticed the bacon wrapper on his arse and reached out to remove it, then with a smirk she withdrew her hand and let the bag remain in place, hoping the grease was seeping right into the fabric.

'Jankowski, good to see you again. Been a long time, huh?' said Wentworth in a loud voice, as he pumped the other man's hand up and down with unnecessary vigour.

Jankowski peeled his hand away and took a step back, looking over Wentworth's shoulder at Alice who scowled ferociously. With a small half-smile, he side-stepped Wentworth, extended his hand and in near perfect English greeted her before turning to Gus and nodding.

Gus smiled back as Alice returned Jankowski's handshake and led him over to a chair between their two desks. She nodded at Sampson who appeared almost immediately with a steaming coffee. Detective Jankowski settled heavily into the chair, sighed, ran his hand over his bald head and studied the pictures on the wall.

Finally, he said, 'This never gets any easier, but at least this time we've managed to reunite some of these children with their parents. Now their healing process can commence.'

Alice and Gus both nodded, allowing him the time to sip his coffee whilst Wentworth tapped his fingers impatiently on the desk, his knee bobbing up and down in rhythmic annoyance as Alice began to brief the two detectives on their investigation.

Halfway through Alice's update the door burst open and in an effervescent wave of expensive scent, DCI Nancy Chalmers burst in waving her arms in all-encompassing greeting as she walked smartly across the room towards the two visitors. 'Oh, I'm so glad you're both here. How was the flight, Jankowski?' She grimaced. 'Awful, I expect. Are the parents settled with their children now?'

Jankowski stood and took two steps towards Nancy, his eyes lighting up for the first time as he stretched out a huge hand which she took between her two smaller hands and gripped tightly. 'It's good to see you again, Nancy, and yes, the parents are reunited with their children, both living and dead.' He grimaced and Nancy patted his hand reassuringly before turning to the other man who'd remained seated.

Flashing an insincere smile, Wentworth said, 'So, you've finally deigned to turn up Nancy?'

'Had a physio appointment, David. Did you want me to cancel it?'

Wentworth shook his head. 'Oh no, of course not, Nancy. Back problems is it?'

Her eyes sparkled with amusement. 'No. Women's problems, David.' She leaned towards him, looking straight into his eyes. 'But don't worry my pelvic floor is in tip top condition. In fact, the physio says if I keep doing my exercises I'll be smoking fags from my fanny again before long.'

Wentworth's smile faded, as a thunderous guffaw erupted from Jankowski. Nancy winked at Alice. 'Come on let's have lunch before we get down to business.'

As the two men left the office, she turned to Gus. 'Wasn't expecting you back till tomorrow, Gus, but it's good to see you back. We'll catch up later.'

CHAPTER 26
Bradford

❛ Look, all I want to know is, what are the implications of them finding those damn brats in Heaton? All I'm concerned, all we're *all* concerned, about is that they can't trace them back to any of us.'

The Matchmaker wanted to tell the old bugger on the other end of the phone to piss off, but he knew that this needed to be handled with care. After all their reputation was at stake here and, as they were all too painfully aware, their business had taken a long time to rebuild after the debacle twelve years previously. Their clientele needed to feel safe doing business with them and it was his job to make sure they did. He didn't like the pompous little bastard but he *was* influential with their other clients, not to mention undeniably rich. His finances had been crucial to them regrouping so quickly.

The Matchmaker had just got back from a lunchtime run when the call came and he could smell the sweat on his skin. He needed to get showered, changed and back to work ASAP. Things were hectic and he couldn't afford to be gone for too long. On the other hand, he couldn't very well fob this client off. He wiped his face and slung the towel round his neck before replying. 'There's no need to worry. We've got everything under control. This was an isolated incident that cannot be traced back to us and certainly *not* to you.'

'Yes, well, you would say that, but I had contact with at least one of those brats and I don't want this coming back to bite me on the ass, forensically speaking that is!'

The Matchmaker bit his lip. He wasn't entirely sure how *clean* the kids had been at the end. He'd taken his eye off the ball on that one. Leaving it to The Distributor to negotiate a safe house had been a mistake and he had no guarantees that established protocol had been utilised after each meeting, but he wasn't going to admit that.

Instead he put on his most disdainful voice and replied, 'We're not amateurs you know. That's why you and your friends are happy to pay the big bucks. You know when you rent from us, you're guaranteed complete removal of *all* evidence. It's part of the deal.'

'Well, just so you know, I've got eyes on the periphery of this investigation so I'll know if you're bullshitting me.'

The Matchmaker laughed, 'And *I've* got eyes *inside* the investigation. Nothing gets left to chance with our organisation.'

'Who *are* you?' asked the other man, his voice quiet.

Again The Matchmaker laughed. 'All you need to know is that I'm extremely well-connected. Even more well-connected than you.'

***

Rosalind Street

The Distributor sat in the stolen car opposite Ishaq Asif's house in Great Horton. Bored, he watched the two stupid loved-up kids heading back down the street, each with bulging Tesco bags swinging from their wrists. Their free arms were wrapped round each other, making them look like a pair of Siamese twins. The Distributor, pissed off by the brooding Adele song on the radio, leaned forward and with half an eye on the red door, fiddled with the dials trying to find Capital. At least it was usually quite lively. The door had remained resolutely shut for the past three-quarters of an hour and he wondered exactly what the brat was telling the police.

Bruce Springsteen's 'Born to Run' flooded the car. As he tapped along to the beat he admitted to himself that it had been a mistake to use Sharon Asif's grotty house as a storage facility. It was cheap, if not cheerful, and he'd enjoyed being able to syphon off some of the rent that he'd have had to pay for a more anonymous place, but as a long-term strategy it had been a mistake. He bit his lip and was cursing his short-sighted greed when the door finally opened. The two police officers stepped forward, turned and the woman spoke to the tall skinny Pakistani, probably the brother, who held the door slightly ajar. At last the brother nodded and shut the door. The two officers walked down the steps and turned towards their car, not bothering to look in his direction.

He pulled balaclava on, slipped the gun into his waistband and, with his hand on the door handle, waited till they started their car. He was just about to open the car door when Jamal and his brother, both wrapped up for the winter weather stepped out of the house and quickly ran down the steps. A black Corsa at the kerb beeped and, before he could do anything, the two of them were inside.

A quick glance down the road told him the police car was still there. Fuck, he'd have to do it now. Quickly he flicked the key in the ignition, opened the window, grabbed the gun from his trousers and took aim. Two shots in quick succession hit the black Corsa sending an avalanche of glass into the car. The two loved-up kids turned, hands to their mouths as The Distributor quickly took off. The boy took a step towards the speeding car and, without thinking, The Distributor poked the gun through the window and fired before accelerating past the police car that now drew level with the Corsa. Glancing in his mirror he saw Tesco bags strewn in the snow and the boy lying on his back, his girlfriend kneeling by his side. Behind them the female officer jumped out leaving the Sikh officer to follow.

The Distributor took advantage of his head-start, screeched down side streets, turning twice before reaching Great Horton Road. He accelerated, and driving on the wrong side of the street, stormed down towards The Mumtaz restaurant, before screeching suddenly to the left at the traffic lights in front of cars that had been intending to go straight. His manoeuvre caused the cars to swerve and three cars collided, stopping the police car from following. Quickly nipping into the Asda car park on Cemetery Road, he parked up between two people carriers. His heart was hammering and he was sweating profusely. He grabbed his belongings, gave the car a final cursory check and left the car park on foot, glad he'd kept his gloves on the whole time.

CHAPTER 27
The Fort

B y the time DC Hussain had contacted The Fort about the shooting in Great Horton, DCI Chalmers had lunched the visitors. Then, reassured by Gus's return to work, had excused herself and departed to oversee a major liaison involving Leeds and Bradford Drugs units. Quickly, Gus updated them on the recent shooting on Rosalind Street and informed them that they were waiting for Jamal and his brother to be checked over at the hospital before they were transported to The Fort for interview.

Jankowski was the first to speak. 'Your detective Compo worked very quickly to identify the children from the Interpol missing children's files. I believe there are only a few still unidentified and he has managed to identify both of the dead children, too.' He inclined his head with a smile towards Compo, who had remained by his computer rather than join the rest of the team at the table.

'Yes, Compo worked overnight yesterday to match the children.' said Gus.

Wentworth, still upset by the grease mark he'd finally discovered on the back of his trousers, snorted. 'Humph, that explains the ripe stench of BO accompanying the bacon smell.'

Turning steady blue eyes on Wentworth, Gus waited till the other man looked away before speaking. 'I think we *all* agree that the smell of bacon butties and the sweat of hard work is a minor discomfort compared to what each of those poor children suffered since their disappearances. If bacon butties and all-nighters get results, then I'm all for it. My team work hard and some of them haven't been home since yesterday. If it bothers you that much we'll open the windows, but what is most important right now is the need to move quickly on this.'

Jankowski caught Gus's eye and smiled before turning to Wentworth. 'Do you see the similarities?' he said

Wentworth frowned. 'Similarities? Not sure I get what you mean.'

It was Jankowski's turn to frown. He tutted dismissively, using his entire body to emphasise his annoyance before speaking again and when he did he enunciated each word crisply. 'DCI Chalmers requested my involvement in this. I suspect because she fears that The Matchmaker and his group have resurfaced.'

Gus looked from one detective to the other wondering what exactly Jankowski meant by this, and feeling annoyed that DCI Chalmers hadn't shared this information with him before she left. He was aware she'd barely had the time but he hated feeling like he was on the hop.

Wentworth nipped his trouser leg between his index finger and thumb and gently tugged it up before crossing his legs. His lips pursed up and he glared at Detective Jankowski as if he was a stool specimen.

'Why in heavens name would they regroup in *Bradford* of all places?'

'Why wouldn't they choose Bradford?' said Jankowski, 'Liverpool and Hull are close enough. Most trafficking security is concentrated down south and major motorways make transporting children north or south very easy from Yorkshire. Plus, their overheads will be lower.' He smiled and Gus could tell by the anger flickering in his eyes that he didn't rate Wentworth. He warmed to Jankowski.

Seemingly sensing the other man's antipathy, Wentworth flushed. 'I think you're looking for connections that aren't there. We all feel bad about not getting the entire ring twelve years ago but you can't keep imagining links that aren't there. This isn't a very organised group is it?' He splayed his hands in front of him 'For God's sake, they wouldn't have used a bloody druggie whore to house their assets if they were experienced would they?'

Jankowksi sipped his coffee, holding Wentworth's gaze over the top of his mug, then very quietly said, 'Assets?' He placed his mug deliberately on the table and leaned toward Wentworth. 'You mean *children*.' He raised his hand and punctuated each word with his pointing finger, 'Never, ever, forget: these are children. Poor defenceless children, not fucking assets!'

Silence resonated round the room, then Gus cleared his throat and turned to Jankowski. 'Perhaps you could tell us what happened twelve years ago?'

Jankowski pulled his gaze away from Wentworth and leaned forward in his chair, his fingers steepled against his chin. 'Twelve years ago, a major international paedophile ring, based in the Cambridge area was identified. Despite our best efforts, we were unable to apprehend the ringleaders.'

Wentworth then took over to explain how things had gone wrong for the investigation. 'We got a lucky break when the wife of the man known as The Treasurer, James Clegg, came forward with evidence. Cathy, his wife, agreed to maintain her normal life whilst we tried to get more information about the ring.' He shook his head 'We managed to prosecute many very high profile clients, judges, barristers, senior consultants, politicians, and of course, James Clegg.'

Jankowski slammed his fist on the table. 'The boss of the organisation called himself The Matchmaker. Can you believe it? What sort of sick fuck calls themselves The Matchmaker when they're selling kids to adults for sex? The Provider acquired the kids from Eastern Europe and The Facilitator arranged the meetings between the children and the clients. Poland was his main hunting ground but we never managed to identify or catch him.' He shifted uneasily in his seat.

Clearing his throat Wentworth said, 'James Clegg was in fear for his wife and child's safety so he gave us zilch and the clients knew nothing of use about the organisers so although we locked over twenty paedophiles away for a very long time we didn't get the head of the organisation. We've been waiting for them to reform, but I'm not convinced *this* is the work of The Matchmaker.'

Jankowski, on the fingers of one hand counted off each point as he made it. 'We can't ignore this. Firstly, these Eastern European children are all disenfranchised in some way; either they are Roma or very poor with little recourse to the law. Secondly, they are being trafficked, seemingly in groups, to the UK. Thirdly, we have, what appears to be, systematic abuse of by multiple perpetrators. Fourthly, both Europol and Interpol have flagged up an increase in child abductions in Eastern Europe over the past three years. Fifthly, I don't believe in coincidence. Do you?'

Gus bit his lip. No, he didn't believe in coincidence either. Jankowski hadn't given any hard facts, yet both he and Nancy seemed to be in agreement on this one. He turned to Compo. 'Get what you can from the files about this case and let's consider it as an option.' He rubbed his thigh surreptitiously under the table before standing up. 'Now gentlemen, I've got a dead prostitute's son to interview. If you want to observe, follow Alice.'

***

The corridors echoed with their footsteps as Alice guided Detective Jankowski and DCI Wentworth toward the observation suite. At the other end of the corridor a door opened and their interviewee, Jamal Asif, jeans sitting uncomfortably low on his hips and head bowed, entered the corridor accompanied by both an older Asian man and a constable. The older man wore a western suit with a tie and a prayer hat. He sported a permanent scowl on his face and his arm was draped round the younger boy's shoulders. As they approached, Wentworth who'd already expressed his reluctance to observe the interview cursed and turned abruptly on his heel and retraced his steps. 'Forgot my phone. I'll catch you up.'

Mumbling something in Polish under his breath, Jankowski smiled at Alice. 'Mostly he's an idiot but, occasionally he's an excellent detective and so I give him the benefit of the doubt. He thinks Nancy and I are wrong about this being the work of The Matchmaker and so he won't invest his time.'

He shrugged. 'We are not wrong so I *will* invest my time.' He tilted his head towards Jamal who had entered the interview room. 'The attack on this young boy demonstrates that he must be in possession of some very important information.' His lips tightened, 'and this time The Matchmaker will *not* get away.'

Alice ushered him into the observation suite with its hard chairs and listening equipment and, grimacing at the stale air resulting from too many sweaty bodies, unemptied bins filled with discarded food scraps and the gritty, almost tangible stench of coffee grounds, she reached over, lifted the bin and placed it in the corridor. Then extracting a lavender room spray from her handbag, she sprayed it round the room looking slightly embarrassed. 'I always carry one of these.'.

Jankowski settled down, arms folded over his skinny chest, his eyes boring through the mirror as if sheer will power alone could get him the information he desired.

'I hope he can tell us something.' said Alice, 'But remember, the first part of the interview will be about his mum's murder, not the abducted children or the attack outside his brother's house.'

***

The streetlights clicked on just before the first drops of rain began to fall, turning the pavements into treacherous slides for the unwary pedestrian. Gus had just nipped into the major incident room for some painkillers before interviewing Jamal. Against his better instincts, he glanced over and saw a light in his sister's flat. He sighed heavily and raked his fingers through his tight dreads. He knew that later, when he found the time to analyse his emotions, he'd feel angrier by his sister's betrayal than by his wife's defection, and that in itself concerned him.

He heard a throat being cleared in the exaggerated manner of someone wanting to gain your attention, without being so crass as to intrude in your thoughts. Lifting the coffee mug to his lips, Gus swigged back his pills, grimacing as cold, bitter coffee flooded his mouth. Turning around, he rested his aching thigh on the low window sill. 'Hi, Compo, you ok?'

Compo bit his lip and moved his weight nervously from one leg to the other. His eyes darted around the room checking that they were alone. 'I just wanted to say, I'm sorry I embarrassed you earlier.'

'Embarrassed me?'

Wringing his fingers, Compo clarified. 'With the visiting detectives, you know?'

Realisation dawned. 'Oh, do you mean that smarmy git Wentworth and his stupid comments about bacon smells?'

Compo flushed. 'And BO, sir. He said I stank!'

Taking two steps towards him, Gus flung his arm round the shorter man's shoulder. 'The man's a pillock, ok? You've been on the job in this office in front of a damn computer screen for twenty-four hours and that's what the arse focusses on?' He gently shook Compo. 'It was you working through the night that got those kids matched to their families quickly. *That's* the important thing.' He paused, catching Compo's eye. 'Now, you've done your job. Go home, get some sleep and tomorrow the bacon butties are on me.'

Smiling lopsidedly, Compo raised one nail bitten finger. 'Just got one little girl to match, sir, then I'll go.' He turned away and then turning back his normally cheery face dark with tension he said, his voice was so low Gus had to strain to hear him. 'I tried to grab an hour last night but every time I closed my eyes, those little faces kept swimming in front of me.' He wiped his sleeve over his eyes briefly. 'Does it get any better, sir?'

Gus squeezed his arm. 'You know what? It might take a while but what *will* help is the fact that you've done your bit to help those kids. It's the only thing to cling to.' He released Compo's arm and lowered his own voice. 'And believe me, I know. I still relive that thing with Greg. Every damn night I waken up and they're all dead and I'm still alive.' His mouth tightened briefly. 'But now I'm back at work …and life goes on.' He knew it was crap, but if he said it often enough, who knows, one day it might be true.

A sound from behind made him spin round. DC Sadia Hussain stood in the doorway. Gus raised an eyebrow at Compo in a 'how long has she been there gesture?' In return Compo pursed his lips and shrugged.

'Em, excuse me, DI McGuire, but DS Cooper asked me to tell you they're waiting for you in Interview Room Two.'

Gus studied her tall slender frame and perfect complexion for a second, before moving past her and through the door. This was the new DC. The one Alice didn't rate very highly. He smiled. Alice was a stickler for being a team player and this Sadia had got off on the wrong foot with her. He suspected more sparks would fly between the two before long. Two steps further down the corridor and he turned to face her with a frown. 'Was it you who witnessed the attack on Jamal Asif?'

116

She nodded briefly. His blue eyes bored into her face until she flushed. 'Are you ok?'

Again, she nodded, but remained silent.

'Anything worth knowing before I go into the interview?'

Her eyes flicked up and to the left as she thought about his question, then she reluctantly shook her head. 'No, sir. We were parked too far back to see the attack clearly.' She grimaced. 'Should've checked the bloody parked cars before we went in, though.'

Gus shook his head. 'Don't be silly. That's guilt talking. You'd no reason to check the parked cars. I wouldn't have thought to check them either on a routine call. Let it go and move on, ok?'

Her mouth drooped sulkily and his eyes narrowed. She'd need to lighten up a bit and take advice if she was going to fit into his team. 'I mean it. Forget it and move on. You're no good to anyone brooding about mistakes anyone could've made. Don't be such a bloody diva.'

The sulkiness left her face to be replaced by outrage. Satisfied that he had provoked a reaction, Gus nodded briefly and as he left the room, he heard Compo say. 'He's right, you know, you can't dwell on the little parts of the picture when there's a whole painting to finish.'

She snorted. 'Who the fuck are you, anyway? Leonardo Da Vinci?'

Then, just as the door was about to close behind him he heard Compo's quiet response. 'Well, you're definitely no Mona Lisa.'

Laughing, he headed along the corridor. Good for Compo, sticking up for himself with Hussain. God, was he glad to be back at work!

***

The tall man pacing the small square that constituted the largest interview room in The Fort paused when Gus and Alice entered. Painted nondescript beige and lacking character it did nothing to calm a nervous interviewee, but then, on the whole, the design was functional, with the purpose of aiding the extraction of confessions from villains.

Jamal was slumped in the plastic chair. With his legs sprawled under the table, he barely glanced at them, but the tall man extended his hand and introduced himself. 'I'm Jamal's brother, Ishaq Asif.'

Gus took the slightly sweaty hand and shook firmly. He gestured to an uncomfortable-looking red plastic chair next to the younger boy. 'Sit down, Mr Asif. I'm DI McGuire and this is DC Cooper.' Alice held out her hand. The man looked at it for a second before pointedly ignoring it. He pulled out the chair and sat down next to his brother.

Gus winked at Alice. They were used to sexist arseholes and Gus knew Alice would be fuming about the handshake slight. He also knew that she wouldn't let it affect her dealings with the man. Moving his chair away from the table to allow him leg room, he sat down and waited till Alice had pulled her chair right up to the table and rested her elbows on top.

'I'm very angry about the attack on your brother, too,' said Gus. 'I've been informed that the hospital checked you over and, apart from mild shock, you are both ok. Is that right?'

The older man nodded sternly.

'We're conducting this interview in two parts, Mr Asif, and because we think the shooting is related to the second part of the interview, we'll discuss that then, ok?'

Ishaq Asif looked puzzled, 'What do you mean the 'second part'. Surely it's all related to that whore. It was probably some supplier wanting paid that shot us.'

Gus blinked, momentarily thrown by Ishaq's words, then said, 'That's what we need to determine, so shall we crack on?' Leaning over, he pressed the recording equipment and asked each person present to state their name for the record. Then he sat back, arms crossed and waited as Alice flicked through the folder she'd brought in with her.

Ishaq Asif glanced at Gus, who met his gaze but remained silent. Frowning, Asif tapped his fingers on the table. Ignoring him, Gus focussed on Jamal, who stared at the wall above Gus's head. Jamal's eyes were red-rimmed, and his nose looked raw as if he'd rubbed it too hard with a coarse tissue. Gus wondered if his slumped posture indicated defeat, grief or shock or, indeed, a mix of the three.

'How long are you going to keep us here?' said Ishaq in a strident voice. 'We've already been waiting for an hour and, now you're here, you're not even speaking to us.'

Gus bit the inside of his cheek to stop himself for intervening and watched as Alice smiled, laid the folder on the table and carefully positioned it before she said, 'I was just refreshing my memory before I got started, Mr Asif. We'll not keep you any longer than is necessary.'

Mr Asif looked at Gus. 'Aren't you doing the interview?'

Shaking his head in a flurry of dreadlocks, Gus smiled. 'No, Mr Asif, DS Cooper's my best interviewer and so she'll be leading on this.' He cocked an eyebrow. 'No objections, I hope?'

The other man looked as if he'd like to complain but, finally shaking his head, he clasped his fingers on the tabletop and waited, the lines on his face expressing every ounce of frustrated anger he felt.

Jamal, with what appeared to be a huge effort pulled himself up and leaned heavily on the table, his eyes meeting

Alice's. 'Where are the kids? My brother and sisters, are they ok? Can I see them?'

Patting his arm gently, Alice said, 'Your brother is in BRI at the moment. His nappy rash was severely infected, but he's on antibiotics and will soon be released into the care of a foster parent. Rehana and Maryham are fine. They're with a foster carer but you'll be able to see them later, ok?'

Rubbing his sleeve across his face to soak up the few tears that rolled down his cheek, Jamal nodded and slumped back in his chair.

Ignoring Ishaq, Alice looked directly at the younger boy when she spoke. 'Jamal, you know your mother was found murdered on Sunday morning?'

She waited but got no response. 'Jamal?' she said firmly. He looked up and nodded.

'You've got to speak for the tape, Jamal.'

Reluctantly, Jamal spoke. 'Yeah, I know. Good fucking riddance to her.'

Jumping to his feet, his voice sharp, Ishaq said, 'Jamal!' He looked at the police officers. 'He doesn't mean that. He's just upset. Despite her obvious flaws, she was still his mother.' Turning to Jamal, he said something in mother tongue.

Jamal cowered slightly in his chair.

Gus looked from one brother to the other, fleetingly wondering just how scared Jamal was of his brother and wishing he'd got a translator in. What had Ishaq said to Jamal to provoke that reaction? After all, Ishaq Asif was much older than Jamal. However, on balance, Gus felt that Asif was just being over-protective *and* it was only a few hours since they'd both been shot at. They had the right to be a bit twitchy and on edge. In a firm tone, he said, 'Sit down, Mr Asif. You are here as an appropriate adult because Jamal is only fourteen, but you mustn't interrupt the interview unless you feel your brother is becoming unnecessarily upset, ok?'

Ishaq's mouth flattened into a thin line and he slowly sat down. 'Yes, ok, fine.'

Looking at Jamal, Alice continued. 'How did you know your mother was dead, Jamal? Who told you?'

He shrugged. 'Dunno'

Alice smiled. 'Was it one of your neighbours?'

With a sideways glance at his brother, he said, 'Yeah, suppose so.'

'Which one?'

'Dunno.'

'The reason I ask is that none of the neighbours have seen you since Saturday afternoon. I'm wondering how one of them could've told you about your mum if they've not seen you since her death.'

He sniffed. 'Overheard some of them talking in One Stop.' The One Stop shop was a focal point of the small village and was frequented regularly by most of the locals. The owner and the shop workers had been interviewed twice already, the last time being only that morning.

Alice raised her eyebrows. 'Oh, when was that? Because the One Stop manager doesn't remember seeing you or your mum in there since Saturday tea time.'

Ishaq frowned. 'You said Mrs Khalifa told you, Jamal.'

Scowling, Jamal fidgeted on his chair, eyes drifting round the room as though seeking a means of escape.

'We need to know who told you about your mum, Jamal.' Alice said, keeping her tone calm.

Sighing loudly, Ishaq nudged his brother. 'Come on, Jamal answer the question, for goodness sake.'

Tears welled up in Jamal's eyes and when he spoke it was too quiet for the recorder to pick up. 'I found her.'

Biting her lip, Alice said, 'Sorry, Jamal, I'm going to have to ask you to repeat that for the tape.'

His head jerked up. His cheeks a swollen ruddy mess as he rubbed furiously at them with a rapidly disintegrating tissue. 'I found her!'

'When did you find her, Jamal?'

Gus felt sorry for the lad. He knew the sort of life Jamal must have had to date. A drunken mother, no money, no food and now she was dead and his siblings were in care. He handed him a clean tissue. Jamal wiped his face dry and blew his nose. 'Saturday night. Don't know when, about seven, I suppose, before the snow got heavy. She'd left the kids home alone again. I'd told her off about that but she did it all the time. She didn't care about them. All she cared about was getting drunk or high.'

Ishaq glowered at Jamal. 'Why didn't you tell me? I'd have come to you. I'd have taken care of the kids. You know that. You should have phoned the police straight away.'

Gus, cleared his throat and caught Ishaq's eye, silently warning the other man not to intervene. Throwing his arms in the air in disgust Ishaq tutted loudly as Alice continued.

'How did you come to find her Jamal?'

'I was in the Chinky's getting chips and I saw her pass by coming from the King's Arms. She was staggering so I knew she'd had a drink. I finished my chips inside the Chinky's, then I saw one of them alkies that hang around the church staggering up the road after her and I knew she was going to the graveyard.' His face flushed and his fingers clenched on top of the table. 'That's where she always took them for a shag.' Alice pushed a cup of water towards him. He took a drink and then placed the plastic cup back on the table.

'You're doing really well, Jamal.'

'I was angry. She was always leaving the kids. It's not right. They're too little and I knew she'd spend her shag money on booze, not on chips for the kids so I decided to go round to Quarry Street and wait till she'd got paid and make her give me some money for the kids' tea.' He looked round at the three faces round the table. 'So, I waited at the corner of Quarry Street, near Spicy Delight, for fifteen minutes and when she hadn't come back I headed round to the graveyard. The snow had got quite thick by then and when I got there I didn't see her at first and then I looked down and she was there lying near that big broken gravestone, her head was mashed in and she was dead. I could see she was dead.'

He laid his arms on the table and, resting his head on top, allowed great sobs to rattle his bones and wrack his skinny body. Ishaq got up and kneeled beside Jamal with his arms round his half-brother's shoulders. 'Oh beta, you should have told us. You should have told us.'

Gus raised an eyebrow at Alice, indicating she should allow Ishaq to calm Jamal before she continued. Observing them, Gus could clearly see the love and care that flowed between the two brothers. He could almost forgive Ishaq his earlier sexism on that basis alone – almost, but not quite.

When Jamal was calm, Alice said, 'I need to ask you a few more questions. Are you able to continue?'

Eyes glazed with worry, Ishaq frowned at her. 'Can't you give him some time? You can see he's upset.'

Alice met his gaze calmly. 'I have a murderer on the loose and someone just this morning tried to shoot you and your brother. I don't have the luxury of time. If Jamal could continue, it would be helpful.'

Jamal shrugged his brother's arm off his shoulders and straightened in his chair. 'It's ok, Ishaq. I'm ok. I'd rather get it over and done with.'

Alice smiled. 'Good boy, Jamal. This is really brave of you and we appreciate it.'

Taking another sip of water, Jamal looked expectantly at Alice.

'Did you see anyone when you walked round to the graveyard?'

He shook his head and then belatedly glanced at the recorder and added, 'No.'

'Ok, Jamal, you mentioned earlier that you saw a man follow her round. Did you recognise him?'

Jamal screwed up his face. 'Not really.'

'Could you describe him?'

Jamal pursed his lips. 'Old. Fortyish probably. Tall and bald with a long dark coat.'

'Would you recognise him again, Jamal?'

Jamal shrugged. 'Doubt it.'

Alice shuffled the folder on the table in front of her and said, 'Do you have a phone, Jamal?'

'Yes.'

'So why did you not phone the police or an ambulance for your mother?'

He froze, his face expressionless for a second and then he hung his head and mumbled, 'I was scared. I saw she were dead and I just ran off.'

Alice's tone dropped and became almost caressing. 'Where did you go Jamal? You'd just found your mother dead, so where did you go?'

He sniffed and lifted the tissue to wipe away a stray tear. 'I went to Frankie Robb's house in Frizinghall. He's my mate from school.'

'Just write his name and number down here, will you Jamal?' and she pushed a pad towards him. He took his phone out and scribbled a number and address on the paper. She ripped the sheet off the pad and handed it to the uniformed officer that stood by the door. 'Check this out, please?'

Returning to the table, she sat down. 'What time did you arrive at Frankie's?'

'Probably eightish. I walked down through Heaton woods.'

'Jamal, you said you were concerned about your siblings, so why did you not go back home to take care of them instead of going to your friend's house?'

Sobbing heavily, desperation tingeing his voice he said, 'I was too scared. I thought I'd get in trouble. That you lot would think I'd done it.'

Alice exchanged a glance with Gus. He nodded and Mr Asif, misinterpreting the nod, thought they could go. He stood up and turned to Jamal. 'Come on then, Jamal, let's go.'

Gus stood. 'Sorry, Mr Asif, but we're not quite finished yet. We've still got a few more questions to ask Jamal, but we're going to get in some drinks and sandwiches for you before we move on. Halal?'

Nodding half-heartedly, Ishaq slid back onto his chair as Gus and Alice left the room.

'What do you reckon?' asked Alice.

Walking slowly down the corridor, his shoulders hunched, Gus ran his fingers through his dreads. 'You know what? I reckon Jamal knows more than he's letting on and we'll need to tease it out of him carefully.' He took a further few steps and then added, 'And I'm not sure that Ishaq being in the room will help Jamal share everything.'

They were halfway along the corridor when they heard the interview room door open. Gus turned back and saw Ishaq Asif closing the door quietly behind him. He walked smartly along the corridor towards them.

Wondering what had made the other man follow them into the corridor, Gus leaned against the wall. When Ishaq drew near he glanced from Alice, who remained expressionless, to Gus who smiled encouragingly. 'Is there something you need to tell us, Mr Asif,' asked Gus.

Shuffling his feet slightly, Ishaq Asif sighed heavily. 'I think there is something that I'm not aware of and I'm concerned that Jamal may need some sort of legal representation?'

'Well, Mr Asif, it's entirely up to you of course, but at the moment Jamal is only helping us with our enquiries and you, as his responsible adult, will be able to request legal representation at any time.' Gus placed a reassuring hand on the other man's shoulder. 'I know it's very stressful and upsetting for both of you, but why don't you eat some tea and then we'll continue in a bit?'

'I also wondered about my cousins, detective inspector?'

Gus frowned. This was the first he'd heard of any cousins. 'Which cousins?'

'Jamal's half-siblings are also my cousins. Didn't you know?'

With a glance at Alice, Gus raised his eyebrow. Alice shook her head and Gus turned to Mr Asif. 'Maybe you should explain what you mean?' he said.

Ishaq screwed his eyes shut for a second, as if to clear his mind. 'Jamal and I share a father. My mother died a long time ago and our father now lives in Pakistan with his third wife.' He glanced at Gus who nodded to show he understood.

Ishaq continued, 'When my father divorced Jamal's mother, she became dependent on drugs and alcohol. Whilst he lived in Bradford my father managed to keep her partly in check, but when he moved back to Pakistan things got out of hand.'

He snorted and glanced round the corridor. 'She married my father's younger brother, Khalid. Unfortunately, he was not a good man and was happy to encourage his new wife's addictions. Khalid is the father of her younger children.'

'But, he's dead now, is he?' asked Gus

Ishaq nodded. 'Yes he died two years ago.' he laughed humourlessly, 'of a drug overdose. This was before Iman, her youngest, was even born. Sharon,' he hesitated, 'didn't cope well. I'm afraid she became more and more addicted and erratic. My wife, Asma, and I tried our best. We sent food back with Jamal for the little ones and twice we contacted social services.' He snorted in annoyance. 'For all the good that did. Anyway, I am the little ones' closest living relative and I want custody of them.'

Gus released a long breath. 'Well, Mr Asif, I can't help you with that: you're going to have to contact social services. First you need to eat and then we need to finish interviewing Jamal.'

CHAPTER 28
Bradford

Y ou did what? Are you a complete idiot? No don't
answer that. Are you somewhere safe?' The
Matchmaker waited for the other man's response
then, tapping his fingers lightly on his desk, said, 'Let me
think.' He tilted his head to one side. Aware of his leg
bobbing up and down, he forced his body to relax. The
bobbing stopped. 'Is the car clean?' He paused. 'Any eye
witnesses?'

Noting the slight hesitation before The Distributor
responded in the negative, The Matchmaker flicked a glance
towards his office door. Last thing he needed was his PA
walking in whilst he was talking to this fool. Reassured that
she was firmly ensconced at her desk in the outer office, he
said, 'Are you sure? It's your neck on the line, after all.'

The Distributor responded in a sulky tone. 'Well, there
were a couple of kids in the street. When I drove past the girl
looked into the car, but it was only for a second and I had a
balaclava on. She can't identify me.'

Standing up and moving over to the window, The
Matchmaker deliberately controlled his breathing before
saying, razor sharp. 'Liar!' He heard the other man's
breathing quicken and was satisfied. 'You shot at the boy,
but, fortunately for you, all you hit was his shopping. What a
debacle.'

'How did you know?' said The Distributor, his voice
shaking.

The Matchmaker laughed. 'Don't you know by now? I
know everything.'

The Distributor hesitated and then asked, 'Will you
postpone the girl tomorrow?'

Lightly tapping his finger on his lip, The Matchmaker deliberated. 'No, we won't cancel our plans. This could turn out alright. It'll stretch the police a bit further and they won't be expecting it. After all, they don't know anything about Cathy Clegg, do they?' He laughed. 'Clean up the house you're in, move to the depot and keep a low profile till tomorrow.'

***

The Distributor had made his way to the depot by public transport. He'd taken a circuitous route, jumping on and off buses and doubling back. The debacle in Great Horton had rattled him and he felt shaky but he knew The Matchmaker would expect him to be on the ball ready for the next day. He'd made a slight detour on his route along Thornton Road to make sure the car he was going to jack for the next day's activities was still in place. Now, looking out the window, the Thornton Viaduct seemed to loom threateningly from the snow-covered fields. Each arch looked like the spaces between a gargoyle's huge teeth. The fields beneath were dotted with children pulling sledges and laughing. On another day The Distributor may have been tempted to go down and get closer, just in case a distracted parent left their child vulnerable. But, not today. Today he was chastened and, though a distraction would provide release, he knew he needed to focus. Pity it was so damn cold. He switched on the portable gas fire and when it ignited, flicked it to full power before making the phone call he'd been putting off since he arrived.

'Everything's in place! It'll happen tomorrow morning!'

'Good.' The Matchmaker hung up abruptly, leaving The Distributor feeling slightly on edge.

***

In another part of Bradford, The Matchmaker slipped the throw-away phone into his inner pocket and re-joined the group of smokers huddled against the cold sleet in the doorway. He didn't smoke but he liked to get down with the trolls occasionally, after all, he often picked up juicy bits of information from the careless mouths of the minions and in this day and age knowledge was key. Subduing his inner exaltation, he turned to the man nearest him, 'Have you heard the one about...?'

CHAPTER 29
The Fort

Gus saw the apprehension in Jamal's eyes and decided to play on that. He pulled his chair under the table, so he was sitting directly opposite the boy, and signalled for Alice to reload the tape and introduce them. When she was ready he began.

'So Jamal, any idea what I'm going to be asking you about?'

Jamal's eyes flitted from Gus to Alice who no longer looked friendly and reassuring. Ishaq frowned but remained silent.

The corners of Gus's mouth turned down. 'No?' He leaned his upper body across the table and looked right at Jamal. 'So, no ideas?'

Jamal shook his head and Gus said, 'For the purpose of the tape, Jamal Asif, in response to my question, shook his head.' Turning back to the boy he continued conversationally. 'So Jamal, what do you know about the twenty children in the attic of your home – two of them dead?'

Ishaq gasped and jumped to his feet. 'What? Are you mad?'

Gus ignored Ishaq and looed instead at Jamal's pale face. The boy's hands shook so much he nearly spilled the remains of his water cup over the table.

***

Nancy opened the door and quietly stepped inside the observation room. Holding her briefcase in one arm, her coat slung haphazardly over the other, she was worried. In the reflection from the one-way mirror she saw the telltale lines that snaked out from her eyes. They seemed dull, their customary sparkle dissipated by the tensions of what had seemed to Nancy, not only an interminable day, but one of the worst she'd experienced since The Matchmaker case twelve years previously.

Even another bout of mindless sex with Charles wouldn't be enough to make her feel better. She felt drained, every sinew of her body cried out in protest and she couldn't begin to think about how Gus must be feeling. For the first time since she'd double-tagged with Gus's dad to convince DCI Bowles to exert pressure on his psychiatrist she wondered if she'd made the right decision. What of it all backfired and Gus ended up wrecked? What if they'd both misunderstood his needs? What if Dr Mahmood was right and Gus wasn't ready? She sighed and shook her head. What the hell was she thinking?

None of them were ready, none of them would come out of this unscarred, but Gus... well, he was special. This could be his salvation. The case that pulled him back from the brink. The case that gave him back his soul after his best friend ripped it out and left him full of guilt, physically compromised and emotionally damaged. She leaned back against the wall, welcoming the soothing lavender fragrance that lingered in the air and allowed her briefcase and coat to slip to the floor. Pasting a customary smile on her face she walked over and sat beside Jankowski to watch Gus interview the Asif boy.

***

'Well, did you know about the children in the attic?' Gus was persistent.

Jamal used his sleeve to wipe the tears from his face. 'Yeah, yeah I did know about them. But I never knew any were dead.'

Ashen-faced, Ishaq rubbed his hands over his cheeks. 'Oh Jamal, what's been going on? Why didn't you tell me and Asma?'

Watching the interaction between the two brothers, Gus's mind drifted to his own relationship with Katie. They'd always been close, always had each other's backs. But now? Well, that was anyone's guess. With effort, he drew his mind back into the stuffy interview room. Jamal and his brother had been well fed. Raja's pizzas, judging by the spicy, cheesy smell pervading the room. They needed information quick and Jamal was their best bet. The earlier attack on him indicated that he knew more than he'd told them so far.

The way Jamal's head swivelled between the detectives and his brother would have been comical in different circumstances. Today, it was sad. No fourteen-year-old should have a mother like Sharon Asif, or live in a house with abducted children in the attic.

'He told me he'd kill my brother and sisters if I told anybody. So, I didn't. I couldn't.' Picking at a ratty piece of wool on the sleeve of his jumper, he looked at Gus. 'They're safe now aren't they?'

'Yes, Jamal, your brother and sisters are safe now. Nobody can hurt them. But you can help those other kids now. If you're brave, that is.'

Swallowing hard, the boy nodded.

'Go on then. In your own words, Jamal, what happened?'

Ishaq hugged Jamal briefly and then let go, moving one hand to rest on his arm. 'Go on Jamal, tell them everything.'

Taking a deep breath, Jamal sat up straight and began. 'One night whilst I was asleep this man came in and dragged me from my bed. He hauled me across the landing and he stank of sweat and garlic. He didn't put the light on, so it was dark. He started to push me down the stairs too quickly and I fell and ended up at the bottom.' He touched his forehead and continued. 'I bumped my head and it was bleeding, but he just laughed. He shoved his fat arms under my armpits and yanked me into the living room. He put the hall light on, but not the living room one so I couldn't see right well. *She* was sprawled on the couch, stoned as usual, and another man was in the corner. He spoke right posh. He said I'd to help the sweaty man and if I told anyone what were going on, he'd give my sisters and brother to the men who liked to do bad things to kids. I knew what he meant. He meant he'd give them to the paedos. Then, the sweaty man made me follow him out the back door. He'd parked a big van in the alley between our house and the ones in front. He opened the door right quiet and when I looked in there were two boys in the back. They were all bloody and crying. He'd put something over their mouths. He told me to take them up to the attic. The next night he came in a black car and there were another two in the boot. Every few nights he'd come. Mostly in the van, but sometimes in a car. He'd drop kids off and sometimes he'd make them have a shower and he'd put new clothes on them and take them away.'

As Jamal continued his story, Gus felt a cold coil of anger in his stomach. These bastards had to be stopped and he was determined to do it. Jamal was on a roll now. He didn't need prompting to continue. It was as if the dam had burst and nothing could stop the lad from spewing everything out.

Aware of Alice's tense body beside him and the distress on Ishaq Asif's face, Gus kept his eyes firmly on Jamal. There was no space for anyone else's emotions in this room. They had a job to do and they owed it to Jamal and the other children to be professional, no matter how disgusted they felt.

Jamal hiccupped and squeezed his eyes tight shut. 'I knew where he was taking them, but I couldn't do owt, and when they came back they were always hurt. I hated that man, but I hated my mum more. She made me empty the buckets of piss and shit and every time that man came he'd look at

Rehana and Maryham. Once I found him right in their room and he was touching Maryham's hair. I told him if he ever went in their room again I'd yell till the whole neighbourhood woke up. He just laughed and kissed her cheek whilst she still slept, but he never went in their room again, 'cos I locked them in at night.' Jamal's fists clenched and unclenched at the memory. His face was a mask of anguish.

Gus poured him a glass of water. 'Jamal, you've done really well, but I need to just ask a few more questions, ok?'

Ishaq, face rigidly angry, squeezed Jamal's shoulders reassuringly and nodded at Gus, silently acknowledging that it was better to for Jamal to continue and get it all out now.

'Did you ever see the posh man again?'

Jamal shook his head. 'No, never, but you know what? He scared me more than the sweaty man. Sweaty man was evil but that posh one… He was worse.'

'Had you seen either of them before?'

'Yeah, sweaty man. I'm sure he worked at the school for a while. Think he was a builder or something.'

'Which school? Your school?'

'Yeah, Carlton Wood.'

'Right, Jamal, can you tell us any more about either of those men?'

'No, except my mum was shagging the sweaty one and he gave her money and drugs for keeping those kids up there.'

'I want you to work with a police artist to try to get a picture of those two men. Will you do that?'

'I'll be able to do that for sweaty man, but I'm not so sure about the other man.' Jamal's fingers worked more rapidly on the piece of wool and he looked down at the table. Gus realised that the boy was terrified and said, 'Jamal, I promise you we'll take care of you. We won't let this man anywhere near you or your siblings.' He paused to allow his words to sink in, 'But, we really need to catch him. You want him caught, don't you?'

Jamal nodded, but his eyes held a glazed look. 'I'll try' was all he said.

Gus, realising that this was as much as he'd get for now decided to move on. 'Now, you mentioned a van and a car. Can you tell us about them?'

Frowning, Jamal thought for a second before replying. 'The van was white with doors that rolled up at the back. It wasn't right big, but it had sort of shelves and on some of the shelves were mattresses. New ones mind, not been used or owt.'

'Where were the children?'

'They were sat on the floor or on one of the shelves. They didn't speak English 'cause I tried to speak to them upstairs but they couldn't understand me.'

'What was the van like outside. Did you get a number pate?'

'Nah, not a number plate, but there was a picture of a mattress on the side and a name. Can't remember what the name was. It was like it was a delivery van for mattresses.'

'Anything else?'

Shrugging, Jamal shook his head.

Ishaq leaned forward. 'Surely he can go now, detective. He's exhausted and he's only a kid. He needs to rest.'

Holding up one hand, Gus smiled, 'Only a few more, Mr Asif, please.' He turned to Jamal. 'Did you see the man who shot at you today?'

'No, it all happened so quickly. We didn't get the chance before he'd driven off, did we, Ishaq?'

Ishaq shook his head. 'All I saw was the black car, like I told the other officer.'

'Ok, Jamal, you need to take a break, but after that shooting today we don't want you to go back to your brother's.' He smiled at Ishaq. 'We've had an officer outside your house all day, but we want to move your family and Jamal to a safe house for a few days, just as a precaution.'

Looking like he would've liked to argue, Ishaq grimaced, but then, with a tired sigh, he nodded.

'We'll take you and your brother to the house. Your wife and child will be brought over, too, and we'll send the police artist to you tomorrow morning.'

Ishaq stood up, but Jamal hesitated and then picking up his phone, he started flicking through it.

Gus sensing, the boy's excitement waited until, face flushed, he yelled. 'I've got it!' A smile stretched over his face as he handed his phone to Gus. Gus took it and saw a photo of a man taken in dim light. He was lying down with his eyes shut in profile, but it was a start.'

'Sweaty man?' said Gus

Disgust on his face, Jamal nodded. 'I took it ages ago when he was asleep in my mum's bed. It's pretty crap because I was too scared to use the flash but I kept it just in case he ever touched Maryham or Rehana again.'

Heart thundering with excitement, Gus smiled. 'You did good, son, you did good. But I'm going to have to keep your phone till our techie expert's had a look at this.'

CHAPTER 30
The Fort

Nancy watched as Gus, unaware of her presence, stood in front of the board that held the photos of the children. Nancy could tell by the way he stood that his right leg was playing up. The sling supporting his left arm was twisted at the back over his shoulder and she guessed he'd only put it on when the rest of the team had gone home. She'd have words with him about that. After speaking in detail to his physio, she knew that, although he needed to strengthen his torn shoulder muscles by letting them support themselves for increasing periods, he also had to support it regularly to avoid over-stretching. She suspected Gus was blithely forgetting to pace himself and was reluctant to show weakness in front of the team.

He stretched out his right hand and traced the faces of each child individually. Nancy knew he would have committed to memory every detail about each child. Seeing his shoulders slump, she frowned and pushed herself away from the wall as he gently lowered himself onto the edge of his desk, arms crossed. Apparently, heedless of the paperwork being crushed beneath his buttocks, he remained engrossed in the photos. Three mismatched mugs stood among the disarray of folders cluttering his workspace. Circular coffee stains adorned its wooden surface with a couple of screwed-up wrappers and a half-full foil pill packet strewn alongside. Clearly he'd been there for a long time.

Summoning a bright smile from her drained reserves, she gently coughed. Gus started and then pivoted round on one heel to face her. His handsome face looked haunted and Nancy shuddered. Doubt clenched her stomach. He'd worn that same look in the hospital six months ago and Nancy wanted to gather him in her arms and rock him like a baby.

Her mind flashed to his mother, one of her best friends. Corrine would never forgive her if she'd made a mistake. Imagining what the tornado that was Gus's petite half-Jamaican mother would do if she hurt her baby, Nancy touched her crucifix. Gus's mum was no pushover. She'd fought her upbringing in a Scottish orphanage to become a paediatrician, first at the Sick Kids in Edinburgh and then at Jimmy's in Leeds, until she'd packed it all in to do charitable work and explore her many artistic hobbies. Nancy was in no doubt that she'd suffer greatly if Gus flipped through coming back to work too soon.

Limping towards Nancy, his face transformed into a welcoming smile. She moved in and hugged him whispering in his ear. 'It's great to have you back. We've missed you.'

When he replied his voice was thick with emotion as he returned her hug. 'Good to be back, Nance. Good to be back.' He gestured to the kids on the wall behind him, his brow furrowed in anger. 'We'll get these bastards. I'll make sure of it.'

'I know you will. Now, what the bloody hell does a girl have to do around here to get a coffee?'

Flinging his head back, Gus guffawed; a sound that lifted her heart. He was so like his big bluff dad in many ways, yet he also had the gentle empathy of his mother. She watched as he went over to the coffee machine and poured them both a brew. When he'd added milk and sugar to hers and carried it back to his desk, she moved over and slid the chair out from the opposite side. Slipping her shoes off, she collapsed into it and with a sigh crossed her feet on the desk, revealing a hole in her tights. With an annoyed tut, she reached down and pulled it, making the hole substantially bigger in the process.

'Maybe just stop pulling at it or it'll unravel up to your armpits,' said Gus.

She cast him a sharp look, then gave up and sank back in her chair, accepting the steaming mug he offered her. 'New on today these were. Damn waste of money.' She took a sip of her drink and spluttered in an exaggerated way before giving him a coy look. 'Bloody awful coffee this, Gus. Got anything to take the edge off?'

Pushing his dreads back from his face, Gus laughed and opening his bottom drawer, he presented her with a bottle of twelve-year aged Glenmorangie Lasanta malt whisky. Pursing her lips, she nodded approvingly. 'Better taste than your dad. I've always preferred a Glenmorangie to a Glenlivet. It's the chocolatey toffee flavour that does it for me. It's like drinking a Crunchie with an extra kick. Humph. But there's no budging the old bugger, dead set in his ways, he is.'

Gus tipped a liberal amount into her mug and a much smaller amount into his own. 'Not sure that this isn't sacrilege, mixing this quality of whisky with coffee. Doesn't come cheap, you know.'

'Ah, I see you inherited your old man's penny-pinching ways.'

When he laughed, she was pleased to note that his face seemed less strained than before. Tipping her mug in a cheers motion, she sipped, content to chat about trivia as, soothed by the alcohol, the tension of the day slowly left her body.

Twenty minutes later she banged her empty mug down on the desk and pushed her feet back into her shoes. 'Right, let's get you home then, Gus my boy!'

Slightly disorientated and relaxed by the small amount of whisky he'd allowed himself Gus looked puzzled. 'Eh?'

Already putting her coat on, she paused. 'Get your coat on. I'm dropping you home. Tomorrow will be another busy day and you,' she said, prodding his chest, 'Need your rest. You still at your mum and dad's place are you?'

Gus looked about to protest, so Nancy cocked her head to one side and raised her eyebrow. Gus shook his head and laughed before grabbing his bag from under the desk. He meekly limped after her. No need to tell her that he never managed to sleep for more than a couple of hours a night.

CHAPTER 31
Shay Lane
Tuesday

Gus's habitual scowl transformed into a reluctant grin that made his eyes sparkle. On entering the kitchen he'd witnessed his tiny mum twerking energetically to Miley Cyrus's 'Wrecking Ball'. His dad, with a decidedly lascivious look on his spherical face made the odd thrusting movement in time to the music and the pair of them lip-synced the lyrics in near-perfect time. Laughing and slightly breathless, his mum stopped when she saw him and hands on her hips, she caught her breath.

'Your mum's still got the moves,' said Fergus McGuire, wrapping his huge arms round his wife's shoulders and hugging her tightly.

Corrine McGuire's face reddened and she wafted a tea towel at him. 'Och, away with you, Fergus. It's you who spins me round the dance floor till I'm all hot and bothered.'

Still grinning, Gus pulled out a chair and sat down at the table. 'Well your twerking looked like it was getting Dad all hot and bothered just now. Since when did you twerk to the radio in the morning?'

Corrine raised an eyebrow and pouted. 'You're never too old to try something new Angus, that's my motto. Scrambled eggs coming up!' She turned to the stove and ferociously stirred the steaming pan that she'd forgotten during her impromptu dance session. The extractor fan made a valiant effort to suck up the thin trail of grey smoke, but the smell of singed scrambled eggs still hovered accusingly in the air.

Gus glanced at his dad who stuck his tongue in his cheek but wisely kept quiet as a plate of brown speckled eggs was placed in front of Gus. Two slices of toast, both bearing the remnants of half scraped burnt ash slathered with yellow and black speckled butter lay, defeated, under the eggs. Thankfully, a large mug of delicious coffee accompanied the burnt offerings before him. If there was one culinary skill his mother had mastered, it was how to make a damn fine cup of coffee.

Casting a sidelong look at his Dad who was hiding his grin behind *The Guardian*, he waited till she'd turned away before quickly slipping half of her loving offering into the dog's bowl, where, after a friendly lick from Heather, his dad's bull terrier, the evidence of his treachery was quickly disposed of.

Fergus winked at him and poured some more coffee. 'How're things going, Angus?'

Twiddling his fork around the remains of his food, he shrugged. 'Compo pulled out all the stops and matched the kids to their families. Alice got the enquiry up and running efficiently. Nancy enlisted help from Cambridge and Poland respectively because she's worried a known paedo ring has reformed and Sharon Asif's son Jamal was shot at yesterday just before we brought him in for questioning. He's given us a few leads on the men who brought the kids to the house. We'll follow up today.'

Both arms extended before him, Fergus shook his newspaper in front of him. 'Even *The Guardian*'s leading on this today. Bet they'll be camping outside The Fort and BRI all day. Bloody vultures.'

Gus groaned. He hated dealing with the press but, when they got wind that he was back at work and leading the investigation, they'd hound him. After all it wasn't so long ago that *he* was the Telegraph and Argus front page news.

With his mum's tuneless humming providing a soothing background noise, he shovelled a few forkfuls of food into his mouth, immediately washing it down with a huge gulp of coffee. His thoughts drifted to his meeting with his wife the previous day, making him scowl. He fixed his gaze on his dad, who shifted uncomfortably in his seat. Reluctantly, Fergus folded his newspaper away and placed it on the red and white polka dot tablecloth. He exchanged a glance with his wife who turned resolutely to the sink and pulled on a pair of rubber gloves preparatory to doing the washing up.

'I dropped in on Katie yesterday,' said Gus

'Aye, we know. Katie phoned last night.'

Remaining stubbornly silent, Gus waited for him to continue.

'Look, I'm sorry, laddie. I should've told you but... well, your mum and I didn't know how.' Hands splayed in supplication, he looked all of his sixty-two years. 'Not when you were in such a bad way.'

Eyes closed, Gus cursed under his breath. 'It wasn't up to *you* to tell me.' He glanced at his mum, who now leaned against the sink, tears in her eyes, wringing a tea towel between her gloved fingers. 'Or you, Mum. Katie and Gabriella were the ones who should have shared their *happy* news. But, of course, they were too cowardly.'

Seeing his mother flinch at his words, Gus was immediately contrite. He jumped to his feet and gathered her in a hug. 'Don't worry, mum. It's really strange but I actually don't care that Gaby's left me. Well, my pride's a bit wounded, I suppose, but to be honest I'm more pissed off that the two of them didn't have the decency to tell me.' He dragged his fingers through his hair. 'Gaby and I were finished a long time ago and quite clearly she had issues with her sexuality. We were going through the motions for months before I killed Greg and, to be honest, it's as well it's over. Time for all of us to move on.' He held his mother slightly away from him and kissed her cheek. 'When I can bring myself to forgive them that is.'

Corrine tutted, and pulling completely away from him she placed her hands on her hips in an all too familiar pugilistic stance. 'Don't you dare say that you killed Greg, Angus

144

McGuire! Don't you dare! You know as well as we do that you had *no* choice.'

Blue eyes flashed, but when he spoke his voice was gentle. 'Hey, it doesn't matter how we dress it up. The bottom line is that I killed Greg,' he held up a finger to stop her from interrupting, 'and I *did* have a choice, no matter what you say. I could have chosen not to save myself, not to kill him, but I didn't.' He smiled. 'And I'll learn to live with it, ok?'

A tear trickled down his mum's face so he dropped a kiss on her corn-rowed hair and hugged her. 'I regret killing Greg, but I don't regret saving myself.'

Lips still trembling, she reached up and cupped his cheek with her palm. 'I'm glad you made the choice you did, darling. I truly am.'

Squeezing her shoulder Gus turned to his dad who had remained silent during the exchange. 'Drop me off at The Fort, Dad?'

With a heavy sigh, Fergus lumbered to his feet and kissed his wife on the cheek. 'Come on then, let's get cracking. You've got some murdering bastards to find and I've got a death by stewing in filth to post mortem'

'What?'

Shrugging dismissively, he said deadpan. 'Death by drowning in bathwater. Daft git! Was probably pissed and dozed off in the tub.'

As his old man left the kitchen, Gus turned to wave bye to his mum. 'No more twerking today. At your age you'll end up causing an accident.'

He quickly shut the door behind him as his mum sent a balled up tea towel flying towards him.

CHAPTER 32
Keighley

The Matchmaker couldn't resist it. He knew it was dangerous, but still he did it... and it was *so* easy. Wearing a hoodie and trackie bottoms he skulked in the dreary early morning drizzle inside the doorway of a charity shop. Already he'd received a couple of pounds from a middle-aged woman in high heels, trotting along to some appointment or other, protecting herself from the sleet under one of those dome shaped clear brollies. With a clear view of Keighley's Wetherspoon's he eyed with interest the myriad of people entering the pub for their early morning breakfast. From retired couples treating themselves to a fry-up, to young singles taking time out for a cuppa and toast on their way to work, The Golden Crown was bustling. The Matchmaker knew exactly what he was looking for and it wasn't long before he saw the perfect candidate.

Yawning as he got out of his blue Fiat, the man ferociously rubbed his face in an attempt to wake himself up. Hair still flattened by sleep, he pressed his key fob and the car emitted a double bleep. It had a dint in the front bumper and suited the Matchmaker's purposes perfectly; nondescript and commonplace. The car owner wore cement-streaked jeans and a dust-infused, mucky, white t -shirt from which muscled arms hung, chimp-like. Following him discreetly into the pub, The Matchmaker was pleased when he saw him join the man who'd driven up in a white builder's van ten minutes earlier. The car owner ordered a full English breakfast with extra toast. Feeling peckish himself, The Matchmaker also bought a full English and paid in cash, before heading over to a table nearer to the door where he could continue his scrutiny of the men. Shortly afterwards a third bloke joined the other two. He was young, clearly the gofer and, despite his slender build, they called him Big Al and clapped him robustly on the back. 'Hey Big Al, want a cop of page three before we go? Set you up for the day, hey!'

'Aw leave him alone; he still thinks tits are for his mammy's milk. Don't you, Big Al?'

The lad grinned good-naturedly. 'Fuck off! I've seen plenty tits you know? And not them wrinklies that your missus has, Bill.'

Bill raised his hands in mock protest. 'Oooh, you've hurt my feelings now.'

Fifteen minutes later, having belched and slurped their way through their breakfasts, rustled through *The Sun* and effed and blinded enough to support the typical builder's stereotype, the three threw their napkins onto greasy plates and headed for the door.

Oblivious to the shadow observing them from the doorway, they walked over to the white van and bundled in. Grinning at his good fortune, The Matchmaker pulled on a pair of gloves and waited for a few minutes before heading over to the Fiat. Taking a small electronic gadget from his pocket, he aimed it at the car. It bleeped twice. Opening the door, he slid behind the wheel and within seconds the engine was running.

With the adrenalin rush quickening his heartbeat, he drove along the A629 towards Steeton, caught the A6034 to Addingham, followed by the A65 to Ilkley and, although the rush hour was abating, he got caught behind a people carrier laden with children and a huge slavering dog that stuck its head out the nearside rear window. Frustrated with the driver's erratic steering he was tempted to peep his horn but caution dictated he swallow his anger Eventually, after what seemed miles, but was in actual fact only a few hundred yards, the car turned off and he took a right off the main road onto Cunliffe Road. Turning onto Springs Lane, he passed Betty's Tea Rooms and continued on till just before he reached Ilkley's pride and joy, the ornate King's Hall and Winter Gardens. Anticipation rising as he neared his destination, he indicated and turned onto the little-used Dales Way Link, with its few isolated houses looming behind the trees that bordered their properties. This was the heart of moneyed Ilkley, home of the west Yorkshire affluent, though the narrow road and potholes would belie it. Eager now, his hands gripped the wheel tighter and he pulled himself forward to peer out the snow-specked windscreen. The wipers left a fuzz of streaked water across the screen, but he was still able to view the narrow road in front of him. He slowed as he approached the huge house that loomed up to the right from behind a tall fence. Dense foliage marred his view of the house, but previous reconnoitres had told him that behind the heavy security was a forbidding building with an attached granny flat in expensive Yorkshire stone.

Aware of the extensive CCTV coverage around the house, he pulled into the side of the road just outside camera range and studied the entrance with its high ornate gates with sloping spikes on top to discourage climbing and the equally oppressive fence that fanned out from the gates and circled the entire property. Amazing what selling your story to the papers can give you.

His breathing quickened. Slamming his fist on the steering wheel he imagined Cathy Clegg living in the lap of luxury, whilst her husband rotted in prison. 'Bitch!' He hated that woman. He hated her spoilt brat and her new life too. But, more than anything, he hated her for being the instrument that caused their downfall twelve years ago. He slid the car into gear and still breathing angrily he moved off. 'Stupid bitch, did you really think we'd let you get away with it? Did you really think we'd let you off the hook?' He laughed aloud, executed a three-point turn in the tight space and drove back towards the main road and Keighley. 'Your time has come, Cathy Clegg. Your time has come and you will pay dearly for your actions!' he said aloud.

When he arrived back in the Weatherspoon's car park he deliberately parked the Fiat two spaces away from the spot he'd liberated it from an hour earlier. A cursory glance around the driver's seat satisfied him that he'd left nothing incriminating behind, so he slammed the door shut and walked away, hood obscuring his face from any CCTV cameras. He felt good. Very good.

CHAPTER 33
The Fort

Holding a plastic bag packed with bacon butties in one hand, his bag hanging over his good shoulder, Gus stood by the kerb, waiting for the flow of traffic to allow him to cross. He'd just left the warm Chaat Café with its mouth-watering aromas and cheery familiarity and was keen to eat a proper breakfast after feeding half his mother's offerings to the dog earlier. His heart sank as glancing across the road he saw the unmistakeable presence of the journos huddled on the pavement outside The Fort. Hopefully they hadn't sussed out that he was senior investigating officer in, what they'd dubbed 'the babies in the attic' case.

'Fucking miserable weather,' said a voice behind him. DCI Wentworth in a raincoat, his breakfast in a similar carrier bag dangling off a wrist that held a massive black umbrella. His smile was much too bright for 8:30 on a Tuesday morning. Gus, mind full of the briefing he was about to conduct, nodded brusquely and concentrated on the traffic. The man hadn't endeared himself to Gus the previous day and Gus didn't have the time or the inclination to offer second chances.

From the corner of his eye he saw a familiar BMW pull onto the road to his left blocking the oncoming traffic and giving him the opportunity to cross the road. His sister, Katie, sat in the driving seat. Ignoring her tentative smile, he glared at her.

'Someone you know?' said Wentworth.

Gus strode across the road, Wentworth following on behind. 'Not any more.'

Head bent against the rain he'd barely reached the steps to the Fort before the flurry of bedraggled journalists flocked round him like flies to a turd.

'DI McGuire, is it true you're leading on the murder at the graveyard and the babies in the attic case?'

Gus's heart sank. He'd hoped for at least a few days' grace, time to find his feet, before being hounded. He lowered his head and ignored them.

'DI McGuire, are you fit for work after the tragic events of last year?'

'DI McGuire, have the children discovered on Sunday been identified yet?'

'Is a paedophile ring at large in Bradford?'

Hunching his shoulders, customary scowl in place, Gus shouldered past them, followed by Wentworth who taking Gus's lead remained silent. Cameras flashed around them and the strident voices vied with one another to be heard. Gus tuned them out, concentrating instead on the children he was desperate to avenge.

Aware of Wentworth following him along the corridor Gus, having forgotten to take his painkillers earlier, felt pain gnawing just below his groin with each step he took. At the far end of the corridor a trio of men stood in a semi-circle, backs to the huge water cooler watching his progress with interest. Gus groaned inwardly when he saw them. There was no way he could access the water to take his medication without interacting with them and he was in no mood for their stupid one-upmanship. DS Steve Knowles was no friend to him and neither were Knowles's two sidekicks, DCs Jazz Panesar and Alfie Redmond. Envious of Gus's place on the university fast track scheme and jealous of his solve rate in the Bradford Major Crime Team, they took every opportunity to taunt him.

The smile on Knowles's stubbly face told Gus they were waiting for him. Straightening his shoulders, he held the other man's gaze as he approached. Tweedledee and Tweedledum, like the idiots they were, cast sycophantic looks to their glorious leader.

As he drew level, Gus nodded abruptly. He'd taken only two steps past them when they burst out laughing and whispering, raising their voices so he would only hear part of their conversation. With the words 'dyke' and 'carpet muncher' hanging in the air Gus clenched his fists. Visions of him landing one on Knowles, breaking his already bent nose and sending his arrogant head flying backwards to rebound, with a sickening crunch, off the wall behind, ran through his mind. He imagined turning his attention to the other two pricks that, master down, would cower like the cowards they were. Only the knowledge that their pet, DCI Hussain, would relish such a reaction from him kept Gus from making good on his thoughts.

A sudden shout of. 'Oi, watch where you're going!' made Gus turn round in time to see DS Knowles bent double and DCI Wentworth hands splayed before him in apology.

'So sorry, didn't see you there. Did my elbow get your stomach?' Wentworth grimaced. 'Fuck, have I winded you?'

Realising who Wentworth was, Knowles red faced and still clutching his stomach backed away, but not before throwing a threatening look in Gus's direction. Gus frowned, wondering what had prompted Wentworth's action. Maybe he wasn't such an arse after all.

Wentworth, checking to make sure he hadn't damaged his bacon butty shrugged and said to Gus, 'Always been clumsy, me.'

CHAPTER 34
Bradford

The space was dire. Damp and smelling of must and cat piss but hopefully it wouldn't be for long. He kicked the grubby settee, releasing a cloud of dust. Fucking crap idea, doing this in such a rush. He's finally losing it, and it's not *his* neck on the line. It's me doing the bloody kidnapping. The Distributor with barely disguised anger, mumbled and cursed.

The plan had been in place for months now. Making the initial contact with the girl had been easy. Preying on her insecurities about the new baby, building up how much her dad loved her and how bad her Mum was for lying, telling her he was dead, not letting her have contact with him.

He liked kids, not just for the money they made him and his friends, or even for the fantasies they fulfilled for him, but also as small people. He was good with them. Got their trust easily, which of course had been beneficial over the years. Pity The Matchmaker had warned him off touching the girl.

Anyway, it was all systems go now. He'd given her a secure pre-paid phone and she'd been keen to meet up with him for short amounts of time. This time he was counting on her sneaking out from that fortress they called home and meeting up with him at the end of the road where there was no CCTV. He doubted she'd tell anyone. Why would she? She knew what was at risk and the last thing she wanted to do was lose the daddy she'd missed for so long. But he didn't want to be hanging around for too long either. Too many nosey parkers in this sort of area. No, she'd better be quick and then they'd be off, change car a couple of times before heading to their final destination and the final reality for little Miss Clegg! He rubbed his hands together and set off, adrenalin pumping at the thought of what was to come.

CHAPTER 35
Ilkley

Molly Graves was fed up. It was half-term and all everyone did was coo over that stupid baby. Her Mum was too knackered to take her anywhere and Granny Jessie only wanted to help with her brother. Never mind, though. *She* had a secret, one that none of them would ever imagine. Not even in a million years. One that was more precious than that stupid bawling kid. Even if Mum and her stepdad, Alex, didn't love her, she knew someone who did. Someone who'd spent a long time trying to find her and who listened to her and wanted to spend time with her.

In the privacy of her en suite bathroom she carefully locked the door before taking the phone from her pocket. It wasn't a fancy one like her iPhone. No, this was a poxy, cheap one, but she didn't care. Her dad had given it to her, besides, she'd not need it for very much longer anyway. Closing the toilet seat she sat down and switched the phone on, keeping her fingers crossed that there'd be a message. The screen flashed and then she smiled. There it was – a text. Her fingers flew over the keys and her message came up on the screen. She raised one fisted hand and punched the air. He was going to pick her up at the end of the street at 10:30. Now all she had to do was escape the grown-ups. That shouldn't be too difficult, for all the attention they'd given her since 'it' was born.

A frown spread across her face for a second. She knew she'd be in real trouble when she got back. Mum was so bloody strict... too strict, always checking up on her and not letting her out of her sight. She shuddered. Too damn claustrophobic, yes, that was the word.

She brightened. It would be worth being grounded, anyway, to spend some time with her dad. The dad her mum had told her was dead.

Flushing the toilet, she left the bathroom and began hatching her plan to get out of the house and away before anyone spotted she was missing. Easy. She'd done it before after all.

CHAPTER 36
The Fort

Fuelled by a bacon butty and strong coffee, Gus leaned against the desk at the front of the room and, despite feeling slightly nervous, was keen to start his first briefing in many months. Compo, sat behind his suite of computer equipment, a splodge of ketchup on one cheek, devoured his third bacon butty of the day. Frowning slightly, Alice scoured the incident board, checking for omissions that Gus knew weren't there. Efficient and intuitive, she'd done a good job in his absence. The newbies to the team, DCs John Sampson and Sadia Hussain, were checking through witness statements and the visiting officer DCI Wentworth hovered at the back of the room. Detective Jankowski was on his way back to Poland, having facilitated the transport of Andrzej Bielski's body on the same flight as his parents. The other children were being repatriated when they were fit to leave the hospital. Gus had never seen so much despair as he did in the faces of the parents. They still needed to ID the dead girl, but hopefully with Europol and Interpol on the case that should be soon. Jankowski had left behind strict instructions to keep him in the loop with the rest of the investigation.

Clearing his throat, Gus rustled his notes and began. 'Any word on the photo from Jamal Asif?'

Sampson stood up. 'It's been shown to neighbours, shops et cetera in the village, but so far no hits.'

'What about Jamal's school and the builders that were there?'

'Schools are on holiday this week so we're still trying to get hold of someone. The head teacher's on maternity leave. We're dealing with the deputy who's acting head and didn't oversee the building work. She's getting back to us as soon as she's found the building records.'

'What about the transit van? Anyone see that?'

Sampson shrugged. 'Vague recollections of a van from a few neighbours, but no sightings of children getting in or out of the van.'

'Shit!' Gus pushed himself away from the table and began to pace. 'Surely someone, somewhere, noticed the repeated presence of a bloody van with a mattress logo on the side.' Dragging his fingers through his hair he stopped. 'Right Sampson, you and her.' He frowned at DC Hussain. 'What's your name again?'

Her eyes narrowed, but she answered promptly. 'DC Hussain, sir, Sadia.'

'Right, you and Sampson will get out on the streets and magic up a sighting of the van and the guy driving it. We need an ID on him ASAP!'

He turned to Alice. 'Al, you still on to observe the child psychologist interviewing the Asif children?'

Grimacing, Alice nodded.

'Right after that I want you to chase up the acting head teacher and follow up on the builders. Compo, I need you liaising with Interpol and individual detectives involved in the original missing kids investigations. We need to know how these bastards get the kids out of their countries without detection.'

Alice raised a hand. 'I'm on that, Gus.'

'What's the status on the other children? Any chance of interviewing them?'

Alice said, 'It looks like our best lead from those kids will be through evidence acquired from their clothes and bodies. None of them are fit to be interviewed and the results aren't back from the lab yet.'

Taking a sip of coffee, Gus turned and tapped the picture of Sharon Asif. 'Now, on to the Asif murder. Anything from the door to doors on that?'

Alice sighed and shook her head. 'Both her and Jamal were spotted in front of the Chinese Restaurant. The restaurant confirms that Jamal bought chips. The King's Arms confirms that Sharon Asif was in making a nuisance of herself at around eightish. She's banned from there so they chucked her out. She went to The Delver's Inn, just down the road, but nobody can confirm she left with anyone. No one's come forward on the hotline either to say they saw her heading to the graveyard.'

Pausing, she shuffled the papers on her desk. 'We *did* get one interesting phone call from the old folks' home that overlooks Sharon Asif's terraced row. An old woman was interviewed by a PC yesterday and couldn't remember anything. She phoned back last night to say she remembers something now, but will only talk face to face.'

Gus shrugged 'Well, I'm not getting my hopes up that she'll have anything concrete for us, but it's worth a shot.' He turned to Sampson. 'You'll manage to fit that in, won't you?'

As Sampson scribbled in his notebook, Gus noticed Sadia Hussain's scowl. What's her problem he wondered? Surely she's not petty enough to resent Sampson having the lead on that interview. After what Alice had told him the previous evening he wouldn't be surprised. If she expected to continue working on his team, though, she better acquire some team spirit pretty damn pronto.

'Anything else?' Gus asked.

'Yes, a car reported missing yesterday fits the description of the one used in the attempted shooting of Jamal Asif. It was discovered in the Asda car park on Cemetery Road. Forensics are on it.' Alice grinned. 'They found a coke bottle filled with piss so maybe they'll get some DNA to go with the fingerprints they found on the underside of the driver's seat, where it looks like someone adjusted the seat.'

'Not to burst your bubble Al, but the most info we'll get from that urine sample will be the sex of the pisser. Urine doesn't carry much DNA. However, let's hope the fingerprints don't belong to the car owner. We could do with a break.'

Glancing round the room, he rubbed his hands together. 'Right, let's crack on.'

CHAPTER 37
Ilkley

Whilst Bradford was all hills and mills and had the gritty patina of a well-used but stoic prostitute, Ilkley was all arty crafty and designer boutiques. Bradford's Aldi, Lidl and pound shops were substituted in Ilkley with Marks and Sparks, Waitrose and Betty's Cake Shop. Dog shit was relegated to its rightful place in pooper scooper bags. The absence of spit or chewing gum on the sidewalks and an abundance of coiffed, manicured women typified Ilkley High Street.

The Distributor, parked in a side street, felt out of place here. Far too posh for his liking. It was nearly time, anyway, so he engaged the clutch and, driving the car he'd scoped out the previous evening and had hotwired this morning, he moved past a gourmet pub called The Duchess of York. The trio of medium-sized residences on his left told him it was time to turn off and within seconds he trundled over a cattle grid and into the sparsely populated wooded area of Dales Way Link, where a near-neighbour lived a good twenty-minute walk away. Very secluded and very lonely, he thought. Especially for a young girl. From the miles of snow-covered fields and moorland sprung the occasional large custom-built house, cleverly designed to reflect traditional Yorkshire architecture.

Here the properties were elevated in price range from expensive to exorbitant and security was de rigueur. Unfortunately, for the owners that is, public money didn't stretch to CCTV cameras on this isolated road. Mind you, strangers stood out like a sore thumb here so he hoped the little bitch wouldn't keep him hanging around. He didn't need the owner of one of the properties further up to pass by and notice him parked here. Peering along the icy road he

161

saw a small figure in leggings, knee-length boots and a red coat approach. With a sigh of relief, he plastered on a smile and started the engine. Molly was right on time.

CHAPTER 38
Heaton

Having gained entry to the Marigold Court Old Folks Home, DC Sampson and DC Hussain stood outside Mrs Louise Brown's flat. The old lady, hunched, with arthritic hands and the cloudy eyes of those with cataract problems, glared at them and shook her head. 'You can't come in you know.'

Sadia shuffled impatiently, but DC Sampson smiled widely and in his pleasantest tone said, 'We won't take up much of your time, Mrs Brown. We just want to chat to you about what you saw.'

Still not giving an inch the old lady glowered at him from behind the half-closed door. 'It's Tuesday! You can't come in.' She said, glancing at Sadia, whose face, Sampson noticed, resembled a skelped arse. What the hell was wrong with the woman?

Sadia moved forward, but sensing that all would not end well if she led the discussion, Sampson nudged her gently out of the way, ignoring her annoyed tut. Once more, he smiled at the old lady. 'I'm sorry, Mrs Brown, I'm not sure I understand?'

Her mouth pursed into lip-sticked creases and in a tone that made no attempt to disguise her annoyance at Sampson's stupidity she said, 'It's laundry day. Every Tuesday. Without fail.'

Sampson shook his head to indicate he still didn't understand.

The old lady sighed theatrically and, with over-emphasised enunciation, said 'Tuesday. Laundry day.' Jerking her thumb towards the lifts, she continued, '*She* takes my laundry every Tuesday.' Then, lowering her voice to a whistling hiss she said, 'But I don't give her my knickers.' She shook her head ferociously. 'No bloody way!'

Ignoring the sound of Hussain's foot tapping impatiently behind him, Sampson said, 'Ok. It's Tuesday and it's laundry day, but I still don't understand why we can't come in for just a few minutes. After all, you requested a home visit.'

A whoosh of air suggestive of recently eaten garlic hit Sampson's nostrils as she all but yelled. 'My knickers are in a bucket.'

Sampson blinked. 'Sorry?'

'I've got my knickers soaking in a bucket so you can't come in. Come back tomorrow,' she said, as if addressing an imbecile.

Momentarily stymied, Sampson gawped at her. Then, seeing that Sadia was ready to step into the breach he wedged himself firmly in front of her again. Dredging patience from a previously untapped source he smiled. 'Am I right in thinking that you're not letting us in because you've got your... er... delicates soaking in a bucket?'

Her over-rouged face split into a huge grin and she gave a guttural whoop of laughter. 'Not sure I'd call my knickers 'delicate', lad. But yes, you've got it at last.'

Risking her garlic breath, he bent his head closer to her. 'Where do you keep your bucket? The one with your...er.' He glanced sideways, caught Sadia's eye and was annoyed to feel himself blushing. 'Knickers?'

'Where do you think I keep them, sonny? In the bathroom. Where else would I keep them?'

'In that case, if we promise not to go near your bathroom would you let us in so we can have that little chat?'

Cocking her head to one side for a second, she considered his proposal. Then, she shuffled back from the door, allowing them entry into her flat. Standing in front of the bathroom door like a sentry on duty, she watched as they settled themselves onto the settee in her living room. The first thing he noticed on entering the flat was the faint smell of mints. The second was the overabundance of greenery. Every conceivable surface boasted a plant of one kind or another, giving the small living room the look of a greenhouse. The gas fire, fastened to the wall beneath a painting of cancan girls in red corsets, blasted out enough heat to allow Mrs Brown to grow exotic fruit, should she so desire. She shuffled in and sat opposite them on her padded high-backed chair. 'Well?'

'You phoned last night requesting a home visit because you had some information for us?'

'Yes, that's right. But, I distinctly remember telling that girl on the phone that Wednesday would be best.' She flapped her hands, a frown flitting across her face, then she said, 'Anyway, it must have been about three weeks ago in the middle of the night. I'd got a dose of diarrhoea.' She leaned towards Sampson and whispered, 'Actually had a couple of accidents, if you know what I mean.'

Despite Sadia's slight snigger he managed to keep a straight face. 'I know exactly what you mean.'

Folding her arms under her breasts, she smiled. 'Well, I were up and down all night. It were fair running right through me and my tummy was sore. I couldn't settle. I saw the lights shine across the curtains and so I looked out and there it was. One of them white vans like my window cleaner has. Only it weren't his, 'cos his is blue.'

'Do you remember what time this was?'

'Yes I do as it happens. I thought it was strange, so I looked at the clock. It was 3:20am.'

'Did you notice anything else?'

'Well, it were there for a while. I saw this man get out the front and move round to the back and open the door. I think he were talking to someone but he could've been on the phone. Those young 'uns are always on their phones these

165

days.' She directed an accusing look in Sadia's direction as if suspecting her of being a prime phone culprit.

Bringing her back on track, Sampson said, 'What did the man look like?'

'No idea I'm afraid. Too dark and besides I don't see right well either. But, I did notice the mattress picture on the side. Thought it were a damn funny time to have a new mattress delivered.'

Realising they'd exhausted Mrs Brown's knowledge of the van and its driver, Sampson thanked her as he and Sadia stood up to leave. With surprising agility, Mrs Brown sprang to her feet, elbowed past Sampson and sprinted to take up her sentry position in front of the bathroom door, as the pair trooped out of her flat.

With the door shut behind them, Sadia burst into hysterical laughter placing her hand on Sampson's arm to support herself.

'Oh, so you do have a sense of humour then, Hussain?' said Sampson, surprised by the change from the dour-faced, monosyllabic woman she'd started the morning as.

Sadia winked at him and straightened up before resorting to her normal stern demeanour. 'Yeah, but don't tell anyone, will you?' She punched him lightly on the arm. 'Bet you're glad we didn't come calling the week she had her shitty knickers soaking in her bucket.'

CHAPTER 39
Ilkley

The baby was screaming and Beth Graves was nearly pulling her hair out. She couldn't remember it being as bad when Molly was a baby. Why was he always crying? Colic, they said, but this was so relentless. She looked down at Sam's scrunched up red face and immediately her earlier anguish was replaced by concern. The poor thing was pulling his little legs up to his tummy and was clearly in pain. She laid him on his back and very gently, with two fingers, pressed on his little tummy following a circular movement round his scabby umbilical cord like she'd learned at baby massage class when Molly had been a baby. His screaming subsided slightly until finally, with a series of tired hiccups, he closed his eyes and fell asleep. Rather than disturb him, Beth covered him with a blanket and stretching herself out on the floor beside him, she fell into a fitful doze with one ear tuned to the rhythmic breathing of her baby.

An hour later, stiff and cold she started awake when Sam began to whimper, his tiny arms and legs building up momentum as they kicked and waved. She straightened herself, rubbed her eyes and gingerly got to her knees before lifting him and moving to the wooden rocking chair to feed him.

Smiling she looked up when the bedroom door opened and Granny Jessie poked her head round. Her smile faded when she saw the look on Jessie's face. 'What is it?'

Jessie waved her hand dismissively. 'Probably nothing, it's just– I can't find Molly. Is she here with you?' Her anxious gaze travelled round the room hoping to see the red-haired girl hiding behind the curtains or some piece of furniture.

167

Beth felt her heartbeat quicken and she stood up deftly refastening her bra as she did so. 'She's not here Jessie; I've not seen her since breakfast.'

'She didn't go to work with Alex then?'

Beth frowned and shook her head. 'No, no. Why would she? She's hardly speaking to him since he withdrew her internet rights for being cheeky the other day.' She handed the gurgling baby to Jessie. 'Can you change his nappy? I'll check outside and then I'll phone her. She can't have gone far. She knows not to wander off without permission.'

Nevertheless, at the back of Beth s mind was the knowledge that her twelve-year-old daughter had been feeling jealous since the arrival of her brother and was playing up. Pushing the boundaries more than usual. But she wouldn't have left the grounds would she? She knew how dangerous it was out there. She'd always instilled the need for caution in her daughter. Surely she wouldn't have risked her safety to go off on her own? Then unbidden the headline from the previous night's news sprung into her head. 'Children found in attic room in Bradford. Paedophile ring suspected.' She flung her hands over her face and shuddered. 'Oh please, not again. Please, God, don't let this all happen again!'

CHAPTER 40
The Fort

DCI Nancy Chalmers threw open the door and stood there until, sensing her presence, Gus looked up. Her face was ashen and her hands shook as she pushed a stray curl behind her ear. Immediately, Gus tried to jump up to go to her but he'd been going over interviews and notes for hours and with the strain of being in one position for too long, his leg gave way on him. Frustrated he slumped back into his chair, as she made her own unsteady way towards him.

'What the fuck's wrong, Nancy?'

Gus watched as her eyes quickly surveyed the room. Compo was fully engrossed in his computer screen with headphones on and his head bobbing to some erratic beat that seemed to send vibrations along the floorboards to his feet. Sadia Hussain, looked up, but when Nancy glared at her, her mouth tightened and she averted her eyes.

Pulling out a chair Nancy plonked herself down. Tentatively stretching his leg before standing, Gus got up and walked over to pour her a large mug of coffee. Noting that her hands still shook slightly he added two lumps of sugar before returning to his desk and depositing the mug in front of her. 'Drink,' he said in a tone that brooked no argument.

As she sipped it, Gus looked over at Sadia, whom he suspected was faking absorption in her computer screen. Pursing his lips, he dipped his hand into his pocket, withdrew a tenner and turned to Sadia. 'Nip over to The Chaat café and get us a bacon butty and some cookies, Sadia.'

Sadia grimaced, whether at his peremptory tone or at the thought of the bacon butty which, Gus acknowledged, some might consider to be an insensitive request to make of a Muslim, or at his peremptory tone, he was unsure. For Christ's sake though, he wasn't asking her to eat the bloody thing.

Huffing, she snatched the money from his hand and left the room.

Nancy shook her head and smiled slightly. 'You do know who she is, don't you?' Gus shrugged. 'Doesn't matter who she is as long as she does her job and doesn't get too nosy.'

Nancy gave an inelegant snort. 'You were just like her when you were a DC. Impatient to move up the ranks and too keen to know everything.' He felt her eyes on him as she continued, 'And it's not a bad trait.' She paused. 'As long as you're on the right side.'

Gus frowned '… and she's not?'

'I don't know. You'll have to find out for yourself.'

Gus sat back down. 'So, who is she then?'

Some of the colour had returned to her cheeks as she placed her mug on the desk. 'She's DCI Hussain's daughter. His *only* daughter. And he's very protective of her. Word is he didn't want her to join the force after her degree, but she was insistent.'

'Shit, I don't need him breathing down my neck on this investigation. It's complicated enough as it is.'

'Don't worry, when I was asked to take her on I insisted he keep his rather large and disdainful nose out of our business and away from *my* team.'

Grinning, he imagined Nancy going head-to-head with the tiger of the station. Gus had had a major run-in with the man just before he'd been injured. A drug bust gone wrong due to the shoddy, gung-ho work of some of DCI Hussain's team (namely Knowles & co). This had led to a minor altercation, which had escalated in part due to Hussain's heavy-handedness. When Gus had intervened, the other man had made some rather harsh aspersions regarding Gus's 'credentials' as an inspector. It seemed DCI Ishmael Hussain wasn't a fan of the fast-track option for officers with degrees. Unfortunately, Hussain was the big boss's favourite. He was trotted out every time Bradford police was accused of racism. Gus wasn't the only one to doubt the man's sincerity or his commitment to equal opportunity, but his misgivings weren't shared by the powers that be.

Face serious, Nancy, placed her elbows on the desk. 'Things have just got even more complicated, I'm afraid.'

Nodding, he waited for her to continue. Biting her lip and drumming her slightly chipped varnished fingernails on the table, she sighed. 'A young girl has gone missing in Ilkley. It's safe to assume she's been abducted.'

Gus frowned and opened his mouth to speak, but Nancy held up her hand to stop him. 'It's linked, I know it is, without even a *shred* of doubt. Jankowski was right and the identity of the current victim confirms it.'

'Who is this young girl?'

Getting to her feet, she paced the length of the room. 'Look, I know you're up to your ears in this investigation. And I know it's a lot to ask of you when you've only just returned to work, but I want, no scrap that, I *need* you on this case. I don't have time to go into everything right now but I want you on the ground in Ilkley. I want you there at the house and the parents will explain everything. Trust me, Gus. This is important and it's got to be kept quiet for now.'

The fluttering in his chest was caused not so much by Nancy's words, as by her tortured expression.

'I need more information than that, Nancy.'

'Trust me Gus, it's better you hear it from the mother, Beth Graves.'

Gus tossed his head, his face sullen. 'For God's sake, Nance, you know how busy we are here. Can't you send someone else?'

She held his gaze. 'I've told you, this is crucial to your ongoing investigation. Just do it!'

Smarting from her harsh tone, Gus snatched the address from her hand, and grabbed his coat and bag. He reached the door just as Hussain, face flushed with exertion, burst through.

'You! With me now!' said Gus.

Sadia barely had time to grab her bag and cast a quick bemused glance at Nancy before trotting out of the room after her irascible boss.

'Where are we going?'

'Ilkley and you're driving, hurry.'

CHAPTER 41
Ilkley

With Sadia proving to be a fast and capable driver, they drove over the tops to Ilkley. Bracken and heather, smothered by snow drifts flashed past the window. It was beautiful and if a child hadn't been abducted, Gus would have enjoyed the drive. However, his head was full of questions. Why was Nancy so convinced this was linked to the current cases? Why was she so shaken? And why break protocol to have the major crimes unit involved so early for a possible abduction.

Thankfully, unlike Alice who always chattered like an express train, Sadia seemed content to listen to the radio, leaving him with his thoughts. Normally, he'd have chosen Alice to accompany him, but Nancy's assertion that he'd been more than a little like Sadia Hussain when he was a lowly DC had made him choose Sadia. He hoped his instincts wouldn't be proved wrong. If she was some sort of spy for her dad, who openly disapproved of Nancy, Gus *and* the major crimes unit, it was wise to keep a close eye on her.

The confined car felt stuffy, so Gus cracked the window open. This earned him a pointed frown from Sadia. Despite himself, he smiled and cracked it another inch. As cool air infiltrated the car, the whoosh of wind drowned out Sadia's annoyed tut. However, seconds later his thoughts were interrupted when his window whirred back up. Casting a sideways glance at Sadia, he noticed the slight smile on her face. *Cheeky bitch used the central control to close my window.* He turned to look at her. She was, despite the sulky look she often carried, quite beautiful. Flawless complexion, long blue-black hair and eyelashes also long and dark that framed deep brown eyes.

Smothering his grin, he resumed his silent contemplation of the scenery for a few seconds before pressing the button to open the window again. The urge to grin increased when he realised she'd locked the passenger window.

Driving through the well-gritted town centre, Sadia turned left at a road leading towards the woods. At the bottom end of the moor, she slowed slightly. 'Sir?'

Gus turned towards her as she negotiated round a parked car. 'Yes?'

'What's the big urgency in Ilkley?'

Gathering his thoughts, Gus rubbed his shoulder. He'd had to strap it up again and it was throbbing like shit. 'A child's gone missing, suspected abduction. DCI Chalmers says this is a 'sensitive case'. That's about all I know. We'll find out more when we get there.'

She checked her rear mirror. 'Haven't we got enough on with the trafficking case and Asif's murder?'

'DCI Chalmers thinks there may be a link between this and the other two cases. Who knows? But, if she wants us on it, it's because it's important?'

Nodding, she turned onto the Dales Way Link. Gus braced himself as they juddered over the cattle grid and studied the isolation that fanned out to the side of the narrow road. The snowy landscape made the area seem even more desolate. The few houses they passed were situated quite a distance from the road. Some people, it seemed, really craved solitude.

They drifted to a standstill, the engine humming gently. Sadia leaned over the steering wheel and peered through the windscreen.

'This is it. What sort of people live here?'

Gus shared her surprise. Not content with just having security cameras dotted periodically up the length of the winding drive, the owners had created a double-gated access. Three-metre high railings spread out from either side of the gate. By the looks of it, they surrounded the entire property. Gus glanced at the slip of paper Nancy had given him. The number and house name tallied with their GPS destination. They'd arrived at Four Oaks.

'Well, I'll be damned!' he said, under his breath.

'So, *this* is more important than twenty abused kids?' said Sadia, her face flushed.

Gus studied her heightened colour and the way her hands gripped the steering wheel with interest. Why the hell was she so enraged by this? Before he had a chance to ask her she thumped the steering wheel with her leather-gloved fist. 'It's disgusting. Someone with a bit of money reports their kid missing and all of a sudden that takes precedence. Couldn't the locals have dealt with it?'

Gus began to reply when she engaged the clutch. Putting her foot down, she wrenched the wheel to the right and swung onto the tarmacked waiting area. Taken by surprise, Gus lurched forward, the seat belt tightened agonisingly across his shoulder. Before he could react, her window whirred open and her right arm extended towards the security bell. His sudden expletive halted her. She turned towards him, mouth open in surprise.

Rubbing his shoulder, he glared at her. When he spoke his words were staccato. 'What. The. Fuck, Hussain? That stupid trick of yours could have landed me back in hospital.'

Under his angry glare, her face blanched.

Gus took a deep breath and when he spoke again his tone was calm. 'Look, Sadia, we're all under a lot of strain at the minute. These cases are hard going.' He paused to adjust his sling, then raised his sharp, blue eyes to meet her gaze. 'You've got to learn to control your reactions. You can't go off on one. Let's get the bigger picture before we jump in with guns blazing, eh?'

He smiled and pointed to her open window. 'You better press the bell.'

Lips tight, she nodded and did as instructed.

A fuzzy voice addressed them through the intercom. Moments later, once they had shown their warrant cards to the minute camera, the first gate slid open. Driving forward, it slid shut behind them before the second gate opened, allowing them access to the curved drive leading to the house.

Gus shook his head. 'How the hell did someone manage to abduct a child from here?'

Looking subdued, Sadia swallowed hard. 'Beats me.'

Following the cobbled drive up to the front of the house, they parked between a Land Rover, and a marked police car. As they got out a uniformed officer approached, hand outstretched. 'Hi, sir. PC Owens.'

Gus, pointing to his strapped shoulder, offered his left hand to the officer, who, with a smile, quickly swapped hands.

'What's going on, Owens?' asked Gus, after introducing himself and Sadia.

'Got a report this morning about a missing school girl; Molly Graves. Then I was told you lot were coming.'

'What've you done so far?'

'Two officers searched the grounds and surrounding area. Sent another one to the neighbours.' He opened both hands wide in an encompassing gesture, 'But, as you can see, the neighbours are miles away. Nobody's seen owt so far. I also sent two officers to Molly's friends' houses.'

As Gus nodded approvingly, the front door opened and a diminutive figure stepped out.

'That's granny,' said Owens.

Telling Owens to request a family liaison officer, Gus, followed by Sadia, walked towards the small porch where a middle-aged woman waited.

CHAPTER 42
Bradford

The transaction had been successful and girl was in their clutches. Now, the exquisite torture he'd planned so carefully over the years could begin. In anticipation, The Matchmaker phoned The Facilitator. When the call was answered, he said, 'She's in the depot.'

The Matchmaker knew that, despite his reluctance to risk what they'd recouped over the years, The Facilitator had the utmost faith in him. After all, where would they be if not for him? The Matchmaker had been the brains behind the operation for so long and, for that, he knew, the other man would allow him this indulgence. It would be so good to make the bitch pay. She'd cost them a lot. Nearly broken them, if the truth were told. He looked forward to making her suffer.

Thinking he heard movement outside his home office, he walked to the door, opened it and glanced down the stairs. They were empty. He stepped back inside, locking the door behind him. The last thing he needed was for his wife to get curious and listen in to his private conversations. 'Let's get this show on the road,' he said, sitting down at his desk.

'We'll keep our distance. The Distributor will take the risks.'

'Oh yes, he'll have to do a lot to do to redeem himself,' said The Matchmaker drumming his fingers on the desk. 'And we'll make sure he does. For now, we still need him.'

A nervous laugh rumbled over the phone. 'Have you sorted things out at your end?'

'The idiot's stupidity has left a few loose ends, but we'll let them play out. Nothing implicates us.'

He hung up and walked over to the mirror. Straightening his tie, he assessed his reflection with a critical eye. Tall, handsome, some might say, debonair. Flicking a piece of fluff from the shoulder of his suit, he smiled. The mere thought of his appointment with the ten-year-old boy made him hard. Leaving his office, he went downstairs and kissed his wife perfunctorily on the cheek. Happy that he was about to devour fresh meat, he headed to their safe house in Leeds. Occasionally, The Provider excelled himself.

CHAPTER 43
Ilkley

The woman led them through to a spacious kitchen without uttering a single word. As soon as they entered the room, she scurried over and sat down at the table. Gus frowned and made a mental note to encourage the family to have a doctor look at her before he left. She looked ready to drop. The last thing this family needed was for grandma to lose it. Heat belched from the Aga that stood, bright red, between bespoke kitchen units. Gus immediately felt at home in the clutter that marked this room as the centre of family life. The large American-style fridge-freezer was covered with pictures of a young girl with curly red hair; petting various animals, in climates as diverse as the snow-capped hills of northern Scotland, the Greek isles and a rain-swept Yorkshire moor.

Well-thumbed books lay across the work surfaces and four pairs of wellies were lined up in size-order by the back door. The window above the sink looked out over a huge garden with what looked to be a mega-sized, snow-covered trampoline in the far corner. Eight chairs stood round a large pine table, which was definitely *not* courtesy of IKEA. One of them was occupied by a man in his late thirties with prematurely greying hair cut close to his scalp. In a second chair sat a woman with short brown hair, breastfeeding a new-born baby. Shirt sleeves rolled up loosely and tie awry, the man stood up, hand outstretched, and introduced himself as Alex Graves, Molly's stepdad. Resting a protective hand on her shoulder, he introduced his wife, Beth. Then turning to the older woman he said 'And this is Molly's granny, Jessie Graham.'

Beth looked up. 'Jessie is my previous husband's mother.'

Gus studied each adult in turn. Alex was clearly distressed. His white shirt had a splodge of what looked and smelled like baby sick down the front. His wife, by contrast, looked uncannily self-possessed. Her gaze was direct, dark and uncompromising and, apart from a tightness round her eyes, it was hard to detect how she felt.

Clearing his throat, Gus pulled out a chair, sat opposite Beth and introduced himself and Sadia. 'I don't know about you, but I'm in dire need of a coffee and I think you all need to keep up your strength.' He turned to Sadia. 'DC Hussain here will rustle up some toast and drinks for us and you can tell me what's happened.'

Sadia's eyes narrowed, but Gus held her gaze, daring her to refuse. Normally he'd have made the coffee himself, but his shoulder was killing and, to be honest, he quite enjoyed winding her up. After a few seconds her shoulders sagged. Pasting on a smile, she picked up the kettle and turned to the trio. 'What'll it be? Tea or coffee?'

As if startled out of her trance, Jessie jumped to her feet. 'I'll do it. God, what am I thinking? I should have offered.' Agitated, she turned to her daughter-in-law. 'You need to keep your liquids up when you're breastfeeding.' She blew her nose on a rapidly disintegrating tissue and took the kettle from Sadia.

Minutes later, with steaming mugs and a plate of buttered toast in front of them, Beth settled her sleeping baby in his pram. Popping a couple of naproxen, Gus observed her sympathetically. 'Tell me what's happened?'

Wringing her hands, Beth said, 'I fell asleep. I fed and changed Sam and then we just fell asleep.' She grabbed her husband's hand. 'He's not a good sleeper, you see. We're all exhausted but I should have used that time to be with Molly.'

Alex put an arm round her shoulders and squeezed. 'Oh, Beth. You can't think like that. Molly knows she shouldn't leave the premises.'

Picking up another slice of toast, Gus said, 'How do you think Molly was taken?' He gestured towards the gates and cameras outside. 'This place is like Fort Knox; so how could the system have been broken?'

Alex sat up straight. 'It couldn't. No way. I own the company and we've spared no expense. There's just no way anyone could have infiltrated the system. I've made sure Beth feels safe. It's what I do. Security is my business and *this* security system is state of the art.'

He pulled the laptop that lay on the table towards him. Pressing a few buttons, he turned the screen Gus. 'I've already set it up. This shows Molly leaving the house at 10:13.'

Sadia and Gus leaned closer and watched. The girl, in black boots and skinny jeans, curls bouncing jauntily, walked down the drive. When she reached the pedestrian gate she hesitated briefly and glanced around. Pulling off her glove, she pressed her thumb to the biometric pad by the pedestrian gate. Before the gate had opened fully, Molly slipped through. They watched her walk slowly along Dales Link Way towards the main road until she moved out of view.

Gus tapped his lip gently with one finger. 'So, Molly left the house on her own.'

Beth looked blankly at Alex and then nodded slowly. 'She must've done.' Her voice rose to a strangled cry. 'Why the hell would she leave the grounds without telling us? Without asking permission? We've drummed into her how unsafe it is outside.'

Gus wondered if perhaps little Molly Graves had got fed up with all the restrictions. Maybe she realised her friends weren't so restricted and had decided to break the rules.

'Did Molly ever express an interest in visiting somewhere locally? Somewhere she might have gone on her own?'

Both Beth and Alex shook their heads. 'No, nowhere.' Beth cradled her face in her hands. 'But she was jealous of Sam.' She grabbed Alex's hand. 'Her nose was pushed out of joint when he arrived.'

Gus exchanged a glance with Sadia, 'And you've phoned round all her friends and given all their details to PC Owens?'

Beth closed her eyes and sighed. 'Yes, yes, yes. I can't think of anyone else to try.'

Gus looked at each of the three faces in turn. He could almost taste their desperation. 'Right then. I'm going to bring my expert in to see if he can identify a weakness in your security.'

Puffing up his chest, Alex said, 'There *is* no weakness. I've told you that.' He gestured to the screen. 'Anyway, we can see that she left of her own accord.'

Beth frowned at her husband, 'Alex, someone's taken her. After she left here someone took her, or else she'd be back by now.'

Gus looked from husband to wife. 'Why would you say that, Mrs Graves? Often when children go missing they're with someone they know.' He inclined his head apologetically to Jessie. 'I hate to ask this, but you mentioned that Jessie is your previous husband's mother. Could Molly be with him?'

A stillness descended on the room. Beth and Jessie exchanged furtive glances. Alex's jaw tightened and his hand automatically drifted across the table to meet Beth's.

Beth leaned forward, her face lined in frustration. 'We're under witness protection and Molly's dad is in prison.' She turned and stared at Jessie. 'Those bastards have taken our little girl.'

As if sensing his mother's anguish, the baby let out a high-pitched shriek that hung in the air like a giant exclamation mark.

'Witness protection?' repeated Gus. He knew it was called UK Protected Persons Service now, but no-one could get out of the habit of calling them WP. For a moment the only sound in the room was the sound of a tap dripping. Then, Gus felt his phone vibrate in his pocket. He pulled it out and glanced at the screen. Sampson. He shrugged apologetically and moved into the hallway.

'Sir, we got the results back on the gun. Compo input it into Interpol's records and the ballistics matches the gun with one used in Gorce, Poland, twelve years ago. Guess what it was used for?'

Gus felt Sampson's excitement reverberate over the line. 'Go on.'

'To shoot an elderly man during a child abduction. The perp got away.'

'Shit! Right, tell Compo good work, then get on the phone to Jankowski; he should be back in Poland by now. Get him to pull the files and send them to us. We need to act fast. Tell him to correlate any other child abductions in the area at that time.' Gus released a slow breath. The links to Poland were very telling. It seemed Nancy was right to think these two cases might be linked. He needed to get more information from Beth Graves.

'Any word from Alice about the bloke in the photo?'

'She's just phoned in. She's heading off to interview the builder who employed him. Er, where are you? Compo said you and Sadia left in a rush. Is everything alright?'

'No. The shit just hit the proverbial fan and, unfortunately, the animal doing the shitting is a great hulking elephant, not a bloody Chihuahua.'

'Eh?'

'Never mind. Can you get Compo to head over here with all his stuff? We've got a missing child, possibly abducted and I need him to hook us up in case we get a ransom call.' Gus reeled off the address and then hung up.

He slipped his phone back into his pocket and took a minute to consider the bombshell Beth had dropped before Sampson's call. Witness protection. No wonder Nancy had been on edge. He ran his fingers through his dreads. She should've warned him to expect this. He'd have words with her on his return to The Fort. A child was missing and he had a really bad feeling about this. The local bobbies had started door to door, but in this neck of the woods it was unlikely anyone had seen anything.

When he re-entered the kitchen, three pairs of panicked eyes followed his progress into the room. He turned his chair round and straddled it, leaning his arm, supported by his sling along the back. He revelled in the slight stretch the position offered his tender thigh and shoulder

'Right, witness protection? I presume you've already contacted your handler about this?'

Beth Graves nodded.

'So, tell me everything.'

Beth shuddered and closed her eyes briefly. 'This is related to those children isn't it? The ones in the attic, I mean. It's all linked, I know it is.'

Gus tapped his fingers on the chair back. 'I don't know, Beth. Why don't you fill me in and we'll take it from there?'

Her hand trembled as she massaged the bridge of her nose. She leaned heavily against her husband and glared at Gus. 'I've already told the police all this. You should have this on file. Why don't you stop bothering us and go find Molly?'

Gus kept his tone calm. 'Look, Beth, I'm sorry if you think we're wasting time, but it's essential that you tell me everything I need to know. It'll be quicker for you to tell me than for me to access your files.'

For the first time Jessie spoke. 'He's right, Beth. Just tell him what he needs to know.'

With a sigh Beth began her story, while Jessie wept silently beside her.

'Twelve years ago I was called Cathy Clegg.'

Gus's eyes narrowed and his gaze remained on Beth as she continued.

'I discovered some awful pictures on my then husband's computer. The vilest images you can imagine. I did the right thing. I went to the police in Cambridge and reported it. It transpired that he was part of a group of paedophiles who abducted and imported children, mainly from Eastern Europe, into the UK. His paedophile ring sold the children or hired them out to the highest bidder. They, in turn, used them any way they wanted. Some made snuff movies. Some uploaded videos.' A single tear rolled down her cheek. 'All of the clients were very rich. Surgeons, barristers, even politicians...'

Gus felt Sadia tense beside him at the table. A quick glance told him she felt as angry as he did. Trying to maintain a neutral expression, he nodded at Beth. 'You're doing really well.' Fuck, what had this poor woman been through? And now this. He knew coincidences didn't happen often in his line of work and his concern over Molly's safety had just spiralled.

Beth swallowed, and linked her arm through her mother-in-law's. 'The police begged me to help them close the ring down completely. They promised me Molly and I would be safe. I did what they asked.' She laughed humourlessly. 'It was clear from the images that my husband's interests weren't young babies, so we knew Molly would be safe from him. That didn't stop me worrying about his friends.' Her mouth curled up as she said the last word. 'I made sure I kept Molly safe. She spent a lot of time with Jessie during those weeks, didn't she?'

Jessie her voice trembling, nodded and said, 'Yes, she did. Of course, I didn't know what was going on at the time. I just thought Beth... Cathy... was ill. She looked terrible.'

Beth leaned over, took a swig of coffee and grimaced. Gus nodded to Sadia who quickly rose and brought her a glass of water. Beth sipped, then continued.

Gus digested the information Beth had revealed. How the hell did she cope knowing her husband was a paedophile? What strain did it put on her to continue living with him, having seen the sort of things he had done? His estimation of the woman sitting opposite increased. 'What did the Cambridge police do next?' asked Gus.

Beth took a minute to compose herself before responding. 'They set up cameras and surveillance equipment throughout our home. They hacked his computer and phone lines. They accessed his work PC and laptop. For seven months, Molly and I lived with him and pretended nothing was wrong.' She looked down and mumbled. 'What else could I do? I'd seen those images. I had to help stop them.' Alex squeezed her arm and she acknowledged his support with a weak smile.

Gus didn't know how to respond to the anguish he saw on Beth's face. What could you say to a mother who'd risked everything, picked herself up and started again, only to have her daughter disappear? 'That must have been sheer hell for you, Beth,' he said at last, knowing his words were inadequate.

Beth snorted and placed her glass on the table. 'Of course, when it came down to it, they were too bloody clever for the police. After all, that *sacrifice,* and the toll it took on my health, they couldn't catch the ringleaders. Oh, they caught many abusers and, of course, James, but the ringleaders remained unidentified. Although the ring was disbanded, I knew they'd regroup. My ex-husband warned me after I'd testified that The Matchmaker would get me. That he'd want revenge. Now he's taking it, isn't he?'

As tears rolled unchecked down her cheeks, Gus's eyes narrowed – The Matchmaker. That was the name Jankowski and Wentworth had argued about yesterday. The name of the man Jankowski was convinced was behind the attic children's abduction. Now it was clear why Nancy had been so keen for Gus to hear Beth's story first hand. Taking a deep breath, he kept his voice calm. 'Nothing's certain yet, Beth. We just don't know enough. We don't even know for sure that Molly's been abducted. She could just be with friends.'

Shaking her head furiously, she glared at him. 'I knew. Deep down in my heart I knew when I heard about those kids in the attic on Monday. It's him. I'm certain. Molly wouldn't go off on her own. Don't you understand? That bastard has taken her.'

Feeling in his gut that she was right, Gus waited till she was calm before asking his next question. 'You said your ex-husband warned you about The Matchmaker. Why didn't he just identify him to the police?'

'According to him, only The Matchmaker and The Facilitator knew each other personally. The rest of them were only contacted online or by phone.' With one finger she traced a bubble of water as it trailed down her glass. 'For all their monitoring and everything the police couldn't seem to access anything to identify the rest of the ring.' She looked at Gus. 'They disappeared without trace.'

Gus sucked in one cheek and bit it as he thought. No wonder she'd gone into witness protection. How could she feel safe otherwise? 'What did your WP agent tell you?'

Beth's shoulders seemed to flop. 'She told us to sit tight and then contacted your boss. She's adamant there's been no breach from their end.'

'I'll need their contact details.'

Beth pushed a piece of paper across the table to Gus. 'She says this is a safe number. Her name is Angelica

Battacharya.' And as Gus scrabbled in his pocket for a pen she added 'You can keep that. I've got a copy of it.'

Gus folded the paper into four using only the fingers of his left hand, like a practised roll-up maker, then slipped it into his trouser pocket. 'If they didn't break the WP, who do you think did?'

Beth blew her nose and shook her head. 'I haven't got a clue. We're always so careful. Jessie, Molly and I left the country for six months. You may not believe it but I was a bit of a celebrity during the trial. Ended up with the press on my back accusing me of being complicit in James's actions. I was harangued on my way to and from court. We had to live in a safe house for months. Anyway, when the trial was over I sold my story to the highest bidder and used the money to change mine and Jessie's appearances. Molly was a baby, so we changed all our names and disappeared. I got a degree and trained as a teacher. I've worked hard. We moved to Yorkshire about six years ago. No-one could have found us.'

'Who knows this?'

'Only us and our contact in witness protection. For God's sake, I only told Alex the truth two years ago, just before we got married. The witness protection people checked him out first.'

If WP were adamant they'd not breached protocol, then it stood to reason that someone from the Graves' home had … *but who?* Was the person even aware that they'd slipped? He decided to pursue that later when he could separate the family. Maybe something would come to light then. But for now, he felt that the sooner he met with this Battacharya woman the better – get an outsider's view of the family.

Jessie began to sob again. Gus glanced at Sadia meaningfully and said, 'Look Jessie, why don't you let DC Hussain take you to your room and you can have a wee lie down. You're exhausted and we need you to have a rest, ok?'

If Sadia was half as good as Alice she'd take the opportunity to get Jessie's take on things. Briefly he pondered the different reactions displayed by Jessie and Beth. Jessie seemed by far the more emotionally volatile, yet he sensed a brittleness underneath Beth's calmer exterior.

Wringing her hands, Jessie reluctantly followed Sadia from the room.

Gus turned back to Beth. 'I want you to think really hard now, ok? Has there been anything strange you've noticed recently? Anyone following you or anything like that.'

The couple looked at each other, then shook their heads.

'PC Owens is going to make sure someone stays outside all night. When the Family Liaison Officer arrives she will be your direct link to me. I need you to tell us immediately if you think of anything, no matter how small, that might have a bearing on Molly's disappearance.'

Beth and Alex looked crushed. Gus wanted to offer some solace but he felt reluctant to be too positive. 'Look. Molly may well have just taken off. Lots of young girls her age do.' But even as he spoke, Gus wasn't convinced. Sometimes in this job you just knew.

Alex's laptop made a pinging sound at almost exactly the same time as a bell sounded in the hallway. Immediately he moved the mouse activating the screen. 'There's a car in the drive with a woman in the driver's seat.'

Gus moved behind Alex to look at the screen. 'It's Janine Roberts,' he said, 'She's the Family Liaison Officer I was telling you about. She's excellent. She'll look after you.'

Alex stood and walked over to a cupboard near the door. Inside were the controls for what Gus assumed was Four Oaks entire security system. Alex pressed a button and the gates opened.

Minutes later Janine, small, plump and homely, entered, her afro covered by a brightly coloured scarf. Her calming presence immediately filled the room.

CHAPTER 44
Bradford

Alice hated schools. She'd spent too many years being shunted from one to another. Her parents had followed one scientific research grant after another, leaving Alice to uproot, re-settle and cope with the ridicule her unfortunate name elicited. Then, to top it all, was the struggle to maintain grades that wouldn't have her parents pulling their hair out, wondering why, with their above-average brains, *their* daughter averaged out at no more than a B.

This one, however, seemed less formal and smelled better than the ones she'd attended as a child. No sweat, no piss, no disgusting boiled veg. Kids these days didn't know they had it so good. Nevertheless, she had to forcibly remove her frown and replace it with a smile. The slightly flustered acting head teacher had struggled through the snow to access the records for the building work they'd had done before Christmas.

'The head teacher, Mrs Graves, is on maternity leave. She deals with buildings.' The woman ran her fingers distractedly through her short spiky hair and opened a filing cabinet. 'It's in her remit, you see. I deal with staff and student absence and she deals with buildings and curriculum. Of course, Mrs Jackson, the administrator, would probably know just where it is, but she's in Tenerife for half-term.'

Alice smiled reassuringly. 'I'm sure you'll find it. Maybe under 'buildings' do you think?'

Flicking through khaki folders that dangled from silver hooks, Mrs Horan nodded. 'Yes, yes, of course. It'll be under B. B for 'Buildings'. That's if she filed a hard copy. You know, nowadays, we seem to rely more and more on computers. Of course, I can't access Beth's computer.'

Finally, her slender fingers found the Buildings folder. She plucked it out of the cabinet. 'Oh dear, it seems rather thin.' As she opened it, a single sheet fluttered to the floor. Picking it up, Alice noticed that it was dated 2010. Heart sinking, she handed it back to Mrs Horan.

'Looks like Mrs Graves didn't keep paper records of the building work? Do you think she kept it in a shared file?'

Seeming flustered, the other woman bit her lip, then moved over to the head teacher's desk. Clearly uncomfortable sitting there, she perched in front of the computer. After a few minutes, it booted up. She typed a few words and a file opened on the screen. With a relieved smile, she said, 'Here it is. Guttering, tiling and an additional classroom added to the annex in the science department.' She turned the screen to Alice, who took a note of the builder's name, address and phone number and left the relieved acting head teacher to shut up the school.

CHAPTER 45
Fagley

Jacko Dinwoodie had been a builder for nearly thirty years, following in his father's footsteps. His office was a small and probably illegally erected lean-to attached to the side of his terraced house. Its position at the end of the row afforded him a large side-garden area denied the other houses in the street. He spent fifteen minutes moaning about the weather and the adverse effects it had on the building trade. Alice listened with impatient sympathy, realising that he was the sort of bloke that would deliberately be obstructive if he wasn't treated with the respect he felt a man of his professional talents deserved. When he finally wound down and leaned back in his chair, tipping it precariously to balance on two legs, he sniffed, looked her up and down and then said, 'Right what can I help you lot wi'? I don't do owt illegal, so I'm betting you're just gonna waste my time.'

Smiling her friendliest smile, Alice wondered how many possible building illegalities she'd find if she looked and said, 'Oh, I hope not, Mr Dinwoodie.' She leaned over conspiratorially. 'You see, we really need your help to find this man and we think he may have helped you out on the job up at Carlton Wood Secondary School. Do you recognise him?' She handed over the photo taken from Jamal's phone. The older man studied it carefully before handing it back to her. Sniffing a glob of phlegm into his mouth, he swirled it round his mouth before swallowing it.

Struggling not to retch, she was finally rewarded by an abrupt nod. 'Yeah, I recognise him. He was one of the subcontractors, I reckon. Lazy sod if you ask me, but I didn't employ him. It were probably Dougie Kaczynski that pulled him in to help with the labouring.' He lowered his voice and winked. 'Between you and me, lass, he probably paid him cash in hand.'

Having retrieved Kaczynski's contact details from Mr Dinwoodie, Alice stuffed the photo back in her pocket, thanked him and left his office, noting that it was marginally warmer outside than it had been in.

***

She found Dougie Kaczynski on a building site in Fagley. The snow had done its worst and the site was a quagmire of cement-stained mud. Alice found it hard to imagine the 20 one-bedroomed homes that Kaczynski assured her would be there before the summer. In direct contrast to Jacko Dinwoodie, Dougie Kaczynski was angular and gave the impression of perpetual motion. His face was almost fleshless with sharp cheekbones and a pointy chin. From his elongated torso jutted blade-sharp shoulders and spiky elbows. Each gesture was delivered with staccato precision. His arms moved around him as he spoke – a windmill on caffeine overload. Ceaselessly he directed his men using the builder's equivalent of semaphore. 'He's going under the name of Sid Smith, probably not his real name. He was employed cash-in-hand for the school job. Didn't work right hard and disappeared after only a few days' work.' Pausing briefly, he scratched his chin and cocked his head to one side. 'Didn't collect his pay for the last day either, from what I remember. Not that he deserved it anyway.'

'You got an address for him?' asked Alice, doubting that any address given would be authentic.

Kaczynski snapped his fingers. 'You might be in luck there, you know? We picked him up near the Odeon a couple of times. And if my memory serves me, the address he gave was in that area too. Hold on, love, I'll just get it.'

Alice, still not completely comfortable with the Yorkshire 'love', bit down a retort. Gus had told her 'love' was used regardless of sex, but it still grated. Kaczynski returned from the makeshift office moments later, a piece of paper with a nearly indecipherable scrawl on it, in his hand. She took the grubby sheet, made sure she could read the address and thanked him. As she left, a sudden thought occurred to her. 'Don't all your workers need to be DBS checked if they're working in a school?'

Kaczynski grinned. 'Yeah, that's right. All of mine are.'

'Even Sid Smith?'

Kaczynski, like a magician produced a piece of paper from the bib of his dungarees. 'Course he was. More than my life's worth these days not to comply with the law. He handed over a DBS certificate with Sid Smith's name on it. The school photocopied them for their records, too.'

'But you still thought he was dodgy?' said Alice, pissed that, whilst she'd nearly forgotten to check the DBS, Kaczynski had been on the ball.

Kaczynski shrugged. 'Maybe. But he had the paperwork and that's all I needed.'

CHAPTER 46
Ilkley

On arrival at the Graves's home, Compo was overcome by an acute case of bashfulness. Never before had he been in such posh surroundings, not even at his graduation ceremony. Thankfully, Gus had appeared at the door as he'd stood, chin hitting his shoes on the drive beside his bashed-up old van. He wanted to rub his sleeve over the more obvious muck and bashes, but realised that, given, the overall condition of the vehicle, he'd be fighting a losing battle. PC Owens helped him into the house with all his equipment and he was soon settled in a spacious room off the main corridor near the kitchen.

Having glimpsed the homely disarray of the kitchen as he walked past, Compo surmised from its neatness that this room, by contrast, was rarely used. He stood in front of the table, a variety of monitors, PC towers and peripherals surrounding him. Spinning slowly on his heel, he gave a low whistle. Wow! This was posh. Every oversized chair and sofa in the room matched. Each had a liberal dotting of plush cushions in contrasting shades. The carpet was so thick he felt himself sink into it with each step he took and the wooden table was so dense he doubted it could be moved by an army. Hesitant to place any of his equipment on its shiny top, he bit his lip. Then, with a deep breath he left the room and hesitantly crossed to the kitchen. Inside, Gus was still debriefing the parents. Shifting from foot to foot, Compo hovered near the door till Beth Graves looked up with a questioning frown.

'Sorry to intrude, but I wondered if you had a cloth or owt to cover the table in the other room? I don't want to scratch it with my equipment.'

Confusion momentarily crossed her face, then, 'Oh, don't worry about it. It's an old thing anyway.'

Catching Gus's grin, Compo raised an eyebrow, nodded and left the room. Bloody hell if that's an old table, his one at home must be positively antique. Wonder if it'd be worth a bob or two?

He called Gus and together they watched the girl press the security button to get out the pedestrian exit and turn left. Within a few yards she was out of sight.

'Right, Compo. We know there's no more CCTV footage along Dales Way Link but what about just at the access point? Is there any there? Can you maybe isolate cars that entered and or left the road in from say nineish this morning?'

Compo, swung round on his chair, plugged in his earphones and began to nod his head rapidly, his fingers flying over the keyboard faster than a granny on methamphetamine.

Gus tapped him on the shoulder and Compo pulled one bud from his ear releasing a barrage of metallic sound that made Gus take a step back. 'Christ, Compo, you'll knacker your ears listening to it that loud.' Compo shrugged. 'Have you hooked up their landlines so we can trace any calls that come through?'

With a smile, Compo nodded, adding, 'And their mobiles, too, boss. Owt else?'

Gus smiled and shook his head.

'I'm going to post it all through to The Fort so I can monitor it from there rather than hanging out here. That ok?'

Sensing the other man's discomfort at his surroundings, Gus nodded. 'That's fine. The FLO's here anyway.'

CHAPTER 47
Thornbury

❛ I'm at this Sid Smith's last known address in Thornbury, Gus. Singh and Dobson are meeting me here.' Alice sat in a pool car, having elected to leave her distinctive Mini at The Fort. Looking across the road she had eyes on the front door of the grubby property just off Dick Lane. How appropriate she thought, her lips curled in distaste. 'The builder, Kaczynski, reckons it's a false address but we've got to try. It's probably a false name, too, but they're checking it out for me.'

After listening to Gus's instructions to be cautious she hung up, flung her mobile onto the passenger seat and humming tunelessly to Mark Ronson's 'Uptown Funk', tapped her gloved fingers on the steering wheel, her eyes never straying from the blue door. Nearby, she could hear the growl of engines at a standstill at the huge Thornbury roundabout, but Hawthorne Lane was quiet. She fidgeted, feeling chilled and wished she'd thought to nip into McDonald's for a coffee before turning off Leeds Road. Seeing Dobson and Singh pull up behind her she realised it was too late to ask them either. Never mind. She didn't mind missing a coffee if they caught this bastard.

Getting out of her car she joined the two constables by the gate to the property. 'I don't really expect him to be in here but if he is, be prepared for him to try to do a runner.'

Singh, tall, gangly and a practised sprinter, grinned. 'Let him try, just let the bugger try.'

Gingerly walking up the slippery path to the door of the ex-council house, Alice was alert to any signs of movement, but the house remained annoyingly still. No curtains tweaked, no lights flickered in the dulling light, no signs whatsoever of occupancy. Slipping off her glove, Alice

197

hammered on the door with the side of her hand, then rattled the rusty letterbox for good measure. Three pairs of ears strained for sounds from within. Nothing.

Then a voice said, 'If you're after that bugger, yer out of luck. Saw him head off that way with one of them roller cases, t'other day, like.'

Alice turned to see a woman, in hair curlers huddled in the doorway of the next door property. Despite the freezing temperatures, she wore a crop top and a pair of skinny jeans. A cigarette hung from her lips. Blowing out a spiral of smoke, she sniffed. 'He was a right tosser, you know. Didn't like the way he looked at my kids.'

'What day did you see him with his roller case?'

The woman screwed up her eyes and flicked ash from the tip of her fag. 'Yesterday, around sixish, I reckon, because it was before I gave the little 'uns their tea.'

'Don't suppose you know where he was going, do you?'

'Nah, he got the bus though. Johnny told me he saw him getting on at McDonald's. Mucky bastard that he is.'

Unsure whether the 'mucky bastard' was Johnny or Sid Smith, Alice thanked the woman and turned to Dobson. 'See if you can get CCTV footage of him from First Direct buses. We might be able to track his movements from here.'

Then with a wink she cocked her head to one side and said, 'You know, I'm sure I can hear someone calling out in there. Can you?'

Following her lead, the two constables, copied her actions then, grinning, agreed with her.

'Well, best check it out then.'

The neighbour watched with interest as Dobson raised a sturdy boot ready to bust the lock open. 'Why don't you just use the spare key?' she said, 'He keeps it under that plant pot 'cause he's always locking himself out.'

Alice ignored Dobson's smirk as he lowered his foot and, retrieving the key, she thanked the woman and unlocked the door. 'Gloves on, boys.'

The yellow light in the hallway barely illuminated the area immediately under the unshaded bulb. Fortunately, Dobson and Singh both carried torches. The trio, Alice in the lead, walked down the hallway opening doors as they went.

Certain that the downstairs was empty, Alice sent the two constables to clear the upstairs, whilst she perused the living room and kitchen. Sid Smith was indeed a 'mucky bastard' she thought, wrinkling her nose against the stale acrid smell of sweat and decomposing food that hung heavily in the air as she poked through his kitchen dustbin.

Satisfied that there were no bills or paperwork in the kitchen to give clues to his whereabouts, she moved into the living room to be met with an avalanche of cluttered dirty dishes and overflowing ashtrays. Again, no clues to his whereabouts jumped out at her.

Dobson called down to tell her they'd cleared upstairs so she joined them. There were two bedrooms and a bathroom. The bathroom, Alice noted, would provide the crime scene investigators with a wealth of DNA. If they were lucky some of it may come in useful for matching purposes at a later date. Whilst Singh got out his phone to make the request for a forensic team, Alice continued to explore the bedrooms.

The largest was clearly where Smith had slept. The sheets, stained with various body fluids, made Alice shudder, but apart from that he'd left nothing incriminating behind. The second bedroom was the cleanest room in the house and had clearly never been used by Smith.

Alice sighed and moved back downstairs to await the forensic team.

CHAPTER 48
The Fort

By the time Gus left the Graves' home and returned to The Fort, his leg and shoulder felt like they'd been savaged by a Rottweiler, yet he'd never felt more alive. Tired, sure, but alive and raring to go. He was determined to find both Molly and the bastards who'd abducted those other kids. Each of their names was indelibly engraved across his heart.

On the drive back, Sadia had maintained a stony silence for most of the way. He'd been happy to ignore her. His mind was buzzing with his own thoughts anyway. Then, without warning, two miles from Bradford, she exploded like a firework. Brown eyes flashed sideways at him as she drove, hands gripped the wheel firmly in the ten to two position. She was pulsating with anger. 'With all due respect, Detective Inspector McGuire, I'm a *Detective* Constable and my job is to *detect,* not to make endless cups of tea and toast.'

Gus noted the formal use of his rank and hid a smile. He wasn't really into the formal stuff. Firmly believed respect was earned, not inherited automatically with a promotion. Angling his body for a better view of her flushed face he listened to her rant, which was suitably punctuated by frequent emphases.

'Have you *any* idea how demeaning it is to be asked – no *ordered* – to make tea and toast like some bloody *lackey*? That, with all due respect, is the FLO's job not *mine* and I don't expect to be put in this position again. I'm entitled to my opinion. I'm not a robot. I have skills and abilities equal to, and in many cases, surpassing the male officers.'

When she finally fell silent, Gus continued to study her. Wisps of dark hair curled at her cheek and her face was flushed a delightful pink. The only things marring her beauty, were the thinned lips and the angry scowl that puckered her forehead, ageing her by ten years.

When she'd finally ground to a halt, Gus rubbed his aching thigh and said in a mild tone, 'Look, Sadia, word is that you have trouble with authority. I get that. I got a bit frustrated myself, with all the red tape shit when I was a DC. However, you don't do yourself any favours by not trying to mix with the rest of the team. In a tight spot they're the ones who'll have your back. They need to feel you'll have theirs, too.'

Tight-lipped she continued to drive. Gus frowned. Was that a glimmer of tears in her eyes? In the fading light it was difficult to be sure. Knowing this was his best chance to pull her into the group he continued, 'Your job is to follow orders issued by your superior officer. In this instance, me. Whether I ask you to make tea, or to mop up a pile of shit, you *will* do it because, rest assured Sadia, it will be because I deign it imperative to the ongoing investigation.'

He paused to let his words sink in. 'You may feel some sort of entitlement because of your dad, but let me tell you now, so we're completely clear about this, I do not, never have and never will hold with nepotism. I'll treat you the same way I treat any of the other officers on this team.'

Sadia snorted. 'My dad's been more of a hindrance than a help with my career. I'm here *despite* him not because of him.'

'Then all the more reason to try to fit in. Prove him wrong. It doesn't matter to me who your dad is as long as your loyalties lie with the team.'

They continued in silence. Gus wondered if he'd hit the right tone with her. He was a bit out of practice. He sensed she could be a good officer if all her edges were smoothed a bit. He'd needed to exert his authority, something he hated doing, but he also needed her on-side.

When Sadia finally pulled into the police yard and parked the pool car in its bay, he turned to her and grinned. 'Just so you know, I'm as likely to make the tea and toast in those circumstances, as to ask one of the DCs to do it. In case you hadn't noticed, I'm not exactly operating with two hands at the minute.'

She paused, her body twisted to exit the car.

'I have many faults, Sadia, but sexism is not one of them, ok?'

She nodded and began to pull herself out of the car.

He sighed. 'And I don't hold grudges. This is done and dusted with a line drawn under it. We move on as if this didn't happen... unless of course you're going to continue isolating yourself?'

Sadia took a deep breath and then slid back into her seat. Her face flushed and her back stiff, she turned to face him. When she spoke it was in grudging tones. 'I'm sorry, sir. I shouldn't have said what I did and I'd like to move on.'

Realising just how much effort that half-apology had taken, he inclined his head in acceptance. 'It's Gus. We're not into formality much on my team.'

Opening the car door again, she had one leg out before she twisted back towards him. Not quite meeting his eyes, she said, 'I know it's not an excuse but,' she risked a glance at Gus. 'I guess it makes me a bit touchy when I think my dad's influencing how I'm being treated by fellow officers.'

Holding her gaze, he smiled slowly. 'Ok, so now we both know where we stand. Prove yourself on my team, Sadia, and you'll get the kudos you deserve.' He held out his hand. Sadia glanced at it and then raised her gaze to meet his. She extended her own hand and they shook.

***

On entering the incident room, Gus was aware of nothing but the building's minute creaks and the soft whirr of Compo's computers, crunching data unsupervised through the night. He was alone and glad of it. Then, moving a few steps into the room using the light from the hallway to guide his path, he heard it; the unmistakeable sound of gentle snoring coming from the chair in front of his desk. He walked closer. DCI Nancy Chalmers lay asleep, half-slouched in the chair, a thick saliva trail hanging from her chin. Her bare feet rested on the desk. Her floral skirt had flicked back, revealing the top of her stockings. She mumbled incoherently in her sleep. Smiling he went over to the coffee machine and flicked it on, before clearing his throat loudly.

Disorientated, she began to struggle upright, wiping the trail of saliva from her cheek with her sleeve. 'What? Who's there?'

'It's just me,' said Gus as the machine gurgled and groaned through its coffee-making cycle. Spying a familiar Tupperware container next to the coffee machine, he grabbed it, deposited it on the desk and flicked on the desk light. As Nancy pulled her skirt down, blinking rapidly against the light, he tapped the tub lightly with one finger. He said, 'Looks like mum's been in with some offerings. We can have a burned biscuit with our coffee. Whoopey doo!'

He plonked a steaming mug in front of her. 'Come on, dunk a biscuit while the coffee's still hot. That way you won't break a tooth.' He moved to sit behind his desk.

She laughed. 'Compo's already eaten most of them. Constitution of an ox, that boy. Good job too, or Corrine would think we don't appreciate her baking skills.'

Looking mournfully at the distorted biscuits Gus said, 'We don't.'

'Now Gus, that's not true. We do appreciate her efforts, it's just the end result that we find less admirable.'

Awkwardly he bent down to pull a bottle of whisky from the bottom drawer of his desk. Pouring a generous shot of twelve-year-old Glenmorangie in each mug, he sat down and waited.

Nancy took an appreciative sip, but avoided meeting his eyes.

'How was Cathy?'

Gus shifted in his chair. He always found it hard to remain annoyed with Nancy for too long. She'd been his mentor since she moved up from Cambridge and he trusted her implicitly. However, he was really pissed off with her right now. He couldn't understand why she hadn't give him a heads-up before sending him off to the Graves's house. When he spoke, his tone was measured and taut. 'You mean Beth. Her name's Beth Graves now. Why the hell didn't you give me the background before sending me off there?'

Nancy's eyes drifted round the room. She sighed and sat forward resting her elbows on her knees, her head bowed. Pulling at her skirt she said, 'I got a shock when her witness protection officer contacted me. I hadn't realised Cathy, I mean Beth, was in Bradford.' She risked a glance at Gus and when he didn't respond she continued. 'Jankowski thinks The Matchmaker is at work again and, to be honest Gus, Beth's little girl going missing just confirms it.'

Gus interrupted her with a 'You don't say.'

Throwing him an apologetic look she continued. 'I wanted you to hear the story from her. Not my version. Cathy – or Beth rather – was the one living through it all. I was just another sergeant making the poor girl go through hoops so we could bring down the ring. But we couldn't even do that. The whole damn investigation was a bloody mess. I wanted you to connect with her without my influence.'

Savouring the warmth of the whisky-laced coffee, Gus relented. 'When she mentioned Cambridge, I wondered if you'd been involved in the initial investigation.'

'I was sergeant. Wentworth was the DI on that investigation. It was fucking awful, Wentworth was an arse and Beth,' she heaved a sigh that spoke volumes, 'poor Beth was a young mother, guilt-tripped into helping us in a tenuous plan to catch the entire team. We knew it was risky and far from infallible. Still, we convinced her she'd be instrumental in bringing down the whole ring. As it was she *did* do a lot of good. We caught her hubby, made the ring untenable so they disbanded and we caught a hoard of influential paedophiles.'

'So how the hell did she get so rich; and why is she a target?'

Taking another fortifying sip of her drink, Nancy placed the cup back on the table before replying. 'Well, some arse in one of the tabloids thought it would sell papers to demonise her. They got in touch with an extreme group, Association of Vigilant Parents. They said she was as culpable as her husband and that her actions in remaining under his roof were tantamount to child abuse. Egged on, and possibly funded in part, by the press, they decided to take out a private case against her and tried to sue her for culpability in child abuse, aiding and abetting a known paedophile and knowingly endangering her child.'

Nancy's face reddened. 'Of course it was slung out as ridiculous. However, the tabloids jumped on it. From the day we arrested James Clegg till the day he was sentenced, Cathy was stalked by those lunatics. They pelted her with eggs when she turned up at court, posted shit through her door. No matter how many times we moved her, they found her.'

'Leak from inside the investigation?'

She shrugged. 'Who knows? But, she was only a kid herself and as the trial date approached, she became more and more aloof.' Frustrated, Nancy slammed her hand on the desk. 'The press didn't like her. Painted her as a cold, unlikeable character and basically made her life hell. The amount of pressure that girl withstood was enormous. Good job James's mother had the dignity to support Cathy.'

'Yes, I wondered about that. Bit unusual isn't it?'

Nancy smiled. 'She was an exceptional woman. She loved her son, but she knew Beth was right to do what she did. Besides, she didn't want to lose her granddaughter either. I'm not sure Beth would've survived if she'd not had that support.'

'And the money to afford that house and Fort Knox security system?'

Sighing, she shrugged. 'She did what she had to. Sold up her house and her mother in law's, signed an exclusive for half a million with one of the tabloids, employed a ghost writer and got a publishing deal for another £100,000 and then disappeared into witness protection. I'd hoped never to see her again.' She smiled, 'for her sake, not for mine. I liked her. For all her youth, she was strong and principled.'

'Still is from what I've seen. Married again and got a newborn baby. A boy called Sam.'

'That's good. She'll need a big support network if The Matchmaker's got Molly.'

Dunking one of his mum's biscuits into his coffee, before lifting it dripping to his mouth, he pondered Nancy's words. 'Tell me about the trial and this Matchmaker arse.'

Closing her eyes, she took a deep breath before replying. 'At the sentencing her ex-husband James yelled an impassioned warning for her to disappear with their daughter because The Matchmaker had threatened revenge on the child. It was awful. He was screaming, tears pouring down his cheek as he was dragged away.'

'Did you believe the threat?'

Nancy looked straight into his eyes. 'I did, Gus. The powers that be tried to brush it off as hyperbole, but I knew.' She banged her fisted hand against her chest. 'I knew in here that it was true. I suspected we'd had some sort of leak in the department, because all the key players, bar James Clegg, AKA, The Treasurer disappeared without trace. There had to have been a leak.'

'Bit of a coincidence that Beth's in Bradford and you are too.'

She laughed. 'You accusing me of being the leak?'

Waving his hand dismissively, he continued. 'No, but I remember someone once telling me that there was no such thing as coincidence in our line of work.' He clicked his fingers, grinning at her. 'Hell, that was you.'

She laughed. 'Yes, usually that'd be right, but in this case, I just don't see how me being in Bradford's linked. I followed Charlie Bowles up here from Cambridge when the DCI job came up. No-one could have planned that. Anyway, witness protection is as tight as a cow's arse. *No one* could know she was here and she's changed her appearance, so that rules out a chance encounter. Besides, The Matchmaker doesn't leave things to chance. This has all been planned.'

'If this is the work of The Matchmaker, then there must be a leak in WP somewhere. I'll have to find it.'

In silence they finished their drinks. When she got up to leave, Nancy turned to Gus.

'When I saw that attic on Sunday and all those children, I *knew* he was back. That's why I called Jankowski and Wentworth. If we don't find that poor kid, I dread to think what these bastards will do to her in revenge.'

CHAPTER 49
Bradford

Gus hadn't been in the Kings Arms for months. Heck, he'd barely had a drink in months, either; not with all the pain meds he was on. But right now he needed one desperately. So despite his misgivings he crossed the road diagonally from the station and pushed past the smokers' club that huddled in the doorway. He didn't recognise any of the faces, so he doubted they were police officers. Once inside he took a deep breath as the heat from the real wood fire hit him. It was busy, but not as busy as he'd seen it.

Standing in front of the bar were the three twats who'd hassled him yesterday in front of Wentworth. He frowned and then, straightening his back he walked over to the other end of the bar and hoped he could avoid another run-in with them. When the barman, Jakey Boocock approached with a welcoming grin and an outstretched hand, Gus grinned back and ordered a half of lager and a double whisky.

'Heard you've been off on sick leave Gus. You back now?'

Handing over a twenty he nodded. 'Yes, back at work now, just got to watch my arm and leg but otherwise I'm fighting fit.' Lifting the whisky to his lips, he took a sip, savouring its warm peaty flavour. A yell from the other end of the bar told him his presence had been noted by the trio of officers. Studiously, he ignored them and downed the rest of his whisky in one, before gesturing to Jakey to refill his glass. 'Same again, Jakey.'

Jakey nodded and then spoke under his breath. 'Those pillocks at the end have been here for hours. If they start owt, I'll toss them out.'

'Don't bother on my account, I'm just here for a drink. Alice been in yet tonight?'

Jakey shook his head. 'Nah not yet. Too early for her.' He laughed 'She's a night owl that one. Never see her before ten.' And he placed Gus's refilled glass in front of him.

Glad to take the weight off his aching thigh, Gus pulled himself onto a bar stool and glanced round the bar. It was a proper old fashioned bar with empty whisky bottles sitting on a shelf that surrounded the entire room. Sepia photos of old Bradford dotted the walls showing images of the old fashioned trams that used to be a frequent sight throughout the city. Ignoring the voices from the other end of the bar rising and falling punctuated by raucous guffaws and pointed stares Gus savoured his drink, knowing that it wouldn't be long before one of them said something directly to him. Pissed off by their pettiness in comparison to the situation of the kids they'd rescued on Sunday and the little girl who, he was sure, had been abducted by the same group of men, he growled under his breath and downed his second double whisky, before catching Jakey's eye again. He pushed his empty glass across the bar. 'Same again, Jakey.'

With a shrug, Jakey filled the glass and placed it in front of Gus. As he turned to serve another customer the noise from the other end of the bar suddenly increased. DC Knowles shouted across the space to Gus. 'Hey, McGuire, how'd you manage to turn your missus into a carpet muncher?'

Gus caught Jakey's eye and shook his head slightly telling him not to intervene. The other men, flushed faces and slurred voices revealing just how drunk they were continued to throw jibes in Gus's direction.

'He's probably not man enough to keep a woman interested. Maybe his butch sister's more of a man than he is.'

Hand clenching round his glass and the muscle in his cheek pulsing Gus took another long sip.

'What's wrong, Angus? Not even man enough to defend yourself?'

'Maybe he's a poof! A fucking shirt-lifter. Maybe that's why she went off with the butch Doctor McGuire, and I don't mean his dozy Scottish Dad either.'

Feeling a hand land on his shoulder and assuming it was Knowles or one of his crew, Gus jerked his arm up and spun round. Unfortunately, with whisky induced disorientation he stumbled, lost balance and fell off the stool. Stepping forward Alice applied her shoulder to his stomach and hefted him upright, her small frame tensing with the effort. Back on the stool now he peered at her through glazed eyes. 'Hiya Al, what're you having to drink?'

CHAPTER 50
Bradford

It was freezing outside but The Distributor didn't care. The gas heater kept him warm and he had the TV for company. Ok, it wasn't The Ritz. He laughed, not unless the Ritz had started putting battered old mattresses on the floor. Never mind: he had his own minibar and it was a damn sight cheaper that any posh hotel would be. A microwave meal and a few cans, that's all he needed. And, of course, he deserved a drink after the stress of the last few days. First the fiasco over in Great Horton with the Asif boy and then today's abduction.

Never mind, it had all gone off without a hitch. Thank God. The Matchmaker wouldn't have been happy if he'd fucked this up, too.

He glanced at the screen that stood on the table. Pity *those* goods were out of bounds, he thought studying the little girl's prone figure. Curly red hair mussed up over the scratty pillow, still wearing her boots, the coverless duvet half falling off her skinny frame. Maybe he should go in and take her boots off for her. Nah, won't bother. Might be tempted to take off more than her boots. Anyway, she might wake up and then he'd have to dope her up again. Best let her wake up in her own time. That way he could avoid temptation.

He stuck his hand down his trousers and lazily scratched his groin with one hand whilst lifting a can of cheap lager to his lips with the other. Itch suitably appeased he lifted nail bitten fingers to his nose, sniffed deeply and frowned. Maybe it was about time he risked the dilapidated shower that was cordoned off in the corner of the room.

CHAPTER 51
The King's Arms

'Fuck's sake, Gus! How much have you had?'

His upper body swayed slightly as he squinted at her.

'Sorry Al, thought you were one of those arses.' He jerked his head towards Knowles and his posse, nearly slipping off the stool again in the process. Alice sighed and rolled her eyes, wishing she'd come to the pub a lot earlier. Tight lipped she glared at the other officers who having noticed his near fall they were now whooping and slapping each other on the back as if they each deserved personal congratulations for Gus's clumsiness.

'Fucking wuss, can't even hold his booze. Total tosser!'

Seeing Alice's stern look sent them into even more uproarious laughter. Disgusted, she drew a bar stool over and pulled herself up. Trying to deflate the situation, she leaned forward to block Gus's view of the idiots at the other end. Ordering herself a pint of lager she tutted when, running the words together Gus said, 'Minesawhisky.'

Putting on her sternest face she prodded his good arm. 'I don't bloody think so, matey you've had enough as it is.' Then turning to Jakey, she said accusingly. 'How much has he had?'

With intense concentration Jakey coiled a bar towel into a cone and stuffed inside a pint glass before corkscrewing it round to dry the glass. He shrugged, refusing to meet her eyes. 'Only two.' Then placing Alice's pint glass in front of her added, '…doubles.'

'Shit, he's on strong painkillers, Jakey. He shouldn't be drinking at all. Bring him a pint of water now, will you?' Then turning back to Gus whose gormless lop-sided grin made her smile despite her annoyance. 'You're not supposed to drink with painkillers. What the hell are you thinking?'

Momentarily sober he stared right at her and enunciated carefully. 'What I'm thinking, Alice, is that I don't *want* to think. Not for tonight anyway. Just for tonight, I want to forget that there are eighteen damaged kids out there and another one out there being subjected to fuck knows what sorts of atrocities, whilst my fucking wife's shagging my sister.' Defiantly, he slurped some more whisky before sloshing his glass back on the bar. Seeing her opportunity, Alice slid the glass out of his reach, replacing it with the pint of water Jakey had brought over.

'Wahay, lightweight poofter can't hold his drink. Look at him, on the water now.'

A glance towards Gus told her that he'd fallen into an oblivious stupor and was completely unfazed by the drunken insults being thrown his way. Jakey, on the other hand had stalked down the bar and was admonishing the men. Egged on by each other, they seemed to be beyond persuasion. A couple, sitting near the fire, sent disapproving glances at them.

'Come on, boys, quieten down, you're losing me customers,' said Jakey

Knowles stretched over the bar and flung an arm round Jakey's neck. 'Aw, come on Jakey, it's just a bit of fun. No harm meant.'

Extricating himself, Jakey leaned away from Knowles's beery breath. 'Final warning, right?'

Mumbling and giggling like flushed schoolgirls caught necking behind the bike sheds, the three men became quiet for a short while.

Alice, using Knowles' quietness as a chance to leave Gus alone for a minute, said to Jakey. 'I'm going to the loo. Don't you dare give him any more whisky.'

She quickly skirted past the men at the bar, ignoring their whispered taunts about her sexuality and how hanging around with a McGuire would soon turn her into a lesbo too.

Minutes later, on her return their volume had increased again as they loudly listing all the homosexual insults their limited intelligence allowed.

Furious now, Jakey vaulted the bar and tried to reason with them, but was largely ignored. Approaching them from the side, Alice grabbed Knowles's arm and spun him towards her, whilst quickly stepping forwards and slamming the heel of her boot into his instep. 'You are well out of order, Knowles and I'll be filing a written report on your appalling behaviour tomorrow morning. So right now I suggest you leave the premises or I'll be forced to arrest you for disturbing the peace.'

His friends circled Alice, invading her space and breathing alcoholic fumes over her. 'Aw get lost, Cooper, we're off duty and we're just having a good time.'

She held her ground. 'You are police officers *all* the time and right now your behaviour is moving into homophobic hate crime territory. Just get out. The landlord's asked you to leave and if you don't, I *will* arrest you.'

Somewhere in his drunken state DC Redmond realised she was deadly serious and grabbed his friends arm. 'Come on Andy, it's not worth the hassle. The bitch will cause trouble. Let's just go.'

With a final glare in Alice's direction, Knowles turned and stumbled unsteadily from the pub. Alice heaved a sigh of relief and turned back to Gus who, head resting on the bar, snored gently.

'Keep an eye on him, will you, while I get my car,' she told Jakey

Minutes later the pair of them pushed a semi-conscious Gus into the back of Alice's mini. 'Talk about playing sardines' said Jakey, as with one final shove he managed to slam the mini's door shut. 'Will you be ok with him now?'

Nodding, she got into the driver's side. 'If he's sick in my car, I'll bloody skin him!'

Grinning, Jakey went back into the pub as Alice turned the car left and headed down Oak Lane till she could cut across to get to Gus's house on Marriner's Drive. Hearing snoring from the back seat, she smiled slightly. Gus had been living with his parents since he got out of hospital but Alice had no intention of taking him back there in this state.

'Don't know if you're ready to move back into your marital home or not Gus, but tonight you've got no option. It's there or the side of the road!'

CHAPTER 52
Wednesday

It was cold and dark when Molly finally woke and she wasn't sure how long she'd been asleep. Her eyes were gritty and her head felt heavy and fuzzy. She lay, eyes straining to see the ceiling that disappeared into darkness high above her. Disorientated and afraid she knew this wasn't her room at home. The dimness made her imagine all sorts of monsters lurking in the oppressive shadows. She didn't really believe in ghosts or monsters but, with a choked cry, she flung the foul smelling duvet over her head to block out the things that loomed unfamiliarly at her, and tried to collect her thoughts.

It was morning when she'd got into her dad's car and it wasn't that much later that he'd veered off the main roads and drove into the countryside. She'd been a bit puzzled because he'd promised to take her to Maccy D's and then shopping, but he'd said they were going to Leeds. Frowning, she tried to remember the journey but as usual she'd been too busy wittering on about her mum and the brat to notice where they were. It wasn't until he'd braked and pulled onto a bumpy little lane surrounded by huge buildings that she realised something was wrong.

'Where are we?' she'd asked straining in her seat to see why they'd driven in here. When he'd turned towards her with a hankie in his hand and the air filled with a metallic antiseptic smell, she'd known for sure that something was badly wrong. Flinching, she remembered his hand coming towards her like it was in slow motion. For the life of her though, she couldn't remember a single damn thing since then. Shivering, she closed her eyes and, wrapping her arms round her body, she cried in the dank, dark room.

CHAPTER 53
Marriner's Drive

Gus woke with a headache to the smell of fresh coffee and the sense that things had changed in his universe. He opened his eyes and realised he wasn't in his old room at his parents' house. For a second he was puzzled, wondering why Gabriella was making him coffee when she hated the smell of it. Then, realisation dawned. Gabriella was gone and he was alone in their marital bed for the first time since he'd left hospital. He screwed up his face and raised a hand to his forehead and groaned.

A vague memory of Alice pulling him out of her mini, pushing him up the hill to the front door and then him violently vomiting in the flower pot next to the open door as she laughed none to gently at him, flooded his mind. Moving even slightly elicited such a pain behind his eyes that he lay, head cocooned in a pillow as fragmented memories of The Kings Arms and Knowles and crew flitted in his head. Shit, he'd really overdone it on the booze last night. He was pissed off with himself because drinking was *not* how he dealt with things. '*Fuck's sake, Gus,*' he admonished, '*get your head in the game.*'

At last, with some effort, he lifted the covers and saw with relief that he was still fully dressed. He couldn't have borne it if Alice had undressed him and put him to bed. Bad enough that she'd rescued him from the pub and got him upstairs and inside the bedroom. He swung his legs round and realised that both his shoulder and thigh were throbbing viciously. A wave of dizziness washed over him. He groaned. When it passed he crawled over to the en suite, turned the shower on, stripped and got in. The warm water flowed soothingly over his shoulder and head for long minutes before he felt able to continue. Finally, nausea fading, he soaped his body, washing away the faint sick smell that hovered around him. Showered and dressed in clothes he'd almost forgotten he possessed, he followed his nose downstairs in search of coffee. Sitting at the kitchen table, one foot on the chair opposite, Alice lifted a slice of toast slathered in jam and margarine to her mouth. She grunted. 'Oh, you're alive then, are you?'

Ignoring her, he made his way over to the coffee machine, poured some into a mug, topped it with a dash of milk and slammed two slices of bread into the toaster. He pulled a chair out from under the table, grimacing when it scraped across the floor, and sat down. Taking a single sip of coffee, he paused before his second, allowing it to settle in his stomach. Then, deciding it was going to remain there, he looked at Alice 'So tell me the worst. Did I do anything stupid last night?'

Face expressionless, Alice studied him for a full minute before grinning. 'Nah, you got pissed, avoided clouting Knowles, puked in a plant pot and slept through the night.' She stood up, grabbed the toast that had just popped from the toaster flung them on a plate and pushed it across the table to Gus with the marg and jam she'd nipped out to get from Sainsbury's earlier.

'To be honest Gus, it's the first normal thing you've done since before, well…' she waved her hand in the air. 'Since before – you know? Take your painkillers and eat your toast and then I'll take you to work. We've got a lot to do today.'

With a melancholy look on his face he stared at the toast. 'I think I'll pass.'

'Like hell you will. Get that damn toast down you, whilst I put my face on.'

A sideways glance at her told him that he had no choice in the matter.

CHAPTER 54

The sharp sleepies dug mercilessly into Molly's eyes making them water. She rolled onto her back, nose wrinkling at the mildew smell and opened her eyes. It was lighter than it had been earlier. Above her she could see huge metal pipes stretching across a stained brown ceiling and meeting the breeze-block walls on either side of the room. As it all came back to her she whimpered and screwed her body into a tight foetal shape. Tears welled from between closed eyes, moistening the harsh crud that had gathered there as she slept. Her mouth felt dry and the lingering clinical taste of chloroform remained. Remembering 'him' her eyes flew open and scoured the large room for his presence. Relieved to see no sign of him, she sat up on the filthy damp mattress, pulled her legs up to her chin and wrapped her arms around them, trying to stop her small frame from shivering.

What an idiot she'd been to believe that horrible man was her dad. She should have believed her mum and gran. After all, why would they tell her he was dead, if he was actually alive?

As she sat shivering and hungry an unwelcome pressure in her bladder made itself felt. She looked round the room, wondering what to do. Finally, she got to her feet and began to explore. The door was a huge metal concertina roll up one like her stepdad had on the garage at his work. She pulled it, but soon realised it was locked or padlocked on the other side. The walls were damp with liquid rust stains streaking them. In places she could see water dribbling down the concrete and puddling in the crevice between the wall and the floor. She followed the water flow backwards and realised that the pipes had sprung leaks periodically where their seals had corroded. A stream of yellowing water flowed along the pipes to the walls reminding her of her pee dilemma.

Moving round to the huge window, she scraped her nails over the thin ice coating. When her hands got too cold, she breathed on the small area she'd cleared before finally wiping the remaining ice away with her sleeve. Peering through the hole she saw snow covered fields undulating away from her. The snowfall had resulted in an onslaught of people congregating on the fields, building snowmen and sledging down the slopes. Looming over the moving dots was a familiar viaduct. Where had she seen that before?

Molly could see sheer icicles dangling from the window sill as she pressed her nose to the gap and strained to see if she could attract anyone's attention. With a sinking feeling in her chest she gulped back a sob, realising she was too far from the fields for anyone to notice her. Her bladder now felt uncomfortably full as she resumed her aimless walk round the room. From nowhere a strange crackle flooded the room, followed by a voice she knew belonged to her abductor; the man she'd so foolishly believed was her father.

'Morning, Molly. Did you have a good night?'

Glancing fearfully round the dimly-lit room, she wondered where the voice had come from. Before she could identify the source he spoke again, his voice sharper and angrier.

'Answer me, girl! Did you have a good night?'

Molly's legs seemed to liquefy as she nodded and then shakily said 'Yyyess!'

She spotted four small cameras, one in each corner of the room. A speaker dangled from the network of pipes.

'If you need to piss use the bucket. I'll bring some food later.' His laugh made Molly's heart flutter. 'Later on you'll find out just how bad things can get, Molly Graves.' With a further crackle of static, the room fell silent again.

Molly stared nervously at the cameras. Her bladder was bursting but she didn't want to go if he was watching. Suddenly all the scenarios her mother had so earnestly warned her about flew through her mind. Any one of them could be more than a possibility. All the stories of children being abducted, ripped from the safety of their families' loving arms by bad men with evil desires buzzed in her mind. She flung herself face down on the mattress and sobbed her heart out, wishing she'd listened to her mum, wishing she'd not been jealous of her gorgeous little brother and cursing the man she'd been oh too willing to believe.

Finally, she sat up, rubbed her raw face dry and began to think. Feeling slightly more empowered, she whipped the filthy sheet from the bed and wrapped it loosely round her bottom half. Then, manoeuvring her knickers and skinny jeans down to her knees before perching precariously a few inches above the bucket, she peed, satisfied that at least *he* couldn't see her privates.

CHAPTER 55
The Fort

It was early and everyone had gathered for the briefing. Although Gus led it, DCI Chalmers stood, arms crossed, in the corner, a serious expression on her drawn face. Everyone knew by now about Molly Graves' abduction and the atmosphere in the room was alert and serious. Gus cleared his throat and began. 'We'll do a quick update on Sharon Asif's murder, the attack on Jamal and the abducted children and then move on to Molly Graves, ok?'

He nodded to Alice, who stood up and moved to the front of the room. 'The gun used in the attack on Jamal and his brother has been identified as the same one used in a fatal shooting in Poland twelve years ago.' Alice glanced at Gus, shifting her weight in her heavy black boots. 'This coincided with a series of child abductions. Detective Jankowksi identifies these abductions as probably being the work of a paedophile ring headed by The Matchmaker. This ring was broken up by Cambridge police in 2003 with the help of the wife of the only member of the ring to be apprehended, James Clegg. This is the first concrete lead on the abducted children in Sharon Asif's house, but more importantly it also links into the current kidnapping of Molly Graves, which Gus will explain more fully later.'

Gus nodded and Alice continued. 'I also observed the first session between Sharon Asif's two daughters and the child psychologist. From what the girls said it seems that although they were aware of the children upstairs they hadn't seen them arrive and hadn't actually set eyes on them. They did hear them crying and were concerned about them but when they mentioned them to their mother she hit them. The psychologist is going to continue with therapy sessions and he will report back to us. The girls are physically thriving in the care of foster parents and so is the little boy, who has been released from the hospital. Although they are traumatised, the psychologist thinks they may survive with minimal emotional damage because they're so young.

'Sessions with the abducted children are less positive. The psychologists involved in those sessions all recommend that we bring in child psychologists from the corresponding countries to work with the children. The need for translation causes additional stress and they are reluctant to continue. I've arranged with Detective Jankowski and the police in Latvia to send recommended experts over. Bradford's chief child psychologist Dr Kaur, will liaise with them. None of the children are fit for travel so they will remain here for the immediate future. It's going to be a long and slow process.'

There was a moment's complete silence as Alice sat down and the officers present processed the information.

Gus stood up and waited a second or two before continuing. 'In terms of Asif's murder, we're no further forward. No one, except Jamal, saw her or anyone else entering or leaving the graveyard. The weather was so bad that the odd few people who were about had their heads down and were focussing on getting home quickly. Forensics has not shown up any significant clues so we're a bit stuck. The only information we have is what Jamal Asif volunteered. To be honest, I think we need to talk to the lad again, but that'll have to wait for now. Alice has got some info on the photo that Jamal took of the man who threatened him and left the children in his house.'

Alice stood up again. 'Been to the school and the builders employed by the school. The bloke in the photo was recognised as a casual. We visited the address he gave and found the premises empty. Forensics are going over it now. However, we did have information that he caught a bus into town at around 6pm on Monday. Compo's narrowing down CCTV footage in the hope we get a hit. Who knows, maybe we'll be able to track him to his current location. We've got a team on that, but anyone with free time should help out there too. Also, got forensics going over the car they found in the Cemetery Road Asda car park. They found a couple of prints on the lever that adjusts the seat so hopefully we'll hit a match on those, either here or through Interpol.'

Gus nodded and moved over to the new board that had been erected at the front of the room. 'Right, that brings us on to yesterday's abduction.'

He pointed to the picture of a young girl with a big smile and curly red hair. 'This is Molly Graves. Security cameras on her home has her leaving the premises around 10:15am yesterday. She hasn't been seen since. The reason we've inherited this case is that Molly Graves and her family were under witness protection and living here under assumed names.

'Her mother was instrumental in breaking up the paedophile ring Alice mentioned earlier. This was a particularly insidious ring that set up an extremely lucrative business enterprise selling and or renting abducted children for high-profile, rich paedophiles. Molly's mum's intel and bravery was key to catching nearly fifty rich and powerful paedophiles in the UK and making it impossible for the ring to continue their operations. The coincidence between the children found in Sharon Asif's attic in Bradford, Beth Graves settling in Bradford, the gun used against Jamal being associated with the initial ring twelve years ago and the subsequent abduction of her child are too coincidental to be ignored. During the initial trial, Beth was on the receiving end of a lot of threats from an extreme group called Association of Vigilant Parents renowned for violent and intimidatory practices. Her husband begged her from the dock to disappear, saying the ring leader, known as The Matchmaker wouldn't rest till he had revenge against both him and Cathy. Clegg believed he'd abduct their daughter in pay back. So, we're taking this very seriously.

'It seems that Molly left voluntarily, without her parent's knowledge, but I suspect somehow their witness protection security was compromised. She hasn't been seen since. Compo, I want you to analyse their security system and get as much access to the stepdad's online activity. WP did all that before he and Beth were married but I want nothing left to chance. We need to rule him out. Alice, Sadia and I are going to re-interview the immediate family and Sampson, you will interview Beth Graves's colleagues, a Mrs Wendy Horan, deputy head at Carlton Wood High school.

'Shit,' said Alice. 'That's Jamal's school and the one where the builder was working before Christmas.'

Gus nodded 'Exactly! It's all getting more and more linked. Witness protection was broken and we need to discover exactly how that was done. Their contact at WP insists the break wasn't from them. I'm meeting with her tomorrow in London after I've interviewed James Clegg.'

CHAPTER 56

I t was cold but at least he'd brought her an extra blanket which he'd bundled through the door with a Morrison's carrier bag containing two snickers bars, two cans of coke and a tube of Pringles. Molly's mum didn't let her have coke, but Molly reckoned she'd be ok with it, since there was nothing else to drink. She lay listlessly on the mattress. She'd got used to its mildewed smell and now, with the blanket wrapped round her as well as the duvet, at least she was warm.

A tear trickled down her cheek, swiftly followed by another, as she thought about her mum and her gran and even that wrinkled red baby with its screwed up face and its nice clean smell. She rubbed the tears away with the back of her hand and blew her nose on the corner of the sheet. It was fully light now and she wondered if she should go over to the window. Maybe someone was playing in the fields outside. Maybe some kids building a snowman or something. She'd just swung her legs over the side of the mattress when she heard a metallic clunk from outside her room. She held her breath and, head tilted to one side, listened intently. There it was again. A grating metal noise, then a big clunking noise followed by a bang. She heard footsteps outside the room. She tiptoed over to the door and pressed her ear to it. Was that voices she could hear?

Another door further along opened. She heard a laugh. She frowned. Then there was the sound of shuffling followed by a high-pitched scream. For a second her heart stopped beating. That sounded like a child. She was sure of it. It was too high to be an adult. She shivered and, clutching the sheet around her, too frightened to move, stood trembling behind her door. Another yelp and then muffled crying. Definitely another child.

A door slammed shut. Metal clanked loudly and more footsteps approached, slowing outside her room. Molly scuttled back across to the mattress and flung herself on top. Heart hammering, she pulled the duvet up to her chin and stared wide-eyed at the door. Muffled thuds came from outside followed by muted voices and a horrible scraping sound. It was the rusty old lock being opened.

With just the tip of her nose and her eyes visible over the blanket, she held her breath, ignoring the burning sensation in her lungs. Slowly, the door swung open and she could see *him* standing there. Then her gaze lifted to the other man. Her eyes widened and her bladder voided.

She screamed and screamed and screamed.

CHAPTER 57
Ilkley

Jessie Graham's granny flat adjoined the main property and was spacious and airy. An imitation wood fire, positioned on the feature wall, threw out some welcome heat. Alice held her hands in front of it and then rubbed them together, enjoying the sensation of warmth flooding her body. The drive to Ilkley had been miserable. The pool car's heating system had given up the ghost before they'd even set off. Despite muffling herself in scarf and gloves the chill air had insinuated its way through Alice's layers and into her bones. When Gus had told her that she, accompanied by Sadia, was to interview Jessie whilst he and the FLO interviewed Beth and her husband, Alice's heart had sunk. Why did she have to get paired up with Ms No-Personality 2015? Alice glanced over at Sadia who, since they'd entered the room, had stood like a sergeant major by the door looking as if someone had set about her face with a wet fish.

Whilst Jessie made some tea, Alice took the opportunity to look around the living room. Bookshelves filled with an eclectic mix of authors including Jean Plaidy, Karen Rose and Stuart MacBride made her smile. It appeared that despite a romantic leaning Jessie wasn't averse to a bit of blood and gore. On the large table near the kitchen, lay a couple of teen books by Sophie Mackenzie and Jane Casey, probably Molly's. Beside them a scattering of pens with floral toppers and a froggie eraser spilled out of a cupcake-covered pencil case which sat on top of a closed jotter. Above the fire was a trio of photographs. The first was of Molly as a baby. The second featured Beth, Jessie and Molly at the seaside and the third was Beth and Alex's wedding photo. A very low key affair, thought Alice judging by the smart but non-wedding-like outfits and the absence of flowers. Jessie had disappeared through one door into the kitchen so Alice reckoned the other doors led to the bedroom and bathroom.

Jessie appeared carrying a tray in shaking hands and Alice rushed forwards to relieve her of the load, carrying it over to the coffee table that had two chintzy over-stuffed Laura Ashley chairs on one side and an equally floral three-seater sofa on the other.

Chattering inconsequentially, Alice busied herself pouring teas into mugs with owls on, while Jessie, with a glance at Sadia, settled herself on the sofa. Pushing Jessie's tea towards her Alice lifted her own mug and perched on the edge of the chair opposite Jessie. Glancing at Sadia, she said, her tone barely hiding her annoyance with her insensitivity. 'Here's your tea, Sadia. Come and join us. I'd like you to take notes whilst Jessie and I have a little chat.'

Sadia opened her mouth to protest but Alice narrowed her eyes and nodded to the sofa. Sighing heavily, Sadia walked round, lifted her mug and moved over to the sofa. Rather than sitting next to Jessie as Alice had wanted, she placed her mug on a rickety table at the far end of the sofa and wedged herself into the corner as far away from Jessie as she could. '*So much for a nice cosy chat,*' thought Alice, as Sadia ran her hands down her trousers and took out her notebook. She looked at Alice, head cocked to one side in a let's get on with it gesture. Alice contented herself with a scowl, which, in Alice's opinion, Sadia deliberately chose to ignore

Turning to the older woman, Alice scrunched forward in her chair. Hands clasped loosely on her knees she smiled. 'I know you're upset right now, Jessie, but you really need to focus for us, so we can find Molly.'

She stretched out her hand and gently pressed Jessie's arm. 'Anything, anything at all that's stuck in your mind over the last few days? Any strange folk around or maybe something Molly said or did?'

Jessie screwed up her face, and shaking her head from side to side she snuffled into a tissue. 'That's just it, there's nothing. Not a thing I can think of. I mean she's been a bit jealous because of the baby, you know? But that's only to be expected, isn't it? A new baby in the house and all our attention diverted. But she's a good girl, is Molly.'

Sadia's phone rang, making Jessie jump. Sadia stood up, mouthing an apology and left the room to answer it. When she returned, Alice could tell from the glint in her eyes that she had something good. Sadia raised her eyebrows to Alice, who gestured that she should continue.

Walking round to the front of the couch, Sadia faced Jessie. 'That was one of the PCs on the phone. He's been chatting to one of Molly's friends, and one of them,' she looked at her notebook where she'd jotted down the name, 'a Chelsea Robson, said that Molly was excited because her 'real' dad was taking her shopping.'

Jessie paled and one hand feebly gripped the arm rest. 'What? Molly doesn't have a real dad.' She flushed and waved her arms in agitation. 'What I mean is, Molly doesn't know anything about her real dad. She thinks he's dead. That's what we told her.' She bit her lip, her gaze going first to Alice and then to Sadia. 'It was for the best. She didn't need to know what her daddy was.'

Hesitating, Sadia flicked a glance at Alice, before continuing. 'Well, Chelsea was adamant that Molly was going to meet her real dad. The PC thinks she's being truthful. Yesterday, he felt that she was hiding something. That's why he went back today.'

Again, Jessie shook her head. 'That's impossible. You know he's in prison.' She flung herself back in the chair, looking like a bedraggled rag doll.

Alice caught Sadia's eye and indicated she should sit down. Taking the hint Sadia resumed her previous position on the sofa, leaving Alice to continue.

Taking a deep breath, Alice waited for a moment before beginning. 'Look Jessie, can you think of any reason Chelsea might have said that?'

Eyes huge and bloodshot, the worry of the past day clearly etched in her face, Jessie looked up and shook her head.

'Is Chelsea the sort to make things up?'

Again, Jessie shook her head. 'No she's the sensible one out of Molly's friends. The worrier. She'd never make up something like this.'

Alice lowered her voice slightly. 'Well, if Chelsea's not lying, it looks like Molly was going to meet someone she *thought* was her father.'

Head bowed Jessie began to weep. Alice stood up and squeezed herself between the two women on the couch. Sadia, whose head had been down as she scribbled in her notebook, her expression hidden by a cascade of dark hair, immediately moved to the chair Alice had vacated.

Clearing her throat, Sadia leaned forward and began to speak, 'Well, you must know something.'

Alice held up a single finger and narrowed her eyes in warning. She put her arm round Jessie's heaving shoulders and squeezed reassuringly. 'We're working on the assumption that Molly's abduction relates to what happened in 2003.' She waited to let her words sink in. 'That means that somehow, somewhere, your witness protection has been breached.'

Jessie gasped, her head jerked up and her hands flew to cover her face. 'Oh my God, no!'

Alice exchanged a glance with Sadia. 'Your key witness protection officer maintains the breach isn't from their side. Do you have *any* idea how your true identities could have been revealed?'

Pale and shaking, Jessie grasped frantically at Alice's hand. 'Oh my God. But that was years ago. I'd never have done it if I thought this could happen. Never. I swear, never.'

From the depths of the house a bell rang, breaking the resultant silence. Sadia, jumped up and cracked the door slightly. She turned to Alice. 'It's just Beth's work colleague.'

Alice nodded and lifted Jessie's cold hands into her own. Looking her straight in the eye, she said in a tone that demanded the truth. 'You need to tell me what happened, *now*. We can't waste time. We *need* to know.'

Gulping back tears, Jessie began to speak. 'It was years ago. Probably about four years. I got a phone call from our operator at witness protection on the burner phone we use. Occasionally, she'd touch base to check that we were ok and to let me know any updates on my son. You know, like if he'd moved prison or whatever, I still write to him. He's my son after all.' Jessie swallowed hard and took the tissue Alice handed her.

Sadia shuffled in her seat as Jessie focussed her attention on Alice.

'It's a real palaver. I have to put my letter in an unsealed unaddressed envelope and then I have to put that in another unsealed unaddressed envelope. Finally, I put both envelopes in a third one. My operator texts a different address each month and that's the one I use on the outer envelope. They check the contents to make sure I've not put any detail in that I shouldn't. They black out anything that might reveal our whereabouts. I don't send photos or talk about anything Molly's involved in: no school plays, no sport activities. I'm really careful. When his letter arrives it's always from a different address and it's usually in a plain envelope, like a bank statement or something.'

Alice nodded. 'That all seems really secure, Jessie, but you were going to tell me about something that happened four years ago?'

With desperate eyes, demanding understanding, Jessie maintained eye contact. 'He's still my son you know, even after all he's done. He's still my son.'

Alice nodded, ignoring the quiet tut from Sadia, but deciding to have words with her about it later.

Jessie sniffed. 'Well, the operator told me James had been attacked by another prisoner and was in ICU in London. He told me he'd be ok and he'd keep me updated. But … you know… I couldn't just sit and do nothing, so I went down to see him. I didn't tell Beth.

'When I got there he was out of ICU and in a side room with a guard outside the door. They'd handcuffed him to the bed.' She blew her nose. 'I stayed in the waiting room until the guard went to the toilet or for a fag break. He probably wasn't supposed to leave, but James was handcuffed anyway. I thought James would be pleased to see me, but he wasn't. He shouted at me and told me to get out. Said I was risking everything and that's what they wanted. I was so shocked, I ran out and came home. I was scared for months after, but then nothing happened and I thought he was exaggerating and so I forgot about it. He wasn't though, was he?'

Alice shook her head. 'Perhaps not Jessie, but we'll investigate everything.

Jessie began to cry again. 'Oh my God, it's all my fault. They've got Molly and it's all my fault.'

Pulling the weeping woman to her chest, Alice jerked her head towards the door, telling Sadia to go and tell Gus what they'd discovered. Talking soothingly to Jessie, Alice rocked her back and forth as if she was a baby. Sadia had opened the door to leave when an explosion rocked the house. Alice quickly sprang up and with Jessie following, she and Sadia ran through the door, into the corridor to the kitchen.

CHAPTER 58
The Fort

DCI Nancy Chalmers gave a perfunctory tap on the door and walked in. DCS Charlie Bowles glanced up frowning, but when he saw who his visitor was, his face immediately transformed to a smile. He pushed the paperwork he was sifting through to one side. 'Hello Nancy, it's good to see you. Take a seat.'

As she walked across the room, Charlie noticed the slump of her shoulders and the dark bruises under her eyes. When she sat opposite him, he could see the tension lines around her mouth and eyes. He leaned forward, pressed a button on his intercom and asked his PA to bring in coffee for two.

Nancy smiled. 'Just what I need, Charlie. It's been a shit couple of days and it doesn't look like it's going to get better any time soon.'

Standing up, Charlie moved round to the front of his desk and resting his bottom on the edge, he stuck his long legs out before him, crossing them at the heel. With his arms folded loosely over his chest he studied her.

'Is it the trafficked kids or the abducted girl?'

He knew Nancy had tried to contact him the previous evening, but he'd been 'unobtainable' when she'd first been notified about the Beth Graves situation. It was too sensitive to put in a memo, so he'd given her the first free slot of the morning.

With a grimace, she said, 'Well, actually, Charlie. The two cases are linked.'

Charlie rested his elbow on his folded arm, raised his hand to his mouth and tapped his lip with one finger. He was just about to speak when, with a perfunctory knock Julia, his PA, opened the door. Using her ample butt to wedge it open, she entered the room backwards carrying a tray filled with coffee, mugs and Kit Kats.

'Oh Julia, you're a bloody star. I love Kit Kats. Thanks so much' said Nancy, her eyes lighting up.

Julia grinned, as she deposited the tray on the coffee table near the comfy chairs. 'You're looking a bit peaky today, Nance, so I thought a bit of spoiling was in order.'

Charlie winked at Nancy and put on a mock pout. 'Hmm, so she gets preferential treatment does she? When was the last time you ever spoiled me?'

Julia threw a disdainful look at Charles. 'Phew, when's the last time you ever looked peaky? You and that fake tan of yours, you look like that bloke off *Bargain Hunt*.'

Hiding the slight spark of annoyance her cheek had provoked, Charlie flung back his head and released a huge guffaw. Best to keep on Julia's good side. After all, she had control of his diary. No need to give her an excuse to scrutinise it too closely, not with all his extra-curricular activities.

Nancy laughed. 'You're a tonic, you know, you really are.'

Julia winked and made her way back to the door, hesitating only when Charlie called her name. 'No interruptions till Nancy's gone, ok?'

Julia nodded and left, closing the door behind her.

Charlie stood up and gestured for Nancy to follow him to the soft chairs. He made himself comfortable, then began to pour coffee. Dropping a single sugar cube into one of them, he swirled a teaspoon round and then pushed the mug towards her.

Nancy grabbed a Kit Kat, ripped the wrapper off, snapped one of the chocolate fingers and rammed it into her mouth. Charlie watched her eat. Her voracious appetite was one of the reasons he was attracted to her. He found it incredibly sexy, the way she embraced the physical world with such fervour.

Lifting a biscuit, he carefully slipped the paper wrapper off and folded it in half. Then slipping a fingertip under the foil flap, he opened it with great care. Placing the chocolate wafer on the tray, he folded the foil in four before placing it neatly on top of the paper. Next, he lifted his biscuit and carefully snapped it in two, shook the excess crumbs off and began to nibble it slowly, interspersing each bite with a sip of coffee as he waited for Nancy to speak.

'It's bad, Charlie. You remember that case in 2003? The one with the paedophile ring? The Matchmaker?'

Charles pursed his lips and thought for a moment before nodding. 'Yes, the one where the wife came forward and reported her husband?'

Nancy nodded, 'Well, she went into WP and now, would you believe it, she's turned up here in Ilkley. It's her daughter who's gone missing. It's looking increasingly likely that the daughter's been abducted *and* that the trafficked children are linked to this.' She leaned forward, eyes anguished. 'That bastard appears to have accessed her new identity.'

Charles, a sceptical look on his face, replaced his mug on the tray. 'Oh come on Nancy, you can't be sure it's the same ring, surely?'

Face completely serious, she bit her lip. 'I've never been more sure, Charlie. I'm convinced.' Hands shaking, she put her half-full drink down, slopping some onto the teak table. Not noticing Charles's quickly hidden glare she continued. 'Never in a million years did I think I'd come across Cathy again – or Beth, as she's now called. And now, here she is. It's bloody awful. As if that poor kid didn't suffer enough ten years ago. It's bloody shite, that's what it is, shite!' She roughly wiped her sleeve across her face to get rid of the tears that had sprung to her eyes.

Charlie walked round the table and stood behind her, his hands gently kneading her shoulders. Staring into space, a half-smile on his face, he said in a voice that, even to his own ears, sounded doubtful. 'Well, maybe you'll have better luck catching him this time, Nancy.'

Shoulders tightening beneath his fingers, she said, 'Thanks for the vote of confidence.' She began to shrug his fingers off but he soothed her with a smoothly delivered 'I've got every faith in your abilities. You know that. Just keep me in the loop.'

For a moment she resisted his ministrations and then as he increased the pressure on her muscles, she moaned and allowed his firm fingers to work their magic.

'How's Gus coping with it all? He's had a busy first few days back at work.'

Eyes closed, she sunk farther into the chair. 'Gus's fine, coping remarkably well. Still looks in pain sometimes but he's focussed and seems to be on the ball.'

'Hmm, well I hope he is. We went out on a limb to get him back to work so quickly. I only hope it doesn't come back to bite us on the arse.'

'Tut tut, Charlie. It won't. Trust me, Gus is fine.'

Stepping away from Nancy, he walked back round to his chair and sat. 'And you're sure this all links back to Cambridge all those years ago?'

She sighed. 'It certainly looks that way, especially now they've abducted Beth's daughter. It's The Matchmaker at work again. I'm sure of it. Gus is trying to get to the bottom of who breached the Witness Protection protocols. WP say it wasn't them and you know how stringent they are, so I suspect the family somehow revealed their true identities.'

Charlie grinned, wiggling his eyebrows nock suggestively. 'Fancy a little, eh… physical activity to get rid of the last of your stress?'

Nancy grimaced and jumped to her feet. 'How inappropriate, Charles. With Julia next door? Yeah right.' She cocked her head to one side and bent over to caress his cheek gently. 'You'll just have to wait till Friday, as planned. Of course, that's if I'm not too busy.'

She snatched up her bag and headed for the door. 'Looks like the shoulder massage and Kit Kat did the business for me. Now you can get to whatever mega complex paperwork you stopped when I came in.' And with a wink, she exited his office.

For a moment, Charlie remained by the coffee table, a thoughtful look on his face. Then, tapping a rhythm on the wood, he inhaled deeply. Nancy had out manoevered him and he didn't like it. He didn't like it one bit. Standing up he moved over to his PC and seconds later, calming flute music flooded the room.

CHAPTER 59
Ilkley

Sadia and Alice, followed more slowly by Jessie, burst into the kitchen. Gus, Janine Roberts, Beth, Wendy Horan, and Alex, mouths agape, stood round the large pine table looking at the scorched remains of a cardboard box that was still smoking in the centre. Gus held up a hand as they entered, stopping them from coming right in.

'There's a metal tin in the middle of the box. We don't know what's in it. Get the bomb squad out here ASAP, Alice.' As Alice scurried out of the room to make the call, Gus turned to the other four shocked adults. 'We better get out of here now. We don't know what other little surprises the bastard who sent this has left.'

Beth gulped and suddenly jumped into action, rushing from the kitchen and up the stairs. 'Got to get Sam,' she shouted, her voice shaky.

Janine, quickly recovering from her initial shock, began to herd the others from the room. Before Alex could follow his wife upstairs, she was running back down with a squawking, blanketed bundle in her arms. Gus quickly herded them through the front door and down to the end of the garden, where he reckoned they would be safe. On Gus's instructions Alice and Sadia ran back and started up the two unmarked police cars that sat in the drive in front of the house. Quickly, they reversed them until they rested half on the cobbles and half on the lawn, throwing up sods of icy grass and leaving huge welts in the turf and. Once there, the Graves family and Wendy piled into one car. Leaving the engine on for warmth, Alice got out and approached Gus.

'Bomb squad's on its way.' she said, as Sadia climbed out of the other car and joined them. Gus, panting with the adrenalin rush, gathered Sadia and Alice a few feet from the car. In the distance they could already hear the sirens approaching. Alice pale and shaking slightly said 'What the fuck happened there?'

Gus ran his fingers through his dreads, 'Bloody bastards left a parcel at the bottom of the drive and Beth's friend brought it into the house with her when she came.'

Alice glanced at the woman who was comforting Beth in the car. 'Yeah, that's Wendy Horan. She's doing Beth's job at Carlton Wood while she's on maternity leave.'

Gus nodded. 'That's right. Anyway, before I had a chance to stop her, Beth began to open it. As she pulled the lid open, there was a flash and a hellish bang. The bastards wanted to frighten her, so she wasn't hurt, but God knows what's in the tin. I'm taking no chances.'

Sadia who'd remained quiet, spoke for the first time. 'I'll get someone on to checking CCTV and their personal security cameras to see who dropped it off. There's no CCTV on this road but we may catch something on the access roads.'

Gus nodded. 'And get forensics here too. They might find something, once the area's been cleared by the bomb experts.'

Sadia walked down the garden to meet PC Owens, who was walking up the drive towards them, having abandoned his car on the lawn near the bottom to allow emergency vehicles access.

Rubbing his shoulder, Gus looked at Alice. 'I got sod all from Cathy and Alex about the WP breach. They're both adamant that they've not breached it in any way. Did you get anything from Jessie?'

Alice explained what Jessie had told them.

'Shit' said Gus when she'd finished. 'Good job I'm meeting with their WP agent tomorrow. I want you to grab Sadia and get over there and re-interview Molly's friend.' He chose to ignore Alice's disgusted expression when he mentioned Sadia. 'Get as much detail as you can. Try to find out how this bloke made contact with Molly and see if we can catch that bugger.'

'Do you think he's The Matchmaker, then?'

Gus shook his head. 'Nah, that'd be too fucking easy. Whoever he is, he's just a minion. Maybe even the same bloke that shot at Jamal.'

He frowned and tapped his lip. 'Get Compo to check CCTV to see if the car abandoned on Cemetery Road has been spotted in Ilkley in the last couple of days. And tell Owens to request some extra bodies to help. When the newspapers get wind of this they'll come sniffing around like dogs after their own arses.'

As Alice walked away, Gus spun on his heel and walked over to speak to the bomb squad officer who'd just arrived in record time. He was just getting out of an open-backed army truck when Gus reached his side.

Extending his left hand to the burly man in army fatigues, he said, 'DI Gus McGuire. Didn't expect you within the hour, but I'm glad you're here.'

The man took in Gus' injured shoulder, smiled and shook Gus's hand with his left one. 'Sergeant Cecil Ormerton.' His voice was pure English public school. He nodded to Gus's strapped arm. 'Looks like you've been in the wars?'

Gus shrugged. 'Minor injury.'

The other dipped his head and moved round to the back of his truck. 'I was on the moors, doing controlled explosives training with a bunch of squaddies when your call came through. Lucky for you, really, or you'd still be waiting.'

Gus grinned. 'Could do with a bit of luck on this case.' He looked into the truck's cabin. 'You on your own, then?'

Pulling equipment out of the truck Ormerton said, 'Someone's heading over from headquarters, but I'll do an initial assessment on my own. If necessary, I'll wait till they arrive before dismantling it. Now, is the house completely cleared?'

'Yeah. They're all waiting in that car over there. Do you think that's a safe enough distance away?'

Ormerton assessed the distance between the house and the vehicle. 'Which room is the package in and where is it located?'

Gus told him. Ormerton nodded. 'If it's at the back of the house they should be fine there for now. Now, tell me about the package.'

Ormerton listened carefully as Gus explained, as succinctly as he could, what had happened. He drew a quick diagram of the layout of the kitchen and the parcel's position on the table.

Finally, the other man nodded. 'Ok, I'll get my suit on and then I'll go in to assess. You're right to be cautious. Nowadays with all this easy access to bomb components and the internet instructions to make the fuckers, it's better to take precautions.'

Gus smiled slightly at the sergeant's swearing. Whistling, Ormerton strutted over to his army vehicle, spoke to another officer on his radio and began to don a padded suit and helmet before entering the house. Gus stood, eyes focussed nervously on the front door. Within minutes, Ormerton was back.

'Looks like a pretty amateurish explosive. Designed to create a loud bang rather than do any actual damage. I can't see anything explosive attached to the tin but I'm going to open it under a controlled unit. Fucks up your forensics I'm afraid but better than getting your balls blown off.'

Feeling his own balls shrivel at the very thought, Gus moved over to the squad car and got in. He wished he'd grabbed his coat from the back of the kitchen chair before he left the house. A few minutes later Ormerton's colleague arrived and the pair of them, similarly clad and carrying a metal structure re-entered the house.

Gus felt edgy. Despite the welcome warmth, he couldn't settle in the car so when he saw PC Owens approach with a plastic mug of steaming coffee and a blanket, he got out. Handing both to Gus, who wrapped the blanket round himself, they leaned against the car and waited. Gus didn't know about Owens, but he knew his own body was tense, bracing itself against the sound of a blast. Fortunately, it never came.

Ten minutes passed, then Owens nudged him gently and nodded to the right. Alex Graves, also coatless, had left the confines of the heated car and was approaching. It was clear from the slump of his shoulders and his nervous glances towards the house that the morning's events had taken their toll on the man. Gus sympathised. He wasn't so emotionally involved, but he still felt like he'd been dragged through a thorn bush in the scud. He was hoping against hope that The Matchmaker, because he was certain that's who was behind this, had contented himself with frightening them with the first big bang and hadn't left any more surprises for Sergeant Ormerton to find.

'Any news?' said Alex.

Gus shook his head. 'No, we're still waiting. The bomb expert's inside as we speak and as soon as he's done we'll send the forensics team in. Maybe you and your family should head off somewhere warm till the house is declared safe.'

Alex thrust his hands into his pockets and shrugged. 'I don't think we want to leave just yet. Beth's feeding the baby and at least they're warm in the car.'

Standing side by side the three men continued their vigil. Then, with a sideways glance Gus said, 'Did you know Jessie visited her son four years ago?'

Alex tensed and then his head swivelled towards Gus. 'What?' He sighed and swept his hand over his hair. 'Christ, she breached the witness protection.'

Gus nodded slowly. 'Looks that way.'

A heavy silence hovered between them, until finally, Alex said in an anguished voice, 'That's why she's nearly catatonic. She's not said a word since we left the house.'

Gus nodded again. 'Probably shock. She'll be ok.'

When Alex replied, it was with venom. '*She* might be ok, but what about Molly? She could be dead for all we know. Who knows what those bastards are doing to her.'

Gus was about to place his good arm round Alex's shoulder, when he heard a shout from the house. Ormerton still wearing his protective clothing and helmet stood at the door. One hand was raised in an unmistakeable thumbs up.

He turned to Alex. 'Stay here,' before walking towards Ormerton, who was divesting himself of his heavy armour as he approached.

'All clear in there now, inspector.'

Gus turned and nodded to the forensic team, who'd arrived a while back and were currently waiting a few feet away. Immediately, they jumped into action. Gus walked over to join Ormerton who'd stopped a few feet away from his truck.

'Find anything useful?'

Ormerton shook his head. 'Whoever sent that parcel is a fucking bad bastard. He left a little gift behind and in my mind it's as bad as a fucking bomb.' He shook his head as if to rid himself of an awful image. Then he pulled his hand out from his pocket and offered his card to Gus. 'You ever need me for anything, call any of these numbers. I'm working here for another three weeks and it would be my pleasure to help bring this bastard down.'

Gus narrowed his eyes. 'What are you not telling me?'

Ormerton glanced back at the house. 'Go and have a look.' He jerked his head back towards Alex, 'But don't let him in till everything's cleared away.'

Gus's eyes narrowed and then with a nod he headed to the house.

CHAPTER 60
The Fort

Sampson, eyes red with tiredness, opened the door to the incident room. It was deserted, except for Compo, who was devouring a tuna mayo sandwich at his computer. Sampson walked over to him. He was wired by a combination of too much Red Bull, caffeine and adrenalin. The brainstorm had hit him minutes ago, just as he finished compiling the file he was about to pass on to Compo.

Now, he stood next to Compo's untidy desk, his face alight with excitement despite his fatigue, and waited for Compo to look up. When he'd explained his idea, Compo, equally, invigorated high-fived him. He quickly dumped his half-eaten sandwich haphazardly on the desk behind him, oblivious to the smear of mayo he left on a file marked 'Urgent and Private'. He wiped his hand down his Rolling Stones T-shirt, Mick Jagger's pouting lips open to receive the large blob of mayo he deposited there. Once he was satisfied that his hands were clean enough, his danced his fingers quickly over the keyboard. When Meatloaf's 'Bat out of Hell' suddenly blared from the speakers, he turned round and high-fived Sampson again, before rubbing his hands together like a Yorkshire version of Fagin.

'Yehaw,cowboy, let's bring 'em in.'

Slightly bemused, Sampson watched as, head bobbing ferociously to 'I'll be gone, gone, gone', Compo uploaded the footage he'd retrieved onto the PC. Maybe it was the Red Bull, maybe it was Compo's infectious enthusiasm, but all of a sudden Sampson found himself executing a complicated riff on an air guitar as Compo worked.

Sampson had been trawling through CCTV footage of the three roads that led to Dales Way Link. He'd been logging each vehicle's details and comparing them to a list of residents' vehicles, in the hope they'd identify the car used to drive Molly Graves away from the area. He'd completed the last tape and had inputted the vehicle reg numbers into the ANPR system and was waiting for it to churn out details of the various cars' whereabouts, when he had a sudden thought. If the Molly Graves's abduction was linked to both the trafficked children and the attack against Jamal Asif, then maybe, just maybe, the abandoned car found in the Cemetery Road Asda car park had been used to stake out the Graves's residence prior to being abandoned.

Sampson realised that if he correlated the movements of *that* car between the time it was stolen and the time it was found, then they'd have a rough idea where the driver had been in the car. Hopefully, that would then throw up areas of interest where they could access CCTV and cross-match to ID the shooter and get some clues to where he was holed up. Sampson didn't know a quick way to do this, however, he knew a man who did. Which was why, half an hour later, while one of Compo's special little computer programmes did its thing, the two of them were letting off steam in the deserted incident room.

That was when the door opened and in walked DCI Hussain. Noticing the senior officer first, Sampson tried to attract Compo's attention by coughing and allowing his hands, mid riff, to drop to his sides. When Compo finally realised, he was in the process of executing an ungainly half-split. Immediately, he toppled over onto the floor, knocked a pen pot off a nearby desk and then quickly scrambled up to silence Meatloaf.

DCI Hussain looked unamused. His body was tense, hands clasped behind his back. His normally patrician face was lined with a frown that started at his forehead and didn't stop. When he spoke, he enunciated each syllable in an accusing monotone. 'What exactly is going on here?'

Sampson and Compo exchanged nervous glances, then realising they were expected to reply, Sampson spoke. 'We just got a bit of a breakthrough and... er... whilst the computer programme was running we thought we'd... em... well, celebrate.' He splayed his hands in an apologetic gesture, while Compo, head bowed beside him, remained silent.

Hussain's eyes narrowed. 'Idiots! I'll be bringing this up with DCI Chalmers. I always thought DI Gus McGuire didn't run a tight enough ship and this just proves it.' He glanced round the room, his mouth curled up in distaste at the less than pristine evidence of hard work. 'I'm looking for my daughter. Where is she?'

Sampson all but saluted. 'Sir, she's in Ilkley with DI McGuire.'

'Hmmph, she'd have been better off here, keeping an eye on you two fools.'

Sampson, slightly narked by the inference that Sadia was superior to him, reddened but stood his ground. 'With all due respect sir, DC Hussain is of *equal* rank to both myself and DC Compton and as such she's not in a position to 'keep an eye' on me.'

Hussain's frown deepened. 'Are you contradicting me, Sampson?'

Compo, agitation making him bounce on the spot, glared at Sampson and said, 'No, no, sir. DC Sampson wasn't contradicting you. You wouldn't dream of it, would you, John?'

'For goodness sake, stand still. Does McGuire not have a single normal officer, other than my daughter, on his team?' And before they could reply he spun on his heel and left the room, slamming the door behind him.

CHAPTER 61
Ilkley

The house was freezing as Gus walked along the hallway, his shoes dripping slush on the highly polished real wood floor. Ormerton had switched off the Aga and the scene of crime officers had been trailing in and out with their equipment leaving the doors open. Before entering the kitchen, he grabbed a bunny suit from the box by the door, hitched his tall frame into it, donned some nitrile gloves and covered his shoes. Ready, he walked through the door.

A very faint smell of burnt cardboard lingered. The exploded box had been moved to the work surface and now all that lay on the table was the tin box that Ormerton had cleared. Gus's jacket still hung on the back of the chair, which was pushed out as he'd left it. He grabbed it and shrugged it over his shoulders. He nodded at Hissing Sid, the senior Scene of Crime Officer, who waved him over to the table where a few scattered pieces of scorched cardboard lay with the red metal tin open in the centre.

'Not a lot we can pull from here really, Gus. Soon as you've seen this *in situ*, we'll bag everything up and be out of your way.'

Gus's eyes strayed to the tin. When he saw what was inside a muscle twitched in his cheek. Now, it looked like they had the confirmation they needed that Molly Graves had been abducted. Tresses of golden red curls, on a scrap of white fabric lay in the centre of the open tin.

'Fucking sick bastard, eh?' said Sid

Gus nodded.

Sid pointed to the pictures on the fridge. 'It's hers, isn't it? That hair'

'Yep, looks like it.' Gus's gaze moved to a scrap of paper that had been unfolded and lay beside the tin. It had four creases showing where it had previously been folded. Gus read the words that were scrawled in red crayon. 'You've got email.'

He turned to PC Owens who had followed him in and now stood at the door. 'Get the family back up here now and see if you can find either DS Cooper or DC Hussain.'

Owens nodded and left. Gus looked at Sid. 'Child's writing, you reckon?'

Sid looked at it. 'Probably, yes. But we'll know more when I've analysed it.'

'Can you bag it open like this? I'll show it to the parents see if they can identify the writing as Molly's.'

'Sure thing.'

Gus turned and saw Alice entering the room. Her gaze immediately fell to the tin and the note. Her hand flew up to her mouth as she took a single step nearer. 'Fuck.'

'My sentiments exactly,' said Gus

He turned to Alice. 'When this lot have gone, I want you to bring the family back in. We need to access their emails. And get Compo here.' Leaving Gus to strip off his bunny suit and flick the kettle on she left.

By the time Beth, Alex and Jessie, accompanied by Janine Roberts the FLO, had returned to the house and settled baby Sam in his pram, Gus had mashed a pot of tea and was busy pouring it into mugs. He sat down opposite Beth. 'I've got something to tell you and it's not pleasant but I need you, for Molly's sake, to hold it together, ok?'

Beth paled and she clutched her husband's hand. With a single nod, she indicated she was ready for Gus to continue. Knowing there was no way to lessen the blow Gus spoke slowly and clearly his gaze never wavering from Beth's face

'We found tresses of curly golden red hair that seems to match that of your daughter. They were in the tin that was inside the cardboard parcel.'

Beth scraped back her chair, rushed over to the sink and vomited. The acrid smell hung heavy in the air, as Alex rushed to join his wife at the sink. Quickly, he rinsed the sick away and took her into his arms. She collapsed against him, shoulders heaving for a few seconds and then, abruptly straightened and walked back to the table. Wordlessly she sat back down. Meanwhile, Jessie sat at the other end of the table weeping silently, tears flowing unchecked down her cheeks. Janine Roberts had her arm round the older woman's shoulder.

Beth looked at Gus and he resumed. 'We've sent it off for analysis but at the minute we're assuming the hair is Molly's.' he paused. 'There was also a note.' He turned the bag over and pushed the note closer to them. 'Does that look like Molly's writing?'

Beth took a quick glance and nodded.

Gus tapped the bag. 'Then we need you all to access your email. It looks like the kidnapper has communicated with one of you.'

Alex, jumped to his feet and took the laptop from the cupboard that housed the security equipment. Laying it on the table, he booted the laptop up. 'We've not even looked at our emails today. Too busy worrying about Molly.' Then when it was ready he said, 'Whose mail shall I check first?'

'Beth's, I think. If it is this Matchmaker character, then it's Beth he wants to hurt,' said Gus.

With trembling fingers Beth accessed her email. Gus moved round the table to stand behind her so he could see the screen over her shoulder.

'Anything?'

Beth scrolled down her mail and stopped at an email with the subject heading 'I'm coming to get you'.

Gus grabbed her hand as she looked about to open it.

'Wait! Don't open it yet.' He turned to Alice. 'Is Compo on his way?' Turning back to Beth he said, 'I want my IT expert to check this out. I don't want any clues that might lead us to the sender to be erased if we open it without taking precautions.'

Beth sagged back in her chair her eyes never leaving the screen.

Ten minutes later, Gus met Compo at the door. Looking slightly dishevelled, Compo stomped up the steps and into the hallway lugging a huge bag over one shoulder and pulling a trolley case. 'Vultures are gathering out there now, Gus.'

'Suppose it was only a matter of time really. You manage to get everything you need?'

'Yes, brought most of it yesterday but we expected them to communicate via phone. Never mind, I've got all I need here. I'll have to hook up to their PC though.'

Compo shuffled into the kitchen behind Gus. When Gus turned round he recognised the other man's nerves and smiled encouragingly. Compo looked at the spacious kitchen table where Alex's laptop sat and turned to Beth. 'You ok for me to spread out here?'

Beth nodded abruptly and continued to stare open-eyed at the screen whilst her baby nuzzled greedily at her breast.

Compo hooked up various pieces of gadgetry to the computer and then moved back to monitor his own screen. He pressed a couple of keys and then said, 'You can open it now'

Beth, hand trembling, leaned forward and clicked on the email. There was no message, just a video attachment. She glanced up at Gus, who waited till Compo nodded before saying. 'Right, Beth, open it.'

At first it was unclear what they were seeing as the camera wobbled all over the place. Gus frowned as he realised that it was pointing at the roof of what looked like an old warehouse. Then, it panned down and steadied. There in front of the recorder was a young girl with a head full of golden red curls, sitting on a mucky mattress, her knees curled up to her chest, and a soiled sheet draped round her skinny shoulders.

'Molly!' Beth rammed her knuckles into her mouth to stop herself screaming.

Molly's face was tear-stained, her hair dishevelled, making her eyes look huge in her pallid face. A muffled distorted voice addressed the girl and then a figure wearing a Scream mask and a white coverall, walked over to her. She screamed and scrambled back up the bed, her feet kicking frantically against the mattress. When she could go no further, she turned to her side and tucking her head in she curled into a ball. Frantic, hiccupping sobs rent the air. Her shoulders heaved. The figure in the Scream mask turned, sneering into the camera and then the distorted voice spoke, echoing into the kitchen. 'Now you'll see what it is to suffer, bitch!'

As Gus rested his hand on Beth's shoulder he could feel the tension radiating from her. After his experience with his godson Billy, he had some idea what Beth was feeling. He also knew that nothing he or anyone else could do would make this any better for Beth. He could only watch the events on the recording unfold with her.

Scream man grabbed Molly and pulled her upright, as effortlessly as if she weighed nothing. A chair skidded across the room landing on its back at his feet. Holding the girl in one arm, he flicked the chair upright and flung her onto it. In a fluid movement he spun it round, so the frightened girl stared straight into the camera. Then, from his pocket he took out a bundle of cable ties. He yanked her arms behind the chair and wrapped one round each of her wrists. With a vicious tug, he secured Molly to the chair. Then he pulled her legs together and yanked another tie round both feet.

Again he paused for effect, seemingly leering at the camera through his mask. 'Now for the action!' He dug into his pocket again and took out a substantial tool wrap, which he laid on the mattress. With tantalising precision, he opened it and took each item out of its sleeve. One by one he held each tool up before the terrified girl's eyes. With his gloved finger he caressed each blade and sharpened edge before replacing it in the wrap. Finally, he lifted a pair of shears and snapped them open and shut repeatedly, close to Molly's nose. She whimpered and struggled against the ties.

In the kitchen, Beth groaned.

Gus swallowed hard, dreading what this man would do next.

In a weirdly, distorted sing-song voice the Scream man turned to the camera. Snapping the shears open and shut, he said, 'Bitch, you wouldn't believe the damage these lovely little things can do.' He laughed and then moved round behind the chair. Gently he moved Molly's curls to one side, revealing a delicate ear. His head jerked towards the camera, as he opened the shears and positioned them so that Molly's ear lay between the blades.

'Oh my God.' Beth's voice was barely a whisper.

The camera panned in and out as Scream man taunted them. Gus realised that someone else was operating the camera. Probably the elusive Sid Smith, he thought.

Then, with a sudden movement, Scream man jerked the shears backwards catching Molly's ear lobe with the blade. She yelped and a small rosette of blood bloomed on her lobe for a second, before dripping onto her t-shirt. He laughed, low and guttural. Then, casually reached out with one finger, caught a drip of blood on the tip and raised it to the mask. His tongue slithered out from the leery mouth hole and lapped up the blood.

'Mmm, the first taste of revenge. So sweet.' And he spun round, grabbed a handful of Molly's curls and yanked it above her head. The skin on her face pulled taut and her neck muscles pulsed as she strained upwards to try to release the pressure. Tears rolled down her face and dripped off the end of her dimpled chin. With the shears snapping widely behind her, the man laughed again. Abruptly, he whooped in imitation of a Native American warrior and snipped twice. Dancing away from the chair, he held a handful of curls in his raised fist like a scalp. Raggedy clumps of hair fell sparsely around Molly's head. She looked like a bedraggled scarecrow.

Still whooping, the camera followed the almost maniacal man, as he danced round the room then abruptly stopped. 'Rest assured, bitch, this first blood is not enough to calm my unquiet soul. Speak soon.' The screen went blank.

Beth screamed, jumped from her chair and lunged towards the blank screen. 'Molly.' The single word sent shivers up Gus's spine. He moved to help her back into her seat but before he could do so she turned. Face red, eyes flashing she hurled herself at Jessie, her arm outstretched. Her hand connected with the other woman's cheek in a resounding slap. 'This is *your* fault. You just couldn't stay away from that piece of *vermin* could you? Now look what you've done to Molly.'

Jessie lifted a shaking hand to cradle her cheek. Eyes clouded in anguish, she stared at her daughter-in-law.

With flashing eyes, her anger unspent, Beth raised her arm to strike again. Janine sprung to action, but it was Alex who reached her first. He was a second too late to prevent her delivering a second resounding slap to Jessie's already red cheek.

'Come on now, Beth. You can't do this,' said Alex, but Beth shrugged him off and stood towering over the shell-shocked woman.

'Get out of my sight. Just get out of my fucking sight.'

Janine, professionally unflappable, gently manoeuvred the older woman from her chair and guided her out of the kitchen, saying as she went, 'I'll take Jessie to her flat.'

Beth turned to Gus, her face hard and emotionless. 'Find my daughter before those bastards hurt her any more.'

Gus nodded once and turned to Compo. 'Get as much as you can from the recording and the email, ok?' He turned to Beth and Alex. 'Does he have permission to access all your devices?'

Beth waved her hand dismissively. 'Of course.'

'Right, we'll need that in writing. Compo, get on to it, please.'

Relieved to leave the tension that reverberated in the kitchen, Gus walked through to the room where Compo had set up his equipment the previous day. The two officers who were monitoring the phone lines greeted him as he entered. With a tense smile of acknowledgment, Gus said, 'You lot answer to Compo, ok? He's in charge of all things technical. Any activity on the phones?'

The older of the two men stretched his arms out in front of him. 'Not a bloody peep.'

Gus left them, hoping things were quiet in the kitchen, now. Alice, was talking quietly to Beth when he walked back in. Alex, tea towel flung over one shoulder was washing a few dishes and Compo was working some sort of magic on his PC. Gus smiled when he saw that someone had placed a plate of biscuits next to him, which he was absent-mindedly devouring as he worked.

'Beth,' said Gus, pulling a chair out and straddling it. 'I take it, from your reaction earlier, that Alex told you that Jessie visited her son?' When Beth inclined her head, he continued. 'I know you're upset and I know this is a hellish time for you, but there must be no repeat of your behaviour tonight.' Beth refused to make eye contact so Gus continued.

'You want us to find Molly, don't you?' When she responded with a slight nod he thrust his point home 'Well, in that case you won't distract us by attacking Jessie again, will you?'

Her head jerked up and her eyes met his. When she spoke her tone was subdued. 'I won't touch her again. I want you to focus on getting Molly back. That's all I want.'

Gus turned to Alice. 'Can I have a word, DC Cooper?'

Alice followed him into the hallway and as soon as the kitchen door closed behind them, she released a huge sigh. 'That was bloody awful, wasn't it?'

'Emotions are running high.' He raked his fingers through his dreads. 'Hopefully my meeting with the WP agent tomorrow will throw up some clues. I'm also going to visit James Clegg in Littlehey, Cambridge. I want to see if he can throw any light on the matter. Maybe he'll be a bit more forthcoming now his daughter's at risk. You'll head up the briefing in the morning, but before that, I want you to drop me at the airport.

CHAPTER 62
Bradford,
Thursday

A lice manoeuvred down Marriner's Drive to Emm Lane. The road was a death-trap and she wished she'd asked Gus to meet her on the main road. The slight drizzle the previous night had frozen and Alice was sure she was in danger of skidding into one of the parked vehicles. As she finally turned left followed by a right at the traffic lights onto Manningham Lane she heaved a sigh of relief. 'Thank God that's over with. Thought I was going to hit that blue Rover.'

Gus, slowly released his grip on the dashboard and glared at her. 'Fuck's sake Alice, couldn't you have got a pool car? This is thing of yours is like a sardine tin. By the time I get to the airport my leg'll have seized up.'

Alice, glanced sideways at him, lips pursed. 'Stop bloody moaning. At least my Mini smells better than a dead rat's arse, unlike a pool car.'

Gus snorted. 'Dead rat's arse! Now that's funny.' He took out his phone, pressed a speed-dial number and held the phone to his ear.

Alice fiddled with the radio and listened to Gus's conversation with DCI Chalmers.

'Hi Nance, just to update you, I'm on my way to interview James Clegg in Cambridge and then I'm meeting the Graves' WP agent. Alice is leading the briefing.'

She saw Gus head tilted to one side as he listened and wished the traffic light would hurry up and change.

'Janine got the GP to make a house call and he sedated Jessie so hopefully Beth will have calmed down a bit by the time she's awake again. Janine's on hand and is alternating between the main house and the granny annex. Compo's set up base there with another two techies for now, so we're on hand if and when they contact her again.'

Seeing Gus rubbing his thigh, Alice felt slightly guilty that she'd not opted for a slightly bigger pool car. Gus caught her eye and still speaking to Nancy said, 'Hope the media are a bit more lenient with Beth this time around. Can you keep the WP thing under wraps for a bit longer?'

He listened for a few minutes longer and then hung up.

'Looks like the vultures are on the trail. Nancy says they're camped out in Ilkley and at The Fort.'

Alice tutted. 'And you know what that slimy git Jez Hopkins is like. He's got a nose like a cadaver dog in a butcher's; and the morals of one. Remember what he was like last year. Your dad nearly got physical with him when he wouldn't sling his hook.'

Gus looked startled. 'Really?'

Alice flicked him a glance. 'Yeah, really. You were a bloody zombie at that time. The rest of the press had all gone back under their stones, but Hopkins wouldn't let up. Your dad just lost it.' She laughed. 'Mo had to pull him away.'

Gus shook his head. 'Wow.'

Alice, grinned and changed lanes. 'Is someone picking you up at Heathrow?'

'Yeah, I've got a PC for the day. Hope to fuck they've got a pool car. They'll chauffeur me around and then take me to the station for my train back'

'Aren't you flying back?'

'Couldn't get a seat. Catching the train from King's Cross instead. It'll give me a chance to do some paperwork.'

Seeing the sign for Leeds Bradford airport, Alice indicated and pulled in. 'Maybe you'll discover another leak that will exonerate Jessie, but I doubt it. WP are notoriously efficient.'

'Yeah, I think we've found the leak, but maybe we can trace it back from the hospital. Someone must have followed Jessie back to Ilkley.'

'After four years. You'll be lucky.'

Gus shrugged and grabbed his bag as Alice slid to a stop outside terminal one. 'You're in charge Al, ok? Keep things moving onwards. Compo's on with the technological stuff. Sampson's brainwave could point us in the right direction. Make sure the FLO does her job and get Sadia working. Get in touch if there's any action at all, ok?'

Gus jumped out and with a brief wave he was off. Alice watched him for a second before putting the car in gear and heading back to The Fort.

CHAPTER 63
HMP Littlehey, Cambridge

Gus was met at Heathrow by a Welsh uniformed officer called Leonard Marconi. To Gus, he looked more Italian than Welsh, yet his accent was pure Cardiff. Leonard grabbed Gus's bag and flung it effortlessly across his muscular shoulder, leaving Gus feeling slightly wimpish. Apparently not one for a lot of chatter, Leonard headed towards Cambridge's Littlehey prison, stopping at a Little Chef en route for Gus to grab some breakfast. Gus was glad of the quiet to prepare for his interview with James Clegg.

On arrival at Littlehey, Gus felt the institution's inevitable claustrophobia closing in on him. It always unsettled him to think that the prison walls contained a concentration of evil that but for diligent policing and more than a handful of luck would otherwise roam freely in our cities. Prisons dedicated solely to the incarceration and rehabilitation of sex offenders, had, in Gus's opinion, a more malevolent feel to them. Littlehey was no exception. It had a chequered history having once been a boys' borstal until it became a prison and now it housed only category C sex offenders. Max Clifford was one of its more recent inmates. Mixed crime prisons were sparse and restrictive, but despite that, there was some hope. Here, Gus felt nothing but despair, and his hat went off to the wardens who worked here.

Prison Governor Madeline McCulloch was tall and slim with bobbed hair and an expressionless face that brooked no nonsense. Her office was devoid of any personality. Gus felt it was almost as if she'd left her own self at the door and was challenging visitors to find a single iota of character in the room. Probably not a bad ploy for the governor of a sex offenders' prison.

She shook Gus's hand and motioned for him to sit down. Without asking, she poured him a coffee. He inclined his head slightly and in response to her assumption that he'd have coffee, he walked over to the water cooler that stood in the corner of the room, pulled a plastic cup out and filled it with ice cold water, before returning to his seat. Smiling at Governor McCulloch, he rummaged in his trouser pocket till he found his painkillers, quickly popped two from their bubble pack and swallowed them. Sensing the underling annoyance that tightened her face and pulled a frown between her eyes, Gus looked at her quizzically. 'No biscuits?'

McCulloch inclined her head and folded her arms across her chest. Ignoring his comment, she nodded to the pills. 'Pill popping, inspector?'

Relishing the dance they had embarked on Gus smiled. 'Prescription medication, Governor McCulloch. No need to have me thrown in the cells just yet.'

She gave a sudden sharp bark of laughter and unfolded her arms. 'A policeman with a sense of humour? Few and far between in my experience. I know you want to speak to James Clegg, but what exactly can I do for you?'

Gus explained the situation, ending with a question. 'What can you tell me about Clegg? I mean how he is now? What sort of prisoner is he? Who are his friends? What's your gut reaction about him?'

McCulloch rested her elbows on the arms of her chair and steepled her fingers before her lips. She sighed. 'Well, one thing I do know about Clegg is that he'll be gutted to hear about his daughter, absolutely gutted. Throughout his time here, he has consistently adhered to the WP process regarding his mother and child. This news will devastate him.'

She paused as Gus sipped his coffee and frowned. 'Regarding friends? Well, the truth is, he has none. He's a loner. He complies with every request we make and participates in every initiative, but he adamantly refuses to consider rehabilitation. He maintains that his family is safer with him in prison. Anything else, inspector?'

'I'm interested in the knife attack four years ago that hospitalised him.'

Swivelling her chair slightly she pressed a key on her PC and tutted. 'Hm, in my opinion that was a bit strange. There had been no history of aggro between the two prisoners and the attack, by all accounts, was unprovoked. Gordon Redwood, otherwise known as Gogs, was a small-time thief who'd got done for cottaging and grooming underage boys. He'd been due out in a matter of months. He often played pool with James.' She popped specs on the end of her nose and studied her PC. 'He admitted it after we found the blood-covered shiv in his cell. He said, and I quote, *'Clegg dissed my wife'*. Apparently he called her, and again I quote, *'A fat whore who gives blow jobs to black bastards and Pakis down Leith Docks.'* Gogs' wife lives in Edinburgh.'

She leaned back and tapped the leg of her specs on her front teeth thoughtfully. 'That never really rang true with me, though. For all Clegg's paedophilic tendencies, he was an educated man and certainly no racist. I can't imagine him using that sort of vernacular.' She shrugged. 'On the other hand, he didn't deny it.'

Gus sipped his coffee, enjoying the caffeine hit from the smooth blend. 'So, if 'dissing' his wife was a fabricated motive, what do you think the real motive was?'

McCulloch leaned forward. 'That's just it. No one was snitching and Clegg refused to identify Redwood as his attacker. It was all very strange. We put Clegg in protective custody and moved him to another wing, but really, there was nothing else we could do. Redwood got a year added to his sentence.'

'Ok,' said Gus drawing the word out. 'So, what was James Clegg like as a prisoner?'

McCulloch smiled. 'Now, I can tell you *that* Detective Inspector McGuire. James is a model prisoner. Obedient, quiet and toes the line. Keeps himself to himself. He goes for therapy for his 'condition'.' She drew quotation marks round the last word with her fingers.

Gus snorted and mimicked her actions. 'By 'condition' I take it you mean his propensity to defile young boys?'

McCulloch sighed and nodded. 'Exactly. I think it torments him that he has these feelings. He's one of the few sex offenders I've come across who requests chemical castration on a regular basis.' She grimaced. 'The powers, influenced by his psychiatrist's report, have to date, refused this. Physically, he has deteriorated since first being incarcerated and I see no sign of that reversing.'

'My heart bleeds.'

'Well, I can see you're no bleeding heart liberal, Inspector. But these men are under my care and so,' she caught his eye and held his gaze, her expression firm, 'you will treat him with the utmost respect during your interview. He is being punished for his crimes and you will not seek to torment him in any way.'

Gus straightened in his chair and smiled lop-sidedly. 'Whilst, of course, I respect the motive behind your 'directive', I will remind you that I am interviewing him to gain intelligence on a series of child abductions *and* both sexual and physical abuse of the said children. His own daughter has also been abducted. I will use whatever means I have at my disposal to get the answers I need. He could be key to putting the rest of his little gang of merry men behind bars, where they should have been twelve years ago.' He stood, dreads bobbing round his head. 'I'll need to speak to Gogs Redwood too. Any idea of his current whereabouts?'

McCulloch stood and walked round her desk. 'Well, as it happens, you're in luck. Gogs Redwood reoffended and is currently serving an eight-year stretch at Her Majesty's pleasure.'

Head on one side, Gus held crossed fingers up to her. 'Please tell me he's in Littlehey.'

McCulloch threw back her head and laughed. 'He certainly is. I'll arrange for you to see him this afternoon. He's got a therapy session that can't be changed this morning.'

Gus rolled his eyes, but said nothing.

CHAPTER 64

Opening her eyes felt like the most difficult thing Molly had ever done. She'd wakened a few minutes previously with the sinking dread that the horrible man in the Scream mask had come back while she was sleeping and she didn't even know if it was night or day. She remembered him slitting the cable ties on her wrists and legs, fluttering his fingers in a cheerio gesture and saying, 'Can't wait to see what fun we'll have tomorrow, Molly, can you?'

For ages after the roll down door had clanged shut behind her tormentors, she'd been too scared to move from the chair. Her soaking jeans clung to her legs and an acrid urine smell assaulted her nostrils. Finally, the robotic voice had beamed eerily into the room, telling her to get off the chair and sit on the mattress. Legs stiff with cold and fear, she'd hobbled over and perched on the edge, away from the area where she'd weed when Scream man came in. Reaching behind her, she'd bundled up the sheet and scrubbed the damp mattress with it, before tossing it on the floor. Then, using her old trick with the blanket, she'd peeled her sodden jeans and pants down her legs and over her feet. Shuffling over to the barely aired radiator, she'd draped them over it.

The sudden sound of the doors opening had her running, stumbling as she went, back to the mattress. *He,* the one who pretended to be her dad, had come into the room carrying a plastic bag. He'd thrust the bag at her, handed her a bottle of water and two pills and told her to swallow them. Too scared to object Molly had put them into her mouth, one at a time and swallowed them. Maybe they were poison and she'd die. She didn't really care right then. All she wanted to do was see her mum, or if that wasn't possible, curl up into a ball and pretend this wasn't happening.

'Eat,' he'd said and left. She'd eaten an egg and cress sandwich from the bag and wrapped herself tightly in the duvet and blanket and that was the last she remembered.

Now, she listened to the quiet drip of water from the leak and strained to hear signs that she wasn't alone. There were none, so she slowly opened her eyes and without moving the rest of her body she scanned her peripheral vision. Winter sunlight shone through the windows casting shadows that she identified as belonging to the chair and table. She appeared to be alone so she stuck her skinny arms out from under the blankets and then when the cold air hit them, quickly pulled them back under the covers and shimmied herself to a seated position, keeping the blankets tight round her small frame.

For a long time, she sat motionless, her eyes vacant, then nature's call made her shift to the edge of the bed till her feet in their mucky socks dangled over the edge. She wriggled forward till her toes swung just above her boots and pushed herself off the bed, hooking her toes into them and shuffling over to the foul-smelling bucket that stood in the corner. She hoiked her blanket up, held on to it with one hand and positioned it round her thighs with the other, before squatting over the bucket. She'd nothing to wipe herself with so when she stood up a warm trickle dribbled down her leg. Feeling dirty for doing it, but with no option she used the corner of the blanket to dry herself.

Shuffling back to the mattress, Molly touched the area where she'd weed earlier. It was nearly dry, but it stank like the boys' toilets at school. She curled her nose up, bent over, yanked the carrier bag onto the mattress and plonked herself down before rummaging inside. He'd left her crisps, more Snickers bars, a Mars bar, a packet of Jaffa cakes and some cans of Pepsi. She ran her tongue over her teeth. They felt furry and the taste in her mouth made her feel sick. Maybe if she had something to eat she'd feel better. She took a packet of crisps, a can of Pepsi and the Jaffa cakes from the bag, and placed it at the top of her mattress before crossing her legs and snapping open the can. Her nose crinkled as the fizzy liquid tickled her nose.

With indifference she opened the crisps and shoved a few in her mouth, chewing slowly before swallowing them. Then, she stuffed a Jaffa cake in her mouth, washing down its gluggy sweetness with another sip of Pepsi. Her head throbbed from when he'd yanked her hair up from her head and a small scab had formed on her ear where he'd nipped it with the shears. Remembering her snipped hair, she lifted her fingers up and ran them through the uneven greasy mess that sat roughly over her tingling scalp. Her eyes narrowed and under her breath she said, 'Bastard, fucking bastard!' The unfamiliar words gave her strength, as she repeated them. 'Bastard, bloody, fucking Scream bastard!'

She punched the mattress once, then again and again and again until her breath came in rasping puffs. Molly knew what the Scream man did. She'd seen bits of it at Charlotte's house when she had a sleepover once. Charlotte's big brother had let them watch it. She'd been terrified, but she hadn't shown it, not in front of Malcolm. No way was she going to let him call her a baby. She frowned. It *had* been scary though, she remembered the music and the way Scream man just suddenly pounced. She shuddered. At least this Scream man hadn't killed her. She put her head to one side remembering his tool bag and thought, '*Not yet, anyway.*'

After she'd finished her unhealthy breakfast she felt a bit better. '*Probably the sugar rush,*' she thought, recalling her mother's words when she'd got a bit giddy after eating Smarties. She shuffled back off the bed and over to the radiator. Her jeans smelled bad, but they were nearly dry. With a few contortions she managed to pull them back on and immediately, despite their rich aroma, felt better. She slipped her feet into her boots and walked over to the huge window with her laces trailing behind her. The window was covered in a velvety sheet of ice, so Molly, standing on tiptoe, leaned up and breathed on it through her cupped hands till the ice began to melt. Then taking the edge of her blanket, she wiped at it till she could see through. It was snowing. A real blizzard so hard she could hardly see beyond the window. Her heart sank. No-one would be out there in that.

She sighed heavily and turned away tapping her foot impatiently on the concrete floor. That was when she remembered the slamming doors and cries she'd heard yesterday before Scream man came in and cut her hair. She was sure it had sounded like other kids. She tapped her foot again and then turned to her right and went over to the breeze-block wall and began to bang on it with the flats of her hands. She cocked her head and listened... Nothing.

So she banged and banged again and then opened her mouth and yelled as loudly as she could. 'Halloooooooooo!' Again nothing. The palms of her hands stung and her throat felt hoarse but still there was no response. Frustrated, she lifted her foot and kicked the metal pipes that ran from the radiator, up the wall and along the tall ceiling. A loud echoing crash made her jump as the metal reverberated. With a smile, she kicked and kicked them again and again and again, till her foot throbbed. Then, in frustration, she strode back to the mattress flung herself down and began to sob so loudly, that at first she didn't hear the distant metallic sound. When it finally penetrated her grief, she sat up, rubbed her eyes and looked round the vast space. Then, forgetting her blanket and her bruised foot, she ran back over to the pipes and kicked them again.

She waited hopping from foot to foot, her hands nervously pulling at a tuft of hair. There it was again, another clink of metal, someone else was there. She kicked her pipe again and waited for the clinking reply. There it was.

Grinning she kicked again and then putting her mouth near the pipe, she shouted. 'Halloo, who are you?'

The pipe clanked again, then with her ear to the pipe, Molly heard a very faint voice. 'Hallooooo!' Molly kicked the pipe, her heart beating excitedly. 'Hallo, I'm Molly who are you?' Then she heard the unmistakeable sound of the door along the corridor scraping open, followed by a bang and a scream and finally the sounds of the door scraping shut again.

Moments later the voice of the man who wasn't her dad came through the weird tannoy system. 'You little bitch! Try that again and they'll be punished, ok? No more shit from you, you little cunt. And don't forget I can see you.' And with that, the camera placed high on the wall, spun round with a creak. 'Get back on the bed, right now.'

Molly stared defiantly at the camera for a second and then, shoulders slumping, she walked back to the bed and sat down. She'd forgotten he could watch her and now he'd hurt the other kid. She wrapped her arms round her body, rocking back and forth, as hot tears ran down her cheeks. Why were they doing this to her? Why had they recorded her tied to the chair? Then it clicked. They were going to send that recording to her mum. Something halfway between a groan and a snort of relieved laughter gurgled in her chest. If they sent that recording to her mum, then she'd get the police to look for her. All Molly had to do was make sure that the next time Scream man came she had a clue to give her mum. Thinking back to her Jane Casey books, she realised what her protagonist Jess Tennant would do. She'd find a clue and then find a way to deliver the clue.

Pulling the blankets right over her head, Molly clenched and unclenched her fingers until she was exhausted. She would stay on the mattress for a while and then risk going back to the window. After all, he couldn't watch her all the time could he? She knew the window was her best chance.

She'd been sure when she'd looked out yesterday that she'd recognised the area. All she needed to do was work out where they were before Scream man came back.

CHAPTER 65
HMP Littlehey, Cambridge

Pleasantly surprised by the absence of the odour of male sweat and over-cooked meat and veg, Gus sat on an uncomfortable red, plastic chair in the interview room. A clean pine detergent smell lingered in the room, making Gus think it had been recently mopped. Maybe we should employ these cleaners at The Fort. He'd been impressed by Governor McCulloch's demeanour during their interview. She had a difficult job to do in impossible circumstances and he felt she did it well. The men in here, regardless of their crimes, were under her care and, as unpalatable as their crimes were, they were entitled to her protection.

The door opened to admit an emaciated male with a receding hairline, a stoop and a permanent tremor in his hands. His pallor had the unhealthy tinge of a man who saw too little sunshine. He shuffled over, hoiking up jeans that kept slipping down his skinny hips and sat down in the chair opposite Gus. His eyes flicked from Gus to the floor and back again with the occasional spin round the perimeter of the small room. The guard who'd accompanied him in backed out of the room saying, 'Just give us a knock when you're done.'

Keeping his gaze focussed on the man opposite, Gus nodded. He'd tried not to build a mental picture of Clegg, but even so he was shocked by how different he looked from his trial photos. He let the moments stretch until Clegg could stand the silence no more and shuffled briefly on his chair, before speaking in a rapid panicked rush 'What's happened, why're you here?'

Gus took his time before answering. He leaned across the table and in a low firm tone said, 'Look at me, James.' He waited till the other man lifted his gaze to meet his steady eyes. Almost immediately, they flicked away again. Gus clicked his fingers and the other man's gaze lifted again. 'You need to look at me, ok?'

Clegg nodded and with obvious effort kept his gaze on Gus. All the while his hands kneaded the fabric of his jeans in his lap.

'Your daughter has been abducted and an email video of the perpetrator slicing off her hair has been sent to your ex-wife.'

If it was possible, Clegg's face paled even more. 'No.' His trembling hands flew to his greasy hair and raked through it, his face contorted in pain. As his eyes began to flick round the room, Gus clicked his fingers again. 'Focus!'

The word was like a gunshot in the quiet room and Clegg, visibly jumped before his gaze returned Gus. Breathing heavily, he tried to speak but his words came out rough and muddled as if his throat was parched. Silently, Gus pushed a plastic cup of water towards him. 'Drink, then speak.'

With hands barely able to hold the cup he lifted the water to his dry lips and drank. Replacing it on the table, he began again. 'It was my mum, wasn't it? That's how they found them.'

His voice held desperation and Gus knew that this man would give him any information he had, if it helped to find his daughter. He nodded. Clegg moaned deep in his throat before straightening in his chair. 'What can I do?'

'Tell me about the day Gogs Redwood shanked you.'

Involuntarily, Clegg rubbed his side. He'd been stabbed repeatedly by a prison-made shiv and lost his spleen as a result. He'd be on medication for the rest of his life. He swallowed. 'Gogs never said so, but I *know* he was paid to do it. See we got on ok, me and Gogs.' His kneading hands took on a new fervour. 'They arranged it… *He* arranged it.' His voice lowered. 'The Matchmaker.'

'How could The Matchmaker have arranged it?'

Running his hands through his hair again, Clegg hesitated. Then, he took another faltering sip of water. 'He's got contacts everywhere.' He straightened in his chair again. 'He … no not just he, but we… the organisation had many contacts in high places. At least one of them was high up in the police force. I'm sure of it, but I've got no proof. That's how they escaped, The Matchmaker, The Provider and The Facilitator. None of us knew each other, but The Matchmaker.' He stopped his kneading action and tapped one finger on the table for emphasis. '*He* knew everyone. He was the lynchpin that kept everything running.'

Resuming his kneading motion, he continued. 'I'm certain he paid Gogs to do this to me, in the hope that my mum would break the witness protection,' he bowed his head and groaned, 'and the stupid bitch did.'

Gus gave him a moment to recover.

'You're sure there was no other reason for Gogs Redwood to attack you?'

Shaking his head slowly side to side, Clegg propped his forehead on the table and sobbed.

Despite his knowledge of the atrocities this man had committed Gus felt sorry for him. His anguish was clear. Gus leaned over and squeezed his arm until he stopped crying. 'You're going to go back to your cell now and you're going to write down every single thing you can remember about The Matchmaker or the others and the things you did. I need names, places, feelings, hunches, anything. Your daughter's life is at stake, ok?'

***

Gus's head was throbbing. He'd escaped to grab some lunch, giving the Governor time to organise his interview with Gogs Redwood. He'd already delayed his return train to Bradford by two hours and was determined to catch the later train and he'd had to push his meeting with Battacharya back. He desperately needed to get back, but not until he'd found out what Redwood had to say for himself.

Unlike Clegg, Redwood had the cocky stature of a recurring offender. He was likeable and probably popular among wardens and fellow prisoners alike.

'What's up?' His Scottish accent was undiminished by his years in an English prison. Taking the chair, turning it round and straddling it so his tattooed arms rested across its back, he studied Gus across the table. Gus, leaned back casually in the chair ignoring the twinge across his shoulder. He'd taken his strap off for this interview, determined to show no weakness. He grinned at the prisoner and flung a packet of twenty cigarettes across the table.

Gogs's eyes lit up. One colourful arm snaked out and snatched the cigs quickly, before Gus could reconsider.

'I need you to cast your mind back four years to the time someone contacted you and arranged a substantial payment in exchange for you jibbing James Clegg in the spleen.'

Proudly displaying a set of yellowed ferrety teeth, Gogs said, 'Don't know what you mean, inspector.'

Gus nodded. 'Ok, so when I tell my colleagues north of the border where the money in a certain bank account really came from, you'll still have no idea what I'm on about?'

Gog's eyes narrowed fractionally. 'You lost me, mate, sorry.'

Gus winked at him and touched the side of his nose with his finger. 'Oh, I get it. You're trying to keep quiet about the large payment that went into your account in 2012, am I right?'

Nail-bitten fingers rasped Gog's stubble as he considered his options. Gus raised an eyebrow and smiled. 'Police Scotland accessed your bank accounts. They've reported unusual spending by your wife.' Gus took a sip of the lukewarm coffee he'd brought in in a Styrofoam cup. 'The purchase of a new car... a Porsche, I believe. A large deposit on a house in Morningside *and* a holiday booked to Disneyland, Florida. You can explain it all away, can you?'

Gogs's face flushed. 'Stupid fucking bitch, I told her to lay low and not draw attention to herself. What the fuck's she thinking?'

Gus kept his smile hidden. He'd not had the chance to liaise with Police Scotland on the matter and he'd fabricated everything he'd just said in the hope that Gogs was stupid enough to take the bait. He leaned forward and made his final thrust. 'The thing is, I can arrange for a blind eye to be turned, if you come clean about this, ok?'

Gogs glanced round the room.

Smelling the scent of fear on him, Gus continued. 'If you don't co-operate, we'll drag your wife through the courts. Your kids'll go into foster care and well, with you being in the nick, it'll not be too hard for them to get a court order to take them away from her permanently now, would it?'

Gogs swallowed and scratched his groin in agitation. 'Fuck man, this is crap. Fucking crap.'

Gus nodded, arms splayed before him, his expression sympathetic. 'I know. It stinks doesn't it? But it doesn't have to be like that. Just tell me what you know about the bloke that paid you to jib Clegg and I'll make it all go away.'

Gogs rested his forehead on his arms and then, abruptly his head jerked up and he looked straight at Gus. 'Ok, ok. I found a note under my pillow one day telling me what I had to do and how much I'd get paid for doing it. If I was up for it, I had to drop my dinner on the floor that night and someone would contact me with more instructions.'

'How did you get paid, Gogs?'

'Fifty grand deposit and fifty on completion. I reckoned it was worth a year on my sentence.'

A hundred grand to the likes of Gogs Redwood must have felt like winning the lottery. No wonder he'd done it.

'Well, at that point I didn't know the target was going to be Cleggie. I didn't mind him really, even if he was a nonce, you know?'

Gus wondered what went through Gog's mind to allow him to label James Clegg a nonce, but to absolve himself of the same title. Perhaps it was best he didn't know. Feeling slightly nauseous with the whole business, he leaned forward and rested his elbows on the table. 'Hurry up, Gogs. I've limited time at my disposal.'

Gogs sighed. 'Well, I dropped my dinner that night, but nothing happened. I thought it was someone taking the piss. Then about two weeks later another note appeared under my pillow. This time it told me to get my wife to check our account. I phoned her the next day and when she checked there was fifty grand in our account. So I was committed.' He sucked air through his teeth. 'Anyway another few days passed and then I got another note under my pillow. My instructions were clear. Stab repeatedly, lower belly. Enough to get him into a proper hospital away from here, but not enough to kill him. Still didn't say who, though. It was like the fucking tooth fairy, you get me?'

'I only ever got 10p from the tooth fairy, Gogs, not fifty grand.'

Gogs snorted with laughter, phlegm rattling in the back of his throat. 'Me too. Till now. Anyway, the next night I got a shiv. The note just said the name and 'Tomorrow'.' He wrinkled his nose. 'So, I did it.'

'So who was your mystery tooth fairy?'

'You what?' Gogs looked startled.

'Who was leaving you the notes?'

He shrugged. 'Dunno. Could've been anybody. Another prisoner, a warden, anybody.'

Gus leaned in closer, his tone conversational. 'But who do *you* think it was?'

Gogs glanced away, nervous now. 'Reckon it must've been one of the guards. Who else could it have been? None of the prisoners could get the notes to me. No way.'

Gus nodded and stood up. 'We'll need access to your account Gogs, and you better be prepared to testify to this in court.'

Gogs looked alarmed. 'But, I thought you were going to pull strings... get me off?'

Rapping his knuckles on the door Gus turned. 'You testify in court and we'll see, ok?'

In the corridor outside Gus stretched. He wasn't looking forward to telling Governor McCulloch that she now had a major investigation of corruption amongst her guards to conduct.

CHAPTER 66
London

The Starbucks in King's Cross concourse was busy with commuters, tourists and the few homeless people who had, somehow, evaded the various police patrols that roamed the area to evict buskers, beggars and the like. Gus bagged himself one of the comfy seats in a corner near the window overlooking the concourse and sat with his cappuccino and pesto chicken panini.

He felt vaguely nauseous and put it down to a desperate need for carbs to counteract the fatigue of his early start and the intensity of the various interviews he'd conducted. He took a deep bite of the panini and savoured its rich flavour as he waited for his contact from witness protection, Angelica Battacharya, to turn up. He'd asked her to meet him here because he'd had managed to book a seat on the next train back to Bradford at 19:05.

He was early and when he finished his food, he slumped back in his chair, sipped his coffee and watched the world of King's Cross unfold before his eyes. The young couple, eyes bright, arms entwined tightly round each other's bodies taking a fond farewell, the dumpy woman in the red raincoat held together by virtue of its wraparound belt, her bosoms spilling over the top, as she nervously glanced at the huge clock near the meeting place. Her eyes darted back and forth between the passengers exiting the barrier. And the scruffy youth, headphones jammed in ears, shoulders slumped oblivious to his surroundings engrossed in the beat that pumped into his head.

Gus finally began to relax and had soon drifted into a light doze. The sound of someone clearing their throat in an exaggerated fashion above him startled him out of his reverie. Abruptly, aware of the slaver dribbling down his cheek, Gus jerked upright to grab the napkin off the table, only to be stabbed by a piercing pain in both his shoulder and thigh simultaneously, that caused him to yelp and fall back into his chair. The tall Indian woman in her thirties standing next to him frowned, and then, quickly plucked the napkin from the table and handed it to him, before pulling out the red leather chair opposite him and sitting down.

She waited till he'd wiped his cheek and slowly struggled into a more upright position before thrusting her hand out. 'Hi, I'm Angelica Battacharya and I sincerely hope you're DI Angus McGuire?' She tilted her head to one side and looked at Gus through shiny walnut-coloured eyes.

Gus returned her handshake with a frown. 'How the hell did you know who I was? Oh, and it's Gus, by the way. Can't stand Angus.'

Tapping the side of her long nose with one finger, she grinned. 'My powers of deduction know no bounds.' Then with an infectious grin she added, 'Actually, I googled you before I left the office.'

Gus inclined his head in a touché gesture and braced his hand on the table ready to make another attempt at standing. 'What'll you have to drink?'

Shaking her head, she stood up. 'After your previous attempt to stand up, I think it's better if I went. I'm gasping for a coffee. It's been a hectic day. What do you want?'

Relieved not to have to risk embarrassing himself again, Gus said, 'I'll have an americano and a bottle of water if you don't mind.' He struggled to get his wallet from his back pocket, but with a wave of her hand Angelica told him to put it away and she joined the mercifully short queue. As she waited in line, Gus tentatively swivelled his shoulder. Grimacing at the sharp pain that the manoeuvre elicited, he surreptitiously tried to massage his thigh back to life.

On her return Angelica deposited the tray with their drinks and two plates, each containing a double choc chip cookie. 'I need a sugar rush and I thought you might, too.' She said, gesturing to the cookies. Tilting her head to the side, her smile revealing a perfect set of even white teeth, she leaned forward and lowered her voice. 'You know, if I were you, I'd be a bit more discreet at massaging your thigh. From a distance it looks like you're, em, well, you know?' And she wiggled her perfectly plucked eyebrows salaciously,

Gus, who'd just lifted his coffee to his lips, jerked, spilling some of the hot liquid onto his saucer and released an explosive bark of laughter. 'Christ, does it?' And he glanced round nervously.

Opposite him Angelica chortled, her brown eyes sparling with laughter, 'Watch you! I'm only joking.'

Caught slightly off guard by the woman's openness he studied her for a second. A slight smile hovered on her lips and her eyes sparkled with amusement. She cocked her head to one side. 'Not what you expected, hmm? Didn't expect someone with a slightly bawdy sense of humour?' she pretended to cringe and then shrugged. 'Life's too short to be serious all the time and in my job you realise that pretty damn quick. It's my coping mechanism and you won't be the first person to be offended.'

Gus flung his head back and laughed. He liked this woman with her down-to-earth, no airs and graces approach. 'I was surprised, not offended, Ms Battacharya. It's refreshing to meet someone who's not up their own arse the entire time. You've certainly broken the ice, but unfortunately we need to get down to business as I've got a train to catch in forty minutes.'

Face serious now, she lifted her cookie and began to nibble before she spoke. Gus took the opportunity to pop his painkillers.

'My department is not responsible for the leak, Gus.'

Gus nodded. 'No, I don't think you are either, but we needed to cover all the bases.'

She quirked an eyebrow. 'The mother-in-law?'

Gus sipped his drink. 'Educated guess or evidence?'

She smiled. 'Deduction based on my extensive investigation since we were alerted to Molly's abduction.' She paused, placed her cup and cookie on the table, wiped her fingers on the napkin and began to count off the points on her fingers. 'One, she was notified of the attack on her son four years ago. Two, the idiot who notified her told her which hospital he'd been taken to. He was disciplined for that error of judgement, by the way. Three, mother's instinct: no matter that your son is one of the most reprehensible deviants around, he's still your son. How did I do?'

Gus, lips narrowed said 'Spot on. But you're sure there were no other possible leaks?'

Before he'd even finished the question, she shook her head. 'Absolutely not. Witness Protection is sacrosanct and access to information is confined to the agent in charge of that case. Documentation is coded with numerical references to each 'client'.'

'What about the police? What access do they have?'

Again, Angelica shook her head. 'None. Even if the highest ranking officer in the land puts in a request for information on particular clients, both they and their request are scrutinised thoroughly by an independent body and over ninety per cent of requests are denied.'

'What about officers involved in the original investigation?'

'Again, they have no information about the relocation programme. They will probably know that the client has been put under witness protection but as soon as their protection is activated all contact – and I mean *all* contact – with their previous life ceases.'

'But, Jessie Graham still sent and received letters from her son?'

Angelica's mouth hardened into a straight line. '*That* decision was against normal protocol and it was opposed at various levels of the process, but unfortunately both Jessie and the daughter-in-law, refused to go into protection if their wishes were not implemented. As such we took extreme precautions to preserve their new identities.' She shrugged. 'However one cannot plan for human frailty.'

'What were the precautions?'

Angelica opened her laptop and accessed a file. She smiled at Gus. 'After I open this file I have three minutes to tell you the contents before it will be deleted from my laptop, so don't interrupt, ok?'

Impressed, Gus nodded and Angelica pressed a button. 'The agreement was that there would be no actual visitation. Contact was limited to a monthly letter from her to him and vice versa. The rules were as follows. One, she typed her letter, omitted details of family life other than a single reassurance that 'his daughter was fine'. No references to weather, locations or activities considered to be of regional relevance, no photos. In short, nothing very much. Two, she put her letter in three separate envelopes. The first and second envelope had no address the final one had a PO box address which varied regularly. She was notified of changes to the address by phone call to her unregistered phone. When her letter arrived in the PO Box the initial envelope was incinerated. The letter was assessed by three separate agents to ensure she'd not inadvertently left any clues in the communication. Then another PO box address was put on the second envelope. The same procedures occurred on receipt of that and sometimes that PO box was in a foreign country. The third and final envelope had James Clegg's handwritten address added, written by a different person each time, and was posted from a different location each time.'

She glanced at Gus who gestured for her to continue. 'James Clegg's letters to his mother underwent a similar process in reverse and were often edited if he complained about treatment or anything emotive. In actuality, the records show that he refrained from complaining *and* was at great pains each time to tell his mother he was fine and sorry and, that at all costs, she must adhere to the WP protocols and to take care of his beautiful daughter.'

She snapped her laptop shut and looked at Gus 'No leaks from our end, apart from that stupid mistake of telling his mother which hospital he was in.'

Gus shrugged. 'That one mistake was enough, though.'

Angelica bowed her head. 'It seems like it. I hope you find that little girl, Gus, I really do!'

CHAPTER 67
HMP Littlehey, Cambridge

Governor McCulloch opened the top drawer of her desk, took out a framed photograph and gently traced her finger over each of the three faces. She'd learned long ago not to display any personal items in her office, not just so the prisoners didn't have a way into her inner psyche, but because her male contemporaries, in the main, seemed to view any 'feminine' affectations as a sign of weakness, and *weak* was one thing Madeline McCulloch was not.

Ruthlessly, she'd worked her way up the ranks from warder in a women's open prison in Stirling to one of the highest ranking prison officers in the UK. She had often demanded her family uproot themselves so she could go and do the trouble-shooting that had got her where she was today. She was fiercely protective of them, refusing to bring anything of them into her workplace. And just as ferociously she didn't take her work place home with her in the evenings. Her one concession was the photo she now held in her hand and kept zealously hidden in her locked drawer. It worked on the whole, but today had been a bugger.

She'd spent hours with her deputy in a locked room after DI Gus McGuire had dropped his bombshell and they'd narrowed it down to the possibility that one of her three most trusted and experienced wardens had taken a bribe that led to James Clegg being shanked and hospitalised. They'd contacted and interviewed two of the three but then had been unable to get a hold of Felix Broadfoot, the most senior of the trio. He'd been on holiday and should have reported for duty on Monday, but had failed to show. He wasn't at home and he hadn't answered his mobile.

McCulloch, had been forced to hand it all over to the prison authorities for a full internal investigation and now she nursed a sick feeling in her gut. She was almost sure that neither of the other two officers were involved and she hoped the investigation would prove that. However, her gut also told her that Felix Broadfoot was involved and now, not only had a little girl had been abducted, but he had aided and abetted child traffickers.

She sighed and rested her forehead on her hand for a second. When she'd narrowed it down to Felix she'd made some discreet enquires and had discovered that he put himself up for more than the normal amount of overtime. Then her deputy had revealed that there were rumours about a gambling problem and the breakdown of Broadfoot's marriage.

In the dim light of her desk lamp, she slipped her shoes off and wiggled her toes, before stretching her shoulders. Finally, with a sigh, she moved the mouse to activate her PC. She couldn't put it off any longer: she had to email DI McGuire with her findings. She picked up the lists that she had prepared for McGuire and sifted through them one last time before scanning them, ready to attach to her email. Pressing send she exhaled. Who the hell had put Felix up to delivering those notes to Gogs Redwood, and, worse still, that shiv? She shuddered at the thought of the resultant uproar if the media got access to this information. As if the prison service wasn't in enough disarray as it was.

CHAPTER 68
Bradford

The train journey had been long and the confined leg room made his thigh throb so much that when the journey finally ended he hobbled from the train, each step painful. For the last forty minutes of his journey, heavy sleet had been falling and as he alighted at Frizinghall Station, the platform was slick with a slight covering of snow. His feet nearly gave under him and he slipped jolting his shoulder painfully. Hesitantly, he limped down the stairs and barely managing to hobble over to the car without scrunching his face in pain. He was relieved beyond measure when he saw that he didn't need to squash himself into Alice's Mini for the second time on one day.

He'd barely opened the door when she spoke. 'You look rough.'

Gus edged his leg into the car and slowly eased his bottom onto the seat. Releasing a thankful sigh, he closed his eyes, pulled the seatbelt gingerly over his shoulder and clicked it in place. 'Not done my physio exercises since Monday and it's caught up on me now.' He glanced at her from the corner of his eye as she edged left on Manningham lane to head back to The Fort. 'I'll get up and go for a swim tomorrow morning.'

'Well, see that you do. We can't do with you being immobile,' she said in a motherly tone.

Gus smirked, turned to look out the window, and said, under his breath, 'Nag, nag, nag, that's all I get.'

'If your shoulder wasn't in that damn sling, I'd thump you for that, Detective Inspector McGuire.'

Gus grinned and turned towards her. 'Right, what's going on? Any word on Gogs Redwood's account?'

288

Alice shrugged. 'Don't know why all these fucking criminals are so smart, you know. Sadia's been on it and was getting the run around with the banks soooo...' she held her breath and kept her gaze firmly ahead. 'She went to her dad and got him to light a fire under their arses and we finally got some info.'

Gus released a slow breath and counted to ten before replying. 'What possessed her to go to Hussain for God's sake? Does Nancy know?'

Alice shook her head. 'Nancy was uncontactable, so she used her initiative... and got the results.'

Gus nodded. 'Yeah, yeah, you're right. What did she find out?'

'Well, not a lot, as you'd expect really. The deposit was made from the Royal Bank of Scotland to The Clydesdale Bank by a Robert C. Nesbit.'

'Aw, for fuck's sake! Talk about taking the piss. Rab C. Nesbit? Really?'

Alice nodded. 'It gets worse. Rab C's account was bogus. The funds had basically been sent round the block, to accounts under the names of every whimsical character the bastards could think of. The most the IT department could discover was that they'd originated in some dodgy account in the Canary Islands that has since been closed. So, basically a dead end.'

Gus tapped his knee in agitation. Alice glanced at him.

'Er, before we get back I probably should let you know that DCI Husain had a bit of a go at Sampson and Compo earlier. He's complained to Nancy.'

'And?'

'Well, apparently he caught them dancing with 'Bat out of Hell' blaring, in the incident room.'

Gus raised his eyebrows. 'Now, that I'd have loved to see.'

Alice grinned. 'Yeah, well Hannibal Hussain lived up to his name and nearly ate them alive. They'd had a bit of a techie breakthrough and our intrepid duo decided to celebrate with a bit of air guitar strumming to Meatloaf.'

Gus shook his head 'That bloke's got no sense of humour, fucking arse!'

'Yeah, but now we owe him for the bank stuff and so Nancy couldn't just tell him to butt out. Compo and Sampson are a bit worried you'll be pissed off with them.'

'As if,' said Gus, as they pulled into The Fort car park.

On entering The Fort Alice headed with her customary enthusiasm for the stairs whilst Gus, who'd only just managed the short walk from the car, headed for the lift, saying he'd meet her upstairs. By the time Alice had run up the three flights of stairs and burst into the investigation room, he was lying on the floor, his plastic physio band stretching from his thigh to the leg of his desk. With a pained grimace on his face, he executed a series of exercises. Alice grinned when she realised that the music blaring out from his PC speakers was Meatloaf.

Panting slightly, a sheen of sweat on his forehead, he said, 'Thought I'd welcome my rock star detectives back in style.'

Laughing, she headed over to put the coffee on. 'They'll be here soon. Mo's dropped off a delivery; fancy a samosa?'

At that minute the door opened and Sampson and Compo, both looking sheepish, entered. Ignoring their surprised expressions, Gus continued with his exercises. A big grin spread over their faces when they realised what music was playing. From the floor, Gus winked at them. 'Welcome back, boys. Heard you had a bit of a run in with Hannibal while I was away.'

Hearing Gus's teasing tone, Compo's shoulders relaxed. Then, his nostrils flared and he headed across the room like a sniffer dog. 'Samosas?'

The microwave pinged. 'These are for me and Gus. Get your own. That is, of course, if you can put your air guitars down for a minute.'

As Gus finished off his thigh exercises and began his shoulder ones, Compo and Sampson faffed about near the microwave. He was half-way through his second rotation and could already feel the tightness lessen when Sadia came in. Seeing Gus mid-stretch she hesitated, then, straightening her spine, she walked over and stood in front of him.

'Sir, earlier today I broke protocol, in the absence of both yourself and DCI Chalmers, by asking Hannibal Hussain to lend his weight to my request for information re the bank account in Scotland. I am sorry if this was the wrong thing to do, particularly in light of his arsy behaviour earlier with Compo and Sampson.'

Gus studied her for a minute, his face expressionless. 'Did you just in the space of two sentences call your *own* father and superior officer both *Hannibal* Hussain *and* an arse?'

Sadia's face reddened. 'I'm sorry, sir.'

Gus waved a hand in the air and winked at her. 'Welcome to the team Hussain... at last. Now, have a samosa and let's get down to business. It's late and we all need to sleep at some point tonight.'

The air smelled nicely of samosas and fresh coffee and despite the whirling snow that fell relentlessly outside Gus and his team felt warm and satisfied. Some things were coming together for them and that was good. Sampson pointed at the triangle he'd drawn on the map.

'Compo and I followed the CCTV footage of the Asda car backwards to the time it was stolen and although the driver was smart enough to avoid being captured directly on the cameras, I think he fits the description of Sid Smith, on all the wide indicators of build and colouring and stature. He's been busy as you can see. A lot of activity in the Ingleby Road, Cemetery Road areas and on up to Great Horton and along Thornton Road. He filled up at the self-service Asda petrol station where we found the car.'

In full swing now, Sampson's arm gestures became more pronounced, making Gus smile, happy that his protégé was in the zone. With a quick glance at Compo, whose face full of samosa, he nodded encouragingly for Sampson to continue.

'But, what we found interesting was that he's made a couple of forays to Ilkley and we've caught that car on CCTV heading into Dales Way Link three times in the past two weeks. On each occasion, he was caught exiting the road around fifteen minutes after he entered. The last time was on the morning of the shooting at Jamal Asif's brother's house.'

They all studied the footage for a few minutes more. Then, turning to Sampson, Gus said, 'Good work, John. Looks like our man took a drive-by to check out the location. Any chance of enhancing it further, Compo?'

Compo jerked his thumb at his computer that was purring away happily in the background. 'On it, boss, but I don't hold out a lot of hope. The footage is crap.' He moved from his slouched position to a more upright one, pulled his hat down more firmly on his head and sniffed. 'John's not finished yet.' He practically bounced up and down on his seat. 'Go on, John, tell him the rest.'

Face flushed to be on the receiving end of more attention, Sampson shuffled his feet and studied the floor for a second. When he raised his head a slight frown flitted across his forehead, before disappearing as he started to speak. 'Well, we ran the number plates for all the cars that didn't belong to any residents, or couldn't be identified by them, and two stood out.' He nodded to Compo who flicked a switch, making the interactive whiteboard split in two. On one side was a photo of a green Renault Cleo and on the other a blue Fiat. Both vehicles had been snapped turning into Dales Way Link. Using the laser pointer Sampson indicated the Renault

Cleo and Compo immediately focussed in on the driver's head. He was wearing a hat pulled well down over his forehead and a scarf bundled over his mouth.

'This vehicle was reported stolen from a Rhodesway, which is slap bang in the middle of the area the shooter was recorded in. This footage was taken at 10:10 on Tuesday and the car exited the road at 10:32.' Again Compo homed in on the front of the vehicle.'

Sadia gasped. 'There's clearly a passenger in the front.'

Compo zoomed in more. 'I'd say it looks like it's Molly. Those curls of hers are a bit of a giveaway.'

Leaning forward, eyes narrowed, Gus studied the still. 'Yes, looks like it, Compo. Have you two been able to get a current location on that vehicle?'

'Working on it, Boss.' Said Compo, grabbing the last samosa and taking a huge bite from it, sprinkling an avalanche of crumbs down his front.

Alice looked at the other vehicle. 'What's the story with the Fiat, John?'

Sampson grinned. 'Well, this was pure luck really. We popped the reg in the system and a curious incident report was flagged.' He nodded to Compo who obediently replaced the green Renault with footage of the blue fiat in a car park. Sampson pointed his magic dot at the car entering Dales Way Link. 'This was taken at 8:57 on Tuesday morning. The Fiat exited the road a mere seven minutes later. What's interesting is that on Tuesday evening this car was reported as being stolen from the Wetherspoon's in Keighley.'

He paused and looked round the room, his face alight with anticipation. 'And returned there, too, later on that same day.'

Sadia's mouth turned down. 'What do you mean?'

'Well, it actually wasn't reported as 'stolen' it was reported as being *moved*. The owner parks his car in the same spot every day, has his breakfast with his work mates and then gets in the works van to head off to their building site. He swears that when he returned, his car was in a different parking place. He insisted on looking at the Weatherspoon's cameras and sure enough his car was hotwired not long after he left in the works transit and returned later. Bit of a coincidence, huh?'

He nodded towards Compo again, who brought up another image. 'This is the man doing the hotwiring,' said Sampson.

Alice frowned. 'You know, I'm not sure those two are the same bloke. The Renault driver seems shorter and burlier than the second. The second one looks more toned and possibly taller. Maybe the first one's an accomplice. Maybe we've got eyes on another member of the team.'

A buzz of excitement went round the room. Gus stood up and executed a left-handed high five with his two officers. 'Great work lads, great work. Now, can you get the two images cleaned up for us, Compo, and get one of the experts in the tech team to have a look see what they can come up with. Sadia, get forensics to check out the blue Fiat and see if you can get someone in the Wetherspoon's to give us a better description of this man.'

Sadia, arms folded, looked thoughtful.

'What's up, Sadia?' asked Gus.

'I agree we can't ignore it, but I don't get why he'd drive to Beth's two hours before Molly's abduction. Seems a bit risky to me.'

'Maybe it's a false lead. Maybe it is just a coincidence, but we need to follow it through. In my experience coincidences don't happen very often for no reason.'

Gus smiled at her and then addressed the rest of the room. 'Anything else?'

'I've got a message that Jamal's friend wants to come in. His mum says he's got some information for us, so I've arranged for them to come in tomorrow morning. I've also got them doing another run round the Heaton area to see if we can get any more info about either the kids or the Asif murder. Got Customs running through their records for around the time the kids were abducted. See if we can get some leads from them.'

'Right, if that's all, we'll meet back here 8am tomorrow, ok?'

CHAPTER 69
Bradford
Friday

Gus slipped into the pool, savouring the warm sensation of water sliding over his shoulders as he dipped beneath the surface before starting a slow crawl to the other end of the pool. He was used to the surreptitious glances of the other swimmers as he walked from the changing rooms into the pool. Their curious eyes were drawn to the knotted angry scarring that cabled in jagged lines across the front and back of his shoulder and along the top of his left thigh, but as soon as he was in the water, he forgot about them and concentrated on stretching his healing muscles. Two lengths of front crawl were all he could manage at a time. Then, he swapped to breast stroke, which stretched the muscles but didn't cause as much discomfort. He continued at a steady pace, feeling the residual tension brought about by his previous night's tortured dreams drain away as he cleaved through the water.

Half an hour later, showered and dressed, he paused by the water fountain to fill his bottle and slugged back his pain relief before heading back to his car. Frosty patterns decorated his windscreen and he knew he'd have to scrape it for the second time that morning. Cursing, he pulled on some gloves and did a half-hearted scrape using his left hand, before deciding to huddle in the car with the heater full blast until the ice had melted enough to sweep away with his wipers. Getting behind the wheel, he flexed his shoulders and thigh muscles before turning the ignition on and felt slightly more heartened when 'Uptown Funk' blasted from the Capital FM followed by Herskey and JoJo's irreverent humour. Finally, windscreen clear, he tentatively manoeuvred out of the car space.

Today was the first time he'd driven himself since his injures and judging by the pain every time he pushed the clutch in and wrenched the wheel with his right arm, he wasn't ready for it yet. He'd have to give it a miss for now, he decided as he drove away from the University Pool at the bottom of Great Horton Road and, with a fresh burst of pain, veered onto Shearbridge Road. Driving up Legrams Lane, he noticed a new Polish shop had opened which prompted him to wonder if Jankowski had got any new leads for him. He hoped, too, Madeline McCulloch would have something for him from Littlehey; and maybe some of Compo's computer programmes would have come up with the goods. He indicated right onto Ingleby Road, groaning as his left shoulder burned, and wishing he'd asked someone to drive him or booked a taxi.

By the time he edged his way through the gates and parked next to Alice's mini in the reserved parking he knew that all the benefits from his early morning swim had been eradicated by the drive back to work. Resigned to another day of pain, he edged his way out of his car and took the lift up to the incident room. He'd no sooner got in when his phone rang. Shrugging out of his jacket and looping his bag over his chair he sat down at his desk, booted up his PC and answered his call.

'You got something juicy for me, Jankowski?' He listened for five minutes and when he hung up he was grinning. He glanced round the room and saw that everyone was there. Compo, as usual, was behind his PC with his mouth full of sausage roll, judging by the flakes of pastry down the front of his smiley face T-shirt. Alice was flicking through the faxes that had arrived last night and Sampson was going over the CCTV reports with Sadia.

Gus filled his mug with coffee and raised his voice. 'Listen up! Jankowski's come up with something. Going back over the reports from the Polish abductions, Jankowski noticed no less than six references to a large truck bearing the logo 'Cosy Nights' on the side. He then cross-matched this with the 2003 abductions and discovered that there were references to a similar truck then too. So, he got on to Customs to verify. Turns out they have references to this truck entering and leaving through Calais on corresponding dates. The thing is,' Gus paused and looked round the room at the expectant faces, 'there's no such business registered in the UK or in Poland or in any other country it drives through between the UK and Poland. Looks like we might have got a lead. Let's get our Customs on to it. Sampson you get on to CCTV. See if we can spot this van heading up north from Dover or from any of the other ferry ports.'

As Sampson took a note in his book, Gus continued. 'Also, when Jankowski looked at the repatriated kids' files, he discovered that there were another two boys reported missing at around the same time. He's sending us the details. Looks like we may still have at least two other children to find, as well as Molly.'

Alice moved to the front of the room and turned to face the other detectives. 'Just gone through the faxes sent by Governor McCulloch. She's tentatively identified the warden she thinks facilitated Gogs Redwood's attack on James Clegg. A Felix Broadfoot. An internal investigation is ongoing and she'll keep us updated. Apparently, Broadfoot was due back to work after a holiday but hasn't turned up yet.'

'Get a warrant for Felix Broadfoot's bank accounts. See what that throws up. Ask McCulloch if she's already got them. I think she'll share if she does.'

Alice turned to Gus, her face flushed. 'But, another bit of interesting news, which may or may not mean anything, is that one of the officers that investigated the attack on James Clegg was…' she turned to her colleagues, 'Any guesses?'

As they all shook their heads, she smiled and announced, 'DCI Wentworth.'

Gus raised his eyebrows. 'Well, well, well, that's interesting, Al. Doesn't prove anything, but it is a bit of a coincidence, isn't it? He was involved in the initial investigation and everyone concerned seems to think there was some sort of leak from above.' He walked over and refilled his coffee cup. 'Put in a request, via Nancy, for Wentworth to come and assist. Now we know there's a link to Cambridge, it's perfectly natural to request his assistance. And if he's here under our noses we can keep a bit of an eye on him.'

Alice frowned and pulled herself up onto a desk. 'You know, he was a bit weird when we had Jamal in for interview. I was taking him and Jankowski to the interview suite when Jamal and his brother were in the corridor and Wentworth really abruptly turned and headed back the way we'd come, saying he'd left his phone in the meeting room. Thing was, I know he hadn't because as the doors swung shut behind him, I saw him speaking on his phone.'

'Right,' said Gus, 'we won't jump to conclusions, but we *will* investigate this. Compo, get what you can on Wentworth. Now anything else?'

Alice raised a hand. 'Mrs Robb, the mother of Jamal's friend, Frankie, has phoned in again. She says she's on her way in with her son because he's got something to add to his statement.'

Gus quirked his head to one side. 'You'll deal with that, Al?'

She nodded.

Gus flicked through the report that Governor McCulloch had sent, absentmindedly sipping his coffee as he did so. Alice's phone rang and after a quick glance at caller ID she answered it. She turned to Gus. 'That's the FLO from the Graves' house. Jessie Graham went out for her usual morning walk in the woods at the back of their house and she's not back yet.'

'Is that unusual?'

Alice nodded. 'Janine says so. Says she's usually gone no more than an hour but it's been three hours now and Beth's worried.'

Sadia raised an eyebrow. 'Even after yesterday's temper tantrum?' When she'd heard about the incident the previous day, Sadia had voiced her lack of sympathy for either party

Gus shook his head slowly from side to side. 'You really do need to work on your compassionate side, Sadia. Course she's concerned about her. She's the closest thing to a mother Beth's got and though she flipped yesterday I'm sure she's worried about her now.'

He turned back to Alice. 'Tell them to get one of the local PCs to have a look for Jessie in the woods and I'll head over to Ilkley with Sadia in a bit. Should touch base with them anyway. I want to show Beth the photos of Gogs Redwood and the prison warden Felix Broadfoot to see if she ever came across either of them.'

He turned to Compo. 'Anything from the video email?'

Compo laid down his bacon butty, sucked ketchup from his fingers and pressed a few keys. 'This is the best I can get it. I'll put it on the whiteboard so we can all see.'

They sat down and watched the screen. 'Don't forget we're looking for clues to where this building is. What sort of building it is, anything at all that gives us a clue, ok?'

Compo slowed the footage right down so they could focus scene by scene. 'The beginning bit of the video, with whoever's doing the filming being all over the place, shows us the ceiling. I think it's a warehouse with that sort of high ceiling and breeze-block walls.'

Alice pointed. 'Look, the walls are all stained brown as if the pipes have leaked and the paint's flaking. I reckon it's old warehouses.'

'Could be a mill,' said Sampson, 'there are a lot of them in Bradford and some of them are disused.'

'Get warehouses and mills checked out, say, within a ten-mile radius of that area you pinpointed yesterday, for starters,' said Gus, 'but hold on a second to see if we can get any other clues from the footage.'

'The next bit was very focussed on Molly and the bloke in the Scream mask. I've tried to focus in on him where I can, but I've not found much as the overall covers his clothes. He's wearing gloves, so we can't even be one hundred per cent sure of his race. He's pretty average build. There's a flash of a necklace. Gold, I think, but that's the best image I can get.' They focussed on the slight flash of gold that protruded under the mask. He's wearing a watch. You can see its shape under the gloves but no chance of IDing the make or owt. And of course his voice is distorted, although I've sent it to the voice people to see if they can clean it up or hear any other identifiable background sounds.'

Compo fast forwarded the recording till just after the Scream man cut Molly's hair. 'When he starts to dance around, after the hair thing, whoever's recording moves with him and focusses in so we get quite a good view of this.' He pressed a button and an enlarged image of a huge window with the Scream man framed in front of it flicked onto the screen.

'It's iced over, so it must be freezing in there, but someone's obviously cleared a bit of the ice off because you can just about see out the window. Looks like it's quite high up, but when you focus into the distance you can see this. It's some sort of structure in the distance, but it's too hazy to be clear what it is. But, what's also interesting is what you *can't* see. There doesn't appear to be any houses or buildings in the foreground. Any idea what it is?'

Compo moved the frame in and out for them, but nobody could identify it.

'Never mind, when we get a list of possible buildings it might help narrow down the list a bit.' Gus slapped Compo on the back and continued. 'Listen up. Watch that film again and again, when you've got a spare minute, ok? You might be lucky and just catch something. Compo send it to the Polish officers. Edit it so it only shows the images of the room and ask them to see if any of the children can identify the room or give us any more information on it. Some of them won't be able to do this, but try. At this stage anything's worth a shot we need to find out where they are. They may have been held there at some point.'

Gus's phone rang at the same time as Alice's. They exchanged a glance and answered. Then, with a quick look at Sadia, Gus grabbed his jacket and his bag from his chair and headed for the door. 'Come on, Hussain, you're driving. They've just found Jessie Graham.'

CHAPTER 70
The Fort

Alice walked into Interview Room Six, the one they used for interviewing children. It was bland but lacked the residual sweaty odour that hung like dirty laundry in the other rooms. A sofa and two padded, supposedly comfy armchairs surrounded a small coffee table and replaced the hard wood tables and functional plastic of the other rooms. In one corner was a cupboard containing anatomically correct dolls, toys and leaflets concerning children's welfare.

Alice smiled and extended her hand to the tense mother whose unrealistically long bleached hair that fell to her waist in perfect crinkled curls. She perched on the very edge of the sofa, looking as if she was ready to set off at a run if a sudden noise disturbed her. Alice turned to the gangly youth, wearing jeans and a hoodie, who slumped beside his mother. 'Hi Frankie, good to see you again. Your mum says you've got something you want to add to your statement.'

Frankie grunted and glared at his mother from the depths of his hood. His mother nudged him, smiling apologetically at Alice. 'Tell her, Frankie. It could be important.' She turned her head to Alice and shrugged. 'I never liked that Jamal, you know. Not ever and his mum was nowt but a whore.'

Frankie rolled his eyes. 'It's not Jamal's fault his mum's a whore.'

'Don't you use that word, Frankie Robb.'

Alice heard Frankie mumble something that to her ears sounded very much like 'Well you just did.' And, she had to admit, the lad had a point.

In an attempt to defuse the building tension, Alice cleared her throat and caught the boy's gaze as she placed a small recorder on the coffee table before them. 'I'm going to record this, so I don't have to take notes while you're speaking.' She introduced the people in the room and gave the date and time before leaning back, legs crossed. 'Go on then. When you're ready, ok?'

Frankie glared at his mum. 'It's not important, you know.' His face was screwed up in the insolent look of a teenager, both embarrassed and slightly afraid. Alice had seen the look before and sympathised. It wasn't easy speaking to the police and it was always worse in the presence of a parent.

Finally, Frankie sighed and leaned towards the recorder. 'Jamal told me he did it.' He leaned back and gazed round the room, as if he'd said all he was going to say.

Alice waited until she was sure he wasn't going to expand on his statement. She glanced at Mrs Robb, who was nodding her head vigorously in an 'I told you so' manner. Alice cleared her throat again and tried to catch Frankie's eye. 'What exactly did Jamal say he did?'

The boy breathed out an exaggerated nicotine breath and rolled his eyes again.

Alice wanted to give him a shake and tell him to get on with it, but instead she pasted on a smile and said in a reasonable tone. 'I know this is all a bit of a hassle for you, but you need to expand on what you just said. What did Jamal say he did?'

With an exaggerated sigh Frankie rested his elbows on his knees and stared right at Alice. 'He said, 'I battered the old bitch to death in the graveyard', that's what he said. He said he fuckin' battered the old cunt to death in Heaton graveyard.'

'Frankie,' said his mum before Alice had a chance to continue, 'don't you dare use that language.' She smiled apologetically at Alice.

Frankie scowled. 'She asked me what he said and I told her. Now you're telling me off for swearing.' He huffed a huge sigh and flopped back on his chair.

Before Mrs Robb spoke again, Alice placed a hand on her arm and shook her head slightly, before speaking to Frankie. 'When did he tell you this?'

Frankie sniffed a phlegmy snort and grinned at her. His mother prodded him with one perfectly manicured finger. 'Stop that! How many times have I told you that's disgusting? Just stop it.'

Frankie sneered at his mother and repeated the phlegmy snort before turning back to Alice. 'That night. The same night he did it. He came straight to my house, he'd swiped a bottle of vodka from One Stop and he told me. Then we got pissed, ok?' He stood up and stepped towards the door.

Alice moved between him and the door. 'Sit back down Frankie, I'm afraid I've not finished with you yet.'

Hands thrust deep in his pockets, he turned and flung himself back onto the sofa with such force it moved back a foot, making his mother screech as she nearly toppled from her perch on the edge of the seat. 'Little bastard,' she said, glaring at him.

Frankie grinned and with a half-sneer curving his lip looked up at Alice. 'Come on then, get on with it. I don't have all day.'

Alice stared right back at him and then in a stern voice said, 'You've got as long as I need, ok? Unless, of course, you want me to detain you for perverting the course of justice? Which, so you're clear, *would* mean throwing you in a cell.'

'Fuck's sake! Talk about the fucking Nazis.'

Alice sat down. 'Just answer my questions and you'll be done quicker.'

He nodded.

'Right, I'll ask again. When exactly did Jamal tell you he'd 'battered his mother'?'

'That night. I've already told you.'

Alice smiled sweetly. 'When exactly did he tell you? Was it as soon as you answered the door, or after you'd drunk the vodka?'

'I opened the door, and he was pumped, bouncing up and down on the doorstep. So, I asked him what was up and he said, '*I've done it. I've fucking done it, battered the old cunt over the head with a stone in the graveyard and she's dead.*' Then he pulls the vodka from his pocket, opens it, takes a swig and says '*Come on mate, we're celebrating.*''

'Had he been drinking before he knocked on your door?'

Frankie thought for a second then nodded. 'Yeah, the bottle was only half full and he was slurring his words an' all.'

CHAPTER 71
Ilkley

The ancient pool car had only just begun to warm up as Sadia pulled into Dales Link Way and even from this distance, Gus could see that the news vultures had descended on their carrion. White vans were abandoned at intervals half-off the road, their tyres sunk centimetres deep into the snow, evidencing the length of time they'd been stationed there. The layers of snow on the un-gritted path had been smoothed to ice rink standard by the unprecedented flow of traffic.

Sadia slowed and looked questioningly at Gus. He gestured for her to pull over to the side. As she slowed, he felt his phone vibrate against his leg. Frowning, he retrieved it and glanced at the number. Shit! Dr Mahmood. A quick glance at his watch told him he was late for his appointment with her. Taking a deep breath, he answered with a gruff 'Hallo.'

'You do realise that you're now forty-five minutes late for your appointment?' She spoke without preamble and her arctic tone made him flinch. He imagined her standing by her desk tapping an impatient finger on her phone.

Injecting as much regret into his voice as possible, he turned away from Sadia and addressed Dr Mahmood. 'Look, I'm really sorry, but something came up and I forgot to cancel.'

Her voice came back at him with all the force of a slapped face. 'I thought I made it clear. Cancellations are not an option. Be here at 6pm or I *will* revoke your fitness to work status.'

Gus began to reply but was met with the distinctive sound of the call being terminated.

Sadia glanced at him. 'You ok?'

Lips set in a grim line, he nodded abruptly and set his phone alarm for 5:15. 'Just the bloody mind police on the warpath.' He punched in the Graves' number and requested immediate access before indicating to Sadia that they should drive on. As they approached the drive, the car was immediately besieged by a flurry of yelping reporters leaning in to take photos.

Sadia, cursing under her breath, tried to maintain her speed but it was impossible with pack of determined bloodhounds, baying around the car. Then, as the gate began to open in front of her she accelerated loudly and, with a greater speed than Gus would have risked with the journos in front, moved forwards. Two PCs walked out to push the reporters back, allowing the first gates to close behind them before the second set gave them access.

Instead of entering the house, they were directed round the side and followed the constable who guided them towards the large gate at the back that led into the woods.

'SOCOs are already there, sir. Just walk straight ahead a couple of hundred yards and you'll see the cordon.'

Gus nodded his thanks and, wishing he'd brought a heavier coat, pulled his collar up to his ears and braced the blizzard that swirled around them. Before he reached the scene, he heard his father's Scottish brogue reverberate through the trees and groaned. He'd hoped to avoid his father's parental concern since he'd moved back into his own home, but now he had no choice. He knew his dad would make a complete mental inventory of Gus's appearance to report back to his mum and would, undoubtedly, also comment loudly on anything that popped into his mind. Gus could only hope that he'd refrain from embarrassing him completely.

Signing into the scene, they suited up. Gus, feeling like an abominable snowman in light of the frigid conditions and driving snow, walked over the markers left by the SOCOs.

Within a few seconds they found themselves in a clearing where a white tent had been erected. He opened the front flap and poked his head through. 'Alright to come in?'

His father's huge frame turned towards him and his voice rumbled like thunder. 'Well hallo, Gus laddie. Nice to see you. Wish the circumstances were better though. Such a shame, such a shame.'

The head SOCO waved them into the tent and, after donning their forensic suits, Gus moved over to his father. Down on one knee, his arm resting on the other, Dr McGuire looked like a huge, artistically positioned yeti. Clad from head to toe in a forensic suit, with his head tilted towards the body, he was completely white. It was only when he turned back to Gus that his spherical, ruddy face broke that illusion. 'Couldn't have happened very long ago. Gunshot wound to the side of the head, blood spatter in the snow and,' he pointed to the other side of the tent, 'indents in the snow indicating someone walked off that way. Unfortunately, the snow's filled most of the prints, so not sure how much use they'll be.' He turned back to Jessie Graham. 'I'd say death was instantaneous.'

Gus, hands thrust deep in his pockets, looked down at Jessie, feeling sad that she'd been caught up in this and hoping she'd had the chance to make up with her daughter-in-law before she died. He stepped onto a tread that took him nearer to the snow-filled footsteps. One of the SOCOs knelt before the footmarks with a little brush in her hand. She glanced up as Gus approached. 'We might be lucky here. There *might* be a print in the ice under the fresh snow.'

Thrusting his good hand in his pocket and trying to ignore the insidious cold that penetrated the flimsy nitrile glove he'd managed to pull over his bad hand he inclined his head in acknowledgement. Another SOCO approached, holding a plastic bag containing a single sheet of paper. 'This was thrown on top of the body.'

Gus took the bag and read the words on the paper. Again they looked to be written in a child's hand. 'You've got email!' read Gus. Eyes narrowed, he handed the bag to Sadia. 'The bastard's playing with us.'

He thanked the SOCO, laid a hand on his dad's arm. 'Text me when you have the PM time and I'll be there.'

Gus began to retrace his steps when his dad spoke. Unfortunately, despite his obvious attempts to whisper, his voice seemed to reverberate around the small forensic tent. 'Are you ok, Angus? I mean...' Doctor McGuire struggled to a standing position and shuffled his feet. 'I mean with all this Gabriella stuff.'

Gus saw Sadia's curious look and felt his face redden. The last thing he needed was a public dissection of his wife's sexuality. When he replied his voice sounded strained, even to his ears. 'Not here, Dad.'

His dad reached out and placed a hand on Gus's arm. 'It's just your mum,' he shrugged his huge shoulders, looking like a sad Pierrot marionette, 'She worries. That's all.' His voice lowered, 'and so do I.'

His father's despondent figure pulled at Gus's heartstrings and his shoulders relaxed. Of course they were worried. They loved both him and his sister and this thing with Gabriella must be really awkward for them. He patted his father's arm and grinned. 'Honestly, Dad, I'm fine. Gabriella and I weren't getting along anyway. But, I'm not going to pretend that Katie's betrayal doesn't hurt, because it does. I just need some time. Tell Mum that. Oh and tell her thanks for the biscuits she dropped off. Compo devoured them.'

Seeing the relief flood his dad's face, Gus turned with a wave and indicated that Sadia should follow him. Together they headed back to the house. 'Looks like we've got another video to watch.'

CHAPTER 72
Ilkley

Even after only a few days, Gus could see the effects of the strain on Beth. Her cheekbones jutted like razors over deep hollows and tension furrows were etched under each eye. The skin of her forehead stretched paper thin and translucent, like an icy Norwegian fjord, but still she sat erect, expectant almost, in front of the table, her hands clasped tightly before her, with her husband's arm stretched stiffly across her shoulders. In the tense atmosphere, the kitchen clock continued its bizarrely cheery tick tock, accompanied by the low hum from the fridge.

Beth's eyes bore into Gus's. 'She's dead isn't she?'

Gus held her gaze and nodded briefly. 'Yes. Gunshot wound to the head.'

Beth bit her lip and nodded slowly. She sniffed once and abruptly wiped away a single tear. Gus waited, conscious of her grief and reluctant to cause her any more distress. He knew he'd have to question her, but five minutes would make little difference.

An angry frown settled on the bridge of her nose. 'This is all about revenge, isn't it? Revenge for breaking up their sordid paedophile ring. They've waited twelve years and now they want to take everything away from me, just like I took their disgusting money-making perverted business away from them. First Molly and now Jessie. Who's going to be next? Alex or even my baby?'

Gus placed his hand on her arm and squeezed slightly. Immediately, Beth jerked away and jumped to her feet. Dragging her fingers through her dank hair, she glared at him. 'Why are you here? You need to get out and find those bastards. Go on, get out. You need to find them before they hurt Molly.'

Alex jumped to his feet and tried embrace his wife but she pulled away, continuing to glare at Gus. Janine, the Family Liaison Officer, bustled over a mug of tea in one hand. 'Here, Beth sweetheart, take this.'

Beth, a look of sheer desperation on her face, glared first at Janine and then at the proffered mug. Without warning she snatched the mug from Janine and in one smooth swivel, she spun round and threw the mug at the far wall. It smashed sending porcelain shards flying through the air. A brown splodge of tea circled the wall like a piece of abstract art, before beginning its meandering trickle to the skirting board below.

No one spoke. Alex looked helplessly at the wall and Janine, never breaking stride walked over to get a cloth from the sink. Sadia, Gus noted, followed her and the pair began to clean up whilst Beth stood statue-still, staring expressionlessly at the mess she'd made.

Gus remained seated, but gestured to a chair. 'Sit down, Beth. We're doing everything we can, but we do need to talk to you.'

She hesitated and then slowly, robotically, pulled out her chair and sat back down.

Meeting her eyes, Gus said, 'Did you get the chance to make up with Jessie before this morning?'

Beth's eyes narrowed. She scraped her chair back from the table slightly and extended her arms in front of her, crossed at the wrists as if she expected to be handcuffed. 'What! So you think I did it, do you? You really think I'd take a gun and shoot Jessie, the one person that's stayed by my side all this time?'

Gus shook his head. 'That's *not* what I meant Beth. I know you didn't kill Jessie. I just hoped you'd had a chance to make up before her death. Did you?'

Beth's arms sank back to the table and her head fell forward as if its weight was too heavy for her fragile neck.

'Yes. Yes we did. We spoke last night, or rather early this morning. She would never deliberately have put Molly in danger and I know it. I'll never forgive myself for hitting her.'

'Your daughter is in danger, just as her son was when she went to him. You both acted like the protective mothers you are. Jessie knew that. She knew she'd put Molly in danger and she understood your anger.'

'Doesn't excuse my actions though, does it?'

'No, but at least you got the chance to make up and that's important. Now, Beth there's something I have to show you.' He took out the plastic bag containing the note found at the scene. 'Is this Molly's writing?'

Beth read the note and blanched. She nodded. 'Yes that looks like Molly's writing. Have you looked at this email yet?'

Gus shook his head and gestured towards the laptop that sat on the table. 'My experts have. As you know all activity on your laptops and phones is being monitored. They're enhancing it as we speak, but I've not seen it. I want you to be aware that it does show Jessie being shot, but I need you to watch it to see if you can add anything. Do you think you can do that, Beth?'

She picked up a glass of water, took a sip and then reached out and squeezed her husband's hand. She nodded. 'Let's just get on with it.'

Gus nodded to Sadia, who left the room returning seconds later with the on-duty tech officer. He drew the laptop towards him and quickly pulled up Beth's emails. There it was, under the subject heading. 'You've got new mail.'

He clicked on the attached video. Jessie, wrapped up in a red winter coat with the hood up, strolled through the woods behind the house. From the looks of it she was heading back home. The person videoing seemed to have come through the woods from behind her and was stepping in her

313

footprints. The footage was blurry because of the blizzard, but it was clear Jessie had no idea she was being followed at first.

Then, something flew through the air and hit her squarely between the shoulder blades. It was a snowball. Jessie spun round and peered through the blizzard, back towards the trees she'd just passed. Then, as if she couldn't see anyone, she turned back to continue her walk, but another snowball flew through the air, catching her this time on the side of her face. She turned round and started to speak 'What do you…?'

Her voice tailed off and she raised a gloved hand to her mouth and began to back off towards the house. 'Go away, go away, there are police just over the fence, you know?'

A guttural laugh that Gus recognised from the previous tape drifted through the speakers and then there he was, moving ahead of the camera, in a black coat. He turned his head back to the camera showing the Scream mask that covered his face then turned back towards Jessie. Slowly he advanced, forcing her backwards until she stumbled against a tree. Then from the pocket of his coat he pulled out a gun. With one gloved hand he grabbed Jessie's neck and spun her away from the tree. She tripped, but he yanked her back up and turned her so her back was to the camera. 'Zoom!' he said.

And then he placed the barrel on the side of her head. Jessie looked up at him for terrified seconds, her hands scratching uselessly against his. Then a sudden bang and a shower of red joined the white blizzard. He let her fall to the snowy ground and stood directly in front of the camera. 'Second blood! Be warned! My unquiet soul is still not satiated. Who'll be next, bitch?'

For stunned seconds everyone just looked at the blank screen, then Gus spoke. 'We'll get this enhanced, Beth, but do you have any idea who the man in the Scream mask is?'

Wrapping her arms round her shivering body as if for warmth, Beth turned stunned eyes on Gus and shook her head.

Gus persisted. 'Look at his height, his build, the way he moves. Does any of it look familiar?'

He gestured to the tech to replay the recording, instructing him to stop before the actual gunshot. 'You too, Alex. Study this carefully. Does it ring any bells?'

They watched the recording twice more but neither Alex nor Beth could add anything.

Concealing his frustration, Gus, taking Sadia with him, left the Graves' home, promising to keep them updated of any new developments.

CHAPTER 73
Bradford

Gus had bitten his tongue to avoid a string of profanities leaving his mouth when their car had been mobbed by journos on leaving the Grave's place. He was now distinctly disgruntled. Ever-conscious of the fact that time was running on and, although they were making progress on the case as a whole, they were still no closer to finding Molly. He dreaded to think what The Matchmaker had in store for her next. He was under no illusion that both Molly and Beth Graves would have to endure a whole lot more before this was finished.

There had been a thaw between him and Sadia since their run-in the other day and he appreciated the effort she was making to fit in with the team. She had the makings of an excellent detective. Her tenacity would stand her in good stead and if she could just quell her propensity to judge and condemn she'd be an asset to his team.

They were almost at The Fort when Gus's phone rang. 'Yeah, Compo, what's up?'

Gus listened, ignoring Sadia's questioning glances as she drove. He flipped his phone shut, exhaled and leaned his head on the rest. 'Find a place to turn round. We're heading back to Ilkley.'

'Bad news, sir?'

'You could say that. Compo's found some encrypted images on Alex Graves's computer hard drive.'

She flicked a glance at him. 'And? Are you going to tell me what they are?'

He nodded slowly. 'Child pornographic video files and photos.'

'Fuck!'

'My   sentiments   exactly.   Fuck!'

CHAPTER 74
Bradford

The Matchmaker's Decompression Room, or what most people would call 'Man cave' was similar to the original one he'd had built in his Cambridge home years previously. It was a necessity. He loved his wife but, as he knew only too well, unless he had his own space to decompress when the tension got too much, he'd take it out on her and that just wasn't on. This space was his and his alone. No-one else had access and he invited no one else in.

Here, he had his heavily protected equipment with enough encrypted files to upset a huge number of Britain's richest and most influential figures. Then, of course there was the gym area in the corner and his en suite. Up here, he could be self-sufficient until his darkest moments dissipated, leaving him free to return to family life.

His wife didn't question his withdrawal, relieved that he'd found a way to deal with the darkness that took him over body and soul. Now, he stood naked at the window looking out over the moors from his three storey home, enjoying the warmth of the central heating drying the sweat on his body after his workout. The contrast between the warm room and the blizzard that had darkened the sky and covered the moors with a heavy fall of snow made him smile. Up here looking out over the wilderness he felt very Heathcliff. There were no other houses around and he was so high up, that apart from the odd pigeon, no one could see him.

They'd had a busy morning, him and The Distributor. It had left him pumped, so he'd come straight home rather than heading into his work in Bradford. Now he felt more composed. They'd done what he set out to do. He laughed aloud, remembering the shocked look on The Distributor's face when he'd pulled out the gun. When he'd pulled the trigger he'd nearly ejaculated there and then. God, but it had felt good. He pursed his lips, remembering the other man's frightened expression as they'd retraced their steps. The stupid fucker had been trembling like a baby by the time they'd hiked back down to the main road. If he wasn't careful, The Distributor would find himself dispensable. Rubbing his hands together the Matchmaker wondered how Beth Graves felt right now. The net was pulling in behind her. There was no escape for her now, and she knew it.

Humming under his breath, he watched his semi-erection become flaccid in his reflection, before padding over to the shower and flicking the temperature dial to cold. Thirty seconds of freezing water, followed by twenty of very hot before he soaped himself all over, rinsed and stepped out to towel himself dry. Barefoot, he shrugged on a hoodie and pulled on a pair of trackie bottoms.

Sitting at his desk he rested his legs, crossed at the ankle on his desk and phoned into work. 'I'm working from home today' he told his long-suffering PA. 'Direct any calls here.' He flicked the sound system to quiet and leaned back steepling his hands across his chest as he listened to the waves of gentle music that filled the room.

Finally, relaxed, he turned his attention to work and pulled open the drawer where he kept his supply of untraceable phones. He selected the correct phone and dialled. Within three rings he was connected.

'How are things with our accounts?' he said without preamble.

The Facilitator hesitated and The Matchmaker could hear him moving and then the gentle click of a door. 'Right, I'm in my office now. Things are fine, as you'd expect. The Provider has managed to locate the necessary produce in Poland and is at present en route to the UK. He should be here before the weekend, in time to meet our orders. The respective clients have initiated their deposits and we're all systems go.'

The Matchmaker rocked back in his chair, smiling widely. 'Fantastic! Things are certainly moving along nicely.'

The Facilitator cleared his throat. 'Em, I wanted to talk to you about that. Don't you think that we should cool things down until after the current orders have been fulfilled?'

The Matchmaker frowned and his voice became icy. 'What do you mean?'

'Well, we're creating a bit of a stink right now. First with the kids in Heaton and The Provider having to acquire more stock at short notice, then with Molly and now Jessie. Just thought it'd be sensible to back off until the current order is fulfilled.

'Back off?'

'Well, obviously we fulfil our existing orders and work towards fulfilling future ones – keep the money rolling in. But I just thought maybe we should just forget about our revenge for now. '

He allowed a frigid silence to drift down the phone. He knew The Facilitator was weaker than him. He knew he'd be sweating like a pig right now and he used his silence to threaten him even more, to back him into a corner and make him work.

When The Facilitator broke the silence his voice was rushed and pleading. 'What I mean is, why don't we just get rid of the kid? Maybe even use her first, Client 51 likes that type after all, and then just get rid. That'll teach the bitch *and* it'll be payback for us.'

The Matchmaker's leg began to bounce up and down, his face taut and pinched. 'I hope you're not suggesting we let the bitch off with just losing her brat?'

'No, no. Of course not. But maybe, just for now, we could back off for a bit. Let things cool down, let her stew in her grief and then move on to the next stage.'

The Matchmaker laughed. 'No fucking way! We've waited too long and we're going to end it, just like we agreed. We're going to leave the bitch with nothing. Not a fucking thing, just like she left us.' His voice quietened to a chilling whisper. 'We're going to systematically destroy every part of her family, bit by bit and she's going to know that she's responsible for it.'

He heard The Facilitator swallow, then he said, 'I'm not sure I can do the next bit.'

The Matchmaker issued a snorting laugh, 'Course you can. I've got the utmost faith in you. You concentrate on your side of things and leave me to take care of everything else.'

Ending the call, The Matchmaker threw the phone on his desk and with an abrupt toss of the head he stood up and began pacing. 'Bloody weaklings. I'm surrounded by bloody weaklings. Not one of them prepared to take a risk to defend our honour.' He stripped off his clothes, strode over to the chin pull and began to do pull-ups, his face strained, veins standing out on his neck as his biceps bulged.

CHAPTER 75
Ilkley

W hen Gus and Sadia arrived back at the Graves' home, Alex was in his office. The FLO, Janine, let them in and after greeting them with a worried frown, Beth called her husband to come through. 'He doesn't like to be interrupted when he's working but under the circumstances I'm not sure he's managing to do very much work anyway.'

Sadia exchanged a glance with Gus who looked stern and uncompromising. His customary easy smile banished for now. The sickly sweet smell of baby puke combined with dirty nappy pervaded the kitchen as Gus explained why they had returned so quickly.

Beth jostled the baby on her hip, her face ashen, her lips thinned to a hard line across her face. Alex, by contrast was flushed and waved his arms about in agitation. 'You can't be fucking serious, what the fuck. Why are you wasting time on me when you should be looking for Molly?' He turned to Beth 'You don't believe them do you?'

Beth dipped her head and began to walk from the room, ignoring her husband. 'I've got to change Sam's nappy.' As she walked from the room, avoiding her husband's gaze, Janine followed her.

Gus called her name and Beth turned round. Expecting tears or rage, Gus was shocked to see instead, Beth's neutral expression. He glanced at Janine who shrugged slightly and then stepped closer to Beth, saying, 'Look Beth, let me phone someone for you. You shouldn't be on your own. Not with all this going on.'

Beth flinched. 'What? I take it that 'by all this' you mean the fact that, somehow I've managed to marry a paedophile for the second time or the fact that he's probably responsible

321

for taking my daughter from me, as well as murdering my Jessie?' Beth pointedly held Gus's gaze until he looked away.

Sadia nodded to the Janine, who stood uncertainly by the open door. 'Get her friend, the deputy head teacher over here pronto, ok? Her name's Horan I think.'

Talking gently to her baby, Beth walked upstairs without looking back. Alex, still proclaiming his innocence, followed her to the bottom of the stairs and then hesitated before shouting up to Beth. 'I've never looked at any of that filth, Beth. I never would. I swear I haven't and I'd never *ever* harm Molly or Jessie.' He waited for a reply but when there was none forthcoming he continued. 'Beth, Beth, you should move in with Wendy Horan till all this is over. DI McGuire will offer you protection at their house.' Head tilted to one side, he waited for a reply, but when none was forthcoming, he shrugged and nodded briefly at Gus before continuing to the door. 'Might as well get this over with.'

CHAPTER 76

Molly, wrapped in the grubby duvet, stood on tiptoe atop the thick metal radiator pipe and hefted herself onto the wide window sill. She leaned forward on her knees till her mouth was close to the frozen window. Then she pursed her lips into an O-shape and breathed on the heavily frosted glass. The ice crackled and fractured into small, wet jigsaw pieces which she impatiently wiped away with her sleeve. She pressed her forehead to the pane and peered through the small hole she'd made. It wasn't big enough to see much so she jumped down and looked around the room. When she saw the empty Pepsi bottle, she grinned. That would do the trick. She picked it up, took aim and tossed it onto the sill before clambering up after it. Lifting the bottle, she unscrewed the lid and used the rim to scrape a wider hole in the ice. A few minutes later, she'd cleared most of the ice and despite her frozen fingers, she was happy.

The activity was a welcome distraction to the monotony of her day. She'd not seen anyone since the previous night, when *he'd* turned up with a soggy sausage roll, a little lamp that he placed next to her bed and a heater. He'd plugged both items in and told her she should be 'grateful' to him. Molly didn't like the way he'd said 'grateful', nor did she like the look on his face.

Anyway, the heater had made absolutely no difference whatsoever to the temperature. Initially, she'd been happy with the items. She didn't like the dark and it was freezing, even with the extra blanket. However, after he'd gone, she'd realised that the addition of a heater and lamp probably meant she wasn't getting out anytime soon. She'd flung herself down on her bed and cried for a long time, until she fell into an exhausted sleep. Finally, she woke up with a cold nose and the new day well underway. Her eyes rested on the lamp. It was switched off. She'd left it on when she went to sleep. Quickly, she scooted across the mattress and pressed the switch. A faint yellow glow immediately came on. That meant *he* must have been in here when she was asleep. Molly shuddered at the thought of that creepy man watching her and suddenly her small body was infused with a desire to do something… anything, to get out of this horrid room. She'd peed in the bucket, noticing it was empty. Another sign that *he'd* been here. Stuffing yet another Snickers bar in her mouth, the thick chocolate clogging her throat, she vowed never to eat another one for the rest of her life. Then she began to plan.

Panting slightly after her exertions, Molly craned her neck to see out the window. Snow had fallen heavily overnight and the fields were blanketed in soft white. In the distance troops of miniature people in bobble hats and winter coats with scarves swinging from their necks frolicked in the snow. She sighed, imagining their whoops of glee as they slid down the gentle undulations that led to the valley. She wrapped her arms round her skinny frame and watched as snowmen appeared on the distant fields and the unblemished snow became a maze of footprints and sledge trails.

Molly saw a girl that looked about the same age as her, wearing a similar red coat and blue bobble hat. She was with another girl, probably her sister and they were taking it in turns to slide down the slope. Molly got on her knees and stretched her neck to see if she could see where they finally stopped.

It was then that she noticed the viaduct thrusting out of the valley like a huge snake on legs. She held her breath, hands on either side of her head and peered at the structure. She recognised it. She'd seen it before with her mum. Now, she knew where she was. She knew *exactly* where she was. Now all she had to do was get out.

CHAPTER 77
The Fort

The earlier snowfall had increased to a blizzard and Gus was glad to be back at The Fort. The business with Alex Graves made him feel slightly dirty. He hadn't really considered the man a suspect, partly because he knew he'd been strenuously vetted by the WP programme. The Incident Room was buzzing. The new information had taken the investigation forward and everyone was on a high. Even Sadia had gone to get everyone's sandwiches with good grace. The only downside was that the journos had picked up on their quick return to The Graves' house and some had followed them back to The Fort. Fortunately, Alex had been content to sprawl along the back seat to avoid being seen by them.

'Right, while we're waiting for Alex Graves' lawyer to turn up, is there anything else going on I need to know about?'

Alice, who'd just walked into the room, spoke up. 'I've just taken a statement from Frankie Robb, Jamal's friend. He said Jamal admitted that he had, and I quote, 'fuckin' battered the old cunt to death in Heaton graveyard'. Thing is, he seems quite convincing. It only came out because he had a row with his own mum and said, and again I quote, 'Maybe I should do what Jamal did to his old mum and crack you over the head with a stone.' His mum, understandably, was shocked and quizzed him some more about it. Eventually he admitted that Jamal turned up with a bottle of vodka swiped from the One Stop shop to celebrate killing Sharon Asif.'

Gus puffed out his cheeks. 'Okay. That's a development I didn't see coming, Al. Bring him in with his social worker, not the brother. I want him on his own, don't want him feeding off his brother's bravado.' He sighed, 'It all adds up though, doesn't it? The stories from his neighbours saying he was playing up over the last few months, throwing shit-filled nappies and empty bottles into their gardens. Poor bugger was crying out for help. We'll play that line with him when we bring him in and, if he admits it, we'll have a word with the CPO, see if we can get him a good deal. He's only a kid and no kid should have had to put up with the shit he did.'

Alice nodded, 'I'll go get him myself, Gus. You gonna interview him?'

'We'll do it together, ok? After I've interviewed Alex Graves. Wait an hour before you go get Jamal. Get the social worker briefed and a duty solicitor who has experience with kid's law in place first. I want to be up-front with them from the start.'

He walked over to Compo, who was nodding his head to some heavy bass beat that thrummed through the floor despite him having earphones in. Gus placed a hand on his arm. Compo jumped spilling Tango from the can he was holding over Gus's hand. Chewing the lump of Mars Bar that was in his mouth and swallowing it quickly with a quick swig of Tango to ease its passage he jumped from his chair and tried to wipe Gus's hand with a scrap of ketchup-covered tissue he found on his desk. Gus waved him away with a grin and licked the Tango off instead. 'Calm down, Compo. Look, just wondered if you'd got any more information on those files you found on Graves's laptop.'

'Just working on that. They've been well encrypted. Almost missed them. And I'm having a hard time working out where they originated. They've been bounced all over the place. They're weird. I sent them off to the sex crimes unit to see if they rang any bells with them, but I've got nowt back yet. I'm gonna keep on with this.'

After checking carefully for stray food debris, Gus sat on the edge of his table and lowered his voice. 'Compo, is there a chance those files could've been planted on the laptop?'

Compo pushed his chair back and looked up at Gus his eyes sparking with interest. 'What are you thinking, boss man?'

Gus carefully moved the remains of a sausage roll to the back of Compo's desk and leaned in closer. 'Look, this is probably just me over-reacting but I just wondered, what the chances are of the same woman managing to marry two separate paedophiles?'

Compo's eyes widened and he snapped his fingers to show he was on Gus's wavelength. Gus smiled and continued, 'Then, I thought about something Beth said this morning after Jessie was shot. She said this was all about getting revenge on her.'

Compo snapped his fingers again. 'Of course, first he captures Molly, then he cuts off her hair then he kills Jessie. So, maybe, just maybe, he planted incriminating images on Alex Graves' laptop, knowing we'd find them. The bastard's slowly but surely isolating Beth. He's taking his revenge slowly and surely.'

Gus glanced round the room, 'Look Compo, we don't know this yet. We've got no evidence, so I want you to look forensically at everything to prove it one way or the other, ok? If he is a paedophile, I'll have the bastard. But if he's not I want you on the case, because you're the best there is.' He patted the other man's arm. 'But this stays between you and me for now, ok? Till we know one way or the other. When I interview him, I'm going to go in hard, as if we've got no doubt of his guilt. Got to keep things above board in case he's guilty.'

Compo winked, 'You can count on me.' and he put his earphones back in and pumped up the volume. Gus stood and stretched. Grimacing, he limped over and got out his elastic physio band and, ignoring the bustle around the incident room, he began to methodically do his exercises, allowing his mind to drift as he worked.

By the time he'd finished an idea had occurred to him. He jumped to his feet groaned at the pain and yelled over to Sampson. 'Hey Sampson, get on to Customs North and South and check if they've eyeballed that Cosy Night van. Also spread that around patrol and motorway police. If the business doesn't exist, the only van with that logo will be the one belonging to our gang and considering we've just relieved them of most of the kids they may be urgently acquiring more. Get on the phone to Jankowski and tell them to monitor clusters of missing children, boys or girls.'

Gus turned to the room at large. 'Any ideas how they get the kids past Customs?'

***

Gus, a brown folder under one arm, walked into Interview Room 2 followed by Sadia. Hunched over the table, Graves restlessly peeled the label off a half-empty water bottle. Eyes completely focussed on his task, he didn't react when Gus pulled a chair out, flung the folder down and sat down opposite. With raised eyebrows Sadia sat next to Gus. Gus took his time, letting the tension build, then, banged his hand on the table. Graves jumped and his gaze flew to Gus's face.

'Look, you've been caught fair and square,' said Gus, his face stony cold. 'The evidence is on your laptop. You've not got a leg to stand on, so you might as well just admit it.'

Graves' lawyer, Jacob Foreman, a tall stern man in a funereal suit with an incongruously bright pink polka dot tie, looked down his nose. 'My client declines to comment, other than to maintain his innocence in this matter.'

Gus' blue eyes sparked angrily at the lawyer then turned to laser straight into Alex's. Each word he spoke was incisive. 'This is no time to remain passive. The evidence is here on the files taken from your laptop.' He tapped the folder that sat between them on the table. Shall I show you the images? The filth that you stored on there. The things you did to those children?'

Alex, dropped the bottle and let it bounce onto the table with a slight bang. Rubbing the palms of his hands over his face, he shook his head quickly from side to side. Then with a sigh he took his hands away and looked at Gus, his hand plucking nervously at his ear lobe. Gus scraped his chair back from the table and began pacing the room.

'Speak to me! Tell me all about it. Your nasty little perverted fantasies. The disgusting things you did to those kids and shared with the other nonces. How it felt when you abducted your own stepdaughter and murdered Jessie.'

Alex dropped his head into his hands and moaned.

'You have not arrested my client in relation to, either the abduction of his stepdaughter or the murder of Jessie Graham, so restrict your questioning to the data found on his laptop.'

Gus glared at the lawyer. 'Would you like to see the images your client had on his laptop?'

Mr Foreman shrugged nonchalantly. 'Not my thing.'

Gus jumped to his feet fists clenched by his side, eyes narrowed. Sadia who had sat quietly till now turned to the lawyer and before Gus could speak said, 'No, *your* thing seems to be specialising in getting the bastards who sodomise and rape kiddies off, isn't it?'

Mr Foreman turned a steely gaze on her and, raising an eyebrow said, 'If you can't control yourself, officer, I *will* terminate this interview.'

Gus turned to Sadia and frowned a warning. She shrugged and lowering her eyes issued a mumbled apology.

Alex's sobs broke the tension in the room. 'I didn't do this. I didn't upload or download any images and, to be frank, if I had, do you really think I'd have let you have access to my laptop? I'm a security expert. I could hide anything I didn't want you to see so deep you'd need to tunnel to Australia to find it.'

As he spoke snot dripped down his nose to the edge of his chin. Foreman, surreptitiously moved his chair further away from his client's. Mouth screwed up in distaste, he dropped a tissue onto the table near Alex.

Gus sat down and taking a deep breath, lowered his tone. 'All I'm telling you is, that if you come clean with us about this stuff on your computer and help us find Molly it'll be better for you.'

Face wiped clean his head jerked up. 'If I knew anything that would help you find Molly I'd tell you. I love that girl like my own, ok? Now I've nothing more to say.'

Gus pushed his chair away from the table and nodded to the PC who waited by the door. 'Take him back to his cell for now.'

***

Alice and PC Singh walked Jamal from the lifts through the fourth floor corridor to the interview room. Despite her diminutive figure, Jamal felt shrunken beside Alice. He was tense and, despite being aware that he was clenching and unclenching his fists, he couldn't stop himself. He tried to walk with a swagger, but his heart wasn't in it. He was scared and all he wanted was to see Ishaq. Ishaq would sort everything out. He'd explain how bad it was for him and the kids. He'd make them understand that he hadn't meant to kill his mum.

He'd just been so angry. She'd laughed at him and said she wasn't giving him any money. He'd flipped then and just grabbed the stone. He hadn't meant to do it, it had just happened and then it was too late.

Alice pushed open the door of the interview room and smiled at the two women who waited inside. 'This is Amy

Winters, Jamal. She's a lawyer who specialise in children's law. You've already met your social worker, Naila Siddique. I'll leave you for half an hour or so.' She turned to the lawyer. 'We've already read him his rights. Let me know when you're ready. I'll bring some drinks when we come back.' She squeezed Jamal's shoulder as she left.

Naila, a small slender woman wearing a salwar kameez but no head scarf, jumped to her feet and walked over to Jamal. Gently she took his arm and led him over to the table. 'Sit down Jamal. Both of us are here to help you, ok? But you need to tell us what happened.'

Biting his lip, Jamal sat down on the edge of the chair between the two women and risked a glance at his lawyer. She was tall and, although she didn't smile, Jamal thought her eyes looked kind. She smelled nice too, like strawberries.

With her black ringlets bobbing, Amy nodded at him. 'I'm here to get the best outcome for you, ok?' She waited for his nod before continuing. 'Well, you need to tell me the truth. Did you do it? Did you kill your mum?'

Jamal nodded once then began to sob. Naila handed him a tissue and both women waited. When he was calm enough to speak, Jamal looked at Amy through reddened eyes. 'What's going to happen to the kids if I go to jail?'

Amy frowned and said, 'Your siblings will be taken very good care of Jamal. You mustn't worry about that.' She smiled. Jamal thought her dimples were very pretty and he immediately felt a little better.

Looking straight into his eyes Amy continued, 'It's time for you to tell your story Jamal. You're only fourteen and your school and your neighbours and your big brother all say you're not a bad lad, and we want the best possible outcome for you. In order to do that you need to tell us everything. The fact that you co-operated with the police earlier is a good thing and that you helped them with their investigation into the children they found in your attic.'

She paused and adjusted the papers that were strewn over the table before continuing. 'You need to start at the beginning and tell us everything about that night and then when I have everything I need we'll bring the police back in and they will conduct a formal interview. I'd like us to co-operate with them again. But, for your sake Jamal, you must tell me everything. No secrets, huh?'

When Jamal nodded, she crossed her legs and opened an A4 pad of paper and they began.

***

'Forensics have come through on the gun used to kill Jessie Graham. The bullets match the ones retrieved from the shooting at Jamal's brother's house in Great Horton,' said Sadia

Gus smiled. 'Great, it's all coming together now. Let's keep on it. When Naila and the lawyer are finished with Jamal we'll get on with the interview. Don't want to hang about on this one.' He grabbed his elastic physio band and began his exercises, barking out orders at the same time to distract him from the monotony.

The door opened and almost immediately the room fell silent. Gus, still on the floor beside his desk mid-stretch, paused then he heard a voice cutting through the room like a laser. 'I'm here to speak to DI McGuire, Sadia. Where is he?'

From his position on the floor, Gus saw Sadia shuffle her feet under her desk. From his vantage point, he smiled, noting that even her smooth calf muscles tensed in reaction to her father's voice. Deciding to put her out of her discomfort, Gus raised his voice. 'I'm here, DCI Hussain.'

The man took two steps towards Gus's desk and stopped abruptly. His mouth became pinched, as he looked down his patrician nose, his head swivelling from Gus's smiling face to the elastic band round the desk leg. His voice when he spoke came out like a stuttering firework. 'What exactly do you think you're doing, McGuire?'

Gus continued to smile amiably. 'Physio exercises, sir.' And he demonstrated with a diagonal stretch that pulled his thigh muscles taut and deliberately held the stretch for the count of ten.

A muscle played on Hussain's cheek. 'Do you *really* think the investigation room is the place for this sort of nonsense?'

Gus was saved from answering by DCI Chalmers' arrival. She bustled over and stood between the two men, gesturing to Gus to continue his exercises. When she spoke her tone was brisk. 'What brings you here, Imran?'

Turning to face Nancy, Imran looked her up and down, his disapproval of her colourful floral dress demonstrated by the sneer in his eyes as they slid up her frame. 'I wanted to bring McGuire's attention to the behaviour – in his absence yesterday – of two of his officers.' Gus who'd used Nancy's arrival as a distraction to get to his feet glanced over at Compo and Sampson, both of whom had tensed on Hussain's arrival. Their wary glances swung between Hussain and Gus. Gus winked at them and stepped forward to stand beside Nancy. Nancy continued to smile and raised one eyebrow in a questioning manner indicating Hussain should continue.

Arms behind his back, legs apart, he stood erect and glared at Compo and Sampson. 'I'm very sorry to have to bring this to your attention, Chalmers. Yesterday, I found two officers from your team behaving in an inappropriate manner.'

Nancy raised one hand and stepped closer to Hussain. 'Were they abusing prisoners? Or maybe the public?'

Hussain tutted and shook his head, but before he could speak she continued.

'Maybe they were doctoring evidence or conducting some other nefarious and illegal activity?'

'You are trivialising untoward behaviour, Chalmers and that's not on. If you weren't so... erm... close, with DCS Bowles, I'd be in his office now making a formal complaint.'

Nancy blushed at his sneering use of the word 'close', then shrugged noncommittally. 'Of course, you must do as you see fit, Imran. Although, I hardly think that two officers who'd been on the job for over fourteen hours non-stop and who had just uncovered two very important leads that pushed our investigation forwards, jamming out for ten minutes in the *empty* investigation room, is a major transgression.'

She grinned, 'Hell, if I'd been here, I'd have joined in myself.' She turned her back dismissively on Hussain, who opened his mouth to reply. Before he could speak however, Nancy turned back and glared at him. 'Especially in light of the fact that two of your officers are currently under investigation by internal affairs for their behaviour towards a fellow officer in public. An incident to which we have numerous witnesses.'

Hussain frowned. 'What are you talking about? I thought we'd agreed to brush that silly incident in the pub the other night under the carpet. I've spoken to the officers involved.'

Nancy turned back and smiled. 'Yes, we did have a *verbal* agreement. Nonetheless, I covered my back by taking witness statements just the same. Like you, I don't like my police force being brought into disrepute.' She stepped closer to Hussain and continued. 'I'd thank you to clean out your own stable and allow my officers to behave as efficiently and impeccably as they always do. And I include in that statement their momentary release of healthy tension through a jamming session. Now if you'll excuse me, Gus has an arrest on the Sharon Asif murder to make.' and she all but shepherded Hussain out of the room.

When Hussain and Nancy had left, Sadia released a long breath and turned to Gus, her face flushed.

'Look, about my dad ...'

Gus interrupted. 'Look, when we're at work, he's not your dad. He's a senior officer. It'll be easier for you if you keep that distinction in mind, ok?'

She nodded and turned back to her computer screen. 'Yeah, especially if he's going to be a dick!'

CHAPTER 78
The Fort

Gus and Alice looked through the one-way mirror at Jamal, Naila and Amy. Jamal looked like he'd been ravaged by a Pitbull. His face was mottled. As they watched, his fingers worried at a ragged hole in the sleeve of his jumper. Alice moved away and pumped some money into the vending machine. When the can of Pepsi Max thudded out, she picked it up. 'That's for Jamal. The others don't want a drink. You ready, Gus?'

Gus nodded and together they left the room and approached the interview room. Rolling the tension from his shoulders, Gus hesitated then opened the door. As soon as it opened, Jamal's head jerked up and Gus saw that he'd bitten his lips to a scabby mess. He smiled at Jamal, patted him on the shoulder and walked past to take the seat opposite. Alice placed the can in front of Jamal and joined Gus at the other side of the table.

Gus looked at the three people sat opposite. 'Are we alright to continue?'

The lawyer nodded, adjusted her pad on the table and sat back. Gus nodded to Alice who inserted a tape in the recorder and introduced the participants before Gus took over.

'Ok Jamal, we've already got on file your previous statement relating to the weeks leading up to and including the period of incarceration of the children in the attic at 9 Inkerman Street. In this interview, we want to focus on the day and evening of the death of your mother Sharon Asif. Is that clear?'

Jamal nodded and his solicitor nudged him. With a smile she gestured to the recorder. Jamal sighed and said, 'Yes, I understand.'

Gus leaned back, stretching his legs under the table and keeping his body as open and unthreatening as possible. 'When was the first time you saw your mother, Sharon Asif, on Saturday the seventh February?'

Jamal's fingers continued to pluck at the woollen fabric of his jumper, his head remained bowed as he spoke. 'I stayed at my mate Frankie Robb's place on the Friday. Went there straight after school and stayed over till the Saturday. Then he was going to the football and I knew I should go back and check on the kids. I never liked to leave them with her for too long.'

'When you say 'her', Jamal, do you mean your mother?'

'Yes, my mother.' He sniffed and then wiped a tissue over his nose and eyes. 'When I got in, they were watching telly in the living room. She was lying in her bed, wearing that bloody dressing gown and a short nightie. She stank. The whole fucking house stank… piss, sick, shit… everything. Imran's nappy was full and even *he* stank. His little Babygro was covered in muck and shit, but there was nothing else. I changed his bum. It was sore, so I slathered Sudocrem over it. *She* didn't buy that for him. Mrs Khalifa next door gave it me. *She* never bought owt for us.'

Jamal paused, his fingers working like a piston on his jumper. His eyes were glazed and he stared blankly at the ceiling. Gus exchanged a glance with Naila, who gently placed her hand on Jamal's arm.

'You're doing really well Jamal,' she said.

Jamal swallowed before continuing. 'I woke her up – my mum that is – and told her I'd used the last nappy. Told her she needed to buy more. She just grunted, so I got a cup of water and threw it over her.' A faint smile flickered at his sore mouth, before his eyes clouded over. 'She was mad then. She jumped up. I could smell the sweat and booze and… sex on her.' Jamal's fists clenched on top of the table. 'Fucking whore bitch! She grabbed my wrist.' His fingers moved from the jumper to the skin underneath, Gus could see the yellowing remains of a bruise on his wrist. He leaned over and touched Jamal's arm with one finger.

'Jamal, I can see an old bruise on your wrist. How did you get that?'

Jamal stared up at Gus with a frown. 'I just told you. She did it. She grabbed my wrist and twisted like she always does.' He stood up quickly. Turning round he hoisted his jumper up to reveal a series of bruises on his skinny back. 'She did those too, kicked and punched me for waking her up.'

Gus released a long breath. 'Ok, Jamal you can sit down, love.' He glanced at the lawyer whose face revealed her shock. Gus knew that things had changed dramatically. Jamal now had a motive and possibly an excuse for killing his mother. Gus inclined his head towards Naila. 'I'm going to terminate this interview for now, Jamal, because you've made allegations of abuse by your mother and shown us injuries we previously didn't know existed. What will happen now is that a doctor will come in and do a medical examination to document your injuries. You'll have some tea and then we'll continue,' he looked at his watch. 'Probably tomorrow now.'

Confusion clouding his face, Jamal looked from Naila to his lawyer for corroboration before giving a single exhausted nod.

Gus noted the time and signed off from the tape.

***

As Gus and Alice walked along the corridor, leaving Jamal in the capable hands of his lawyer and social worker, his phone vibrated in his trouser pocket.

Rummaging awkwardly Gus found it, glanced at the screen and scowled. 'Shit, that's my alarm to remind me I've got to go see the shrink. Drop me off will you, Al.' He flexed his bad shoulder. 'I discovered this morning that I'm not fit to drive yet.'

'Sure,' said Alice, changing direction and heading towards the escalator, with Gus following behind, cursing under his breath.

When they got in Gus said, 'What the hell's so funny?'

Alice pouted and looked toward the roof of the lift. 'Not a thing, Gus. Not a thing.'

Lashing snow made the short drive along Manningham Lane and onto Bradford Road, in rush hour treacherous. Gus spent most of the journey cursing and bemoaning the stupidity of psychiatrists and their unreasonable demands on patients who were perfectly fine, whilst Alice smiled and ignored him.

She followed him into the waiting room and was introduced to Gus' soulmate Nemo. Alice, like Gus, took a liking to the hulking fish and seemed happy to entertain him whilst Gus was with Dr Mahmood.

Force of habit had Gus walking towards his chair and focussing on the damp patch on the wall above Dr Mahmood's head, whilst she sat behind her desk and, elbows resting on her chin, studied him. 'How have you been, Angus?' she asked.

Gus pursed his lips and shrugged. 'Busy, very busy. In fact, so busy I'm going to have to cut this appointment short. I've got lots to do.'

Dr Mahmood, stood up and walked to the front of her desk. Placing her hands on her hips, she stared so hard at him that he almost flinched. When she opened her mouth to speak, Gus expected an avalanche of annoyance but, instead, she spoke very quietly. 'The thing is Angus, it's not up to you when this appointment terminates.' She held up two hands palms facing upwards. 'You see these two hands of mine?'

Gus directed his gaze to her hands and then immediately swung his gaze back to his patch with a curt nod.

She continued. 'Well, these hands carry a heavy weight on them. Do you know what that weight is?'

Gus shook his head, suspecting he wasn't going to like whatever revelation she was about to make.

Dr Mahmood lowered her voice even more. 'It's the weight of power. I have power over many things Angus. However, the power pertaining to *you,* is my ability to revoke your fitness to work status, should I deem it necessary.'

Gus narrowed his eyes and directed his gaze straight at her.

She inclined her head, in what Gus could only describe as a regal fashion. 'I have no desire to revoke that status, Angus.' She said, moving round her desk and sitting back down. 'Nonetheless, I will not accept tardiness or a 'no show'. I'm aware that in your line of work, there are occasions when you may need to postpone our appointment and that's fine. However, you will have the courtesy to notify me to schedule an alternate time. Is that understood?'

Gus had the grace to acknowledge that he had been rude to her and that he should have set his phone alarm for his earlier appointment. He would still have needed to cancel, but it would have been courteous to contact her first. He nodded and said, 'Perfectly.'

With a smile she said, 'Right, let's crack on. How have you found your return to work? Be warned, I expect a proper answer this time.'

Gus bit his lip and then described his working week in detail.

Afterwards, he felt a lot of the tension he'd carried into the room had dissipated.

Dr Mahmood looked at him across the table with narrowed eyes. She shook her head slowly from side to side and then rested her forehead in her hands. 'If you'd only loosen up about your accident like you did just now about your current case, I'd be a lot happier with your return to work.'

With a slight smile Gus said, 'I'm fine. Honestly. Being back at work is all the therapy I need.'

Dr Mahmood exhaled a deep breath. 'I'm not one hundred percent sure of that. At some point you will have to let it all out in order to heal. I only hope it doesn't break free when you're in a compromised position.' She reached across and flicked the mouse to bring her diary onto the computer screen. Monday 8am suit you?'

Gus took out his phone and made a show of setting his alarm for it. 'Fine.'

***

Laden with bacon butties and chocolate chip cookies newly bought from Chaat's, Alice and Gus went into the incident room and deposited their goody bags on his desk.

'Dive in, troops!' Gus glanced round, spotted Sadia sitting at her desk, phone glued to her ear. He walked over and dropped a greasy paper bag on top of her desk. 'Egg for you.'

Sadia looked up, her brown eyes flickered momentarily in confusion and then she mouthed 'thank you.'

Gus gave a single nod and walked back to his own desk grabbing the last bacon sandwich and shouting to Compo to get the coffee on.

When she'd finished her phone conversation, Sadia sidled over to Gus. 'Thanks for the egg butty. I didn't order one.'

Gus glanced up and wiped ketchup from his fingers. 'You're welcome. No one ordered owt.' He grinned. 'You could say impetuosity got the better of me.'

As he looked up at her from beneath his dreads she grinned at him. Her almond shaped eyes were huge and lidded by lashes that, on anyone else, he'd have assumed were false. On her, he knew they'd be natural. Her smile revealed perfectly white teeth with an endearing overbite at the front. He stared at her, then shaking himself he turned back to his paperwork.

Sadia laid her hand on his arm and squeezed lightly. When she spoke, the carefree tone of minutes ago was replaced by an urgency that immediately had Gus's full attention. 'That was Janine, Beth's FLO on the phone. Two things. Well three really, first DHL just delivered an identical box to the one that came the other day. They've obviously realised that, now the press have taken up residence at the gate, they can't drop things off so easily.'

Gus's blue eyes narrowed as she continued. 'Janine has contacted forensics and, as a precaution, she's left the box in the middle of the garden with a PC on guard. The second thing is that Beth's moving in with Wendy Horan, her deputy head, for now. She's requested police security, but won't countenance a safe house. She said she's not ever doing that again.' Sadia sighed, 'And the third thing is, she's relieved Janine of her duties. Said she's fed up with having a minder and it's causing her too much stress.'

'Ok! Get a police presence at the deputy's house and get a team to go over it for security. I want a panic alarm in each room and I want the premises covered front and back twenty-four seven.'

He put his hand into his pocket and fingered the card Sergeant Ormerton had given him. 'Tell forensics not to touch the box. I want it checked over by my contact in the army before they touch it. Does Beth know it's there?'

Sadia shook her head. 'No, Janine opted to keep it quiet till she'd heard from us.'

'Good, tell her to try to keep Beth there for now, but away from the windows if possible.'

He picked up his phone pumped in Ormerton's number and gestured to Sadia to get her coat. 'Get a squad car. You can come with me. Compo, tell Alice I'll be back ASAP.'

CHAPTER 79
Ilkley

Blinding sleet and icy roads made the drive to Ilkley take longer than Gus had anticipated. When they pulled into the drive, the reporters, remembering Sadia's earlier impatience, crowded the sides of the vehicle, but wisely left the front free.

Gus grinned at them through the side window as they swept through the first gate into the area he privately thought of now as 'the paddock', before being buzzed through to the drive. The forensic team had arrived and Gus saw an army vehicle parked near the door. He got out of the car and raised his arm in greeting to Ormerton who strode towards him.

Ormerton shook Gus's hand vigorously. 'No bombs or explosives of any description this time. The bastard clearly didn't want to risk damaging the contents of the box.' His eyes narrowed. He hoiked, deep in his throat and spat a glob of phlegm onto the snow in a gesture that jarred with his posh accent. 'Fucking animal!'

'Is it bad then?' asked Gus.

Ormerton nodded abruptly and glared at the gob of phlegm before kicking some fresh snow over it. 'Best go and see for yourself. I've extended my stay by a few days. I've taking a bit of a shine to those buns called fat rascals in Betty's cake shop down the road.' He grinned '...and, of course, the rather less fat, but just as delicious Charlotte, who works there, is an added attraction. Call if you need me,' he said and saluted Gus, before climbing back into his truck and driving off.

Gus, face grim, headed round the corner to the white forensic tent. Sadia trailed behind, muffled in a huge Puffa coat that dwarfed her slender frame. Before he pulled the flap back he glanced towards the kitchen window where

Beth was silhouetted, holding her baby against her shoulder and staring straight at him. Wendy stood beside her, but he could tell from Beth's body language that any comfort from her friend had been rejected. He raised a hand in the air and waved it once. Beth nodded slightly in response and kept her gaze locked on him as he suited up. With a deep breath, Gus stood aside allowing Sadia to precede him into the tent. Hissing Sid walked towards him and shook his head. 'Doubt we'll get much from the box or its wrappings but we wanted to let you see it *in situ*.'

Gus approached the box, pre-warned by the solemn expressions around him that it would not be pleasant. The SOCOs had left the box open on the snowy ground. Gus looked in and saw a white sheet of folded paper. A quick glance at Sid gave him permission to lift it and open the sheet. It was written in the same child's hand as before, but with a darker colour, and in ink, rather than crayon.

Sid saw Gus's frown as he studied the message. 'You've got new email.'

Gus glanced up and then followed his gaze back to the box where a pad of cotton wool covered whatever lay beneath. A muscle twitched in Gus's cheek as he leaned over and with his gloved fingers lifted the pad.

'We reckon the note's written in blood, Gus!' said Sid as Gus looked at the small item lying in the box.

With an abrupt nod Gus turned to Sadia. 'Get the techs to access Beth's email, ASAP. I need to know what's on it.'

Sadia turned to do as he'd asked whilst Gus spoke to Hissing Sid.

'See if you can get a DNA match on that quickly, will you?'

Sid nodded and gestured to one of his team to bag the box up.

CHAPTER 80
The Fort

S ampson slammed his phone down, jumped up and punched the air. 'Fucking ace!'

Alice glanced up and smiled. 'Good news, John?'

'Hell yeah. Customs have only just gone and identified a lorry with the logo Cosy Night on the side. It's been logged getting on a ferry bound for Hull from Rotterdam. It's due to berth at 9pm. Bingo!'

His flushed, excited expression was contagious, so Alice stood up and high-fived him. She knew that the incident with DCI Hussain had affected Sampson. He'd seemed down and a bit wary since then. Hopefully this would set him back on the right path. 'Get on the phone to Gus. He'll be chuffed to get some good news. Tell him I'll organise a search warrant for the lorry and a police team from Hull to apprehend it and the driver, in liaison with the customs crew.' She put her head to one side. 'I'll warn them to expect you to co-ordinate the operation and bring the driver back to Bradford. Take PC Singh with you.'

Sampson paused as he lifted his phone to his ear, his jaw nearly hitting the floor. 'Me?'

Alice paused and then said, 'You did good to get that alert up and running as quickly as you did. We could so easily have been too late. You deserve the chance to follow your lead through to the end. Gus is all about that, you know?'

Sampson turned away to make his phone call to Gus revealing a tell-tale blush running up his neck and to his ears, which Alice found very endearing.

CHAPTER 81
Ilkley

Gus left the forensic tent and immediately his eyes were drawn to the pale face at the window. Beth's eyes pierced him, drawing him towards her despite his reluctance to pile yet more horror on her shoulders. How much more could she take? Her daughter had been abducted, her mother-in-law murdered and her second husband was under suspicion for possessing pornographic images of children. Now this.

He and Sadia began to walk through the sleet to the kitchen door. He felt his phone vibrate. 'Hope this is some good news,' he said to Sadia and angled himself away from Beth, who continued to watch them from the window. 'Sampson?'

Hearing Sampson's report lifted Gus's spirits and he allowed himself a few seconds of elation before he updated Sadia. Then, he told her the bad news. 'Looks like they've bailed Alex Graves, and he's coming back here. Maybe it's just as well Beth's moving out. She won't want to see him.'

'Hell no,' said Sadia her nose crinkled in disgust. 'It's not right is it? That bastards like that get to roam our streets.'

Kicking the snow aimlessly, his shoulders hunched, Gus agreed with her. He hated it when the legal system let criminals loose. However, he'd enough time on the job to realise that it was pointless letting these things get in the way of an ongoing investigation. He shared these thoughts with Sadia and then bracing himself, he continued towards the back door and into the kitchen where Beth waited.

Beth led them over to the table, carrying the baby who appeared blissfully unaware of the trauma surrounding him. She sat down and looked at Gus. The shadows under her eyes were even more pronounced and her frame looked fragile with her bulky cardigan dwarfing her. Her hands rested on the table clenching and unclenching, her knuckles protruding like blunt herbivorian teeth. Gus pulled out a chair and sat opposite her.

'It isn't good Beth, not good at all. He's left another message and our techs have already watched the email video he sent. I don't want you to watch it, ok?' His blue eyes held her gaze steady and strong, but he knew already that she wouldn't listen to him. Beth chewed on her lower lip, dislodging flakes of dry skin tinged with blood. Gus flinched as the sight evoked memories of what he'd seen in the box. She reached across the table for her laptop. 'You can't stop me from looking at it, can you?'

Gus shook his head. 'No, Beth, I can't stop you. I can only advise. But,' he flicked a glance at Sadia. 'If you choose to watch this, we will do all we can to support you, ok?'

She swallowed once and smiled thinly. When she spoke her voice was hoarse, 'Thank you.'

Gus nodded and moved round to stand behind her, as she accessed the recording.

It opened with the camera operator panning round the warehouse room where Molly had been filmed before. Gus, eyes narrowed in concentration, saw the huge window with its puddle of ice scraped off. The camera zoomed onto the chair with little Molly sitting, legs tied to the chair legs and a rope round her middle. This time her hands were free. From nowhere, manic laughter erupted followed by the image of the man wearing the Scream mask bouncing into the frame. His voice was again distorted when he spoke.

'Come on Molly, sweetheart. Tell mummy how much you miss her.' He slid behind Molly and ran his fingers through her savaged hair, lips close to her ear as he spoke. Molly flinched, but kept looking at the camera. He prodded her and his voice rose an octave.

'Come on tell her!'

The muscles on Molly's throat spasmed as she tried to swallow. Then, after another prod, she spoke. 'Mummy, I'm sorry I ate the sausage roll. I'm still veggie. I love veggie food. I won't eat any more meat.'

Scream man slapped her across the face, making her head ricochet back. A drop of blood gathered at the corner of Molly's mouth. He lurched back from her, threw back his head and guffawed. 'Stupid bitch! She's losing it. Fucking veggie indeed. You would make her a fucking veggie. Well, let me tell you, bitch, she'll be eating meat before too long.' He laughed again and looked towards the camera. 'Get it? She'll be eating meat before too long?'

He turned back to Molly and said, 'Tell her what I told you to say.'

Molly, despite her tears, glared at him and lowered her head. 'He says this is all your fault, mummy, and he'll be coming for you soon. 'Her voice cracked. 'He says he's killed Grandma Jessie. Has he mum? Has he?'

Gus felt Beth tense and made to stop the recording.

'Don't!' The word came out like a bullet and with a final glance at Beth, Gus allowed his hand to fall to his side as the recording continued.

Scream man's laugh drowned out Molly's sobs. When he finally stopped laughing, he walked out of the frame, returning seconds later with his tool bag. He laid it on the mattress and unwrapped it. Slowly and deliberately he withdrew scalpels and knives and saws. One by one, he pressed each against Molly's cheek just hard enough to leave an indent, before removing it and replacing it in the bag.

Finally, he chose a tool and raised it to the camera.

Recognising the clippers, Gus flinched.

Scream man, head on one side, his voice echoing eerily said, 'This one I think, don't you?'

A voice of assent drifted from behind the camera. Scream man, beckoned to the camera man to zoom right in on

Molly's crotch. A wet patch grew on her jeans and urine dripped to the floor. 'Disgusting child. Just like her fucking mother. She'll pay for pissing herself.'

With no warning, he grabbed Molly's right hand and strapped it to the chair arm, using a roll of duct tape he'd extracted from his pocket. She tried to jerk her arm away but he was too strong for her.

Gus groaned and glanced at Beth. Her hands were clenched tightly together. He flicked a glance at Sadia, who stared back wide eyed. Inhaling deeply, Gus laid his hands on Beth's shoulders and squeezed as if he could absorb her pain.

On the screen, Scream man placed the clippers round Molly's little finger. Molly looked straight at the camera. Tears coursed down her raw cheeks, her voice wobbled when she spoke. 'We're all square, mummy. Remember, we're all square.'

Then, he pressed the handles together.

Molly's scream reverberated round the kitchen and her small, delicate pinkie fell to the floor.

A whooshing sizzle coated the screen in darkness. The leaky tap's rhythmic drip punctuated the air of desperation with inappropriate frivolity. Beth stared at the fizzing screen, hands twitching ineffectually in her lap. Wendy wept quietly beside her, tissue held tightly against her nose. Then, abruptly, Beth scraped her chair back and jumped to her feet. Her motions were erratic and uncoordinated. Quickly, she walked to the pram, checked the baby and then grabbing the handles, she swivelled the pram round and clumsily manoeuvred it towards the door. Wendy Horan jumped to her feet. 'Beth what are you doing? Come and sit down?'

Beth shook her head and shrugged the other woman's arm off her shoulders. 'Leave me alone. I need to get out of here. I'll come to yours later, ok?'

Gus stood slowly and walked over to Beth, who glared up at him, her eyes shining with unshed tears. 'Beth, you can't just go. We need you to help us. We need you to tell us what you can about the tape.'

Beth took a step towards him, her eyes flashing. She prodded his shoulder. Gus bit back a grimace of pain as she spoke. 'You need to catch those bastards. That's what you need to do. What fucking good are you doing hanging around here? You need to get off your arses and find them. Before they hurt her any more.' Then, she was crying. Great heaving sobs lifted her chest up and down.

Gus put his arm round her shoulder and gently led her back to her chair, whilst Wendy repositioned the pram. He nodded to Sadia and mouthed the word 'coffee.' Sadia immediately moved to the kettle and began filling it. Gus fleetingly remembered the last time they'd been in this kitchen and he'd made that same request. Sadia had been reluctant to comply then, but now she worked quietly without protest, her brow furrowed in a worried line. It was hard to believe only a few days had passed since then.

He'd been reluctant for Beth to view the tape initially, however, in retrospect, he was glad she had. It had thrown up some things that needed clarifying and he was sure she could help.

Sitting opposite her, Wendy Horan by her side, he said, 'Beth, there were some things Molly said in the tape that we need you to consider. I'm going to ask you to watch it again and tell us if there's anything, anything at all, that we can use to pinpoint where they've got Molly. Can you do that?'

Beth wiped her sleeve over her eyes and swallowed. She turned to Wendy and mouthed 'sorry', before taking a deep breath and turning back to the screen. 'Go on, play it again.'

Gus pressed play and they watched the recording again, stopping just before the final scene.

For a minute, Beth remained quiet, then. 'We're not vegetarian. Molly's a chicken or beef burger girl. She loves her meat. Don't know why she'd say those things about being veggie. It doesn't make sense does it, Wendy?'

Wendy shook her head. 'No it doesn't. Remember when we took her for lunch at that lovely little veggie café in Thornton. She kicked up such a fuss, we had to take her to McDonald's on the way home.'

Beth smiled. 'Yeah. Such a little drama queen, isn't she?'

Wendy squeezed her arm. 'Yes, a real live wire.'

Beth lifted a shaking hand to her forehead and swept a tendril of hair back. 'I'm tired, Wendy. Really tired. I don't know how much more I can take.'

Sadia placed steaming mugs on the table and sat down beside Gus. She looked at Beth and said, in a tone Gus had never heard from her before, 'You need to rest Beth. You're in shock and your body's shutting down. The best thing you can do for Molly now is rest. Believe me, I know what shock can do to your body *and* mind.' She smiled at the older woman. 'Drink your coffee, I made decaff, and then let Wendy take you and Sam back to hers. Get some rest. When Molly comes home she's going to need a strong mother there to look after her.'

Beth studied Sadia's face and whatever she saw there seemed to reassure her for she smiled weakly, lifted her drink to her lips and nodded. 'Ok, DC Hussain, you win.'

Gus looked at Sadia, wondering what Beth had seen in her to make her give in. As he watched her, Sadia flushed and looked away.

CHAPTER 82
Hull

Sampson and PC Singh had broken all records to collect the necessary documents to hotfoot it up to Hull in time. Sleet and traffic build-up had made conditions hazardous. However, a bit of weather wasn't going to stop them and PC Singh, flashing lights on and accelerator pedal pressed to the floor, got them to the docks in record time with only a few near misses to their names.

Warrant in his pocket, a determined look on his face and purpose in his stride, Sampson marched across the Customs area at Hull docks, hand outstretched to greet Matthew Dubois, the customs official who had secured the driver of the Cosy Nights lorry. Before long, Dubois had guided them inside and updated them on the apprehension of Devlin O'Rourke.

Sampson and Singh, steaming hot chocolates in their hands, were just beginning to thaw out as they observed him through the one-way mirror. Sampson, seeing O'Rourke sprawled nonchalantly in the plastic chair, felt a sudden surge of anger flooding his body. The memory of the children found in Sharon Asif's attic merged with the image of little Molly Graves and the insouciant demeanour of the man in the room incensed him. He turned to Dubois. 'Does his passport seem legit?'

Dubois nodded. 'The local police are running it through HOLMES as we speak.'

Sampson took his phone from his pocket and texted the name with a request to cross-reference the name with Interpol, to Compo.

'You seized the lorry?'

Dubois hands behind his back, and, as was the habit of many short men, rocked on the balls of his feet in an attempt to expand his body space. He glanced sideways at Sampson, looking mildly pissed off. 'Of course. Forensics are on their way; we know how to do these things in Hull.' He jerked his thumb towards the window, 'He's not the first trafficker, excuse me, *suspected* trafficker, we've caught.' He winked. 'We know our job here, son.'

Heat spread over Sampson's cheeks. He quickly side-stepped the confrontation he felt was coming, by moving back from the window. 'Shall we let him stew for a bit whilst we have a look at the lorry?'

Dubois held his gaze for a second and then relented, 'Come on then, this way. We've had the dogs out but they're acting strangely. Asked the forensics to get a move on in case there's someone inside the lorry. But we needed to wait for the warrant. Kids, is it?'

Sampson nodded once and Dubois nodded back. 'Thought so, the kids always have a bigger impact don't they.'

Sampson, Singh and Dubois walked along a chilly tunnel that acted as a funnel for the cool sea breeze. It led to a huge hangar, lit with strobes that flickered irritatingly and a combined smell of salt air and oil layered the atmosphere. It was empty, except for the lorry bearing the red Cosy Nights script, flashed on a yellow background on the side panel. It stood in the middle surrounded by various suited-up forensics folk, ready to open the back of the lorry.

Sampson knew the sniffer dogs, in light of the previous detonation in Ilkley, had checked for explosives and found none. They were clear to go ahead now and open the lorry.

Sampson handed the warrant to a detective sergeant from Hull who swiftly read it and then with a perfunctory nod, signalled for the forensic team to begin. Sampson and Singh suited up and waited by the plastic crime scene tape that marked the periphery, held up by a series of traffic cones.

The team sprang into action with an energy that left Sampson breathless. Two suited figures converged on each side of the lorry. One jumped agilely into the cab, carrying a huge case of tools. Two technicians shimmied on their backs under the lorry, wearing goggles and head torches. Another two swabbed and photographed the external areas before raising the roll up door to the storage space at the back.

Sampson, on tiptoes, strained to see inside, but even with the assistance of the extra strong lights that flooded the cavity, he could see only a pile of mattresses laid flat in the truck bed one on top of the other. Each was separated by two metal prongs that created a bed frame for each mattress. Sampson's heart slowed. He'd been half expecting to see a huddled group of malnourished traumatised children cowering in the corner, a stream of steaming excrement flowing down to the door as testament to their suffering. Now that he'd been denied the image he'd mentally prepared for, he felt a curious disappointment tinged with relief.

A yell from the lorry's bowels accompanied by frantic activity – smothered conversation and suddenly a masked earless bunny head was at the door, eyes flashing, hands frantically waving.

'Ambulance, now!'

And then a human bunny chain was sliding mattresses out of the lorry, placing them gently on the floor and the most surreal scene Sampson had ever witnessed unfolded before his eyes. Mattresses were unzipped and flipped open, revealing child-sized hollows within. Inside each was a sleeping child attached to a ventilation system that was in turn connected to an oxygen cylinder, nestling in a separate hollow next to the child's ghostly frame.

Sampson's hands raked through his hair. Ten fucking mattresses, ten children. Fuck, fuck, fuck. Disregarding the preservation of evidence, the SOCOs scurried to care for the children while ambulances screeched to a halt at the entrance to the hanger. In stunned silence the SOCOs stepped back and were replaced by paramedics who ascertained that all ten children were still alive. A spontaneous cheer erupted as the last child, breathing independently although still unconscious, was transferred from his cushioned coffin to the ambulance.

CHAPTER 83
Bradford

'That bitch got the latest little offering then, did she?' The Matchmaker laughed and rubbed his hands together. He and The Facilitator were back in the same hotel room as before. The Matchmaker had arrived first, making sure he wasn't followed and as usual his hat and scarf made him virtually unidentifiable. Lucky really, as he was almost certain he'd seen a lackey of that prude DCI Hussain escorting a barely-legal hooker into one of the rooms further down the corridor. He imagined how Hussain would look if he told him that his favourite officer was knocking off prossies in his spare time. He smiled inwardly. Hussain would look down his patrician nose as if he'd just encountered a foul smell. If it wasn't for the existence of the daughter, Sadia, The Matchmaker would doubt that Hussain had ever got down and dirty in the bedroom. Too bloody stuck-up to indulge in the baser activities of mere mortals.

The Facilitator looked tense. As well as his crumpled clothes and obvious fatigue, The Matchmaker thought he carried a defeated air. He wondered if the last few stressful days, although integral to their plan, had knocked The Facilitator off kilter. They'd discussed it all thoroughly and The Facilitator had agreed that a smokescreen was their best protection. So, that's what they'd implemented. Soon the 'truth' would be revealed. The Facilitator could breathe easy then.

As the other man paced the room, The Matchmaker's eyes narrowed. He had to stop him from flaking out. Keep him on board. God, why couldn't the idiot just grow some balls. Did he always have to be the one carrying everything?

The Facilitator stopped pacing, and avoiding The Matchmaker's gaze, he replied abruptly, 'Yes, she got it. But you need to start playing this safely. You're getting too hell-bent on revenge. We've got business commitments to meet and that's got to be our priority. The Provider is off the radar, so we don't know where our next shipment is and we've got orders to fulfil.'

The Matchmaker's fists clenched. He stepped closer. 'Watch your tone! I've worked on this business for two decades. It was my brainchild and I don't need reminding about my obligations to our clients. *You,* on the other hand, seem to need reminding about who salvaged the debacle when James Clegg got caught. I'll get my revenge on that bitch because she *needs* to pay.' He grinned and backed off slightly. 'Don't forget, I've got my finger on the pulse. I know that the police are dithering with that damaged DI McGuire floundering around. Humph, it's laughable, really.'

The Facilitator flinched. 'He doesn't seem as out of the game as you think. He seems on the ball, organised, efficient. Don't underestimate him. That could be our undoing.'

The Matchmaker grabbed The Facilitator's shoulder and squeezed lightly. 'Don't be such a wimp. We're into the endgame now. When I've got my last revenge we'll relocate and continue as before. We'll be in the clear.'

The Facilitator jumped to his feet, rubbing his hand over his short hair. 'For God's sake, can you hear yourself? We've left a whole load of soiled goods in an attic for the police to find. We've attempted to kill Jamal Asif, abducted Molly Graves and proceeded to amputate parts of her body. Oh and did I mention we killed the kid's granny too. Do you really think Gus McGuire, will let all that slide? Because I don't. He seems far too efficient and driven for that.'

The Matchmaker sat down on the uncomfortable desk chair and crossed his legs. With one hand slung behind him resting on the tabletop, his tapping fingers were the only indication of his anger. He waited till The Facilitator looked away before speaking in a controlled tone. 'Don't *ever* question my actions. Things are under control and I'm nearly done. Two more days and operation 'Annihilate Beth Graves' will be over. They can't link any of us to those brats and our client's confidentiality is intact. We're fine, ok?'

The Facilitator, head down, said nothing. Then the Matchmaker's phone rang. Eyes resting on The Facilitator's bowed head, he answered. As he listened, his fingers tightened on the phone. Abruptly, without speaking, he hung up. The Facilitator met his gaze as the Matchmaker said, 'Our eyes on the ground say The Provider's truck has been stopped in Hull. He's been arrested and is en route to Bradford.'

The Facilitator visibly paled. 'And I suppose you can you sort *that* one out too?'

The Matchmaker cursed and began to pace in the confined space. Finally, he spun round on his heel. 'We'll cut him free. We'll begin to relocate tomorrow, ok?'

CHAPTER 84
The Fort
Saturday

Gus walked into the interview room with Alice. Jamal, his lawyer, Amy Winters and Naila Siddique, his social worker, were already sitting at the table. Jamal was slumped in the chair, his head bowed. His shoulders were tense and his fists were clenched by his sides

Gus pulled out his chair, turned it round and straddled it, leaning his arms across the back rest. 'You ok, Jamal?'

Jamal's head jerked up and his eyes flashed venom at Gus before he resumed his previous position. Gus blinked. Wow! What the hell had caused this sudden animosity? He flicked a glance at Naila who shook her head, clearly as puzzled as Gus by the boy's reaction.

'Did the doctor check you out, Jamal?'

Jamal shrugged. Naila nudged him gently with her elbow. 'Come on, Jamal. Tell DI McGuire how you are.'

Jamal's gaze remained on the floor. 'You tell him, if you're so keen.'

Amy Winters butted in. 'The doctors have catalogued Jamal's injuries and have accessed his medical records and have found evidence of significant injuries that may indicate long-term abuse. There are no immediate concerns over any of his injuries and he's fit to interview.'

Gus smiled at her and then turned back to Jamal. 'What's up, son? Are you frightened?'

Jamal snorted and pushed himself upright, his eyes sparking. 'I'm not your fucking son, ok? And yeah, I am fucking frightened. You lot are all bloody bastards. I don't fucking trust any of you.' He jumped to his feet and towered over the table, glowering at Gus.

Naila stood up quickly and grabbed his arm. 'Come on Jamal, what's got into you? This isn't like you. Inspector McGuire wants to help you.'

Gus held Jamal's gaze and waved a hand at Naila telling her to stand down. What the hell had happened to this kid between yesterday and this morning? Was it that they'd discovered the extent of his injuries? Gus didn't think it was that and he really wanted to find out what was causing the boy to act so aggressively.

Naila plonked herself on the edge of her chair. Amy leaned forward and spoke sharply. 'Sit down, Jamal. This isn't helping you.' Jamal glared at her, his chin thrust forward, then he slumped back into his chair still glaring at Gus.

Gus pressed his lips together wondering how to proceed. Eventually, his voice calm and low he said, 'What's up, Jamal? Yesterday you left here happy to work with us, knowing we were going to do our best for you and now,' he splayed his arms, palm up before him, 'you're acting like we're the enemy. That tells me something's happened to upset you. What the hell is it?'

Jamal chewed on his lip and sniffed. His leg juddered up and down, his knee banging periodically on the table.

'He's one of you lot. The fucking bastard who brought those kids to our house is a fucking stinkin' pig.' Without warning, Jamal jumped to his feet and before any of them could stop him, he punched the wall.

Gus, open mouthed, swung his gaze to Alice who looked as stunned as he felt. Naila, after a single shocked glance at Gus, approached Jamal and put her arm round his heaving shoulders. She guided him back to his chair. Gus nodded to the constable by the door 'Get an ice pack and call the duty doctor please.'

Jamal lowered his head onto his arms on the table. His injured hand was grazed and beginning to swell. She pushed

361

a tissue through the gap between his head and his arms. Jamal snatched the tissue and with his forehead balanced on the edge of the table blew his nose and used the tissue to wipe his eyes before thrusting the sodden rag on the table.

Gus waited till he'd quietened down and had an ice pack on his hand. 'Jamal, did you see the man who brought the kids to your house? The one in the photograph at the police station?'

Head still on the table, Jamal spoke in a mumble. 'Not the one in the photo. The other one. The scary one who came that first time.'

'Jamal, where did you see this man?'

Jamal jerked his head toward the door and said grudgingly. 'Just out there in the corridor.'

Gus raised his eyebrows and looked at Amy and Naila, who both looked shocked. What the fuck was going on? Gus felt like his head was about to explode. He mentally counted to ten and then said calmly, 'Jamal, you told us previously that you could hardly see the other man. That you couldn't describe him to us.'

Jamal slammed his uninjured hand on the table. 'Fucking knew it. Knew you lot wouldn't believe me. You always just want to protect each other.'

Gus reigned in his emotions, said, 'Look, Jamal, it's not that we don't believe you. It's that we need to be clear about this for the tape. What you've just told us is really serious and we need to get it right, ok?'

Jamal nodded and scrubbed his sleeve across his face. Naila handed him another tissue.

'Right,' said Gus. 'Tell me how you know the man in the corridor was the same one you saw in number 9 Inkerman Street.'

Jamal glanced at the interview room door as if scared the man would walk through.

Gus said, 'This is in confidence, Jamal. Until we've investigated this, we'll keep this between us. You're perfectly safe.'

Jamal glanced at Naila who gave him a reassuring smile. He began to speak, hesitatingly. 'I didn't see him clearly that time, you know. But there was just something about him. The way he held his head and that.' He scrunched his fingers together and rested them on the table. His eyes flicked between Amy and Gus. 'It were him, you know. I'm certain. It were his voice too. I *know* it were him. It were his voice. Posh an' all… and his watch. Only a posh fucker or James Bond would have a watch like that.'

Exhaling heavily, Gus looked at Amy and Naila. He jerked his head to the door and then turned to Jamal. 'DC Cooper will stay with you for a minute, Jamal. I just want to have a quiet word with Naila and Ms Winters.'

Jamal snorted. 'Cooking the fucking books, covering your arses.'

Gus could detect anxiety in Jamal's eyes. He smiled slightly at the boy's bravado and pushed himself off the chair and walked to the door. 'I won't let you down, Jamal. If a police officer is involved in this, then I'll find him. You have my word on that.'

Once in the corridor, Gus raked his fingers through his hair and looked from Naila to Amy. Both women looked shocked. Gus gestured down the corridor and led them into an empty interview room. Again, his fingers raked through his hair. 'This is a fucking mess, isn't it?'

Amy pulled out a chair and sat down. 'Well, seems to me that if my client is right and he *can* identify a police officer as the man behind this child trafficking, then he needs to be in protective custody. Away from Bradford.'

Gus sat down opposite her and clasped his hands on the table. 'Look, let's not get ahead of ourselves. Jamal's description is sketchy to say the least. Let's try to identify the person in question as quietly as we can before going official. Jamal's fine at the moment with Alice.'

Amy frowned. 'Yes, but if the man he saw also saw him, he could be at risk.'

Gus nodded. 'I agree and that's why we need to narrow this down as quickly as possible. You two walked with Jamal through the station. Let's see if you can come up with a list of officers you saw on the way back to the interview room. Then, I can get their photos for Jamal to identify.'

Amy's eyes narrowed. 'You think he's lying, don't you?'

Gus looked straight into her eyes and shook his head. 'No. No, I don't get the sense that Jamal's lying. I get the sense that he's petrified because he thinks he saw that bloke.' He paused, 'I only hope to God he's mistaken. However, I don't think he's lying. Now let's sit down and get this sorted.'

He pulled out a chair, sat down and took out his notebook. 'Right, think back to who you saw on your way back to the interview room. Remember, it may have been admin staff or other lawyers or anybody. Jamal wouldn't necessarily know which were police officers and which weren't.'

Amy snorted. 'Clutching at straws, Gus clutching at straws.'

'Damn right I am.' Said Gus. 'But not for the reasons you think. I hope Jamal's right so we can nail this bloke. However, I would prefer it not to be a serving police officer, for obvious reasons.' He crossed his legs and rolled his aching shoulder. 'However, police officer or not. I will do my damnedest to send the guilty person down for as long as I can.'

Naila pulled a pad out of her handbag and said, 'Right, let's get started.'

Fifteen minutes later, Gus studied the list of names that Naila and Amy had produced.

'Any you think capable of this, Gus?' asked Naila.

Gus shook his head. 'God, Naila. There're some arses on this list, Knowles for one, but none I believe could do this. However, you know as well as I do that sometimes the most successful criminals are those we'd least suspect.'

Amy stood up. 'I want to get back to my client, can you expedite your investigation into this so we can get him out of here as quickly as possible?'

Gus nodded. 'I'll get Compo on the case. We still need to finish the interview regarding his mum. I think we should get it over with and sent to the CPS. I'll get Alice to finish up interviewing him with DC Hussain. After that get Jamal out of here for some lunch. Be back by 1pm. By then, hopefully, I'll have some photos to show him. Sadia can take you down the back way, so you'll avoid seeing anyone.'

***

Gus' heartbeat sped up. They were close. Things were coming together beautifully now. First Sampson locating the truck in Hull and then Jamal recognising one of the men in the station. Ok, not so good news that one of the key players could be a police officer, but it didn't matter to Gus. No matter who the bastard was, Gus would see he went down for a long time for this.

As Gus paced the interview room, Compo cross-referenced the enhanced images they'd obtained from the recordings. He'd also printed off photos of all the officers on the list Naila and Amy Winters had given, ready to show Jamal later.

When Sampson burst into the room to say he'd deposited Devlin O'Rourke the truck driver in Interview Room 2, everyone crowded round him. Gus slapped him on the back. 'Well done, Sampson. You did good. What's the update on the kids?'

'They're all fine. Traumatised, of course, but physically they're ok. We got them in time and Detective Jankowski is working with missing persons in Poland to try to repatriate them.'

'Right,' said Gus. 'Grab a drink. We'll let O'Rourke sweat for a bit, then I want Alice and Sadia to observe whilst you and I interview the bastard, ok?'

Alice raised her eyebrow. 'Sampson?'

Gus grinned. 'Yeah, Sampson. Jealous, Al?'

She laughed at his teasing tone and shook her head. 'No offence Sampson, but he's a bit green for such a key interview, don't you think?'

'God, Al. You get promoted for five minutes and you think you know better than me?'

'No, it's not that.'

Gus cut her dead with a dismissive wave of the hand. 'Sampson did the bust. He deserves to be there and he'll learn from this. I'll lead. Now head up and make sure everything's in order. I want this to run as smoothly as a stripper on a pole.'

Gus could tell Sampson was a bit nervous about doing the interview, but the lad deserved it. He'd hotfooted up the motorway in crap weather, had witnessed first-hand what O'Rourke had done to those poor kids and was still standing. Gus had to admit that the boy did look a bit frazzled and the bags under his eyes told Gus that Sampson had probably not slept well the previous night. Still he was here, stoically waiting for Gus as he limped along the corridor. When he drew level with Sampson, Gus smiled. 'You ready?'

'As I'll ever be, I suppose.'

Gus remembered how nervous he'd been at his first big interview – A woman who'd killed her husband by slicing his throat because he said her new dress made her look fat. 'You'll be right, let me take the lead.'

Together they walked through the door. Gus thrust it open so hard it bounced off the wall a few times before Sampson gently clicked it shut. A uniformed officer stood against the wall unsmiling and still and the duty solicitor, a man named Cadbury, sat beside O'Rourke. Gus noticed that Cadbury had angled his chair slightly away from his client. Gus thought Devlin O'Rourke looked too big for the chair he was sitting in. He hoped he felt as uncomfortable as he looked. O'Rourke's hands, cuffed in front of him, rested on the table. His face remained impassive as Gus scrutinised him. A few days' stubble covered his lower face and his heavy brows made his eyes look hooded.

Gus strode round to the other side of the table and made an exaggerated show of sniffing the air. 'Fuck's sake, it stinks in here. When's the last time you had a bath?' he rested his fists on the table and leaned over O'Rourke, 'or is that just the stench of fear?'

Sampson followed Gus round the table, pulled out a chair and sat. Slowly scraping out his own chair, Gus kept his eyes on the prisoner. O'Rourke's expression slipped into a sneer but he didn't reply to Gus's taunt. Holding Gus's gaze, O'Rourke leaned back, legs spread widely revealing a bulging crotch covered in tight jeans. He allowed his cuffed hands to slip loosely between his legs.

When Sampson had set up the recorder, Gus introduced those present and re-read the prisoner his rights before beginning. 'You're well and truly fucked now, aren't you? Found in possession of a truck load of sedated kids hooked up to oxygen and hidden in cut out mattresses. What's the betting the DNA found on those kids in the attic will be a match to yours? Yep, you're fucked.' Gus grinned at O'Rourke. 'Care to tell me how those children got in your lorry?'

O'Rourke tensed one arm so the muscles rippled up his arm, giving the impression that his snake tattoo was alive and ready to pounce on Gus. He smirked 'No comment!'

Gus shrugged, his expression bored, as he slipped a packet of chewing gum out and offered it to each of the room's occupants, pointedly omitting to offer any to O'Rourke. 'Of course, the fingerprints we found on the oxygen bottles and the hoses match yours, so there's really no doubt that *you* hooked the kids up. The big question is, how much of the rap are you prepared to take for the whole operation? Give us The Matchmaker and maybe you could spend your sentence in solitary away from all those other prisoners who, despite their own transgressions, still adhere to a moral code that compels them to want to castrate kiddy diddlers like you. What do you say?'

The sneer remained in place. 'No comment!'

Gus popped a stick of chewing gum in his mouth and chewed, before speaking again. 'Well, I'll just offer the same deal to one of the others you know. Maybe the one that we picked up in Thornton. The one who had Molly.'

O'Rourke's flinch was fleeting, but Gus noticed it with satisfaction. 'Oh, didn't I tell you? We've got Molly' Gus tapped the table with one finger. 'You're not the only route to the big man, you know. Oh no. Whichever one of your little band of merry men squeals first, is the one who'll get the best deal.'

O'Rourke lifted his hands and rested them on the tabletop. He began to scratch his wrist with a rasping sound, releasing a flurry of dry skin.

'Fuck off,' he said, but Gus was sure his tone was less certain than before.

Gus looked pointedly at O' Rourke's wrist. It had begun to bleed slightly now. 'Oh, ok.'

Gus stood up and moved to the door with Sampson following, before the other man turned slightly in his chair. 'Let me talk with my lawyer and then we'll talk a deal.'

'Really? Well, you can talk to your lawyer for as long as you like; as for the other, well, I wouldn't hold my breath if I was you. First piglet to squeal gets the deal... Oink, oink.'

***

It had been snowing for hours. Gus had got nothing useful from Devlin O'Rourke so he'd been put back in the cells where he could wallow in his own filth. Now it was time for Gus to speak with Jamal Asif again. Armed with the photos in a manila folder, Gus and Sadia entered the Family Interview Room where Jamal waited with his solicitor, Amy Winters.

Amy looked up when he came in. 'Look Gus, I know this is important but as soon as Jamal's IDed the man he saw, I'm taking him back to the children's centre for the night. The weather's not improving and Jamal needs his rest. He's frightened and tired.'

Jamal sniffed. 'Am not frightened. Just let's get on with this. Let me see the photos.'

Gus took them out the folder. Sadia switched on the recorder and Gus introduced those present before handing the pictures over to Jamal. He explained, for the tape, that Jamal had been given fifteen photos to look at.

'Take your time Jamal, there's no rush. It's important you don't make a mistake, ok?' said Sadia.

Jamal nodded and began to look at the photos one by one whilst everyone else looked on. Finally, he got to the last one. He looked at it and then scowling he flung them all on the table.

'He's not there. I knew you lot would all stick together. He's not fucking there.' And with no warning he scraped his chair back and jumped up abruptly, sending his chair flying and glared at them. Amy gently led him back to the chair that Sadia had set upright again. Tears poured down his cheeks and his shoulders heaved.

Gathering the photos together into a pile, Gus tried to think. He had no doubt that Jamal was telling the truth. So, who the hell had he seen? Who the hell was The Matchmaker? He waited till Jamal hiccupped to a halt before speaking. 'Look Jamal, the photos we showed were only of the people Ms Winters and Naila could remember passing in the corridor in the way back. We're not giving up on this. I'm going to see if I can do some more prying to find out who else was around at the same time as you and we'll bring you back in tomorrow to look at more photos. We're not doubting your word, nor are we trying to cover up. If the bastard who did that to those kids works in this police station, in whatever capacity, we will find him and we *will* punish him. You have my word on that.' Gus thrust out his hand towards Jamal who glared at it for a good ten seconds before grudgingly taking it and giving it a quick shake.

'Now Jamal, I'll send a sketch artist over this afternoon and I'll come by some time tomorrow with Naila and Ms Winters to show you some more photos. I don't want you to talk about this to anyone. No point risking word getting to him.'

Gus was frustrated. His gut told him Jamal was telling the truth, but he was running out of options. He hoped the sketch artist would come up with the goods.

***

Gus was frustrated. He'd got nothing more out of O'Rourke; and Compo was still running possible locations in Thornton. He felt like the day had been wasted and all the while Molly Graves was enduring God knows what sort of trauma. By the time it'd got to 5:30pm, he'd told everyone to pack up and get home and he'd left to brief Nancy before leaving himself.

The walk back through Lister Park made Gus's thigh ache unbearable, but at least it cleared the caffeine fuzz from his head. Snow fell in vertical sheets, covering Sophie Ryder's *Minotaur* and *Lady Hare* sculptures with a frosting that made them look vaguely aggressive, in a comic book way. By the time he reached Marriner's Drive, he was wet, cold and dragging his leg slightly. His shoulder muscles bunched together like a clump of herniated intestines. When he finally reached his drive, he sighed deeply, bit his lip and almost crawled up the steep slope, before falling through the door into his hallway. Slamming the door shut behind him he lay on the carpet and allowed the welcome warmth of his central heating to engulf him, as he painfully massaged life back into his dead thigh.

Showered and medicated, he lay on his couch flicking through the TV channels – a spare part in his own home. He wore a pair of trackie bottoms and his oldest t-shirt, one with Bob Marley's righteous dreads flowing across his chest. If he turned his head slightly to one side, the faint whiff of Gabriella's overly-expensive perfume wafted into his nostrils from the cushion cover. Cursing, he pulled the cushion from behind his head and lobbed it at the telly, knocking over the framed wedding photo that taunted him from above the screen. Of course, it hit the table as it fell and shattered, sending slivers of glass all over the carpet. Cursing some more, he pulled himself up and bending to pick up the frame, stood on a shard of glass. Hopping into the kitchen, he lobbed the frame and photo into the bin, before slapping a plaster on the blob of blood that had appeared on the sole of his foot.

Focussed now, he dragged out the hoover and cleared up the glass. Then, black bin bag in hand, he sauntered round the living room, tossing in the few photos of Gabriella that remained. Satisfied, he surveyed the room with a grim smile. He gathered up the floral cushions that had always given him a headache and tossed them in the bag too. Next went in the stupid John Lewis paintings that he'd always hated because they had no meaning, other than they matched the wallpaper. What the hell was that all about? Buying random pictures of squares because they matched the colour of your walls?

With a sudden whoop, he hurried into the hallway and opened the cupboard under the stairs. He knew it was in there. *He'd* refused to get rid of it and Gabriella had refused to hang it. Stretching right to the back, he finally found what he was looking for. A few seconds later, he exited the cupboard, a stray cobweb hanging from his dreads and a smile on his face. In his hands was a huge picture frame. Holding it out at arm's length, he studied it for a minute and then he went through to the living room and positioned the picture where the discarded canvases had been.

He stood back, arms folded across his chest and studied the charcoal sketch of Bob Marley. Each of his dreadlocks had been sketched in the form of a serpent, intertwining in a sinewy riot of life. He stretched out a hand and touched the inscription at the bottom of the drawing: 'To my best friend, Dread McGuire, love you mate, Greg.'

He was just wiping away a tear, when he heard hammering on his door. Who the fuck could that be? Before turning away to answer the door, he cast a final glance at the picture and in a quiet voice said, 'Love you too, mate.'

Walking along the hallway, the security light illuminated a quartet of familiar heads against the pane. He flung open the door and cocked an eyebrow at the four people huddled on his doorstep, shivering and covered in snow.

Alice's huge eyes peered out from between her oversized black bobble hat and the coils of her equally large scarf. 'We walked all the way here from The Fort, Gus. We're frozen and wet and sooo tired and…' she hesitated, 'we brought provisions.'

The last sentence was delivered in triumph. On cue, Sampson and Compo stepped forward brandishing bulging bright orange Sainsbury's bags. Sadia stepped forward and pushed a bottle, tightly wrapped in the same familiar orange plastic into his hands '… and libations!' she said.

Gus grinned. 'Funny, I don't remember inviting you lot over.' He shrugged and unwrapped a bottle of Glenmorangie. 'But what the hell, come in, let's have a party.'

Alice kicked slush from her Doc Martins and stepped through the door, followed by the others. 'We got snowed in, Gus. Traffic's at a standstill on Manningham Lane and we couldn't face hanging out at The Fort all night. You don't mind do you?'

She shrugged out of her coat, thrust it at Gus, kicked off her boots, rubbed her hands together and marched through to his living room.

'Fuck's sake! You've given the place a makeover since the other day.' She flung her small frame onto the couch and, head on one side, studied the picture on the wall. 'Better taste than Gabriella, I have to say.'

Sadia who'd followed Alice through more hesitantly, stood transfixed, hands on her hips before the picture. When Compo and Sampson joined her, she turned to Gus her brown eyes glistening with unshed tears. 'That is gorgeous, bloody beautiful. I once saw something similar online. It was of Marc Bolan with his curls drawn as serpents. It was great. But this?' She shook her head 'Phew, this is amazing, what a talent!'

Gus felt himself choking up, but he managed to smile. 'Yeah, Greg, the artist, was really talented and I was lucky to have him as my best friend.'

Alice reached out her hand and squeezed his arm. 'He was lucky to have *you* as his best friend, too, you know?'

Gus tilted his head to one side and laughed humourlessly. 'Yeah? So fucking lucky I killed him!'

Alice shook her head and jumped to her feet, standing right in front of Gus glaring up at him. 'Don't you go all fucking maudlin on me, Dread McGuire. You were there for him *always*. Do you think he'd have been able to live with himself if he'd survived after killing little Becky and Billy? No fucking way.' She prodded Gus firmly in the chest '*You*, on the other hand, can and *will* live with yourself, because you know you did the only thing you could in the shittiest of circumstances, ok?'

Gus looked down into her fierce little face, and then glanced round at the other three members of his small but very effective team. Sampson, Compo and Sadia looked embarrassed, but each of them held his gaze. He smiled and slung his arm round Alice's shoulder. He pulled her towards him, in a quick bear hug, before spinning her towards the kitchen. 'Go get glasses, we've got a fine malt whisky to open in Greg's honour.'

Alice grinned and got the glasses. An hour later the phone went and Gus, as mellow as his whisky, picked up. 'Yoll? Hey Naila, how're you?'

As he listened, his expression became serious. His forehead creased in a frown and he stood up and began to pace the room. 'Shit, are you sure? Ok, thanks.'

He released a huge breath and turned to face the others. 'Naila's just remembered who else she saw when she was with Jamal and you'll never believe who it was.'

CHAPTER 85
Ilkley

Scrunched up on the sofa in Wendy's front room, Beth gazed unseeingly at the fading embers in the fire place. She hadn't slept the previous night. Her thoughts kept replaying that awful moment when Scream man snipped off Molly's finger. Molly's scream, even now, reverberated in her ears. She was thankful to Wendy and her husband Paul for putting her and Sam up, yet she felt she was intruding. Paul was kind, but despite her dazed state, she was well aware of the concerned looks that passed between the couple. Now, Wendy had sent Paul off to Morrison's. Beth felt guilty at hounding him out of his house, yet at the same time she knew he was probably secretly relieved to get away from the oppressive atmosphere.

She cradled a mug of cold coffee with a scummy milk layer on top that rippled every time she moved her hand. Wendy reached over and took the mug from her, before picking up a log and throwing it onto the fire. Beth didn't respond. Sam slept soundly upstairs and Radio Four played gently in the background. Wendy sat back down opposite her, her eyes worried. 'What are you thinking?'

Eyes huge and dark-rimmed, Beth turned to her. 'Why did Molly go on about being veggie? It makes no damn sense.'

They sat in silence for few minutes. Then Beth turned to Wendy her face serious. 'That's it. Molly was giving us a clue. She was telling us she's near South Square café in Thornton. That's why she went on about being veggie. That must be where they're keeping her, she must have recognised the area. Why else would she say that stuff? And what was it she said at the end – *we're all square* or something like that.' Beth jumped up, grabbed her phone from her bag and with trembling fingers called Gus.

CHAPTER 86
The Fort

Despite the litre bottle of Glenmorangie that they had demolished the previous night, Gus's team were energised. The phone calls from Naila and Beth had injected some purpose into the investigation.

The snow had continued to fall steadily overnight and Gus had issued sheets, blankets and towels to his team and was pleased they'd come over. Until Naila's call, the atmosphere had been jovial and, for Gus, their presence in his home and the addition of Greg's picture had obliterated all lingering traces of Gabriella.

Now, after a fry-up provided by Sampson and a trek through the crisp snow, they were back at work and the buzz in the incident room was almost tangible. Frissons of excitement seemed to ricochet off the walls, sparking adrenalin as it went. Gus barely noticed the tension in his shoulder and thigh as he watched his team work. The smell of coffee combined with the sweat of hard work was like perfume to him. He knew they were getting somewhere. Compo had initiated a geo-profile programme to try to locate the hazy images they'd extracted from the kidnapper's recording. He'd limited it to a ten-mile radius round South Square in Thornton. One of the images, Compo reckoned, was of a distant bridge type structure, but unfortunately they couldn't make it very clear.

Pouring himself a mug of black coffee and downing his pain meds Gus turned as Compo banged him on the shoulder. Despite having breakfasted at Gus's house not an hour earlier he held a bacon butty in one hand. Gus grimaced slightly, as a dollop of brown sauce landed on his T-shirt. Seeing Compo's flushed face, he just picked up a tissue and mopped up the spillage without saying a word.

Compo's woolly hat was pushed so far back on his head it was barely holding on. Strands of brown curls escaped, making him look a combination of a scarecrow and a mad scientist.

'Finished the analysis of those images on Alex Graves' PC, Gus. Looks like they were bounced around about a trillion times, but I eventually got it. He didn't upload the images. They were planted.'

Gus frowned. 'Planted?'

'Yes, I've not finished investigating yet, but it looks like they were uploaded to his PC by a third party who, wait for it, uploaded them from the police child sex offenders' image database. They then bounced it around the globe and finally inserted it into his hard drive. Clever.' He bit into his butty. Gus tried to ignore his masticating jaws and the contents of his mouth as he continued. '…but, although it was clever, it weren't next level clever, you know?'

Gus grinned and shook his head.

Compo swallowed a large mouthful, coughed dislodging splatters of soggy bread over Gus and said, 'Well, too hard for *you* to do, but quite easy for the likes of me.'

Alice who'd wandered over to listen hid a smile and winked at Gus who ignored her.

'What are you saying, Compo?' asked Gus.

'Well, it's almost like whoever put those images on Graves' PC, weren't right bothered about us realising they'd been planted. Maybe even wanted us to find that out.'

'Hmm.' said Alice, 'that adds up really. It's another way of punishing Beth isn't it? Sow the seed of doubt about her current husband. Torture her by thinking she'd exposed her family to a paedophile, not once, but twice. Clever really.'

Gus perched on the edge of his desk. 'Sounds logical. My only worry is why would they make it easy for us to find that out, Compo?'

Compo shrugged, took another bite of his butty and chewed. 'Obviously either they're just not that computer savvy, or, like Al said, they wanted us to know they'd been planted.' He frowned. 'But if they could hack our databases to get the images that indicates a greater computer awareness than the way they uploaded it to his PC.' He shrugged again. 'Don't know what to say, Gus.'

Gus tapped his finger on his lip, then took a slurp of coffee, turned to Alice and said, 'We better let him go. Get that arranged through his solicitor and then contact Beth to explain the situation. Oh, and let the officers keeping an eye on her know to expect him to turn up there. Meanwhile, Compo, you keep on with that and see if you can come up with anything else, ok?'

Gus had printed off more photos to show Jamal, including an image of DCI Wentworth. Sampson looked at it. 'Do you think it's him, Gus?'

Gus shrugged. When Naila had described the other officer to him the previous night, he'd known immediately it was Wentworth. Whether or not he was The Matchmaker remained to be seen. Although, Gus acknowledged internally, it would be a whole lot better for Bradford if the dodgy officer came from Cambridge. 'I don't know. I bloody hope not, but I don't know. It could have been him Jamal saw and he was around during the initial investigation in Cambridge.' He shrugged. 'We'll have to wait and see.'

'Yeah, but it would be better if it was him, rather than one of our own, wouldn't it?' He flushed 'When I say better, I mean for us. Not for the kids. Fuck nothing could make it better for them but …' his voice trailed off.

Gus squeezed his arm. 'I know what you mean, Sampson. But no matter who it is the shit's going to hit the combine harvester with a vengeance.'

Sampson sniffed, 'Well if we're employing combine harvesters, sir, I know which body parts I'd like to see hit those blades.'

Gus bit back a laugh and moved to the front of the room. 'Right, listen up. I want everyone to leave the room except Cooper, Compo, Hussain and Sampson.'

The officers sifting through and inputting data, paused and looked expectantly at Gus.

He raked his hand through his hair. 'Now!'

At once a hustle of activity ensued as the officers left the room. When the door closed behind the last one, Gus turned to his small team. 'This is big, ok? Fucking big and we've got to make it airtight.'

They all nodded.

'Compo, I need you to make our entire PC trail invisible and inaccessible to anyone outside this room – including DCI Chalmers.'

Compo saluted and turned to his computer, clacking the keys at a rate of knots.

A smile flicked quickly over Gus's face and then just as quickly disappeared to be replaced by a worried frown.

'I know I can trust you. That's why you're here. However, this is sensitive, in capital letters. Alice, as soon as I've briefed you all, I want you to personally contact DCI Chalmers. Don't do this on the phone. Find her and speak to her face to face.'

Alice nodded. In the ensuing silence, Compo's computer pinged making everyone jump. Then three things happened almost simultaneously

Firstly, a collective indrawn breath, secondly every phone in the room simultaneously began to ring and thirdly the door burst open and one of the officers who'd just been evacuated burst in. 'Sir, you'll never guess what's happened!'

Gus answered his phone, listened and then turned to the officer with a curt nod 'I've just heard thanks.' He turned and grabbed his coat. Scooping the manila folder with the photos off his desk, he thrust it into Sadia's hands. 'Get these photos to Jamal. I want an ID, ASAP.' He turned and headed to the door. 'Come on, Sampson and Alice, with me. The officers guarding Beth Graves are dead.

CHAPTER 87

Molly, curled in the foetal position under the duvet, with only her face visible, stared, through red-rimmed eyes, at the wall. She felt numb. Her entire body was ice-cold and the shivers that wracked her body, had only recently shuddered to a stop. Now, the only sensation that registered in her head was the dull throb in her bandaged hand. Time and time again, she saw him place the snippers round her pinkie. She could still feel the sharp, almost unbearable pain that followed when he pressed the handles closed and her finger fell to the ground.

Within seconds he'd picked up from the floor the small cook's blow torch, an exact duplicate the one her mum had for her famous creme brûlée. His horrid Scream mask face loomed towards her. His laugh was wild and scary and then... the stench of burned meat accompanied by unimaginable pain, then darkness. When she woke, it was dark and she was on her own, lying uncovered on the bed. A bandage had been unskilfully wrapped around her tender hand and blood was seeping through its folds.

That had been yesterday morning, yet the pain was still there. She'd dozed off and on all day and most of the night. Now, she felt hot and feverish. She knew she should eat something from the bag the other man had brought, but she couldn't face it.

She looked at her hand as if it was an alien part of her body she'd never seen before. It would never, ever look the same again. Her finger wouldn't grow back. With tears trickling down her cheeks, she reached for the bottled water that someone, probably the creepy bloke, not the masked maniac, had left beside the mattress. She locked the bottle under her arm to hold it steady and using her good hand, she opened it. Balancing the bottle in the space between her crossed legs, she scooped up the pills that had been left beside the bottle and flung them into her mouth. Grimacing at their sour taste, she flung her head back and swallowed them down with a glug of water. Awkwardly, she replaced the lid and let the bottle fall to the floor, before edging her way under the duvet and pulling it up over her head and round to meet under her chin. She knew now that there was no way she was ever getting out of this warehouse alive. No way she'd ever see her mum or her dad or her grandma or even the squealing brat. Unable to stop herself, she let hot tears dribble down her face until her pillow was soaked.

CHAPTER 88
Bradford

Gus, face pinched, leaned forward in his seat, as Sampson edged his way down Oak Lane and onto Manningham Lane which, thankfully, had been gritted. The roads were quiet and Sampson made good tracks onto Keighley Road, past The Branch Pub and The Hop in Saltaire and onto the bypass where the traffic thickened. Alice perched on the back seat stretched her belt till she could lean, her arms one on each of the front seats. She poked her head through the gap between the two. 'Fuck, Gus. This is shit. Just fucking shit.'

Gus nodded abruptly and pulled his jacket round so he could retrieve his phone from the pocket. 'Al, get on to the officer in charge and find out all you can about the scene. I'm phoning Compo.'

Alice leaned back and made the call, whilst Gus waited for Compo to pick up. 'That you, Comps? I know we've not had a firm ID from Jamal, but I want you to ask around. See if anyone knows where Wentworth was last night and the day of Molly's abduction. See if you can get some sort of alibi for him.'

Compo's reply was slow to come, then in a strained husky whisper, he said, 'Ok, I'll attempt to expedite that last instruction immediately.'

Gus frowned. What the fuck was Compo playing at? 'You ok, Compo?

'Not completely, sir. No, I'm not on my own. DCI Wentworth is here in the office now. Shall I tell him you'll contact him when you're free?'

'Christ, Comps, he's in the office with you? You need to engage him in conversation, ask him casually where he was last night and then check it out.'

Gus heard Compo swallow hard. He knew Compo and Wentworth had got off to a bad start but he needed the information. Compo would just have to man up and get over it.

CHAPTER 89
The Fort

Compo tried out a few different smiles and settled on one that felt manageable, before standing up and walking over to where DCI Wentworth. Wentworth studied the investigation board, one arm folded over his chest, the other bent upwards from the elbow. With one hand cupping his chin, he tapped his lower lip rhythmically with his index finger. Compo approached, tugging the hem of his t-shirt with one hand as he shifted from foot to foot. His manic grin still pasted on his face.

Wentworth glanced at him. 'Yes?' his tone was supercilious and immediately made Compo want to run back to his computer, where he'd be in control. Mindful of Gus's instructions, though, he manned up.

'DI McGuire's been called away, but I'm under strict instructions to look after you. Can I make you a coffee?'

Wentworth spun round on his handmade Italian leather shoes and with a slight frown, studied Compo. Compo immediately flushed. His grin stretched even further across his cheeks.

Wentworth shrugged and turned back to his perusal. 'Yeah, a coffee would be good. Hot and black, soon as you like.'

Compo barely managed not to salute before ambling over to the coffee machine. With relief he released his rictus smile as he pushed the appropriate buttons and waited till the rich dark liquid filled the mug. He opened and closed his mouth to relieve his cheek muscles, before reinstating the grin. Lifting the mug, he slowly carried it over to Gus's desk, where Wentworth now sat. He noticed that the other man was flicking through the few files Gus had left on his desk. Eyes narrowed Compo glanced at Gus' computer screen and was relieved to find that flashing on the screen was the icon asking for Gus's access codes. Wentworth hadn't managed to get into sensitive records, thank God! With barely a dribble, Compo deposited the mug on the desk and then, at exactly the same moment as Wentworth did, he noticed the mug's slogan. 'I'm the Office Queen and proud of it!'

Wentworth snorted. 'Not the most appropriate mug for a visiting senior officer, is it?'

Compo all but snatched the mug back, stumbling over his words as he did so. 'I'm sorry, I never thought. I'll change it, sir'

With a magnanimous wave of his hand, Wentworth said, 'Don't bother. I've become used to slumming it since I came up to Bradford. Compared to the Indian restaurant, and I use the term *restaurant* very, very, loosely, I visited last night with DCI Chalmers, this is positively silver service.'

Compo relaxed slightly and replaced the mug. 'Oh which restaurant was that then?'

Wentworth sipped his coffee experimentally before replying. 'Mumtaz, I believe. Bloody expensive but, would you believe, they didn't even serve alcohol. What sort of restaurant doesn't serve alcohol?'

Compo, head on one side, replied, deadpan, 'A Muslim one, sir?'

Wentworth made an explosive sound from his mouth. 'Bloody stupid if you ask me. Half the people in there weren't even Muslim. Where the hell is their customer service? The whole British concept of 'the customer is always right'?' He took another sip of coffee, 'And the food was too bloody hot. I spent most of the night on the toilet last night. I, for one, won't be recommending that restaurant to anyone.'

Compo realising he'd got the information Gus wanted relaxed his grin slightly. 'Well sir, with all due respect, Mumtaz has won many awards and is considered to be one of the best Asian restaurants in Yorkshire.' He made to walk back to his computer, then hesitated, 'There's a huge sign at the entrance explaining that it is a Halal restaurant and therefore alcohol-free. Perhaps you need glasses?'

Wentworth spluttered on his coffee, but Compo ignored him and picked up his phone to text Gus with the information. He reckoned Gus could confirm Wentworth's alibi with DCI Chalmers.

CHAPTER 90
Ilkley

A s they drove into Wendy Horan's cul de sac, Gus noticed that, though it was less private than Beth's street, Roseberry drive had a decidedly posh feel to it. The detached houses were spaciously placed with long flowing drives punctuated by well-tended evergreen trees and perfectly positioned windows to allow complete privacy from the neighbours. Of course, today the evergreen branches were hanging low with the weight of the snow. As a teenager, Gus would have delighted in using his extra few inches in height to reach up to twang the branch sending an avalanche of snow over his much shorter sister. He doubted Katie would be any more impressed if he repeated those actions today.

Gus could already see the dead police officers' car. It was parked in front of number 44 with a swarm of crime scene investigators doing their stuff around the vehicle. As they pulled in behind a SOCO car, the mortuary van, carrying the two deceased officers drove off. Gus's stomach clenched as he steeled himself to get out of the car and engage with the first responders. He walked over to an officer with a pale strained face and introduced himself and his team before ducking under the crime scene tape and donning protective coveralls. A female officer from Ilkley approached him, hand extended, face serious.

'Inspector Jain?' Gus gripped her hand and nodded towards the house. 'What's inside?'

The officer grimaced. 'Not good, not bloody good at all.' She kicked a chink of ice that lay on the frozen path. 'Two dead bodies in the living room, both shot. The pathologist is just finishing up the paperwork for the two dead officers.' She swallowed hard and directed her gaze away from Gus before continuing. 'There was a woman upstairs with a syringe hooked up to her arm. She's drugged and groggy. We're not getting a lot of sense from her, but I reckon she's your Beth Graves. The paramedics are just getting her ready to take to the BRI now.'

'And the baby?' asked Alice.

Inspector Jain's lips tightened and she shook her head.

Gus exhaled slowly. The Matchmaker was really escalating now. He presumed the two dead bodies downstairs were Wendy Horan and her husband. Shit, the death toll was increasing by the minute. Shoulders hunched, he wondered how Beth was feeling. How the hell had he managed to kill the two officers and creep into the house, kill the Horans and drug Beth without alerting anyone? Just as he was considering just how much heat he'd get from Nancy, he felt his phone vibrate. Nancy! Gus braced himself as he answered. For a good minute he listened, then said goodbye, promising to phone her back when he had anything to report.

'Nancy's just got back from informing the officer's next of kin. They've called in an emergency pathologist from Leeds to do the PMs and Nance says she'll attend,' Gus told Alice.

'She give you much heat?' asked Alice,

'No more than I can handle. Although I suspect Bowles is being an arse and the press office is on at her to get a quick result. Lucky she knows what we're up against or she'd be hauling us across the coals.'

He turned to Sampson. 'Make sure the door-to-doors are activated. I want to know how he got to our officers. Someone must have seen something.'

Gus turned to see two paramedics wheeling Beth out of the house. She was hooked up to a drip with her eyes closed. A sudden shout erupted from behind the crime scene tape and a figure wrenched himself away from the police officer who tried to detain him and began to sprint towards Beth.

The officer beside Gus started to sprint towards him but Gus grabbed her arm. 'It's her husband, leave him. Let him go with her.'

Gus reckoned Beth Graves could do with as much support as she could get and now her husband had been cleared of possession of child pornography, he was best placed to provide it.

The paramedics glanced over and, when Inspector Jain nodded, they allowed the now weeping man to climb into the ambulance before closing the doors and driving off.

Gus turned back to Jain. 'Did you find a baby?'

Jain bit her lip and shook her head. 'No, you best come see the scene for yourself. There was a baby's travel cot in a single room with a note left on top.'

Gus and Alice followed Inspector Jain up the steps leading into the house, following the blocks placed by the SOCOs. 'Take me to the baby's room first,' said Gus.

Jain walked to the inner stairs and began to climb them, followed by Gus and Alice. The room she took them to was large for a single and was obviously the spare room. A single bed stood under the window. The duvet cover and curtains matched and a dressing table and single wardrobe stood to one side. Next to the bed stood a travel cot. A suited SOCO approached and showed Gus the bagged note. As he looked down at the travel cot with the hand-knitted baby blue blankets thrust roughly aside Gus's heart sank. Alice craned over his shoulder as he read the note. '*Number two down. Wonder how hard it'll be to snip a baby's little, bitsy pinkie. Maybe I'd be as well opting for the whole hand. You've got email!*'

Alice shuddered. 'Fuck's sake, Gus, we've got to close this down.'

'Do you think I don't know that, Al? Maybe you think you'd be better in charge.' As he spun on his heel to retrace his steps he saw the surprise on Alice's face and felt like an arse. What the hell was he playing at, letting his emotions take over like that?

He headed downstairs to the living room, his shoulders hunched and his fists clenched tightly inside his coat pocket. As he approached the open door the cloying metallic smell reached him. Immediately, his stomach spasmed and his heart began to thump uncontrollably in his chest. Bile rose in his throat and he felt the colour drain from his face. He felt like he'd been thrown into some sort of time warp. He felt like he was back with little Billy trying to staunch the flow of blood. Half-turning to Alice, he gestured for her to go in and stumbled away toward the kitchen where the back door stood open.

Slumped against the door frame shivering, Gus gulped in huge breaths of frosty air. Closing his eyes, he slowly sank down on the back step where he remained until a huge, firm and wholly reassuring hand descended on a shoulder like one of those grab machines at the funfair. Instantly, the smell of blood was replaced by his dad's familiar tobaccoey, Old Spice smell. Gus turned glazed eyes to his dad, whose striking blue ones twinkled back at him. With the tightly fitting white hood circling his face, he looked like a white smiling moon.

'Och, son,' said Fergus, and his huge arm engulfed Gus in a hug. Tears sprang to Gus's eyes. He knew his dad understood exactly what he was feeling and he was grateful for his support.

'Come on, laddie, we'll go in together. You'll be fine,' said Fergus

Gus breathed deeply and then, helped by his dad, got to his feet. 'It was the smell. Soon as it hit me I was back in that room with Billy and Becky and Greg.'

Dr McGuire dipped his hand into his pocket, rummaged for a second and then produced a pot of Vicks. 'Here, dab a bit under your nose and the blood smell won't be so bad.'

Face still pale, Gus smiled weakly and dabbed a liberal dose of menthol-scented goo above his upper lip and, with a firm nod, they walked back down the corridor.

When they arrived in the living room, Alice looked at Gus with anxious eyes and then, with a nod, turned to Dr McGuire. 'Hiya Doc, here's body number one.'

As Alice moved away from the door, Gus saw a man's body prone on the floor with blood pooling under his head from what appeared to be a gunshot wound.

Taking a hard swallow as his dad knelt beside the body, Gus turned to Alice. 'Wendy Horan's husband?'

Alice nodded and pointed behind to the second body that lay on the floor near the settee. 'And there's Wendy.'

Gus sighed and looked back at his dad, whose bulky frame was struggling to stand. Extending a helping hand, Gus smiled as his dad grunted to a vertical position.

Still looking down at the body Fergus began. 'Hmm, cause of death – gunshot wound to the head. Rigor's not set in, so fairly recent. From the position of the body and the slight bruising around the neck I'd say he was grabbed by the throat from behind and shot by a right handed person, then dropped on the floor.' He moved over to the second body and grimaced. 'The perpetrator probably almost immediately swivelled and shot her in the stomach. She didn't die immediately like her husband, but bled out.' He shrugged probably was unconscious within a few minutes from loss of blood. I'll know more after the PM, which I'll do this afternoon.'

He turned to the SOCO who hovered nearby. 'You can bag them up now, Charlie...' Then, he turned concerned eyes on Gus. 'Do yourself a favour laddie and send someone else to the PM.'

Gus had always had trouble at PMs. But, he made a point of attending them in person. He saw it as part of his duty to the victims he represented. However, on this occasion he knew his dad was probably right. Besides which, he had a psycho to catch. 'OK, but when you get the bullets I want them expedited to ballistics. Oh and get that time of death narrowed down, too.'

Gus and Alice left the Horan house and walked towards their car.

'If The Matchmaker is Wentworth we need to pin down his movements. Compo texted saying he was with Nancy last night, but that doesn't let him off the hook – yet. He could have done it later. We need TOD to rule him in or out,' said Gus.

Opening the driver's door Alice looked across the car roof at Gus. 'Should we let Nancy know our suspicions?'

Gus shook his head 'No, not yet. We need more on him. A positive ID from Jamal would be good. I'm going to start surveillance on him.'

'Tricky without letting Nance know first.'

'Yeah, but if we've got it wrong, the buck stays with me.' He rapped his fingers on the roof. 'Let's get back to The Fort and check out the email.'

CHAPTER 91

It wasn't the screeching of the roller doors that wakened Molly but an altogether different sound. At first she thought she was dreaming and lay still under the duvet reluctant to waken up and find herself still in the freezing cold warehouse. Then the noise got louder and more insistent. Maybe it was the other kids from the other room through the pipes. She shook her head. No, they weren't babies and this was definitely crying... a baby crying.

As realisation flooded through her she sat bolt upright and peered round the room. Where was the sound coming from? Then, in an instant she was out of the bed, ignoring the cold concrete on her bare feet as she stumbled towards the cardboard box that lay in the middle of the room, a couple of carrier bags beside it. Instantly, she was on her knees and peering into the box. Seeing the small fists pumping the air and the red screwed-up face of her baby brother sent a balloon of despair into her chest. Sniffling back her tears she lifted the small squirming body wrapped in unfamiliar blankets and snuggled him tightly to her chest. Rocking back and forth, the squirming bundle in her arms, she wept uncontrollably.

When the baby's cries had reduced to mild hiccupping whimpers, she held him away from her. His small face puckered at the sudden lack of body contact and he started to cry again. Gently, she laid him back in the box and leaned over to open the carrier bags. Newborn nappies, baby wipes, a couple of little baby suits and some baby bottles filled with what she assumed was sterilised water and small tubs with measured milk powder inside. A voice boomed into the quiet. 'It's your job now to look after your brother. Heat the water in the mini microwave, add the powder and feed him.' Molly recognised the voice as that of her pretend dad. Her bottom lip curled up in disgust and, heart thudding, she glanced round the room and saw a small microwave on the floor next to the electric fan heater. She sighed in relief. At least she'd be able to feed Sam. As she looked down at the whimpering child she felt less lonely. 'Don't worry, Sam. I'm here now. I'll look after you.' And she busied herself heating up milk for him.

CHAPTER 92
The Fort

The atmosphere in the car on the way back to The Fort was low and the mood hadn't dispelled by the time they arrived. DCI Wentworth had left an acidly worded letter of complaint against Compo, which Gus immediately deposited in the bin. Compo meanwhile looked contrite until Gus nudged him good naturedly. 'Don't let the bastards get you down, Comps. He's an arse. Now let's watch the Matchmaker's latest recording.'

Looking relieved, Compo turned back to his computer and set up the footage to run on the large white projection screen at the front of the room. The image was dark, with falling snow obliterating most of the shot. Then, it focussed in on the profile of the two officers sitting in their car, before falling to a sheet of white as the camera presumably pointed downwards. Seconds later, it panned up again showing the driver's window sliding down, before zooming onto the driver's face. The officer looked surprised and his lips moved as she spoke.

Compo paused the footage and fiddled with the controls. 'Seems we've no sound I'm afraid,' he said pressing play again. 'Wonder why?'

Immediately, the driver's expression changed and a spurt of thick liquid spattered over the dashboard. Her head ricocheted backwards before slumping towards her chest. The second officer, who'd been half swivelled round in his seat, reached over to his partner, but almost immediately, he too ricocheted back and a floret of red bloomed on his chest.

The camera panned up and settled on the car clock, which read 22:15. After a slight jolt the camera followed a pristine snow carpet up to the Horan's front door. Gus watched as a gloved hand extended in front of the camera and pressed the doorbell. As Gus's team watched, Paul Horan opened the door slightly, with only his head visible. His face registered surprise, probably at the camera, and it seemed like he tried to slam the door closed. Then, Horan appeared to reconsider and allowed the door to open fully and the cameraman stepped inside and followed Horan he backed into the living room. The camera briefly panned to the wall clock and hesitated there for a few seconds. It read 22:20. Gus saw Wendy Horan jump to her feet and move towards her husband. However, as she moved, a sudden spurt of blood came from Paul Horan's head and he fell to the floor. Almost immediately a second shot hit Wendy in the chest sending her to the floor, too.

For Gus it felt like he was watching a horror movie in slow motion. The cameraman's actions were almost carelessly casual; as if the lives of the two officers and of the Horans were worthless. Gus glanced at his team and saw that each and every one of them had their eyes, shining with horror, glued to the screen. It would be his job to harness their shock and transform it into determination to catch this bastard.

The camera operator retraced his steps into the hallway and proceeded upstairs. Entering the room where Beth Graves lay, he zoomed so close to her sleeping face, that Gus could see a globule of moisture in the corner of her mouth. Then, from the angle of the camera, it appeared he'd laid it down on the bed. When he picked it up again a few seconds later and zoomed onto Beth, Gus saw the decompressed syringe hooked up to her arm. Gus dreaded to think what the syringe had contained but he knew the hospital would analyse it.

The Matchmaker, for by now Gus felt sure that's who it was, backed from Beth's room and entered the one where baby Sam slept. Without preamble, the cameraman focussed momentarily on the sleeping child then he lifted him and left the room. Abruptly the footage stopped and for long seconds nobody in the investigation room spoke.

Then Gus turned to Compo. 'Get this enhanced as clearly as you can. Anything we can get on this man the better. See if some sort of gait analysis will give us anything on his height. Get a lip reader in to see if we can find out what the officers or Horan said to him.' He turned to Sampson. 'CCTV footage from around 9 to 11pm last night, Sampson.'

Sampson nodded and scurried over to his desk. His movement seemed to galvanise the rest of the team who immediately sprung to action.

Gus looked up as Sadia came in. She stood leaning against the door her eyes locked on Gus, a manila folder hugged tightly to her chest by whitened knuckles.

'You ok, Sadia?'

She nodded and stepped towards him. 'Just been to Jamal with the rest of the photos.' She bit her lip.

Impatient, Gus waved his hand in a get on with it gesture. 'And?'

She swallowed and handed him the folder. 'He IDed the top photo. Was very insistent too.'

Gus glanced at her before taking the folder. Her eyes flashed with a mixture of what looked like excitement and dread. Gus felt his heartbeat increase in direct response. He flicked open the folder. His eyes widened and he glanced again at Sadia. 'And he was 100 per cent sure?'

Sadia held his gaze and gave an abrupt nod.

Shit, this was much worse than he'd anticipated. He needed complete lockdown on this till they were sure. He punched his fist lightly on his thigh and sat down at his desk. Sadia remained standing in front of his desk. Wordlessly he gestured the chair opposite him and Sadia almost fell into it. 'Let me think for a minute,' was all he said and he leaned back in his chair and closed his eyes.

After ten tense minutes, he reopened his eyes, pushed himself from his chair and cleared his throat loudly out attract everyone's attention. In a serious tone he said 'First up, I need to clear the room of all personnel not on my immediate team.'

The officers in question looked at each other, then with a few moans about making his mind up whether or not he needed them, they left the room.

Gus glanced round at his team. Alice, looked at him expectantly from her desk. Sampson, near the coffee machine, stood uncertainly, a mug in his hand and Compo continued working on his computer as if Gus hadn't spoken. With a rueful smile, Gus acknowledged to himself that he quite probably hadn't heard him. Seeing Gus looking at Compo, Alice got up and pulled one of his headphones from Compo's ear. 'Boss man wants a word, Comps.' Quickly straightening himself, Compo pressed a key and then removed the headphone from his other ear.

'I'm not going to give a big preamble about discretion and secrecy. You're all on this team because I trust you. So here goes.' He moved to the centre of the room. 'The picture I'm about to show you is the person Jamal IDed as being The Matchmaker.' He waited to let his words sink in and then turned the photo so they could all see it. The resultant gasps were expected. This was momentous, so Gus let them have time to process the implications. When silence fell across the room he continued. 'Our investigation from here on in will be scrupulous and detailed, but there will be no leaks.' He scanned the shocked faces before him. 'I need a complete background on him. Compo, can you do that without instigating any red flags?'

Uncharacteristically motionless, Compo gave an abrupt nod. As he leaned towards his computer, it broke the silence with a resounding ping. He glanced at the screen and, momentary inertia banished, jumped up, punching the air. 'Got a hit, Gus. Got a fucking hit on Molly's whereabouts.'

Immediately the entire team rushed over to Compo. He stabbed the screen with his stubby nail-bitten finger. 'There, fucking there! Look there's South Square café, there's the viaduct and there is Prospect Mills.' Compo pressed a key and a series of lines and trajectories showed on the screen. This is her view from the mill. I reckon she's on the top floor probably third window along.'

Gus gripped Compo's shoulder tightly. 'Well done, Compo, bloody well done.'

He turned to his team. 'Right Sampson, you're going to the PMs. Alice you're coordinating back-up and firearms unit from here. Get Chalmers here and update her. We need to track our prime suspect. Meanwhile, Sadia and I will head over to Prospect Mills. Get things moving ASAP. We've no time to spare and we don't know exactly how many men he has under him.'

He'd just finished speaking when the door burst open. Beth and Alex Graves burst in. 'I demand an update now!'

Alex was grubby and distraught, Beth pale and drawn. Gus had no time for distractions so he turned to Sampson and spoke quietly. 'Keep him away from us without revealing anything, before you go to the PM.'

Sampson nodded and moved over to lead the Graves to a seat in the room. Leaving Alice and Compo to help Sampson, Gus and Sadia sidled out of the room and ran to the car park.

CHAPTER 93
Bradford

S leeting snow and pile-ups were not conducive to getting anywhere very fast. Gus sat on the edge of his seat peering through the windscreen where snow splatted like massive birds shitting in unison. Then, a loud boom reverberated throughout Rhodesway. Gus slammed the palm of his hand on the dashboard and cursed. Sadia started, but was too scared to take her eyes off the treacherous road. 'What's up?'

'Did you hear that bang?'

'Yeah, rotten day for a wedding, if you ask me, but you got to hand it to them. They're not letting the weather get in the way of their celebrations.'

Gus snorted, blue eyes flashing. 'That's not wedding fireworks, Sadia. There was only one bang. Give it a minute and there'll be one more bang and then nothing. It's the bloody Bradford drug lords letting their runners know the drugs have been delivered.' He ran his fingers through his dreads, 'which means, as it does twice a month every fucking month, CID will be running around like Pomeranians with hair straighteners stuck up their arses trying to locate the big ones. Which means, in turn, that our back-up will be severely diminished because that idiot, Hussain won't prioritise our operation over his.'

Sadia's mouth made an almost perfect O.

With a quick glance at her, Gus said 'I'm sorry I shouldn't have said that about your old man. That's not good.'

Sadia shrugged and when she spoke her tone was bitter. 'I've lived with him for twenty-five years. You don't think I know how stubborn and focussed he is? He can't *ever* deviate from a previously determined course of action. Surprised he's lasted so long in the job really. Oh no. Shit!'

At her last words Gus directed his gaze back to the road and saw a huge, unpassable gritter turn into the road in front of them.

He flung up his hands. 'Would you believe it? Now they bloody grit!'

Sadia clenched her teeth and turned off down an even narrower side street. 'I'll cut down here and, fingers crossed, we'll be able to get onto Thornton Road at the bottom.'

Half an hour later, they approached the huge mill on their left. Despite being set back off the road it dominated the landscape, looming threateningly over the pub on the main road in front of it.

Sadia drove past the entrance to the Mill's pot-holed car park as Gus peered up at the huge blank windows. 'What's the plan?'

Gus gestured ahead. 'Pull into the South Square car park and we'll walk back. We'll see if the pub's open and if they've noticed owt.'

The Flappit Hen pub was dully lit and, despite the roaring fire in the grate, the air held a distinct chill that was matched by the frosty look the barman gave them on their entrance. He paused half-way through a lacklustre polish of the bar and straightened up to his full five foot three inches. When he crossed his over-worked tattooed biceps over his chest, Gus was reminded of Popeye. The barman's bald head glistened slightly in the overhead lights and his frown was venomous as his gaze shifted between the two police officers.

Gus smiled. 'I'd like to speak to the manager, please.'

'Why?' The other man turned his sneering gaze to Gus and tensed his bicep making the red swastika symbol on it dance.

Gus inclined his head. 'Nice ink, crap sentiment.'

The small man made a growling sound in his chest. 'You don't like it, you know what you can do?'

Gus grinned at Sadia whose face had tightened in anger. He shrugged. 'Oh, suppose it'll be something dully predictable as befits someone of your limited capacities like 'piss off back to your own country'. Am I right?'

Face twisted in rage the other man pressed his knuckles down hard on the bar and made as if to vault over, when a sharp voice preceded a taller man through the door. 'What have I told you about causing trouble, Jemmy? If you can't get on with my customers, you'll have to look elsewhere for a job, brother-in-law or not, ok?' When Jemmy nodded, his face still distorted in anger, the taller man jerked his head through the door. 'Take a fucking break.'

When Jemmy had sidled away Gus looked at the other man. 'Nice staff you have. Welcoming.'

The manager shrugged and offered his hand. 'Laurence Carmichael. He's not my first choice of employee, but family is family. What can I do for you? I take it you're on duty?' and he quirked a questioning eyebrow.

Gus took out his warrant card. 'Yeah that's right. DI McGuire and DC Hussain. Wanted to ask if you've noticed any activity in the Mill behind the pub recently.'

Laurence snorted. 'There's always activity there. If it isn't kids pratting about, it's druggies, or teenagers shagging. Always summat going on back there.'

Sadia pulled herself onto a bar stool. 'Inside the Mill or just in the car park?'

'Both really. Usually in the car park but they sometimes manage to get into the ground floor. Can't get any higher up though. It's all blocked off and the lifts don't work.'

'Mind if we have a look from one of your upstairs windows?'

'Nah, help yourselves.' He called Jemmy back to the bar, lifted the bar flap and gestured for them to follow him through a narrow hallway and up some stairs on the right. At the top of two flights they came out on a dimly lit chilly landing. Laurence yanked a door open and gestured for them to precede him into the room. In the middle was a double bed with a dated floral duvet cover on it. Mismatched curtains hung at the window.

Gus moved over and pulled the curtains back. He and Sadia looked down into the Prospect Mill's car park. The snow had been compacted in places and in others there was clear evidence of old tyre tracks

'Looks like there's been a lot of vehicular activity down there,' said Gus standing on tiptoe. 'There's a car parked right in the corner too.' He glanced at Sadia, who despite being a good six inches taller than Alice, was having difficulty seeing out the window. 'You're probably too short to see it from here.'

Sadia pushed herself up with her knuckles on the window sill and craned her neck. 'Yep, you're right. Do you think it's his?'

'Don't think so, but that doesn't mean he's not driving it.' He stared over at the gaping Mill windows. 'We're at the wrong side to see anything. Any signs of life would be at the other side near the fields and the viaduct.'

Sadia jumped off the sill and turned to Gus. 'What shall we do? Backup's at least twenty minutes away.'

Gus sighed and turned to the door. 'Let's take a gander round the car park at least.'

Sadia moved to join him, but Laurence who was now peering down into the car park spoke. 'There's another car just turned in and parked up out there.'

Gus and Sadia ran back to the window in time to see a tall man, face muffled in a scarf, slam the door of a red Mini shut and stride across the snow to the roll up concertina door of the mill. He bent and did something near the bottom of the door, then, with a quick glance around him, flipped the door up a few feet, ducked and went in, lowering the door behind him.

Gus barely glanced at Sadia before taking off, coat flying behind him as he thundered down the stairs shouting instructions to her to put a stick of dynamite up someone's arse to get the team there ASAP.

Sadia, grabbing her phone from her pocket followed more slowly, dialling Alice's number as she moved. When Alice replied she quickly filled her in on what they'd discovered, explaining that Gus had hared off to the Mill. Alice cursed and, as Sadia exited the pub, she cursed too, because all she could see was Gus, dreadlocks flying as he rounded the corner into the car park, slipping slightly on the icy path as he went.

Running after him, Sadia saw him flip the roller door up. He extracted his extendable baton from his coat pocket before stepping through. He turned back waved at her then lowered the door slightly behind him.

What the hell was she supposed to do now? Sadia hesitated, uncertain whether to follow Gus or wait to direct the back-up. Still undecided, she moved towards the red mini. She had a hunch it didn't belong to the driver, so she texted the reg through to Compo and then did the same for the other vehicle that stood in the corner. It was clear by the height of the snow around the tyres that this vehicle had been parked up since the previous afternoon at least.

Finally, fearing that Gus may need help, she phoned Alice and told her she was following him in as there appeared to be at least two people in the building. When Alice directed her to stay put until back-up arrived she switched her phone to silent   and   hung   up.

CHAPTER 94
Thornton

Vague sounds reached Gus's ears as he stood just inside the doors trying to get his bearings in the near-dark. He frowned in concentration, trying to identify them. They came from above – metal on metal. Gus nodded, realising it was the sound of the industrial lift creaking its way slowly upwards. So, Laurence had been wrong. The lift did work, but Gus knew he couldn't risk calling it back down: he'd have to use the huge concrete stairs and hope the sound of his footsteps wouldn't echo upwards.

By the time he reached the first floor, his thigh was throbbing with a vengeance. The steps were wide and uneven meaning he couldn't set a proper pace and the lack of light made it hard going. He hesitated in the stairwell listening for signs of activity. A sudden screech of metal from upstairs told Gus that another roller door was being opened. He slowly began to edge himself up the stairs. He didn't hesitate on the second landing, but continued up to the third floor.

In front of him was a huge metal door. He edged slowly over and pressed his ear to the cool steel. He wasn't entirely sure but he thought he could hear muffled sounds from within. His gut told him this was the right level. Slowly, hoping they'd oiled the hinges, Gus turned the handle and pushed the door open. Thankful for the silence that accompanied this action, he stepped inside the gloomy corridor, closing the door quietly behind him. He moved quickly into the shadows at the side of the corridor and looked around. Someone had fitted dull night lights periodically along the corridor and they sent semi-circles of amber across the floor. Along one side of the corridor were a series of rooms barricaded off by huge wooden batons criss-crossing their metal doors. Along the other side were a series of roller doors. The one nearest the entrance was open, but the room within was in darkness. Further along, a thin glow shone from beneath the third door indicating that the room might be occupied.

Gus crept slowly towards the open door. Keeping his back to the wall, he crab-walked along till he reached the gap. Quickly, he dipped his head into the room, did a rapid scan of the room's sparse contents and, seeing it was empty, stepped inside.

In one corner stood a chemical toilet beside a grubby shower cubicle. In another corner stood a bed with the covers flung back. On a shelf next to the bed a microwave balanced precariously. In the centre of the room was a chair and a wobbly wooden table, strewn with empty cups and pizza boxes. A gas heater was on full blaze a few feet away, but what was of most interest was the TV screen that sat atop a wooden packing case opposite the table. Gus moved closer and saw the screen was divided into two sections. One section showed a room of similar size to the one he was in. Inside was a group of around ten children, huddled together in the corner seemingly clinging to each other in terror. Their sexes and ages were indiscernible. Their hair lay matted across their scalps. Gus immediately felt a wave of nausea as the images he'd seen of holocaust victims came to mind. His stomach tightened and his breathing shallowed.

He flicked his gaze to the other section of the TV. The Scream man was jumping around, looming over a child that Gus identified as Molly only from the bandage round her right hand and her clothes. Her shorn hair was matted, her cheeks hollow and her eyes huge and frightened. In her lap, she held a bundle of rags that Gus barely registered until a small hand escaped and waved for a moment in the air. Molly tenderly replaced it within the covers. It was Beth's baby, Sam. Gus began to back towards the door watching the screen as he saw a second man who matched the description of Jamal's pursuer, begin to set up the camera on its tripod. Scream man paced the floor and appeared to be screaming periodically at Molly, who rocked her bundle to and fro, tears pouring down her cheeks.

As he passed the table, Gus grabbed the bunch of keys that lay half-hidden under a newspaper and crept along the corridor to the next room. Pressing his ear to the door he heard silence and, reassured that the men in the room further down, would be occupied for some time, he reached down and studied the lock at the bottom of the door. On his second attempt he unlocked it. He opened the door a few feet and ducked through.

It was then that he heard movement in the corridor and a male voice. One of the men had left Molly's room and was walking towards him. Gus quietly closed the roller and darted into a dark corner. Placing a finger on his lips to tell the frightened children to be quiet, he waited, holding his breath and hoping that whoever had moved along the corridor wouldn't glance at the TV screen and notice Gus in the corner.

The children seemed to sense that Gus wasn't one of their attackers and remained still, their frightened eyes piercing him in the semi-dark. After a few minutes, he heard whistling followed by footsteps walking past the room he was in. He released a slow breath and then crept slowly over to the children. 'Are you English?'

One of the older boys shook his head. 'Polski.'

Gus put his finger on his lip once more. He had no time to assess their injuries or their state of mind. He needed to get them out of there as fast as possible. He pointed to the door and mimed opening it, then replaced his finger on his lips. The older boy whispered to the other children in Polish and then nodded to Gus. Gus moved closer and held out a hand to the smallest child. Her eyes whipped to the older boy who said something, patted her back and nodded. Tentatively, she took Gus's hand. He smiled at her, and gently squeezed her trembling hand. Gus pointed to another of the smaller children and mimed holding hands with the little girl. The older boy seemed to understand Gus's intentions and quickly paired up the other children. Gus moved to the door and rolled it up. He poked his head into the corridor and listened. Then, turning to the older boy gestured him forward. Gus showed him the door at the end and indicated that on his say so they would go through the door and downstairs. The boy nodded and spoke to the other children in a low voice.

Gus made his way to the huge metal door and opened it. Then, he waved his hand to the boy who quickly pushed two children out of the room towards Gus. Gus waved again and two more followed. When they reached the door Gus pushed them towards the stairs and said, 'Run.' Within a few minutes all but two of the ten children were running down the stairwell towards where, Gus hoped, Sadia waited.

Gus glanced along the corridor, wondering why the last two children hadn't appeared yet. The older boy, poked his head out and gestured Gus to come back.

Heart pounding, Gus crept back to the room. Inside he saw the older boy trying to lift a slightly younger girl to her feet. The girl looked barely conscious and was acting like a dead weight. Gus's heart sank. What could he do? She probably shouldn't be moved, but the two men in the other room had at least one gun between them. She couldn't stay there. Making an instant decision, he hefted her into his arms, and jerked his head for the other boy to follow. When they reached the stairwell, Gus draped the girl over the boy's back and said, 'Go, go.'

Nodding, the boy linked his arms round the girl's legs and began to climb down the stairs as quickly as he could. Gus waited till he'd rounded the corner.

Sweat dripped from his dreads as he whipped them back with a flick of his head. He made his way back along the corridor, rolled the door down in the hope the missing children wouldn't be noticed. He moved on to the room where Molly and her baby brother were being kept. He strained to hear what was happening behind the door but only the deep rumbles of The Scream man's rants reached his ears. Gus's mind flicked back to the last time he'd been outside a room where a raving man held hostages. He was damned if the outcome was going to be the same this time.

The faint strain of the lift moving reached his ears and he grinned. Thank God. Back-up was there. He took his extendable baton from the back of his trousers where he'd lodged it earlier. Then, Molly screamed and without thinking, Gus yanked the door up and rolled through it. His extended baton crashing into the camera man's legs. He fell with a shout to his knees as Gus jumped back to his feet and spun towards Scream man.

Molly, taking advantage of the momentary confusion ran towards Gus, the baby bouncing precariously in her arms. Gus shouted, 'Run, Molly, run! The police are outside.'

From the corner of his eye he saw Scream man draw a gun. Gus dived to cover Molly as she crouched to crawl under the door, never releasing her precious bundle. Instincts kicked in and Gus spun on his heel and then dove to the floor baton extended to whip Scream man's feet from under him. The gun clattered to the floor and Gus kicked it away from the camera man, who he recognised as Sid Smith from Jamal's photo, was now edging on to his knees. Gus grabbed Scream man, yanked his arm up his back and cuffed him, before turning to grab the gun. He pointed it at Smith.

'On your knees now. Hands behind your head.'

Hesitating briefly, he complied and Gus slid the gun towards the door, quickly cuffed him. Then he turned back to whip the scream mask off the bigger man.

When he saw that Jamal's ID had been accurate he said, 'No fucking disguises now.'

DCS Charles Bowles grinned insolently at Gus. 'Pity you couldn't find those reserves of ingenuity to rescue your little godson, isn't it?'

Gus clenched his fists and took a step forward but was stopped by slow clapping coming from behind him. He turned slowly to find Alex Graves holding a struggling Molly in one arm and the gun in the other.

Gus frowned. 'What the fuck are you doing here?'

Alex inclined his head. 'Not sussed it out yet, Gus? Didn't think my little double bluff with the planted child images would work so well.'

Alex jerked his head first towards Bowles and then towards Sid Smith 'Cut them both free.'

Gus glared at him and then did as he was told.

Bowles moved over to his bag and extracted another gun and then went over to Alex and high-fived him. 'Good save.'

He turned to Smith, who raised his hand to high-five too, but before he could complete the action, a blast blew him a few feet across the room and a spray of blood covered the floor. Bowles looked down at him with a grin on his face. 'When needs arise, sacrifices must be made.'

Molly was sobbing uncontrollably now and Alex shook her roughly by the throat 'Shut up, or you'll be next.'

Gus glared at them. 'Back-up's on the way. Why don't you just give up?'

Bowles began to laugh. 'No, no, no. That's not how this will play out.' He grinned at his friend. 'What's going to happen is this. Alex here will escape down the external fire escape and over the fields.' And he turned and fired two shots in quick succession into the padlocked chain that locked the fire door shut. It burst open in a cloud of searing metal.

Before Gus had a chance to react Bowles spoke again. 'Of course we've planned escape routes out of Europe, so he'll follow one of those. Your lot will never catch him. Meanwhile, I'll dispose of you and the brat and say he did it.' He pointed to Sid Smith. 'I'll be the hero and our revenge on Beth Graves will be complete and, just so you know before you die, our little ring will continue with barely a blip. Nice thought to take with you to the grave, don't you think?'

Then he grabbed the squealing baby from Molly and her across the room towards Gus. Instinctively Gus grabbed the red-haired girl, then immediately released her and thrust her behind him. As he dived towards Bowles, Beth Graves flung herself through the door and propelled her husband forward onto his knees. Not stopping to wonder where Beth had materialised from or where Sadia was, Gus grabbed Alex's gun as it clattered to the floor. Beth, screaming like a banshee, grabbed Alex's hair and yanked whilst biting his ear. Gus took up the baby, passed it to Molly and quickly cuffed Alex, as Bowles headed for the fire escape.

The fire exit door had slammed shut by the time Gus reached it. He felt the muscles in his shoulder pull as he wrenched it open and darted through. Bowles clattered down the rusty metal steps, braying like a crazed donkey as he ran. Gus followed and began to gain on the older man. A final jump into knee deep snow and Gus was half-stumbling, half-running after him. Bowles turned and pulled something from his pocket. Seconds later a shot rang out and Gus felt a sharp pain in his arm followed by a warm numbness. Fuck. The bastard had another gun. Using his good arm to support his shot one, he gritted his teeth and kept running, determined not to let him get away.

Gus could hear the sound of sirens approaching. His sane mind told him he should stop and let the reinforcements take over, but the visions of the traumatised children he'd herded down the stairs and Molly's scared yet defiant face made him continue. Adrenalin pumped through him giving him the boost he needed to continue running despite the gradually increasing pain in his arm. Why the fuck couldn't the bastard have aimed at his already damaged arm?

Bowles, not too far ahead of him, paused to glance backwards. His face a mask of fury, he turned and stood both arms extended towards Gus, gun clasped firmly between his hands. Gus hesitated, aware of his warm blood dripping onto the snow.

'Really, Gus?' said Bowles, his tone controlled, a false smile on his face. 'You really want a repeat of last year, with you in hospital, or worse, a coffin.' He shrugged. 'The latter option would be my preference, I have to admit.'

'Just drop the gun,' said Gus. 'You're not going to escape now. Surely even you can see that.'

Bowles cocked his head to one side and then shrugged. 'Maybe, maybe not. However, the least I can do is... this.'

And as Gus took a step forward, another shot rang out over the sound of the sirens. This time Gus fell to the ground. Moments later he heard another shot and everything went black.

***

Sadia was halfway up the second flight of stairs when she heard footsteps coming from above. Two children appeared, followed almost immediately by two more and then more. Sadia realised that Gus must have released them and sent them down the stairs. Quickly, she herded them together. Finally, an older boy appeared, panting and sweaty, with a girl dangling from his shoulders. The girl seemed unconscious. 'Fuck!' thought Sadia as, with an ear cocked for signs that the children had been followed, she hefted the girl onto her back and, with whispered encouragement, herded them down to the bottom and outside.

'*Where the hell was Gus?*' she wondered as she did a silent inventory of the pale, wide-eyed faces that looked up at her so expectantly. The girl she'd carried down leaned against wall where Sadia had positioned her. She desperately needed a doctor and Sadia knew that the men could come downstairs at any moment. Where the fuck was back-up? Smiling, in what she hoped was a reassuring manner, at the oldest boy, she indicated the girl and said 'Help me.'

Immediately, he released the small girl whose hand he was holding and stepped forward to help Sadia hoist the girl back onto her shoulders. Glancing round in desperation Sadia noticed a movement in her peripheral vision. With relief she saw that the landlord from The Flappit was waving to her from the window, gesturing that she should bring the children round to the pub. Sadia would have kissed him if he'd been closer. He'd clearly stayed to watch the proceedings when she and Gus had left and now he was providing a lifeline.

As she hurried the children across the snowy car park towards the pub, she noticed the landlord had left his position by the window and by the time they'd reached the main street, he'd appeared helped her bring the children into the pub.

'Phoned your lot, and an ambulance' he said, gazing in horror at the children who huddled together silently by the fire. He'd relieved Sadia of the unconscious girl and now gently laid her on a long settee. Looking down at the girl, he took a deep breath and then exhaled before turning back to Sadia, 'You best go and find your partner, love. I'll get this lot something to eat while we're waiting for the ambulance. We'll be ok here. I'll lock the doors after you.'

Sadia, reached over and squeezed his arm and nodded. She could already hear sirens coming along Thornton Road, so she knew help was near. However, she'd also seen exactly what these men were capable of and the last thing she wanted was to leave Gus on his own with them. What the hell was he doing? With a sinking feeling she realised that if he could Gus would have followed the children out of the mill. So, what the hell was keeping him?

Leaving the pub, she noticed a car with two figures in it turn into the car park. Who was that she wondered? Back-up, maybe. But then why hadn't Alice alerted her that they were so close. She sprinted forward and round the corner into the mill car park just in time to see Beth Graves climb from the passenger side of the car and glance around her. Sadia opened her mouth to shout and then paused. Where was the driver and what was Beth Graves doing here?

Sadia edged forward and watched as Beth walked towards the open roller door and went inside.

'*What the fuck is going on?*' Then, reluctant to let the woman wander into the building unaccompanied, Sadia followed. Re-entering the mill, she heard Beth's hurried footsteps echoing above her. Following as quietly as she could, Sadia had reached the top of the second flight when the first gunshot rang out. Heart hammering, she increased her pace. Then, there was another shot followed by screaming. Not knowing whether to be relieved that the screaming was female or not, Sadia increased her pace and finally, arriving on the third floor, she rushed down the dimly-lit corridor towards the room where a flash of light escaped. Cautiously, she looked into the room and was just in time to see Gus exiting through the fire escape. A wave of relief surged through her body as she realised he was unhurt.

Still wary, she entered the room and, glancing round, she assessed the scene. Seeing that Beth, Molly and the baby seemed to be ok and not caring what state either Sid Smith or Alex Graves were in, she rushed over to the broken fire exit and poked her head out.

Heights weren't her thing so she sent a quick prayer off to Allah and stared down. She could see Bowles, hotfooting across the snowy field. Just when she thought something must have happened to Gus, she saw him half-jump, half-sprawl off the ladder. Relieved, she watched him follow Bowles and swallowing her fear, she tentatively stepped onto the metal landing. It was icy so she gripped the rickety handrail and began to descend, keeping an eye on Gus's progress as she went. The cold metal rail seared her palms as she held on for dear life. Then, she stumbled. Her stomach flipped and a wave of nausea swept over her. She closed her eyes for a second to allow the dizziness to pass and when she opened them again, she saw Bowles turn and face Gus, a gun in his hand. Words left her mouth, but later she couldn't say what they were. As if in slow motion, she saw Gus' left arm jerk and then blood splatted onto the snow.

'Nooooo!'

Bowles laughed and then took off again. Gus stumbled but righted himself and followed. Sadia half-slipped, half-ran the rest of the way to the bottom and had just stepped onto the solid ground when she heard another shot and Gus was lying on the ground, blood melting the snow around him. Like an echo in her brain she was half-aware of the sirens and then a loud hailer voice telling Bowles to put his weapon down.

Finding her feet she ran across to Gus and instinctively felt for a pulse. She could find none so she straddled him and began CPR. Unaware that she was crying, she continued frenziedly till the paramedics edged her out of the way. Soaked and cold, she turned and saw two armed officers guiding a beaming DCS Bowles towards the front of the mill. Unable to stop herself she walked over and spat in his face.

He laughed.

CHAPTER 95
Bradford Royal Infirmary

A crumpled DCI Nancy Chalmers quietly entered the side ward where Gus lay staring at the arctic wall. He hated being here. He'd been remembering the cold snow contrasting with his warm blood pooling beneath him. He'd had déjà vu. He'd thought he was back in Becky's living room with Greg in a rage. He'd tried to roll onto his side, desperate to find Billy. He'd known he had to stop the bleeding. Where was Billy? Then he'd felt a heaviness across his middle and something was bouncing repeatedly on his chest. He'd felt himself fade away and then soft, cold lips covered his mouth, blowing, warmth into him. His eyes flickered but wouldn't open. Warm fingers touched his frozen cheek and soft hair tickled his head as someone began to gently slap him. 'Don't you bloody die on me, Gus McGuire. Don't you bloody dare.' Too many memories from before and he was desperate to get out.

Contrary to Sadia's assumption, his heart hadn't stopped... he'd fainted, like a bloody wimp. Anyway, a through and through wound on his upper left arm, combined with the strain he'd placed on his already injured right shoulder, made it barely possible for him to do anything for himself. Bowles's second bullet had given him a flesh wound to the side and his third had missed. Gus was glad Bowles hadn't been to the firing range in a while.

Sensing Nancy's presence, he turned and met her eye. 'You look worse than I do, Nancy.'

She snorted and moved slowly over to the chair next to Gus' bed and plonked herself down, kicking off her shoes and lifting her feet onto the edge of the bed. 'Feel bloody hellish, too. Can't believe that bastard. I've worked with him for years and never suspected a damn thing.'

417

Gus moved his hand and awkwardly patted her foot. 'None of us suspected, not one of us. Has he confessed?'

Nancy leaned down, rummaged in her copious handbag and produced a half bottle of Glenfiddich. She got up and poured a sizeable measure into the plastic cup that stood next to a water jug by Gus's bed. Toddling through to the toilet, she returned with another one which she also filled. Handing one of the cups to Gus she took a big swig and said, 'Here's to you, Gus. You and your team did well on this.'

Gus took a small sip, shuddered and handed it back to her. 'Not in the mood to celebrate really, Nance.' He smiled 'Anyway you know my tipple's Glenmorangie.'

She tipped her cup at him and then sipped. Gus studied her as she drank. He'd heard the rumours about Nancy and DCS Bowles. His dad had all but confirmed it when he'd visited earlier. However, Gus also knew that Nancy wouldn't let her personal feelings get in the way of securing a sound prosecution.

'What about the kids?' he asked.

'Sadia was coming up the stairs to help you and met them coming down. She escorted them into the car park. Apparently the landlord of The Flappit was still watching from the upstairs window so she waved him down and went back into the mill. He took them into the pub and kept them till the paramedics took over.'

'They going to be ok?'

'They'll be fine. Jankowski's in charge of repatriation. The best thing for them is to get home to their families.' She sipped her whisky. 'As for the mental stuff. Well, who knows?'

Gus hadn't had time to check their physical injuries in the mill, but his own experience told him that the physical wounds would heal far quicker than the mental ones.

'And what about Molly and Beth?'

'Traumatised. Bowles achieved what he set out to do. Beth's got no-one. Jessie's dead, her best friend is murdered and her husband is going down for a long time. He's singing like a bird, by the way. Beth's strong, but how is she going to pull back from this?'

Gus shook his head. He'd been thinking about that before Nancy came in. How was Beth Graves going to learn to trust anyone, least of all herself, again? She'd married two different paedophiles and, although she was in no way to blame for this, he knew she'd blame herself. His thoughts were interrupted when Nancy spoke again.

'You had us worried back there, you know, Gus. Thought you were a gonner.'

With a wry grin he said, 'I come from good old McGuire stock. No way will a couple of bullets stop me.'

Flushed from the whisky, Nancy matched his grin. 'Well, in that case, the sooner you get your arse out of that bed and down to The Fort, the sooner you'll be able to watch me interviewing Charlie.'

Gus snorted. 'You need me to hold your hand?'

'No. I need you to see this finished. Tomorrow, 9am sharp.'

She pushed herself to her feet, downed the whisky Gus had left undrunk and walked to the door and opened it. 'By the way, I've cancelled your appointment with Dr Mahmood tomorrow.' Then seeing Gus's triumphant grin, she frowned at him. 'Back to normal next Friday, though. Get the woman convinced you're ok and stop wasting taxpayers' money.'

Suitably contrite, Gus nodded, relieved when the sudden cacophony of hospital noise was cut off by door swinging shut behind her.

CHAPTER 96
The Fort,
Monday

Behind the one-way mirror, in the tiny viewing room, Gus struggled to get comfortable. In the end, he found that leaning his butt on the table edge offered the most respite from pulling stitches, aches and bruises. He was with Sadia who, from the moment he'd arrived, had refused to meet his eyes. What was that all about? She'd had his back in the mill. He owed her one for that. Surely she wasn't embarrassed about crying when he got hurt. He was pretty sure he'd be in tears if one of the team were injured. Anyway, it hadn't stopped her trying to help him.

Gus's body tensed as the door to the interview room opened and former DCS Charles Bowles was escorted in by a uniformed officer and his lawyer, Vincent Jacobson. Exhaling loudly, he focussed on unclenching his muscles. No way was that bastard going to give him any more pain than he already had. Bowles, although dressed in prison clothes, still looked like the arrogant sod he'd always been.

Nancy had decided to let him stew in the least hospitable of The Fort's interview rooms, and as Gus watched he saw a few chinks appear in the other man's armour. First it was the bouncing of one knee, then when he got no reactions from the arrogant statements he directed at the one-way mirror, he began to tap the table. At first it was a slow rhythm, but as the minutes passed it became more frenetic. After fifteen minutes, he seemed to collect himself. With a final glance at the mirror he, took a deep breath and closed his eyes. Slowly, the knee and finger movements stopped. Gus made a note to advise Nancy to interrupt his relaxation. Setting him off kilter might make him reveal more than he intended.

Gus had thought *he* looked bad, but quickly revised his opinion when Nancy and Alice walked into the interview room.

Nancy's straight back and determined stride couldn't conceal her pallor and the tension lines around her mouth. Bowles kept his eyes closed until she scraped a chair across the lino and sat down. He took his time studying Nancy, and then smirked. Gus's fingers balled into fists. He was relieved that Nancy had insisted that she conduct the interview with Alice. Nancy dragged her chair further under the table and Gus saw her shoulders relax. God knows what internal reserves of calm she was using up during this interview.

'Well, well, well, Nancy.' said Bowles, his smug tones carrying clearly into the viewing room. 'Your golden boy not up to interviewing me?' He rubbed his hands together, 'or did I crack him? I know I didn't kill him or Vincent here would have told me.'

Jacobson, Bowles' lawyer, laid a cautionary hand on Bowles's arm. 'Come on now, Charles. We agreed you'd co-operate.'

Bowles's eyes narrowed, but he didn't break eye contact with Nancy when he answered the other man. 'I will co-operate. I agreed, didn't I? Nevertheless, I want to have a bit of fun, too. After all it might be the last I have for a while.' He cocked an eyebrow. 'That right, Nance?'

Nancy had her back to the mirror, so Gus couldn't see her expression. However, her shoulders tensed visibly before she replied in a conversational tone, 'How could you do this, Charlie? To all those kids, to your wife, to the police force? Tell me how it all came about.'

Leaning back, Bowles crossed one knee over the other and with meticulous care positioned his trouser leg until the non-existent crease lay exactly central to his knee cap. His eyes sparkled with what, in another man, could have been benevolent humour, but in him took on a malevolent air.

'How can you show concern about Hazel when for the last two years you've been happy to drop your French knickers and bend over my desk at the drop of a hat? You were *panting* for me all those years ago in Cambridge and when you followed me up here, you couldn't wait to spread your legs.'

Gus heard Alice's gasp over the speakers and saw Sadia, beside him, cover her mouth in shock. Nancy, except for a slight twitch of her arm, didn't react. 'Good try, Charlie. However, consensual sex between two adults pales into insignificance in the light of over twelve years' worth of child abuse, trafficking abduction, murder and torture, wouldn't you say? So, bearing in mind that your lovely colleagues Devlin O'Rourke, AKA The Provider, and Alex Graves, The Facilitator, are singing like larks and the fact that you shot Sid Smith, The Distributor, in front of witnesses, I'd say you better start talking.'

Bowles tapped the table with his forefinger and pursed his lips. 'You know what Nancy? I don't think I *will* play your game, after all. Do your worst. I've done what *I* wanted. I've had my revenge on that bitch. I might rot in a cell, but at least I'll have the satisfaction of knowing that she's in hell too. Knowing that she alone is responsible for everything; her daughter being tortured, her mother-in-law and her friends dead.' He laughed, 'The stupid bitch married a paedophile, not once but twice. Oh yes, I'll rest easy in my cell knowing that her freedom is as restricted as mine. So from here on in my response to you will be 'no comment, no comment, no comment'.' He folded his arms across his chest, focussed his gaze on a point above Nancy's shoulder and refused to speak.

As Gus watched, Nancy continued with a few more questions. Each time, Bowles drawled an elongated 'No comment.'

Finally, Nancy nodded to Vincent Jacobson, gathered up her paperwork and with Alice following, left the interview room.

Minutes later Nancy stormed into the viewing room. 'What the fuck does he think he's playing at?' she said, dragging her fingers through her hair.

Gus stood and stretched tentatively. 'Doesn't matter, Nancy. O'Rourke and Graves are both talking *and* we've got witnesses to him shooting Sid Smith. He's going down for a very long time. They all are. That's what matters.'

Nancy inhaled deeply. 'And Graves has supplied us with a list a mile long of all their clients.' She bundled her dress between her legs and hopped up on to a table facing the mirror. At Nancy's exit, Jacobson had requested that the recording system be turned off, so there was no sound. It appeared, though that Jacobson was losing his argument with Bowles, who with a grin kept shaking his head. Abruptly Jacobson stood, went to the door and left. Seconds later the uniformed officer returned. Bowles stood, and, with a 'ta ta for now' wave towards the mirror, was accompanied from the room by the officer.

Nancy rubbed her eyes. 'We're starting to arrest the client list today. Believe me, there won't be a political, financial or religious leader in the UK who'll sleep well tonight.'

CHAPTER 97
Marriner's Drive

Gus, still aching, lay on the sofa in his living room, trying to dispel the haunting image of Beth, her daughter and her baby at Jessie's funeral that morning. Mother and daughter clung to each other, frames skeletal, faces pale and expressionless, eyes bleak and empty. Then baby Sam began to cry and immediately they were on their feet both bending over his pram, eyes suddenly alive. Mother and daughter shared a small smile when he immediately quietened at their attention.

Beth had told Gus they were leaving the UK for somewhere warm, somewhere they wouldn't be haunted by their memories. Gus had smiled at them and wished them well, but at the back of his mind he knew their memories would follow them wherever they went. His did.

He sighed and closed his eyes, savouring the solitude of his home. Then the doorbell rang accompanied by a loud familiar voice calling through the letterbox. 'Hallooooo, Angus. It's me and your mum. Got a wee surprise for you, to liven the place up.'

Gus groaned, wishing he could put a cushion over his ears and pretend he wasn't in. As a second round of ferocious knocking began, he pushed himself to his feet and headed through the hallway to the door. He'd no sooner opened it, when a ball of white catapulted itself at him from his mother's arms, barking loudly.

'What the....?' He looked from his father's large, florid smiling face to his mother's beautiful, smooth, grinning one.

'Thought the house might feel a wee bit empty with Gabriella gone, so we got you a wee gift... His name's Bingo.'

Gus looked down at the squirming creature in his arms and his frustration died as the wiggling puppy yapped twice and then poked out a pink tongue and liberally wet Gus's face.

'Aw, he likes you' said Fergus McGuire placing his arm round his wife's shoulders and squeezing tightly. 'Told you it was a good idea, Corrine. It'll help with his therapy.'

Feeling bulldozed, Gus followed his mum through to the kitchen where she began unpacking various meals she'd made. With a sinking heart Gus realised that for the next couple of hours his solitude would be interrupted. He grinned. What the hell. He couldn't do without them… even if he knew that he'd be forced to bin his mother's unappetising concoctions the minute she left. He sprawled on the sofa, dog still in his arms, and allowed his parents to feel useful.

ACKNOWLEDGEMENTS

There are many people I need to thank for managing to finally get *Unquiet Souls* published.

The Leeds Trinity MA (Creative Writing) staff, particularly Martyn Bedford, whose perceptive tutoring forced me to 'raise my game' and who offered invaluable advice on moving forward to publication- thanks Martyn. My fellow MA students, Lucy Brighton, Stephanie Buick, Sam Gardner, Andrea Hardaker, John Harris, Sophie Joelle, Jo Kemp, Lewis King, Becky Leeming, Suzanne Owen, Ken Relf, Wendy Simpson, Kathleen Strafford and Mark Whittle who egged me on to better writing and who played a huge part in the editing process.

Thanks, also to The Barny Bunch (pub quiz Queens), Debbi, Gillian, Helen, Jyoti, Madi, Rhonda and Susan who generously supplied coffee, mirth and the down to earth nonsense that kept me sane.

The Hare & Hounds pub on Toller Lane was my refuge through stormy writing times and its cosy friendly atmosphere made writing *Unquiet Souls* a dream- thank you, particularly, Katie, Adam and Jade.

The Crime Warp team, Roman, Cheryll, Toria, Jacki and Liz, were behind me all the way and I owe a large debt of gratitude to you. Toria Forsyth- Moser, gets a particular thank you for taking on huge chunks of editing and providing loads of constructive advice.

My family, both immediate and extended (of whom there are many), for their unwavering support and encouragement, I couldn't have done it without you and to Dr Nima Poovaya-Smith OBE and Dr Paul Smith, both of whom had faith in me and supported me in this sometimes daunting process.

The biggest thanks goes to Nilesh, Ravi, Kasi and Jimi who are always there being daft, offering support and making me laugh- they believed I could fly... and darn it they were right. I love you now and always.

Unquiet Souls is a work of fiction and as such I have taken creative licence with a few things; the most notable being that The Fort (Lilycroft Police Station) in Manningham is, in reality, an administrative building. Unfortunately, Mo's SaMOsa's is sadly absent from Oak Lane.

Here's till next time

Best Wishes

Liz Mistry

If you want to connect with Liz, you can do so on:

Twitter: @LizMistryAuthor

Facebook: LizMistryBooks

Amazon: https://amzn.to/2xhdOgG

Website : https://www.lizmistry.com/

Made in the USA
Monee, IL
24 September 2021